"LET GO OF ME!" MOIRA CRIED, FALLING BACK WEAKLY AGAINST THE TREE...

"Oh, no," Random said in a low, menacing voice. "I'm going to hog-tie you this time."

"Is that the usual way you keep your women?"

Random jerked her chin up, and his mouth came down ruthlessly on hers. She groaned in protest, trying to move back from him...the weeks of dreaming and longing firing her blood to fever pitch and making her melt into him. Her hands spread eagerly over his chest, feeling the rapid pounding of his heart, the burning heat.

He drew his head away and glared down at her. "When I get you back to the mountains..."

FRANCINE RIVERS
THIS GOLDEN VALLEY

A JOVE BOOK

THIS GOLDEN VALLEY

A Jove Book / published by arrangement with
the author

PRINTING HISTORY
Jove edition / February 1983

ISBN: 0-515-06823-3

Jove books are published by Jove Publications, Inc.,
200 Madison Avenue, New York, N. Y. 10016. The words
"A JOVE BOOK" and the "J" with sunburst are trademarks
belonging to Jove Publications, Inc.

PRINTED IN THE UNITED STATES OF AMERICA

THIS GOLDEN VALLEY

TAHUALAMNE, CALIFORNIA, 1848

Tree branches lashed the man's face as he ran, and his lungs burned like fire. He didn't dare stop. He could still hear the Indians coming after him, and he knew that if they caught him he was a dead man.

And just when he had the information he'd been seeking for months! The squaw had finally told him everything. He had wooed her slowly, and each time they met she had given him another piece of the puzzle, another piece to the map. When she'd told him the last bit of information he needed, he had taken her forcefully, without thought of where they were, his triumph and lust demanding celebration. They had rutted on the grassy knoll, and when she'd cried out with abandon, her intended had found them. As if that hadn't been bad enough, the damn squaw had tried to excuse herself by telling the brave that the tribe secret had been forced from her. She hadn't reckoned on the brave's retribution. He cut her down with his tomahawk and then gave the alarm to the village while she lay bleeding to death on the grass.

Now they were after his scalp.

His strength was giving out. He'd been running for miles, but he was within reach of Barilovich and Heaton, if they were waiting for him as planned. If he could just reach them, he might have a chance, they might all have a chance. Now that he'd gotten what he wanted, now that he knew where the place was, the world and all it had to offer was within his grasp.

If he lived long enough to enjoy it!

They were coming! He could hear them whooping not far behind him, giving voice to their savage intent. He drove himself harder, muscles rebelling, guts churning in terror.

Then they were in front of him. He swung to the right and found his escape cut off there as well. He tried to turn again, but they were all around, closing in, dark eyes glinting with lethal purpose.

The man drew his hunting knife, crouching low, arms spread apart, eyes darting from one brave to another. His heart pounded with fear and exertion. His great size didn't daunt them.

"Come on, you Digger bastards!" he challenged, taking a step toward one and then another, hoping that the sheer ferocity of his appearance gave him some small edge. It didn't. They were on him, first pinning, then tying him down. It came to him then that if it had been any squaw but the old chief's daughter, he might have been killed immediately. But they intended to torture him, to make him suffer for what he had dared, before they dispatched him to whatever final hell awaited him.

He hadn't intended to give them the satisfaction of screaming. But after the first hour, his body fastened to stakes and slowly being skinned, he had given in to the agony. He cursed Barilovich and Heaton for ever having gotten him into this mess. He prayed for death. He begged to be killed. He screamed until he thought his lungs would burst.

Then the firing began. He was only half conscious and delirious, but he heard it. Opening his eyes, he saw the squaw's intended above him, face contorted with hatred. He saw, too, the glint of steel as his own knife was raised and plunged into his midsection. He screamed again, unable to move, feeling his life's blood spilling into the dirt. Realizing his life was at an end, he considered, then rejected prayer. He lay staring into the blazing sun.

Suddenly, another face appeared over him. A white face. And then another. They were the wrong faces, but it didn't matter now. He had to speak, he had to tell them what he had learned from the squaw, or his life would have meant nothing. His lips moved.

The sandy-haired, blue-eyed man bent down, straining to hear the dying man's last words. The young man's eyes widened slowly as he listened and the full realization of what he was hearing struck him. He looked at his partner crouching beside him, who was staring disbelievingly at the dying man. They exchanged looks, eyes blazing with growing excitement.

"It's there . . . end of ledge . . . gold . . . gold . . ."

The man stopped speaking. His breath came out in a long, slow sigh, and then he was still. Dead eyes stared upward.

"Holy Mother of God," the sandy-haired man said slowly, looking at his partner. Before he could say anything more, all hell broke loose around them.

Chapter One

Moira Cavendish stood quietly on the quay in Charleston harbor, looking up at the *Stephen Rule*. Her heart beat fast with growing apprehension and excitement as people buzzed around her carrying out their duties. The almost overpowering smells of fish, spices, damp wood, and sea air filled her senses and exhilarated her.

Why was it everyone thought only men had wanderlust, she wondered with a half smile. The sparkle in her brown eyes would have caused poor Aunt Miranda to worry greatly. As Moira watched, men worked on the rigging, decks, and sides of many ships, readying them for their various journeys. Cargoes were being loaded and unloaded; there was shouting and talking, as well as cursing and laughing. Few women were on the docks, and those that were drew curious attention. Moira, who had worked to achieve her carefully created image, did not entirely blend in with the scene. Yet she was not attracting as much attention as she usually did. Her soft, full mouth curved in a smile.

A crate being unloaded from a nearby ship slipped from the net and plunged into the water, bobbing there while a man from above shouted angry curses at it. Moira scarcely heard, so intent was she on the ship in front of her.

5

It looked trim, neat, and absolutely splendid to her, just as Daniel had said. But of course, neither she nor Danny knew the first thing about boats, so how could they possibly judge how well this one would make the voyage to California? But if the advertisements were to be believed the cabins were spacious, the food excellent, and they would make their way to the western coast of the continent in record time. What more could they ask for? Besides, this was the one on which Danny had booked passage. Had it been a leaky tub, Moira could not have changed her plans.

Gathering her courage, Moira readjusted her drab bonnet. "Well, get on with it, Mory," she whispered to herself, another habit dear Aunt Miranda abhorred almost as much as her ability to find trouble.

Taking a deep breath, Moira walked up the gangplank. The rope railing didn't give her a feeling of security as she looked down at the murky water below, wondering just how deep it was. The planks rattled slightly, increasing the tempo of her heartbeats, and she sighed in relief when she reached the steps that led down to the deck of the ship.

Moira looked down at the broad-shouldered back of a tall, black-haired man in uniform. He was speaking to one of the sailors, and seeing that the sailor's attention had strayed to something behind him, he turned around and looked directly at Moira.

The officer had the most arresting face she had ever seen. Black, curling hair fell forward on his brow, and his face was deeply tanned. Tiny feathered lines radiated out from his brown eyes, and two creases on either side of his mouth verified that he smiled on occasion. He was scowling, looking extremely annoyed with her interruption. His sharp scrutiny of her brought a light flush to Moira's pale cheeks. Obviously, he did not appreciate her arrival at this precise moment, but having come this far, she had no intention of retreating. She swallowed hard and then tipped her chin upward slightly—what Daniel always called her battle stance—and carefully negotiated the steps to the deck. She lifted her skirt slightly, barely showing a slim ankle, which the officer noticed. The dark eyes moved up as he stepped forward, reaching to take a firm hold of her arm.

Standing on the main deck, she felt at a decided disadvantage, having to tilt her head far back to look up the long male length of him and meet his unnerving eyes. He must be the captain, she decided; who else could he be with that commanding, arrogant air?

She didn't speak but stood staring up at him. He raised his brows sardonically.

"Were you looking for someone, miss?" he asked in a deep, resonant voice. The rapid pounding of Moira's heart had slowed to a painful thudding.

"Are you the captain of this fine boat, sir?" she asked earnestly, smiling and batting her lashes. She hoped he would lose the faintly annoyed scowl on his handsome face. He did, but the smile that deepened the creases of his face was decidedly mocking.

"The *Stephen Rule* is a ship," he corrected. "A bark, to be precise. And I'm First Mate Random Hawthorne, at your service," he said, giving her a bow that brought rising color to her cheeks.

"I didn't mean to give offense," she said, hoping he was not one to take it easily. "May I speak with the captain, please? I've business to discuss with him."

His dark brows moved up again. The blond, bronzed sailor behind him listened and watched with obvious interest. Hawthorne turned slightly and dismissed him, then turned back to Moira.

"Captain Thackary is not aboard at the moment. May I be of assistance to you?" he asked politely. He looked her over again, taking in the worn gingham dress, the old crocheted shawl, the drab green bonnet that had seen better days and should have long since been retired to a ragbag.

Moira bit nervously at her lower lip before answering. "I would like to book passage to California," she said finally, holding her breath for his response. He looked amused.

"So you want to join the rush for gold?"

"No. I'm not the least bit interested in gold. I want to go to California because my brother is there," she told him, which was the truth, after all. Part of it, anyway. She put one hand behind her back and crossed her fingers.

"And your parents?"

"My parents were killed in a carriage accident," she said, her voice dropping to a husky softness. It still hurt to think about it, though it had been well over a year now since it happened. It was hard to believe they were gone, that she would never again hear her mother's laugh or her father's gentle teasing.

"I'm sorry," he said, looking faintly sympathetic, but more decidedly unconvinced that what she was saying was the truth.

"You could not have known."

"And your brother knows you're coming? He's meeting you?"

The questions raised her hopes. Surely he would not ask them if he meant to turn her away. There must still be room for her on the boat—ship, she corrected herself. But how was she to answer him? She wanted to keep to the truth as much as possible; otherwise it would be very difficult later to stick to her story.

"We've corresponded," she said, and that was the truth as far as it went. She had written regularly, but Jack hadn't answered recently. "Do you have a cabin for me?"

"No."

"No?" she repeated with surprise. Her eyes widened in growing dismay. "But it's imperative that I leave aboard this ship!"

"There are others."

"But this one is . . . is leaving sooner than the others."

He smiled slightly. "I'm afraid there's no more room, miss. Were your plans made only recently?"

"They've been developing for some time, actually," she said bleakly, wondering what in heaven's name she could possibly do now. If only Daniel had spoken of his arrangements earlier! But he'd been very close-mouthed.

"You should have come forward as soon as we docked, Miss . . ." he said, waiting for her to supply her name. But she was too deeply involved in her own thoughts to notice.

"I would have . . ." She stopped and looked up at him. "If I had been able to raise the money before this morning," she finished, an idea coming to fruition suddenly.

"Well, maybe the next one will have a cabin for you. You

might try the *New York* or the *Trident* over there," he suggested, pointing them out to her.

"I have to go on this one," she told him desperately. "Oh, I know it's foolish, but I . . . I wrote to my brother and told him I would be on the *Stephen Rule*. And if I'm not, he will be worried sick. And I won't know how to find him when I do manage to get to California!" She clutched at her small, worn, drawstring purse and looked up at him appealingly. "Oh, please, isn't there just one small cabin left, sir? Or a hammock? I'd even be willing to share!" A few tears were called for, and she managed to work herself into enough of an emotional state to make them convincing.

He smiled, eyes glinting. "There are only two cabins aboard this ship that are not being shared already," he said mildly. "The captain's and mine. You were saying?" There was a twinkle in those dark eyes. Was the wretched man enjoying this? She tried to subdue a surge of annoyance. Too much was at stake.

"There isn't even one bed left?" she asked, pretending utter naiveté.

"Bunk," he corrected.

"Bunk, blanket, whatever. Not even one?"

He was grinning now. "Just one."

She was afraid to ask.

"I don't think you'd like the company," he added as she tried to read his mind unsuccessfully.

"A woman?"

"Oh, yes. Definitely."

"I'll take it!" she pounced, opening her purse before he could say another word. She handed him the neatly folded bills. He laughed slightly.

"Now, just a minute . . ."

"You have my money," she told him. "May I have my receipt, please?" It was more a demand than a question, and not politely uttered. He laughed, fingering the bills while studying her.

"You're pretty desperate to get to California, aren't you?"

"Yes." She'd already told him as much.

"I'm not entirely sure I should believe anything you've told me up to now," he said, still smiling.

"I haven't told you one single lie," she said hotly, flushing all the way up to her hairline and spoiling everything. She hadn't lied! She simply hadn't told him the entire truth.

"I'd like to know a little more about you."

She readjusted her shawl slowly. The drab bonnet, though it hid an abundance of shiny dark hair, framed a very pretty face, dominated by soulful, wide brown eyes fringed by dark, long lashes. Usually those eyes shone with a high degree of mischief, but for the moment they were subdued. She had a full, pleasant mouth, although a bit too wide, she thought, and small, perfect teeth. Aunt Miranda had told her often that she had a tendency to laugh too much at too little, but then Aunt Miranda scarcely laughed at anything. Life was a serious matter to Aunt Miranda, so how could she judge? Moira's chin was her greatest drawback, for it gave away her innate nature. It was faintly pointed like an elf's. Fine brows winged up lightly when she grinned, giving her a puckish look. Despite those two features, she was considered beautiful by many young men.

Mr. Hawthorne was making a full inspection as she stood before him. She couldn't guess what he was thinking from his inscrutable expression, but she did her best to guess.

"Your name would do very well for a start," he told her dryly after she had failed to answer. She gave a gurgling laugh, eyes sparkling to full life.

"Oh, that's simple enough. Moira Cavendish," she supplied, putting her hand out. He took it, inclining his head slightly.

"Cavendish," he repeated, looking her over more carefully, one brow rising slightly. "We have a Cavendish booked aboard already."

"You do?" She widened her eyes and tilted her head to one side, then slowly withdrew her hand, as he seemed disinclined to let go of it. "Well, there are a number of Cavendishes in Charleston. I shouldn't be at all surprised if one of them has joined in the mad rush to the gold fields."

"And you're not related to that Cavendish, I presume?" he asked, his mouth curving up slightly on one side. He's suspicious, she thought, and wondered just how much more she should tell him to convince him he should let her board the *Stephen Rule*.

"No," she sighed and shook her head ruefully. "I'm afraid not." She sighed again for effect and cast him a look through her long lashes before going on with her story.

"It's all been a terrible ordeal. You see, Jack—that's my older brother—went to California before the rush began. About a year after he left, our parents were killed. I learned from the solicitors that my father's business was badly in arrears and had been for some time. His creditors were content with the building and our house." So far she had stuck to the truth. She took another slow breath. "Everything else was given over to the auctioneer. Not that we had a great deal, you understand, but it was everything that my father and mother had worked for all their lives. I was allowed to keep a few small pieces of jewelry in remembrance of my mother. I sold them so that I would have the money to buy passage on the *Stephen Rule*. All I want is to be with my brother... and not be alone anymore."

Perhaps she shouldn't have added those embellishments; he still looked quite dubious. And his mouth was twitching. Well, some of their things *had* gone to the auctioneer! And she *had* sold some of her mother's jewelry to get money for her passage! But perhaps Aunt Miranda was right—she did have this terrible tendency to exaggerate at times.

"You're had a terrible time, haven't you?" he drawled.

She gave a faint sigh, glanced up, and tried her best to look suitably pathetic. "You can see why it's so important that I reach California aboard the *Stephen Rule*. I've nothing left here, and my brother is waiting for me there."

The other side of his mouth curved up, and the dark eyes sparkled with amusement. "You just might find all your difficulties over when you set foot on California shores." He turned away before she could ask him what he meant by that remark. It was obviously not a reference to her brother. Had she gone too far with those last bits of information? Perhaps she should have been more mysterious, more aloof.

When Hawthorne returned, he handed her a slip of paper. On it were scrawled a few words confirming her payment and passage aboard the *Stephen Rule*. She stared at it dumbly.

"Your receipt," he said mockingly. "Just present it when you come aboard. We'll be sailing in two days... at dawn.

Don't be late, Miss Cavendish. We won't hold the ship for anyone."

She gasped in delight, her brilliant eyes darting up to him.

"Should you change your mind and come to your senses," he continued, "I will refund your money."

"Oh, no. I won't change my mind!" She beamed up at him. "You can't possibly know what a terrible fright you gave me, Mr. Hawthrorne. Telling me you were full to the rafters and there wasn't even a single bunk left anywhere. That wasn't at all kind of you!" she said, laughingly. She started to turn away, clutching the slip of paper in her hand. Before she had gone two steps, she turned back, putting the tip of her index finger to her lips. "May I come aboard early?"

"Early? How early? We leave at dawn."

"The night before. I'm afriad I'm much better at staying up late than arising early."

He grinned. "Indeed? Well, I suppose it could be arranged. I'll warn the watch so you won't be shot off the bow."

"Thank you. I would appreciate that," she said, grinning back. She went up the steps, then stopped yet again. "Oh, I almost forgot. This lady you mentioned. Shall I speak with her? Where is she to be found?"

"Never mind, Miss Cavendish," he said, eyes dancing. "I'll take care of those small details. I'm sure she'll have no objections."

"As long as she isn't Medusa or a leper, I won't have any objections, either. Not a one, I assure you!"

She started down the plank toward the pier, her steps light and quick. Aunt Miranda always scolded her for walking too fast, saying it was the height of indignity to be seen going at such a pace. "For heaven's sake, child, you're supposed to be a young lady, and ladies walk sedately."

"Miss Cavendish," Hawthorne called from the ship. She stopped and looked up at him questioningly. "How old are you, anyway?"

She laughed. "Just shy of eighteen, Mr. Hawthorne." She put a hand on her hip. "But I shouldn't think that would make the least bit of difference."

Hawthorne grinned down at her boldly. "You're absolutely right, Miss Cavendish. It doesn't."

Chapter Two

Moira entered Aunt Miranda's two-story stucco and brick house on Meeting Street by the iron side gate. Coming through the garden, she stood beneath the wisteria-covered arbor and peered into the parlor window to see if anyone was about yet. She drew her head back sharply when she saw Sarah, the black house slave. The wiry, graying woman was busy at the dainty side table beside the settee, carefully lifting and dusting the porcelain figurines before setting them back in place.

Moira was about to dart past the window when she saw Sarah turn and head in just that direction. She drew back again and waited as Sarah stopped to gaze out at the profusion of flowers that splashed their wild, exotic colors about the intricate garden. A marble fountain stood in the center, where the narrow, winding brick pathways met. On top of the fountain a naked stone boy poured out an endless stream of water from his urn.

Holding her breath, Moira waited for Sarah to move away from the window and go back to her duties. She knew very well that if Sarah saw her the alarm would be shouted to the rooftops. She would report it immediately to Miranda, and Moira could just hear the dire warnings.

13

"Dat girl is up to somethin' again, Miz Rutherford! I tell you she's up to the devil again, and it ain't right. You got to do somethin' with her and fast, or else she'll be going straight to hell!"

Having waited a full minute, Moira carefully peeked around the window frame again. Sarah's back was turned, and Moira didn't waste a second. Darting past the window on tiptoe, she almost tripped over some of her aunt's precious potted begonias and stumbled to a stop at the main door that opened into the foyer. She opened it just a crack and listened.

Aunt Miranda was probably still upstairs resting or else having her hair dressed by Mary, the upstairs slave, for no one seemed to be about. Her luck had held, Moira thought jubilantly as she entered the house. Closing the door noiselessly behind her, she scurried across the hall and up the stairs at a run, skirts raised high about her ankles. Just as she reached the landing, she heard Sarah enter the foyer and say something. Moira froze just out of sight and then, hearing Sarah come up the stairs, made a run for her bedroom. She dashed in, her skirts swishing, and locked the door. Leaning back breathlessly, she listened, her ear against the door.

Sarah was in the hallway, talking to herself in a disgruntled fashion. She walked over to Moira's door, and Moira could almost hear her breathing on the other side. Moira put her hand to her mouth to stifle a laugh and waited. The elderly slave went back down the hallway and down the stairs.

Moira let out her breath and then began to laugh, putting her hands over her mouth to muffle the mirth and excitement that was bubbling out of her. She twirled around, arms held out wide. Tossing the old shawl onto the canopy bed, she untied the drab bonnet and cast it aside as well, shaking her dark hair out of its confining bun. She felt sticky from the heat of the day. Her face was flushed and damp, and her hair was curling from the humidity.

It had worked! She was going to California on the *Stephen Rule!* Oh, the look on Daniel's face would be rich to see. He would be furious, absolutely enraged. But she was not going to remain behind with Mama and Papa gone and both of her brothers off on the other side of the continent. If she stayed in Charleston, Aunt Miranda would have her married off to that wretched Charles Beauchamp with his full, wet lips, ever-running nose, thinning hair, and obscene fortune. Money, to Aunt Miranda, was *important*. But it made a dubious bedfellow.

Moira's head buzzed with her plans. *Devilment*, Sarah would call it, and Moira grinned. It would not be too difficult to leave the house with the few things she planned to take aboard the ship. Aunt Miranda usually went to bed by midnight, and she never arose before noon. By that time the *Stephen Rule* would be well out to sea. Nothing could be done about sending her back then.

As for Daniel, he would undoubtedly say all his good-byes the evening before he departed. She would tell him tearfully that she simply couldn't bear to watch him sail away, perhaps never to see him again. He wouldn't expect her to go to the docks with him, and her not going would make him feel very guilty as well, she thought, smiling to herself. It would serve him right for having waited so long to tell her his final arrangements, almost causing her to lose the chance of getting a place on the ship herself. She would make sure to cry a great deal the night before he was to leave, and she would plead for him to change his mind and stay. There was no chance that he would, but his conscience, if he still had one, would smart painfully. Besides, if she didn't cry and plead, he'd become suspicious. She smiled. It would be a simple matter to remain belowdecks until the ship was miles out to sea and there was absolutely no possibility of her returning. When she appeared, he'd probably be standing at the railing, looking back toward Charleston and feeling terrible for having deserted his little sister. Then she'd tap him on the shoulder and probably have to listen to him rant and rave for a full hour.

Stripping off the gingham dress, Moira rehung it at the back of the wardrobe, where it had been hidden for the past three weeks. She put on her green silk robe and pulled the bell cord. She spent the next hour plotting while she luxuriated in a steamy, scented bath.

She found Aunt Miranda sitting in her usual place on the veranda, looking out over the garden. A tea tray was set on the small table before her. She looked up as Moira came out the door.

"You look very charming, my dear," she complimented her niece. "I've always thought you looked beautiful in hyacinth-blue."

"It's my favorite," Moira agreed, sitting in the chair opposite her aunt for the daily ritual. Miranda was pleased with herself about something, which boded no good for Moira. She wondered what announcement her aunt would make in the next few minutes.

Miranda was a pretty woman, petite and fine-boned, very different in temperament from Moira's mother, Faith. Miranda was inclined to be serious, far too serious, and when she smiled, she did so carefully, so that no wrinkles formed on her smooth face. She only laughed under duress, and then it was a light, practiced tinkle that caused the least amount of facial movement possible while sounding absolutely charming to the listener.

She had china-blue eyes and sandy-brown hair, the same coloring as her sister, Faith. Moira took after her father's side of the family. In her early fifties, Miranda did not have a single gray hair on her head. She kept her hair carefully coiffed in a perfect chignon, with soft framing waves and curls about her forehead and temples. The elegant coiffure was achieved with a minimum of one hour at her mirror and the help of a maid.

Miranda's hands were her greatest asset, Moira had always thought admiringly, watching them now as they handled the teapot, cups, and saucers, pouring milk, spooning sugar, setting a dainty butter cookie on a plate, before handing it to Moira. A blue blood to her very fingertips, Miranda had smooth, white, delicate hands with long oval nails buffed to a sheen. Moira thought that Aunt Miranda was very much like the girl from the old nursery rhyme who sat on a cushion and sewed a fine seam, existing on strawberries, sugar, and cream. She used her hands with a skillfulness that would have left even Daniel Webster speechless. She spoke at length on occasion, but her hands spoke volumes, underlinig, punctuating, and italicizing everything she said.

"You look very pleased about something, Aunt Miranda," Moira observed warily.

"Moira, please, put your cup down before you speak. Stop peering at me in that way. It's extremely rude, and I've spoken to you about it before." She smoothed down a nonexistent crease in the black silk dress she was wearing, evidence of Miranda's continuing mourning for her long-deceased husband, Howard Rutherford. When anyone mentioned his name, she would raise her embroidered and lace-trimmed handkerchief and dab lightly at her eyes. It wasn't that she had greatly loved nor now missed the departed gentleman. It was simply a useful pretense she maintained to keep the fortune hunters at bay.

Miranda had no desire whatsoever to remarry. Twelve years of suffering Howard's lusty affections had been long enough, and she felt fortunate that she had remained childless. Howard had died of a stomach disorder brought on by an excess of expensive brandy and left her a fortune. She was content to live quietly in her elegant Meeting Street house beside her illustrious neighbors, growing her precious begonias, attending the opera whenever she wished, working occasionally for charity, and planning her niece's fortunes. It was her purpose in life to see to Moira's future, much to Moira's dismay.

Moira put her cup back in its saucer, set it down, and demurely folded her hands in her lap. Her innocent air was a little too pronounced, and Aunt Miranda pursed her lips, though not enough to crease her skin.

"I've some wonderful news for you, my dear," she said after waiting a full minute. She lifted her hand and made a gesture of positive delight. Moira prepared herself. "Wonderful news," she added, then placed the hand lightly on her breast, as though whatever information she had was causing her heart palpitations. Moira tried very hard to look serious.

"Yes?" she prodded, knowing that was expected. However, one never hurried Aunt Miranda. She took her time pouring some tea, adding a liberal amount of milk, and then stirring in two heaping teaspoons of sugar, drawing out the suspense as long as possible. Finally, she sighed blissfully and took a dainty sip.

"Charles will be joining us for dinner this evening," she announced as though the king of England himself had decided to come to call. Moira let her breath out.

"Oh, how very grand."

"Moira Cavendish! You can show some enthusiasm! Don't

you realize how many intelligent young ladies of breeding in Charleston are simply falling at his feet for a mere glance from him?"

"No, really?"

"Moira," she said warningly, clasping her hands in frustration. "You couldn't possibly do better than Charles."

"I'd like to try."

"Oh, for pity's sake! You have no taste in men. You would chose some handsome insect without a penny to his name! You've your mother's flighty temperament. My sister was a foolish romantic, and it's up to me to see that you have some sense. You must make a proper marriage, or I will never forgive myself."

"I might forgive you," Moira said. Miranda looked at her stonily and ignored the comment.

"What more could you possibly want? Charles has a thriving business, which he inherited from his father. He has a small plantation and an exquisite house here in Charleston with real Queen Anne furnishings, not those terrible imitations—"

"I prefer Colonial myself."

"Moira, do be serious! This is *important!* We're discussing your future!" She sighed, her hands dropping elegantly into her lap like fluttering birds. "I do believe you enjoy upsetting me. Your father always did. He teased me constantly until I was ready to have the vapors!"

"I'm sorry, Aunt Miranda. But Charles Beauchamp is positively repulsive."

"With the fortune he has? How could you say such a foolish thing! And I'm quite sure that if you gave him just the slightest encouragement, he would ask for your hand."

Moira's mouth curved slightly. "I had the greatest of difficulties prying it loose from him the last time he came to call."

Miranda set her cup firmly in its saucer and glared across the table at her niece. Moira smiled sweetly. "What am I going to do with you? Why in heaven's name did your parents have to depart this world and leave *me* to see to your future?"

"You mustn't worry. Things have a way of working out," Moira soothed, smiling mischievously.

"Worry? You're giving me a faint heart, Moira! I have nightmares about you!"

"I am sorry," Moira said sincerely, having no doubts that her aunt was stating the truth.

"You aren't in the least sorry, or you wouldn't do this to me! You'd listen to reason and be a sensible, thoughtful child and marry Charles Beauchamp just as soon as you could arrange for him to ask you!"

"And thus be out of your hair forever." Moira's reply came before she could suppress it. She laughed at her aunt's indignant expression. "Oh, Aunt Miranda," she said, rising and coming around the table to give her an affectionate hug and a light kiss on her soft, powder-scented cheek. "I do love you and appreciate all you've done for me . . . or should I amend that to what you've tried to do for me? You really mustn't worry yourself about my future."

"Someone must worry."

"Why not just let events take their natural course?"

"Natural course?" Miranda sniffed derisively. "That's exactly what I'm worried about. You are a Cavendish, through and through. And there isn't a bit of sense in any of you. Your brother Jack, for example, is God knows where in California, and we haven't heard a single word from him in a year. And Daniel intends to go as well now that gold has been discovered there. I can't stop him! Trying to stop a Cavendish from doing something is like trying to stuff hornets back into a fallen nest. You end up the worse for your efforts. And you! Moira, you're the worst of the lot, I think. A dozen young men are madly in love with you—"

"All 'wild young pups' like my brothers," she said, quoting her aunt's own words, "of whom you heartily disapprove."

"And when a proper gentleman comes to call," Miranda went on doggedly, ignoring Moira's interruption, "you are barely polite to him. You could be settled in a wonderful home with a bright, secure future before you."

"Oh, Aunt Miranda," Moira sighed.

"I do love you, my dear, but you have no common sense."

"I would think that loving me, you would not want to write *finis* to my life."

"There you are again, Moira! You can't take anything I say seriously!" she said, truly vexed. "And your future is serious business. I would never rest in peace if I saw you married to someone like . . . like . . ."

"Someone like my father?" Moira supplied with a smile, not the least bit insulted. "I should feel myself truly blessed if I did. Mama was the happiest of women. She loved her husband."

"She never had a thing. Not really," Miranda sniffed. "They lived well beyond their means for years. It was only a matter of time before their house of cards came tumbling down around their heads."

"She never knew, and Papa always showed her the greatest consideration."

"But what about you and the two boys? You've absolutely nothing except his debts—unless, of course, I were to die, which won't happen for a good many years if I have anything to say on the matter. The boys aren't taking care of their future. The gold rush! You'd think they could pick up gold with their fingers! It's so ridiculous. These young fools should have more sense than to go racing across the continent or around the Horn. And you, with real gold just sitting there right in front of your nose! All you have to do is smile and accept it, yet you refuse! I don't know what to do about you, Moira. Really, I don't!"

"Well, I promise to behave like a perfect lady this evening," she promised, smiling fondly at her aunt.

"I shall believe that when I see it!"

"When Charles tells me again how your begonias, roses, and fuchsias make his nose run, I shall do my very best not to laugh in his face."

"He didn't say that!" Miranda gasped, affronted to the core. But Moira had already walked down the veranda toward the door. "Where are you going, Moira?"

Moira stopped and turned, curtsying low and grinning broadly. "Why, I'm going up to my room this very minute and study my entire wardrobe. I must wear something devastating this evening with dear Charles coming to dinner, mustn't I?"

"The blue watered silk becomes you best," her aunt said.

"But I wore that at the Richelieus' soiree just last week. Charles was there, remember? We wouldn't want the dear to think I had only one presentable gown. He might think I was after his fortune and not his lovable self."

A faint crease appeared on Miranda's brow, a sign that she

was under great strain. "Then wear the yellow taffeta."

"I think not. It makes me look like a daffodil."

Closing her eyes, Miranda sighed heavily. "Then you decide," she relented wearily.

"Thank you, Aunt Miranda. I shall. You're not to worry. I'll wear something that will absolutely put Charles at my feet!" Moira blew her a kiss and swept through the door.

Standing before her wardrobe, Moira lightly tapped her finger on her lips in concentration. Since Jack had left for California she had read everything she could get her hands on about the frontier. She knew Frémont's reports backward and forward. She had read every true and fictional account of the way west. And she knew that there was not much that she owned that would be suitable. She doubted that California women were wearing watered silk, taffeta, or voile this year. Good spun cotton, broadcloth, and lightweight wool were practical and durable. She laid out several day dresses that would have to do, two cloaks, and some bonnets. Then she rummaged through her armoire for undergarments and nightgowns. It took her some time to decide on three pairs of shoes.

Running her fingers along the soft silks and satins of her evening gowns, she thought it a terrible shame that she could not take everything with her. She loved to dress up in her finest. Touching the watered silk, she decided she could be forgiven for taking one gown with her. It was her favorite, a gift from her mother. She couldn't possibly take the petticoats—they would take up far too much room—but she did lay out the matching dancing slippers, stockings, and underthings. The parasol and bonnet with its pretty silk flowers and lace would have to remain behind—they would be ruined packed in a carpetbag.

Folding everything carefully, she arranged it all in two bags she had purchased the week before. She'd had a great deal of trouble smuggling them into the house without arousing suspicion. She'd decided that if she were caught with them she would say the bags had been intended as a present for Daniel and that not a word must be breathed about it or the surprise would be spoiled.

She had almost eight hundred dollars left after the purchase of her ticket. That should see her through for some time once she reached California, and if she needed a few more things she could always purchase them in San Francisco. Jack had said that prices were higher there, but they couldn't be that much higher.

Shoving the carpetbags far under her bed, she brushed off her hands with an air of accomplishment. She sat near the window overlooking the street, her thoughts turning to Jack.

They had not heard from him in a year—thirteen months, to be precise—and it wasn't like him to be silent for so long. Something was wrong; she could feel it. She and Jack had always been very close, though there were five years between them, and she could sense when something was amiss with him. And something was definitely wrong now; she felt it strongly.

When Daniel informed her that he booked passage aboard the *Stephen Rule,* leaving for California at the end of the month, she had been in a panic. She'd known for some time that he was thinking about going to California to look for gold, but Daniel was always makings plans that came to nothing. This time he had surprised her. Actually, she had been shocked, frightened, and then furious. He had deliberately waited until the last week before his departure to tell her of his plans, knowing exactly what her reaction would be. With the loss of their parents only sixteen months ago, Jack gone, and Aunt Miranda pressuring her to marry Charles Beauchamp, Daniel's desertion had come as the last straw.

Her brother hoped to leave with little ado, saying he would come back within the year with his pockets filled with gold. He had expected her to be upset, of course, but he had not expected her to make plans of her own. Moira seemed flighty and irresponsible, and even those close to her failed to recognize the quick intelligence and determination she possessed. Her plans seldom came to nothing, and while up to now they had been of a lighter nature, she knew how to set things into smooth operation. She had no intention of allowing Daniel to sail off and disappear as Jack had done. He was so caught up in the fever of striking it rich that he would probably never write home to tell her he had arrived in California, leaving her to think he had sunk somewhere off the coast of South America!

As for searching for Jack, she doubted heartily if he would even think to do so, believing that Jack could take care of himself. Daniel was not concerned about anything but gold at the moment.

Whatever the difficulties, whatever vapors Aunt Miranda would have, Moira was going to California on the *Stephen Rule*. And she didn't care a fiddle about gold! It was Jack she wanted to find. Family was far more important than any metal on earth, and she had precious little family left.

Leaning back, Moira rubbed her throbbing temples. There was no use worrying about everything at once. She could do nothing about finding Jack until she reached California, and she couldn't avert Daniel's righteous anger nor Aunt Miranda's hysteria when they learned she was aboard the *Stephen Rule*. What she did need to do now was decide what she was going to wear this evening to please her aunt, since anything she wore would arouse the ever amorous Charles.

When Daniel had learned that Charles was coming to dinner, he had taken himself off to a friend's. Moira envied him his independence. Within the first ten minutes of Charles's arrival she suffered numerous sidelong leers and his wet, pursed lips pressed ardently to the back of her hand. It took all her self-possession not to snatch her hand away and wipe it down the side of her sea-green satin gown. She smiled instead, giving him the full force of her charm, curtsying low and telling him how absolutely delighted she was to see him again. And why hadn't he come to call on her sooner?

Charles was so charmed by Moira's little flirtations and attentiveness during dinner that he insisted they all go on to the opera. Miranda accepted immediately for them both and sent a beaming smile of congratulations to her niece. Moira groaned inwardly as another three hours of Charles Beauchamp loomed ahead of her.

When Charles lingered while draping the matching satin shawl around her shoulders, Moira could almost feel his eyes peering over her shoulder and down the front of her dress. She pretended to sway back to be closer to him and stepped as hard as she could on his big toe. Satisfied at hearing his sharp intake of breath, she spun around and cried out in pretended dismay.

"Oh, Charles, have I hurt you? I am sorry. Oh, it was so

utterly stupid and clumsy of me. Heavens, you're quite pale, aren't you? Do you think you should sit down and take a sip of brandy? Oh, what have I done to you, you poor, poor man?" She put her hand to her cheek and then to her breasts, and then clasped them in front of herself in dramatic display. Miranda looked quite grim.

"I'm fine," Charles managed, pale and smiling weakly. "You're as light as thistledown, Miss Moira." He was limping when they walked toward the door. Moira took his arm and smiled up at him, batting her eyelashes slightly.

"You're such a gentleman, Charles. Really, you are." She glanced at her aunt, winked, and grinned wickedly. Miranda closed her eyes and sighed.

During the carriage ride to the theater, Charles managed to revive and reassert himself. Miranda turned her head and looked out the window as the coach traveled along, and, as though on cue, Charles put his clammy hand on Moira's leg. She could almost feel the heat and dampness of those fingers through the layers of material. She shifted; he clung. She asked an inane question that required polite attention from her aunt, and Charles's hand miraculously disappeared, but only momentarily. She felt it again at her waist when they reached the theater.

Turning abruptly, she caught him squarely in the stomach with her elbow. He grunted, and she managed to look dreadfully sorry. It was a second or two before he could breathe properly again, but he managed to greet friends as they entered the theater.

Settled comfortably in the Beauchamp box to the right of the stage, Moira looked around the large theater with avid interest. She loved the excitement, the low rumble of voices, the people in all their silken finery. The men looked so handsome in their dark formal attire and the ladies, like so many birds of paradise in their multicolored gowns, twittered excitedly below.

Moira spotted a familiar dark head, and the color in her cheeks faded. Random Hawthorne, she thought in a panic, jerking her head around toward the stage and quickly lifting her fan to conceal her face. Charles noticed.

"Is something wrong, Miss Moira?" he asked, leaning toward her and taking the opportunity to put his hand on hers again. She scarcely noticed.

"Nothing at all, Charles," she said quickly, her mind whirling. What was the first mate of the *Stephen Rule* doing at an opera? After a moment, she turned her head slowly, careful to keep the fan raised slightly, and looked down at him again. He was terribly handsome.

Hawthorne was with a beautiful woman. Moira looked with curiosity at his glittering companion. She was dressed elegantly in peach silk and lace, and her pale blond hair was arranged to perfection. Diamonds sparkled around her neck. She talked with animation to Hawthorne as he leaned close to her, listening attentively. Moira felt an odd sensation in the pit of her stomach.

She felt Charles's fingers moving up and down her arm. She looked at him with barely concealed disgust; he smiled lasciviously at her.

"You have beautiful skin, Moira," he said in a low, husky voice. "Silken to the touch." Thankfully, the lanterns were being dimmed and the curtain began to rise, making it unnecessary for her to reply. Charles sat back. Miranda was looking at Moira, a faint, satisfied smile on her face.

Several times during the play, Moira stole a look at Hawthorne. He was losing interest in the opera and looking around just as she had been doing, probably feeling someone watching him.

Moira's heart began to pound hard, and she raised her fan again to obscure her face. She pretended great interest in the opera. Surely he wouldn't be able to recognize her as she was now. He had seen her dressed in homespun gingham, with her hair covered by a horrid old bonnet. Now she was in silk, and her dark hair was piled in curled glory on her head, with flowers carefully pinned in by tiny jeweled combs. And besides, the man did have a beautiful companion by his side, so why should he be paying close attention to other women in the theater?

Still, she could feel those dark eyes moving closer and closer. He was not missing a thing, she thought in growing panic. What if by some remote chance he did recognize her? He wouldn't bother to speak with her during intermission, would he? If he did, how on earth would she explain their knowing one another without his blurting out the whole story? Damn Charles for bringing them to the opera! She sat lower in her velvet-covered chair.

Miranda leaned over. "Sit up, Moira. You're slouching!" she whispered. "And do put that fan down. You look as if you're hiding your face!"

Moira leaned toward her, making sure to keep her face averted. "Pardon me, Aunt Miranda? Did you say something to me?" She pretended to laugh in delight with the rest of the audience as some convenient part of the opera was enacted.

Moira's neck and back were aching by the end of the first hour. She had remained still, keeping her face carefully turned so that Hawthorne couldn't get a good look at her. She was so tense and worried she couldn't have told anyone what was happening on the stage below had her life depended upon it. She almost felt it when Hawthorne glanced around the theater again, and she hunched down in her chair. Tapping her fan against her cheek, she feigned concentration on what was happening with the actors when in reality she was rigid with anxiety. Aunt Miranda cast her curious and annoyed glances.

When the curtain came down and the lanterns were brightened throughout the theater for intermission, Moira glanced down and saw Hawthorne rising with his glittering companion. His hand was placed casually at the small of her back, and she was smiling and talking animatedly again. They were heading up the aisle for the lobby. Moira sighed with relief and then turned brightly to Charles.

"Why don't we stay here and chat, Charles?" she suggested in a sultry voice. "We haven't really had much time this evening to do so . . . in private." She knew she was asking for trouble, but what could Charles Beauchamp do in an opera box? She laid her hand lightly on his arm, and he looked so surprised and pleased that she wanted to laugh. But when his eyes dropped slightly to the neckline of her dress, where her soft, round femininity showed her new maturity, she lost her desire to laugh. A good twist of his nose was what he needed.

Amazingly, Aunt Miranda insisted they go into the lobby. "We must greet the Jacksons and the Richelieus. It would be very rude not to say hello, and they might think we were avoiding them."

Moira sighed. Charles looked irritated at his lost opportunity, but before they left the box he took her hand and looped it possessively through his arm. He leaned closer, licking his lips before he spoke in a low, throbbing voice.

"Perhaps we can involve your aunt with one or two of her many friends and then steal a few moments together, Miss Moira?"

Hardly listening, Moira was looking about the lobby for some sign of Hawthorne. His tall, attractive form wasn't difficult to spot. He was standing near the refreshments with his lady friend, who, judging by the increasingly bored expression on his face, hadn't stopped talking. Others had joined them. Unfortunately, Hawthorne did not seem interested in them either, for he was looking around again. When his eyes came too close to Moira for comfort, she ducked down, snapping the delicate gold chain from around her neck in desperation.

"Moira! Whatever are you doing?" Miranda gasped.

"I've dropped Mother's locket," Moira said and pretended to look around on the carpet floor for it while clutching it secretly in her hand. She bent only enough to conceal her face while not drawing too much attention to herself. Charles began to look as well, though apparently he thought the locket had gone down the front of Moira's dress and not to the floor. Angry, Moira straightened abruptly. She cast a nervous glance toward Hawthorne, relieved to find that his lady fair had finally reclaimed his flagging interest. Moira turned and produced the locket.

"Thank heavens I've found it," she said, smiling brightly. "Oh, I feel quite faint, Charles. Could we please go back and sit down in the box?"

"Of course," he agreed with alacrity. His eyes were glittering. He glanced at Miranda Rutherford impatiently. "There's no need for you to worry, Mrs. Rutherford. I'll take good care of her."

Miranda's eyebrows ascended a fraction as she glanced with speculation at Moira. Moira guessed exactly what was going on in that fertile brain and wanted to protest that she was not trying to worm a proposal out of this donkey! All she wanted to do was get away from the lobby and Random Hawthorne. He could refuse her passage on the *Stephen Rule* or arouse Aunt Miranda's suspicions, and she would find herself locked in her bedroom until the ship departed.

Miranda considered her niece thoughtfully. She apparently decided that Moira did look pale and distraught and that it was best to accompany her niece back to the box. After all, it was not proper for a girl of Moira's age to be alone with a man—even in an opera box in full view of an entire theater audience. And Moira's temperament, and her opinion of Charles Beauchamp, being what they were—well, the outcome of a few moments alone might not be a proposal but rather a badly dented male ego, if not the male himself.

Moira was relieved when they finally reached the relative safety of the box. When the opera ended, she managed to delay their departure from the theater long enough to be sure that he and his lady were well on their way. But when they entered the lobby and she turned her head to look around, she saw them again. He was looking toward her.

Charles helped her into the carriage, and she pressed herself back against the seat. Hawthorne was close by. She gave Charles a bright smile when he looked curiously at her. He looked out the window, trying to see what had caused her excitement. He was terribly confused. One moment she was smiling at him in what he could only interpret as encouragement and the next looking somewhere else in flushed agitation. Moira Cavendish was a strange girl, perhaps a little too much like her brothers, but she was certainly a very enticing one. Perhaps a few faults could be overlooked.

Chapter Three

Moira sat on the settee in the parlor, watching her older brother as he explained the complicated new apparatus he had just purchased—one of his pieces of equipment for searching for gold. He threw her an excited grin as he set up the demonstration with the aplomb of a salesman. His blue eyes sparkled, and he raked his sandy-brown hair back from his brow as he picked up the new gold detector.

"You can't possibly be serious about that thing, Danny," Moira said, giving in to a laugh as she watched him.

Daniel's eyes snapped indignantly. He waited with scarcely concealed impatience for her to be quiet before he went on to justify his new purchase.

"Samuel Cadahy told me that no fewer than a hundred men have made a fortune using this!" he told her.

"Samuel who?"

"Cadahy! Oh, never mind! You don't know him. The point is he knows what he's talking about."

Moira's mouth twitched as she tried to look serious. "I find it very hard to believe that you can find gold with a bellows."

"It isn't a bellows! I've already explained that!"

"It certainly looks like one, except for that little box gadget attached to the side there."

"That's the gold detector."

Moira couldn't suppress a gurgle of laughter. "And I suppose all you have to do is walk around California pumping that ridiculous thing and it will suck up all the gold!"

Daniel's face reddened. "It works! Here, just watch!" He dropped half a dozen small pebbles on Aunt Miranda's clean parlor carpet and began pumping the contraption quickly over them. Moira lowered her head and covered her face with one hand, laughing. Glancing at him, she could see that he was deadly serious about this, and she tried valiantly to be so as well. After several long moments of pumping madly, he gave up with a sigh. Rubbing his neck, he looked annoyed and perplexed.

"I don't understand it," he muttered. He shook the thing and pounded it on the floor. He tried it again, but it still didn't work. "It worked when Cadahy did it."

"Undoubtedly," Moira murmured sympathetically and then looked at him with wide, innocent eyes. "It still does work."

"It does?" He peered down at the carpet to find all the small rocks, including one small nugget of gold, where he had dropped them.

"Of course, Danny. It sucked you right in, didn't it?" Unable to stop herself, she burst out laughing again.

Daniel gave her a baleful look. "Shut up, Mory!" He threw the useless gadget back into its box and slumped onto the sofa. He stretched out his long, lean legs and looked sideways at her, eyes glowering.

"You think this is all madness, don't you?"

"I think that thing is almost as mad an idea as that box of California Gold Grease you bought last week," she agreed, smiling affectionately at him. He sighed.

They shared their good looks, but not their coloring. Moira's hair was very dark, while Daniel had inherited their mother's sandy-brown hair and blue eyes. But anyone who looked closely at the two would know they were brother and sister. Moira's schoolfriends had always eagerly accepted her invitations home, for Daniel was charming as well as handsome, and he didn't stop at stealing a kiss on the stairway if the opportunity presented itself.

Daniel grinned sheepishly. "Well, I've brought you a little

present to remember me by." He got up and went to the mantel, where he had left a small brown package with a red ribbon. He brought it back and handed it to her.

She unwrapped it and took out an oval daguerreotype in an intricate flowered brass frame.

"I thought you might want it," he said quietly, watching her.

"It was very thoughtful of you, Danny," she said, sincerely touched by the gesture. She would leave it for Aunt Miranda. It was unfortunate that she herself had not thought to have one done. Now there wasn't time, but Aunt Miranda would have plenty of memories to keep Moira's image firmly planted in her mind, she was sure. Especially when the *Stephen Rule* set sail and Miranda learned her niece was aboard!

Moira gazed at the picture of her brother and felt tears burning. Danny and Jack were very much alike. Jack had been twenty-one when he left home after an argument with Papa; she had never known what the spat was all about, but it hadn't mattered. Jack had headed for St. Joseph, where he joined a small wagon train.

Papa had been very distraught when he'd found his eldest son gone, a curt note left behind. Yet Jack had written as often as possible, and the family had heard from him on a regular basis. There was never any indication that he planned to come home, and, in fact, he spoke of looking for land in California, good farm and ranch land to settle on. Papa had left the room when that letter was read.

While Danny shared some similarities with Jack in appearance, their personalities were very different. Jack was introverted, thoughtful, quick-witted, and equally quick-tempered. He was moody. Mama had always called him her "moon child" because his moods were so changeable. He was also impatient. When he made a plan, he wanted to enact it right away and not wait for a better, easier time. While Daniel conformed to his peers, Jack had often stood alone. He felt things deeply and was surprisingly idealistic. One of the topics about which he and Papa had argued endlessly was slavery, Jack believing that it was as bad for the white man as it was for the black, while his father saw nothing at all wrong with it and even excused it as an economic necessity.

Daniel was charming, full of laughter, and often grossly irresponsible and unthinking. He dreamed for long periods of time about ideas but seldom carried them out. He was optimistic, never thinking that anything could possibly go wrong. Whatever he did, it was always with a crowd of friends. Even now, he was going to California with a dozen of his university friends, who had decided to call themselves the Charleston Trade and Mining Company. Most of the young men were from affluent families who had nothing to lose by the venture, but every penny Danny possessed was going into this scheme. Already he was wasting much of it on ridiculous gadgets like this gold detector.

Yet he could see no chance of failure. Wasn't California a vast territory? And hadn't they been finding nuggets the size of a man's fist? There would be plenty of gold for everyone. He'd come home rich and buy back the family business, the house, and even add a plantation on the Cooper River, or his name wasn't Daniel Cavendish! It might have been amusing if he hadn't been so serious about the whole thing.

"Oh, Danny," Moira said, sniffling. She thought of Mama and Papa, dead in such an unnecessary accident, of Jack, missing, and of Danny, with his grand dreams of making an easy fortune. She thought of leaving Aunt Miranda and Charleston and everything she had ever known, and the tears that came were genuine ones.

Daniel looked miserable and guilt-ridden. He sat down beside her and looped a brotherly arm around her shoulders. She sobbed even harder.

"I'm not going to fall off the end of the earth, you know," he said. "I'm going to write, I promise. And I'll come back in a couple of months with my cases filled with gold dust. Just you wait!"

She glanced up at him through her tears. The sadness was beginning to be tinged with malicious satisfaction at his woebegone expression. Served him right! Wasn't he planning to leave her behind? And write! He'd never written a letter in his entire twenty-one years!

"How can you think of leaving me, Danny?" She sniffled. "You're all I have left."

He looked suitably miserable. "You've Aunt Miranda. She'll take good care of you."

So easy for him to say, the rogue! His expression was already changing, and she could tell his thoughts were on the *Stephen Rule* and California. He had that gleam of gold lust in his eyes.

"I'll worry so much about you."

"I don't see why you should, Mory. I've got everything worked out perfectly."

"I'm sure. And where does finding Jack come into your plans?" she reminded him.

His eyes flickered slightly, but Daniel had always been a fast thinker. "As soon as I land in San Francisco, I'll go to Bootjack, wherever that is, and find out about him. He's bound to be there and to have some perfectly simple explanation for his long silence. Perhaps he's feeling guilty about never having reconciled with Papa."

"Daniel, he still would have written to me. He'd know I'd worry. It's not like him."

Everything was so simple for Daniel. It always had been. When things became difficult or complicated, he simply went on to something else that was easier. And the same would be true in looking for Jack.

Moira sighed. "I hope you're right, and that he's still in Bootjack."

"I am. I'm sure of it. And besides, Jack could always take good care of himself in any kind of difficulty. Even when he created the problems himself," he added, laughing. "Remember that time he took Papa's carriage and raced along the river? He wasn't more than eight. He told Papa he was tying up the reins and the horse took it into his head to run, remember?"

"I was only one."

"And what about the time Harley and Paul Tyler put him in that tree and then bent it back to see if he could fly. He did. For twenty feet before he landed, and hardly a scratch on him. Anyone else would have been killed. Jack's got more lives in him than a cat."

"Nevertheless, I do worry," she told him firmly. "And I will even more about you. Especially when you persist in buying things like that," she said, indicating the discarded gold detector. "How much did that thing cost you, anyway?"

"Not much," he hedged and then quickly changed the subject. "Has Aunt Miranda convinced you that you should marry Charles Beauchamp yet?"

Moira looked up at him, her mouth curving in an expression that told him a great deal. "What do you think? You don't wish him on me, do you?"

Daniel laughed, gave her a squeeze, and then released her. He stood up and walked to the fireplace. She set the daguerreotype on the side table, watching him.

"You could do a lot worse, you know," he told her seriously.

"Tell me how."

"He's rolling in money, Mory. Just think of the easy life you'd have. Magnificent house, servants to wait on you all the time, all the gowns you could ever want, jewels, Europe every other year—everything. You wouldn't have to go off looking for your own fortune like Jack and me."

"And here I thought you were planning to share with me," she told him dryly. "Well, there's one slight problem with your summary of everything I would have with Charles."

"What's that?"

"I'd also have him." She shuddered expressively, and Daniel laughed. Then he grinned wickedly.

"Do what Aunt Miranda probably did with Uncle Howard. Count the imperfections on the ceiling."

"What do you mean?"

He laughed again, finding some private joke very funny. "Never mind. I expect you'll understand it all in a year or two, or maybe even sooner than that if Aunt Miranda has her way. If you can't abide Charles, I'm sure she will scour the city for another proper candidate for your hand in marriage," he told her, imitating their aunt's way of emphasizing certain words and moving her hand. Moira giggled at his irreverence.

He pointed his own hand at her. "She does have your best interest at heart, you know."

"I think she's more concerned with her own peace of mind," Moira said with a slight smile.

"Can you blame her?"

Miranda entered the room, ending that discussion. They

shared a glass of special Madeira before having dinner. Daniel spent the next hour talking animatedly of his voyage on the *Stephen Rule* and California. He had such grand hopes and dreams, Moira thought ruefully. What would happen to him if it all was a great hoax or if all the gold was gone by the time he got there? Daniel was not one who took disappointments well.

"Aunt Miranda, you've been very good to us," Daniel said. "And I do love you very much. But a man must find his own way in life, and it's time I found mine. Don't you agree?" He sounded so pompous, Moira thought.

"I think you're an utter fool, Daniel, but I wish you luck," Miranda said with a sniff.

"You'll change your mind when I send you a bag of gold dust to repay you for the past year."

"Nonsense. You don't have to repay me," she said as though he had insulted her with the offer. "It has been a . . ." She glanced at Moira and then gave a very faint sigh. "Well, usually it has been a pleasure," she amended, and Moira grinned at her.

"Now, Aunt Mandy," she said, calling her by the nickname she had used as a toddler, "whatever do you mean by that statement?"

It was well past midnight when Miranda decided to retire. She embraced Daniel fondly, admonishing him to behave himself, pray regularly for deliverance, stay away from liquor and cards, and write to her often. Daniel assured her he would do all those things. Moira stopped her aunt in the foyer before she went upstairs.

"Aunt Miranda, I do love you very much," she said, tears sparkling in her dark eyes. She hugged the woman and kissed her cheek, drawing a startled look from her.

Miranda patted her niece's cheek fondly. "You can be a trial at times, my dear, but you've made my life . . . interesting. I only want to see you well settled with a proper husband to look after you."

Moira smiled tearfully. "I know. I shall behave, pray regularly, and . . . remember all you've said." She hugged her again and then let her go. Miranda gave her a curious look before going up the stairs. Moira returned to the parlor, and she and Daniel talked for a brief time before he decided to retire.

"The ship leaves at dawn, and I wouldn't want to oversleep," he told her. "And if you cry anymore, I shall have second thoughts about leaving you behind."

She smiled. "You mean you'd take me along?"

He blanched.

"Oh, well, the thought was there, Danny," she said sadly, letting him off the hook so she could spear him later. He embraced her and held her for a long moment. Then he sighed and released her. "Good night, Mory."

"It's good-bye, Danny," she whispered, looking up at him soulfully. "I'm not coming to the ship to see you off. One good-bye is more than enough. But if you don't write, I promise to come to California myself and wring your neck."

He grinned, kissed her on the cheek, and then walked out of the room. Moira waited for a few moments, sitting in the chair near the window and staring out thoughtfully. She started up the stairs and listened at Danny's door. It was quiet within. She doubted that he was asleep. He was probably sitting just as she had done, having his own second thoughts about the venture.

When she reached her own room, Moira quickly changed her clothes from the silk gown to a more practical brown wool dress with a matching cloak and bonnet. She pulled her carpetbags from beneath the bed and put in a few of her cosmetics, a bottle of French perfume, and a toothbrush, hairbrush, and hand mirror.

She had already written a letter of explanation to Aunt Miranda, and this she set on the mantel of her bedroom fireplace. She went to the door and listened for several moments before going out and tiptoeing down the hall. The house was silent. She went down the stairs and out by the side door through the kitchen.

It was some distance to the docks, but she didn't dare take one of the carriages. Someone would be sure to notice it missing in the morning and set up an alarm. It was a cold evening, but after walking for a few minutes she became quite comfortably warm. She was feeling very excited when she saw the ships and identified the *Stephen Rule*.

Daniel would be getting up soon and bringing his possessions down to the ship for stowing aboard. And then they would set off. A few miles out she would let him know she was aboard. She hadn't yet decided how to do this in the most dramatic way, but she would think of something.

Moira stopped and looked up at the ship. The sadness of leaving Charleston was diminishing with the growing excitement of going to California. The ship was quiet now, except for the gentle lapping of the water against the great hull. But in a few hours it would be in full sail, leaving everything she knew behind. It was a little frightening, and for a moment Moira wondered if she should change her mind and go back to the safety and predictability of Aunt Miranda's house.

Shifting the bag slightly, she put her foot on the gangplank and started up. Someone appeared above her and demanded in a hard voice, "Who goes there?"

Moira opened her mouth to speak, but someone beat her to it behind her.

"Hawthorne," came a familiar, deep voice, and she swung around, giving a startled cry as she tipped backward. She released the carpetbags instinctively in an attempt to grab something and heard them splash into the water below. At the same time a strong arm looped tightly around her waist, yanking her forward against a hard, broad chest.

Moira was immediately aware of the smell of tobacco and brandy and looked up at the elegantly attired First Mate Hawthorne. Her heart began to pump rapidly.

"Is the lady all right, sir?" the watch called from above.

"She's fine, Hendricks. I think we startled her," he said, his dark eyes laughing down at Moira. "You'd better fish her bags out of the drink before they sink. My hat as well."

"Oh," Moira gasped, turning in his arms to look down at the bobbing bags. She saw his hat there too. "I'm sorry, Mr. Hawthorne."

Hawthorne didn't release her completely but held her arm firmly in his hand while he assisted her up the gangplank and onto the ship.

"Are those two bags all you're taking with you?" he asked when they were safely on the main deck.

"That's all I need."

"I expected several trunks at the very least."

"Only bare essentials, Mr. Hawthorne. I understand California is a very informal place. And I hardly have much to call my own, anyway," she said, maintaining her ruse of a poor girl going to California to find her only brother.

The watch fished her two sodden bags aboard and left them dripping at Moira's feet. She wondered how she was going to dry everything out, then glanced up and saw that the watch had also handed Hawthorne his top hat. He was holding it between two fingers, looking at it ruefully.

"I'm terribly sorry," she apologized. "It's ruined, isn't it? I don't know what made me jump like that."

"Yes, I wondered about that myself. Almost as though you'd been caught in a crime." There was a hint of laughter in his voice.

"I should buy you a new hat."

"It's no great loss," he said, flicking the mushy thing back into the water. "We'll decide on some agreeable recompense at another time," he said blandly, eyes enigmatic. "But in the meantime, shall I show you to your cabin before another mishap befalls us, Miss Cavendish?" He picked up her bags, and when she hesitated, lifted his brows slightly. "Was there something else?"

She shook her head, feeling very self-conscious. "Perhaps these would be better left up here," she suggested, pointing at the offending bags. "Oh, never mind," she said, stumbling to a halt. "You're right." She couldn't very well hang her things about the ship. It wouldn't be proper, and besides, proper or not, Daniel might recognize some of them.

Following Hawthorne, Moira noticed his broad shoulders and narrow waist and his catlike walk. He had to duck his head when entering the booby hatch that went down 'tween decks. He glanced up at her, grinning, and told her to hold onto the rail and please watch her step. She did, flushing.

It was darker below, with only the pale light of several lanterns glowing dimly. The ship creaked and moved slightly, making Moira remember that she was no longer on land and wouldn't be for months to come. The passageway was long, and there were many portals on each side. The mate walked slightly sideways to avoid bumping into the bulwarks. Finally, he stopped and held both bags in one hand while opening a narrow door with the other. He stepped to one side, and Moira had the first glimpse of where she'd be living until she reached California.

Never had Moira seen such a tiny room. It was just long enough for two very narrow bunks and a small cupboard, which, upon brief investigation, contained a metal chamber pot, washbowl, and pitcher. There was no porthole and therefore absolutely no circulation of air. There was one blanket on each bunk. Nothing else.

"You can stow your belongings under there," he informed her, pointing to one of two small doors that latched beneath the lower bunk. Moira bent and opened it, peering in curiously. It would barely hold her two small bags, she thought disgustedly. She was glad she had not decided to bring more with her.

Straightening and looking around again, she could scarcely conceal the disappointment she was feeling. Daniel had said the cabins were supposed to be spacious. Obviously, either Daniel had not looked at them, or his was larger! But beggars couldn't be choosers, and she'd said she would sleep anywhere.

"Changed your mind yet, Miss Cavendish?" Hawthorne drawled as he leaned against the portal, watching her with obvious amusement.

She glanced up at him and spread out her hands. "It may be humble, but it's home."

He chuckled. "Nothing you've been used to up to now, I would hazard a guess."

Her brows lifted slightly. "It's quite . . ." She looked around again, searching for an appropriate word.

"Cozy?" he asked innocently, eyes dancing.

"Functional," she decided. "But then, who needs a lot of space? I don't imagine anyone spends much time belowdecks other than to sleep, do they?"

"Not if they can possibly help it."

"Yes, well, I can certainly understand that," she said dryly, smiling up at him. "It's unfortunate I didn't ask you to give me a peek at my quarters. I could have brought white paint and wallpaper to cheer it up a bit."

Hawthorne laughed. "Just like a woman to think of redecorating."

"It could use it," she said, looking around again.

"I'll leave you to settle into your new quarters, Miss Cavendish," he said, straightening. She looked at his formal clothes and realized that he must have just returned from an evening out. It was past three in the morning, and she wondered if he had been with the beautiful lady from the opera again or with some gentlemen for a last evening of revelry before setting sail. He had a certain relaxed look about him that bespoke a satisfying evening, whomever he'd been entertaining. Jack and Daniel had seldom had that look after being with their *men* friends, however.

Mr. Hawthorne was a very handsome man, she thought again. There was something about him that made her feel slightly self-conscious, vaguely defensive, and definitely breathless. She thought he'd probably be a very stimulating companion, not at all like Charles or some of the other young gentlemen she had met through her brothers. He wouldn't sniff after a woman's skirts like Charles Beauchamp, nor would he moon over her like some of Daniel's friends.

Moira suddenly realized that he was watching her watching him, and she blushed hotly. His eyes were gently teasing.

"Hasn't anyone ever told you it's dangerous to look at a man with such an obviously speculative gleam in your eye, Miss Cavendish?"

She managed a provocative smile to cover her embarrassment. "What's good for the gander is good for the goose, Mr. Hawthorne."

He laughed low and looked her over slowly, making her skin tingle. "I suggest you limit your virginal charms to young, *untried* men, or you may just find your tender little goose spitted." He gave her a wicked grin and bowed mockingly. "Good day, Miss Cavendish."

Chapter Four

Moira met her cabin mate an hour later. Sitting on the lower bunk, feeling very dejected now that the full realization of how far from home she was going overtook her, she was startled when the door opened. Jerking upright, she cracked her head soundly on the upper bunk. Muttering a sharp "ouch," she rubbed her head and focused on the woman standing in the doorway with one hand on her hip.

Never in her life had she seen such a person! She stared, mouth slightly agape, at the young woman. The low front of her deep rose dress displayed two very white mountains of flesh, forced up by her cinched-in corset. She wore a hat that looked ready to fly away at any moment. Around her slender throat was a black velvet ribbon. Numerous rings sparkled on her fingers, and the earrings she wore made a soft bell-like sound as she moved her head slightly and told the crewman to put her things inside the cabin. Her hair was dark and curly, escaping here and there around an attractive, though cynical, face. She had very pink cheeks, a darkened mole on her cheekbone, and lips painted a deep red. The dark eyes regarded Moira mockingly, and not with any degree of pleasure.

"So you're the chick I'm supposed to nest with," she said

flatly, raising one shoulder slightly in a disdainful gesture. She tapped her foot and then dismissed the bug-eyed sailor with a faint nod of her head and a brief, promising smile. Two cases, a large trunk, a ridiculously frilly parasol, and a box were crammed into the cabin. There wasn't room to move.

Grunting, the young woman, probably no older than twenty-two, righted a trunk, dusted off her hands, and sat down on it. She pulled off her hat and tossed it heedlessly onto the top bunk. The feathers quivered for several seconds.

"I'm Jewel Delarue," she introduced herself. "And whenever you can stop staring at me with your mouth open like a fish out of water, you can tell me your name. It's Marilyn or Maureen or something like that, isn't it?"

"Moira," she said. "Moira Cavendish. And I'm sorry I was staring," she apologized quickly. Where else could she look but at this fascinating person?

"Cavendish? Well, I've known a few Cavendishes," Jewel admitted and then stopped. "But we won't discuss them."

Moira wasn't exactly sure what she meant but decided not to pursue it. She could guess. They sat in silence, staring at one another, both curious. Jewel spoke again.

"We're a mismatched pair if ever there was one. How old are you, anyway?"

"Seventeen. Almost eighteen. You can't be that much older than I am," Moira observed, though it was difficult to tell through all the paint Jewel wore. Jewel laughed slightly.

"A lifetime, at least. Random said you were going to California to meet your brother. Is that the truth, or are you an escapee from a convent or something?"

Moira smiled, eyes impish. "Or something. But it's not a convent. It's an institution called matrimony."

Jewel laughed, and the hardness softened.

"Random," Moira repeated to herself thoughtfully, and Jewel, thinking there was an implied question, answered.

"The first mate. Hawthorne. Unless he's changed his name recently. You never know these days, and most of the gents I know don't use their real names anyway." She laughed at some private joke, but seeing Moira's blank look, went silent.

"Have you got a brother in California? You're surely not going alone."

"I've got two brothers, and one is in California."

"Where's the other one?"

"He's going to be on this ship in about half an hour or sooner."

Understanding dawned on Jewel's face. "And he doesn't know little sister is aboard."

Moira grinned.

"Well, you might just make an interesting cabin mate, after all," Jewel decided. "Is this brother of yours as good-looking as you are?"

"Much more so," Moira said with a twinkle, "and he's charming as well. Has an eye for the ladies," she added. "He's easily distracted." She raised her eyebrows faintly. Jewel grinned.

"And you want me to look after the boy until the ship is under way."

"He's got sandy-brown hair and blue eyes."

Jewel laughed. "Things are looking better all the time." She stood up. "I think I'll go up and take a stroll on deck—just to take a look at the scenery, you know."

Moira grinned in appreciation. "I shall be ever grateful, Miss Delarue."

Jewel shrugged. She gave one look around the cabin. "God above, not even a porthole. We'll suffocate down here," she said and went out the door.

Moira was exhausted. She had stayed up all night and walked to the docks, and now it was catching up with her. There was no point in sitting awake for another couple of hours, stewing over the inevitable confrontation with Daniel. Besides, she was feeling slightly dizzy and thought sleep might help.

Unfortunately, she felt worse when she awoke. The ship was dipping and swaying when she opened her eyes. She sat up, putting her feet on the floor, careful not to bump her head again on the upper bunk. Her stomach was very queasy and growing more so by the minute. The door seemed to roll in front of her.

Jewel came in a few minutes later to get her shawl. She took one look at Moira and sighed in exasperation.

"Not you, too," she said. "Half the ship is seasick."

"We're under way, then?" Moira asked, swallowing hard.

"Oh, yes indeedy, we are. And have been for several hours now. Except for the sailors, the upper deck is almost empty. The rest are—"

"I . . . I don't feel very well."

"No, and you don't look very well, either. Can I get you anything?"

"Well, my brother, for one thing," she said, looking up, her face white and taut. "I'd better face him and get it over with."

"He was a little green around the gills himself when I saw him standing at the rail a while ago. He wasn't only feeling rotten about leaving his poor little sister behind."

"He's going to be very angry."

"You're sure you want to see him?"

"I think I'd better."

"All right," Jewel said dubiously. She pointed toward the cupboard. "There's a chamber pot in there just in case you need it, which I hope you won't. There's little enough air down here without what we have being fouled."

Moira needed the pot. She was sitting on the floor groaning, her legs sprawled out and the pot in her lap, when Daniel threw open the door, hitting her hard in the rear end.

"Moira! What in bloody tarnation are you doing aboard?" he roared at her as he and Jewel managed to barely squeeze into the cabin.

"I'm going to California with you," she said weakly, wishing heartily at that moment that she weren't. The ship dipped again and she moaned, clutching the pot as though it were a talisman. Daniel continued railing at her, showing absolutely no sympathy for her condition. Anger seemed to have cured his own case of *mal de mer*.

"You can't go with me! What in hades am I supposed to do with you? The others are going to be furious. We don't need a blasted woman botching up our plans. Hell, this ship is no place for you! Do you know how many men there are on this ship?"

"One hundred and twenty-two," said Jewel, smiling like the cat who'd swallowed the canary.

"And five women," he said, casting Moira's cabin mate a distressed look. "My sister is a lady," he said emphatically.

Jewel looked down at Moira sitting on the floor clutching

the chamber pot and then back up at Daniel. "You don't say."

"What's Aunt Miranda going to do when she finds you missing?" he raged.

"She has a letter from me explaining everything in detail. And besides, Danny, I think she'll be secretly relieved."

"Of all the stupid things to do!"

"What did you expect me to do?" she demanded, looking up and seeing the cabin tilting above her. She looked down fast. "With Mama and Papa gone and Jack God knows where in California, I wasn't going to just let you sail off into the sunset! You're my last immediate relative."

"I should have guessed," he fumed. "I should have known! This is just like you! And after crying on my shoulder last night and making me feel bloody awful. You were laughing at me the whole time, weren't you, you little witch! I ought to throw you overboard and let you swim back to Charleston!"

Moira gave him a weak smile. "If I could swim, you wouldn't have to throw me in. I'd go willingly, just to get myself on dry land again." She moaned again as the ship rolled.

"Don't expect me to feel sorry for you!"

"Leave your sister alone, you big—"

"Stay out of it."

"You're her brother, aren't you? Have a little feeling for the poor kid. She's feeling awful."

"Not as bad as she ought to feel," he said grimly. "Serves her right, damn it. You've made a mess of my plans, Mory. Do you realize that? Oh, hell and damnation, why did you go and do this to me?"

"You are my family," she repeated stubbornly.

"You had Aunt Miranda!"

Moira sniffed. "Aunt Miranda is a dear, but she's never quite approved of me and you know it. She thinks I'm too much like the Cavendishes and not enough like the Donnellys."

"She offered you her home."

"Probably with some vain hope of reforming me, since you and Jack were already lost causes," she answered more pertly than she felt. She put a hand to her swimming head, as though that might give her some equilibrium. It didn't. "Can we continue this discussion at a later time, Danny? I don't feel very well at the moment."

"Miranda is probably having the vapors!"

"She's probably more than relieved that I'm gone!" Moira repeated impatiently and then moaned again as the ship swayed. "Oh, do go away, Danny, and just leave me alone for a while."

"Why don't you go?" Jewel added sympathetically. "The poor girl..."

"She thinks this is some grand adventure," he retorted.

"That's your opinion, not mine," Moira muttered dismally, feeling her stomach doing the same roll as the ship.

"Leave her alone."

"Stay out of this," Daniel said rudely. "She's my sister, and she's fouled up my plans. I've a perfect right to give her a piece of my mind."

"You've given her more than you can spare already, buster," Jewel retorted angrily. Moira giggled in spite of her misery.

"There! You see! She's laughing! She thinks this is all a big joke," Daniel said indignantly.

"Out!" Moira ordered, pointing a finger toward the portal.

"Moira, I'm not finished."

Moira glared up at her brother. "If you don't get out of here, Daniel Benjamin Cavendish, I shall retch all over your shiny new boots!"

Daniel left.

"Oh, God," Moira moaned. "Whatever possessed me to come on this miserable boat!" She bent over the chamber pot. "I wish I'd never ever heard of the *Stephen Rule*. I think I'm going to die, Miss Delarue."

"Jewel," she corrected, chuckling. "And you're not quite ready for the grave yet, honey." She helped Moira up off the floor and placed her gently back into the lower bunk.

"Some cabin mate you've been stuck with," Moira muttered in self-disgust.

"I could do worse," Jewel said. She lifted the chamber pot from Moira's hands gingerly, looking at it with distaste. "Then again, I could have done a lot better, too," she added dryly.

"Don't take it far. I think I'm going to need it again," Moira warned, putting a limp hand over her eyes.

"If it's any consolation, you're not the only one losing their breakfast."

"Just tell me it doesn't last long."

"A few days . . . a week at the most."

Moira raised herself up on one shaking elbow, almost cracking her head on the upper bunk again. "A week? You mean to tell me I'm going to feel like this for a week?" She plopped back weakly and cried, "Oh, I knew my sins would catch up with me. I should have stayed in Charleston and married horrid Charles Beauchamp just as Aunt Miranda wanted me to. He would have been preferable to this!"

"Beauchamp?" Jewel asked. "Well, dearie, you *are* one big bloody fool." She shook her head. "But then he would have gone on longer than a bout of *mal de mer.*"

The first big squall made believers out of every atheist aboard ship. There was a trembling line of young men outside Father Bartholomew's room next door for some hours. Jewel sat silently in her bunk. Moira was so sick she didn't care what the fate of her soul might be. At one point she prayed the ship would go down and give her eternal peace.

Jewel turned out to be right. Moira was sick for almost ten days before she finally earned her sea legs. She felt and looked like a battle-weary war veteran. She'd lost almost ten pounds, weight that she could scarcely afford to lose, and the loss of which left her listless. Most of her sparkling color was gone, as was most of her spunk. But she was determined to have a breath of fresh, clean air. Though weak, she went down the passageway and climbed the ladder to the main deck without assistance, drinking in the air with a vengeance.

The sun felt like balm on her face, and she tilted her head back to get the full warmth of it. She felt she had escaped a dungeon in which she had been locked up for months. She saw men lolling in hammocks strung about the deck. The ship looked very crowded. Men were everywhere, and most of them were staring straight at her. Some she recognized.

Daniel spotted her and came rushing over, followed by several of his friends from the Charleston Mining and Trade Company. She smiled weakly, knowing Kris Westwood, at least, was happy to have her aboard. John Pratt, Hadley and Paul Tyler, Carl Waltke, and several others crowded around her, all longtime friends of Daniel. Kris was the son of a physician, John of a merchant; Hadley and Paul's family was old money on the Cooper River, and Carl's family owned a pharmaceutical firm. None of them needed to go traipsing off to the other side of the continent looking for fast riches.

The young men ran up to Moira, asking how she was. So did Daniel, his ire temporarily forgotten. While she was sick he had come each day to check on her and see if she needed anything, but her health had been ably ministered to by Jewel Delarue. Moira and the prostitute had become friends during their confinement together. Jewel often left her to go on deck but returned frequently to check on her and encourage her to eat something. Jewel's care and her dry wit were responsible for keeping Moira's body and soul together.

Daniel heartily disapproved of Moira's fast friendship with Jewel, but Moira had simply dismissed his misgivings.

"So you're finally topside," Daniel said, putting an arm around her and smiling down at her. "You've become as bony as a chicken, Mory."

"Shut up, Daniel," Kris said, his grave eyes on Moira. He was one of the young men that were enamored of Moira. "That's hardly what she wants to hear." He smiled at her sympathetically.

"We'll have to fatten her up," Hadley said, giving her a lopsided smile.

"Frankly, I never thought I'd see the light of day again," Moira admitted with a self-mocking smile. "That air smells and feels wonderful."

She closed her eyes, drawing the air gratefully into her lungs.

"Why don't you sit down, Miss Moira?" John suggested solicitously. "There's a barrel over here."

"I've sat enough for a lifetime," she demurred. The young men talked around her as she stood at the rail, staring out over the ocean. There was no land in sight, and the breeze was warm. She felt someone watching her and looked up.

Random Hawthorne was standing near the forward house looking at her. His eyes made an all-encompassing study of her, taking in the sunken shadows beneath her dark eyes, the pallor of her face, the painful slenderness of her young body, her wanness. She couldn't tell what he was thinking, and he didn't approach to speak to any of them. He had duties to perform.

The wind had been with the ship since leaving Charleston, and they were making good time south. During her illness, Jewel had kept Moira apprised of the happenings aboard the ship. Captain Thackary had had difficulties soon after departure, a result of the exaggerated claims about the luxuries of his ship made in the circulars he had posted about the city. He had advertised spacious cabins, excellent cuisine, a sleekly fitted ship that would bring everyone safely into San Francisco Bay in a minimum of time.

The ship was jammed tighter than a Norwegian sardine can. Some men were sleeping in hammocks on the main deck, while as many as three men were cramped into the smallest cabin. The food, though surprisingly nutritious, was absolutely appalling to the taste buds. Captain Thackary, smiling in a perpetual state of brandied goodwill, refused to take any complaints seriously. He had his money and they were all going to San Francisco. What more could anyone ask for? Besides, it was a little late to quibble about niceties, wasn't it?

The captain spent the majority of his time in his comfortable quarters with his bottle, a loaded pantry, and a trunk of books while Random Hawthorne ran the ship. Late at night, when all the passengers were asleep, the captain would come out on deck for his constitutional. If anyone saw him, he quickly retreated to his cabin like a weasel to its hole.

No one wanted to doubt the seaworthiness of the *Stephen Rule*, but during the first rainstorm, not a week out of harbor, leaks had opened up on deck, and the water had poured through onto the bunks 'tween decks.

On calm nights the sheep, pigs, and poultry could be heard carrying on their infernal racket in the livestock closet. Sometimes one could even hear the ax fall and the sudden cacophony of the other residents on death row.

Once Moira was up and regaining her strength and spirits, she spent all her time on the main deck. Daniel began to worry. Whenever she appeared, men both young and old flocked around her like so many seagulls. The princess had appeared, and court was being held near the bow. Moira was thoroughly enjoying herself.

"I don't want you spending so much time on deck, Moira," Daniel told her firmly one afternoon. They stood on the fo'c'sle, the breeze blowing over them. The air was getting hotter and balmier by the day as they neared the equator. "Sooner or later there's bound to be trouble."

"Daniel, you worry too much," Moira said. She hadn't been pleased when he'd told the young men to give him a few minutes alone with her on family business. She could tell by his expression what the family business was going to be her.

"And you don't worry enough. For heaven's sake, Moira, there are five women aboard this ship and a hundred and twenty-two men. That spells trouble."

"I don't see why."

He took a deep breath and looked exasperated. "It's a simple matter of biological urges."

That made Moira smile. She looked up at him. "Do explain, brother dear."

He blushed. "You've an idea what I mean, I'm sure."

"Elucidate, please. I'm not so sure I do." She managed to look very serious and perplexed.

"Men have certain...well, certain needs, and they are bound to begin thinking along...certain lines." He looked thoroughly embarrassed, and Moira's mouth twitched. He saw it and scowled darkly. "You witch! You know exactly what I'm talking about."

"I was just wondering whose biological urges are coming to the surface. I've seen the way you've been eyeing my cabin mate."

Daniel's face darkened even more. "It's bad enough that you're making my life difficult, but you're learning too much. You're a lady! Remember? You're not supposed to know about certain things."

"Being a lady doesn't mean I must be a fool."

"And while we're about it," he went on, ignoring her statement, "you're getting browner than any sailor aboard. And your hair. Can't you bind it back the way you used to and curl it instead of letting it hang down and fly about your face all the time?"

Moira laughed slightly. "This isn't Charleston, and everyone else is getting as brown as me, you included. And if you're worried about my drawing too much attention. I shall be as inconspicuous as a quiet little mouse."

"Oh, Lord . . ."

"Besides, not one man aboard this ship has even tried to lay a finger on me. And that's much more than I can say for Charles Beauchamp in Charleston. This protective instinct of yours is rather late blooming, wouldn't you say, Daniel?"

"Circumstances change," he said grimly. "And something else. I know you like Jewel and she's been good to you, but I wish you wouldn't be quite so friendly with her. She's . . . she's not a lady, and you are," he finished lamely.

Moira understood Daniel's unease. After the first few weeks aboard ship, Jewel had made no bones about herself. She had finally told Moira in no uncertain terms that living for appearances' sake like a nun was not her style, that she had already wasted valuable time and money by not immediately plying her trade. Monique Beaupré was already well on her way to paying for her passage, and here she was empty-pursed. She was sorry if she was shocking Moira, but that was the way life was, and she would appreciate it if Moira left the cabin for a while. She promised to use only the top bunk.

"I like her," Moira told Daniel simply, and it was true. "Besides, she promised not to corrupt me if I promised not to reform her."

Daniel glared in exasperation at his grinning little sister. "Moira," he began, and she was fully aware that he was about to embark on another of his lengthy lectures on proper decorum. He was beginning to sound like Aunt Miranda.

"I find it very hypocritical that the men who enjoy Jewel and her friends so much should so heartily claim to disapprove of her," she said flatly, looking him squarely in the eye. "If you don't approve of her behavior or her business, how can you possibly approve of your own?"

"I haven't touched Jewel!"

"No . . . not Jewel," she said pointedly, looking toward Monique Beaupré. The redhead was talking animatedly to Kris Westwood. Moira looked back up at Daniel, whose face was a fiery, angry red. She smiled sweetly. "You know, Daniel," she said, tapping a finger lightly on his chest, "it's very difficult not to know what's going on aboard this ship. One should remember that when one is so very concerned with another's propriety."

"You're a bitch," he fumed.

"What an unkind thing to say to a sister who is, after all, merely very concerned with her older brother's moral well-being," she mocked, giving him a teasing, affectionate smile.

Daniel decided against pursuing the subject any further. And Moira went on holding court near the bow.

Chapter Five

The further south the ship traveled, the hotter it grew. Red dust appeared on the deck. Moira asked a handsome blond sailor what it all meant. Were they nearing land? Would they put in to shore? Ole Peterson was flattered that Moira asked him for answers. Moira, unknown to him, liked his thick Swedish accent and his pleasant disposition.

The westerly winds, Ole said, brought the dust from the African desert, and if she were interested in hearing stories of that mystical and exotic shore, he would have some free time after nine bells. Moira was interested in everything, but she saw the lusty gleam in Peterson's eyes and also saw First Mate Hawthorne standing at the helm, watching them with a baleful eye. She decided it would be best not to encourage Peterson.

As the heat intensified, so did the foul moods of everyone aboard. Restlessness and discontent grew or shrank in proportion to the velocity of the winds. The wind down, tempers up; wind up, tempers down. Frequently the ship sat becalmed on a blue sea, and then tempers flared and exploded.

Moniqué Beaupré, businesswoman that she was, and her two girls took full advantage of the boredom, offering entertainment at a hefty price in their cabins.

One afternoon, as everyone stood around bored on the main deck, a strange personage appeared from over the side. Moira was on the bow and saw him as he jumped up on the main deck. She stared in astonishment. It was a few minutes before she recognized Bull McBean, a New England sailor renowned for his size and strength, under the Manila-rope wig and beard. Great sail robes flowed about him as he strode up and down the deck. He held a trident raised threateningly in one hand and roared at the startled, confused passengers.

A makeshift throne was set up on the poop deck, and King Neptune's court was opened. Men scattererd as the crew began gathering up the unbelievers. Neptune stared fiercely down on the congregation of grinning crewmen who had been over the equator before and were therefore exempt from the initiation. The captive passengers were decidedly nervous.

"That one first!" Neptune bellowed, pointing with his trident at Lester Aiken, an obnoxious New Yorker who had caused several arguments aboard ship. He was a chronic complainer, argumentative, and thought it hilariously funny to pull chairs out from under unsuspecting fellow passengers. Everyone watched as he was dragged forward and thrust under the ominous eye of the king of the sea.

"Sit down, you bloody landlubber!"

The young man sat, laughing nervously. Neptune stared harder.

"You laugh at the king of the sea?"

"You're no more the king of the sea than I'm the man in the moon!" Aiken said with all the bravado he possessed. The crew gave horrified gasps of well-portrayed fear. Neptune leaned forward.

"Say your last prayer, you miserable wretch, for you've just consigned yourself to the deep. You'll be food for the fish!" He jerked his head in a commanding gesture. "Blindfold him and send him off the port bow!"

Aiken let out a startled cry as two burly sailors grabbed him. His arms were held back while the blindfold was put on. Four sailors lifted him and carried him down the deck, to the astonishment and cries of protest from the other passengers, who knew full well their turns were coming. Aiken was shouting louder than all the rest as he was swung roughly back and forth and pitched high into the air. His arms flailing madly, he landed in a large tub of salt water. The passengers laughed as he ripped off the blindfold and stared around him in red-faced humiliation.

"Shave the landlubber!" Neptune ordered. Aiken was again roughly seized, lathered with smelly grease, and then shaved with a barrel-hoop razor. His face was raw when they finished, and he looked far less bold. He crawled clumsily out of the tub and slunk off, and the next passenger was thrust forward to face Neptune.

"I rule the sea, I cause the winds, and when I order it—it rains!" Neptune roared. A sailor positioned aloft poured a bucket of salt water down on the head of the New Hampshire merchant sitting before the king. He let out a shriek as the water hit him.

"Do you believe, you miserable land-crawling wretch?"

"I believe! I believe!" the drenched merchant said.

"Shave him!"

Kris was dragged forward next. Neptune examined his own fingernails casually.

"Do you have a token for me?"

"A token?" Kris asked nervously, looking around for en-lightenment.

"A bottle of spirits, you bloody fool!" the king roared down at him. Kris shook his head. Neptune looked disgusted and pounded his trident on the deck.

"Shave him!"

Several bottles of whiskey appeared miraculously from the recesses of California-bound trunks. The king drank from each and passed the bottles around.

Daniel was brought forward, and Moira watched nervously as Neptune leaned forward again, trident held upright to one side. Daniel had no bottle of spirits to exempt him from the ritual.

"Do you solemnly swear to drink water when you can get wine?" Neptune demanded sternly. "And do you also swear that when given the choice of kissing a maiden or a crone, you'll kiss the crone?" There was general laughter.

"I swear," Daniel agreed, a lopsided grin on his face.

"Shave the damn liar!"

More passengers were brought forward, bringing bottles with them. French brandy, liqueurs, wine, whiskey, and Southern Comfort were uncorked. Moira estimated that Neptune had consumed fourteen healthy swigs from as many bottles before relinquishing each to the eagerly waiting crewmen and initiated passengers.

Hilarity was reigning supreme. Neptune was having the greatest difficulty staying on his barrel throne, and he wasn't the only one feeling his liquor. Daniel, Kris, Hadley, and Paul were well saturated, sitting spread-legged near the windlass, passing around a bottle of cognac. Other groups of men were enjoying themselves and their bottles as well.

Moira thought the entire affair amusing. One man was throwing up over the rail, to the hardy guffaws of a sailor sitting aloft with his own bottle. Like a bird on a branch, his legs locked him onto the yardarm and kept him from pitching to his death on the deck below.

She had thought herself and the other women exempt from the ritual until some bright passenger shouted: "What about the women?"

She saw the glittering eyes of half a dozen men turn in her direction. "I've no beard to shave off," she said nervously to a sailor walking toward her. Monique's two girls squealingly fled the deck, pursued by a dozen laughing men. Monique herself was thrust before King Neptune, who stroked his beard with caressive lechery.

"No bottle, your kingship," she said, hands on hips, red hair gleaming in the bright sunshine. Neptune scratched his face beneath the lopsided-Manila rope beard. He was sweating profusely in the heat.

"Then do you swear before the company present here today to render your womanly services from here to the Horn?"

"Indeed, I do, your kingship," she said, smiling, and moved her hips with a provocative invitation that made the men whoop with approval.

"Free of charge, of course."

"Nothing doing."

"To one man of your choice," he amended and tapped his chest. Monique swiveled her hips again.

"A king's ransom for a kingly pleasure, I always say, your Majesty," she said with a grin.

"The tub or a kiss, you saucy wench," Neptune finally managed, hiccuping. Monique brushed a nonexistent speck of dust from her low-cut bodice while the men around shouted and whistled.

"The kiss," she decided.

"Come on up!" he roared, pulling the Manila beard down to expose his flushed face. Monique was hoisted up by two sailors. Neptune grabbed her and yanked her down onto his lap. He bent her backward and bestowed a lusty kiss on her mouth, thrusting a hand down the front of her dress.

Moira's face flamed, and she looked around for a means of escape. She darted for the booby hatch, but two sailors blocked her.

"Now, gentlemen," she said cajolingly, backing up a step and bumping into another sailor behind her. She swung around and looked up at Random Hawthorne. He was grinning down at her in a taunting way.

"No need to panic, Miss Cavendish," he drawled. "Everything is well under control."

"It is?" She gulped. "I haven't a token for the king, Mr. Hawthorne."

"Perhaps your brother has something packed away?"

Moira glanced toward Daniel, who was laughing loudly and polishing off the dregs of a communal bottle. He hadn't the least thought of his sister's plight. Perhaps he'd forgotten she was even aboard in his present merry stupor. He didn't look able to stand, let alone come to her rescue. She looked back up at Random. He was smiling wickedly.

"You look worried, Miss Cavendish. Haven't you a scheme to get yourself out of this one?"

Moira let out a cry of alarm as she was lifted high in the air by two sailors answering King Neptune's order to "bring forth the woman Cavendish." She was set down, amid laughter and bold looks, next to a besotted king, who was now leaning very heavily on his trident.

"This one here's a real lady, your Majesty," Ole Peterson yelled. "Take care how you treat her!"

"A right tasty-looking little morsel," Neptune replied, rubbing his hands together and grinning lasciviously. Moria swallowed hard.

"Not all that tasty," she said with a nervous look at Bull McBean, now exposed under the sagging beard.

"Where's my token?" Neptune thumped his trident like a petulant boy.

"More whiskey! More whiskey!" came the chant from a dozen already sodden men. "Whiskey or a kiss!"

"All I have is a bottle of French perfume," she offered desperately.

"Perfume!"

"I understand there's some alcohol in it," she told him, and there was more uproarious laughter.

"Won't do. Won't do," Neptune said, shaking his head. His wig was sliding to one side.

"Will this do?" Random Hawthorne stepped forward and held up a bottle of the finest bourbon money could buy or man could steal.

"By God, that'll do, all right!" Neptune said and held out his hand. The bottle was tossed up, and, drunk as he was, the king still managed to catch it easily. While Neptune took a long swig of his token, Random took Moira by the arm and escorted her into the officers' quarters beneath the helm. When the door was securely closed behind them, Moira let out her breath in profound relief.

"How can I thank you?" she said, turning to smile up at him. She stopped. He was leaning back against the portal, arms crossed over his chest, smiling in a way to set her heart pounding. Her eyes widened as they met the gleaming darkness of his.

"You should have stayed in your cabin, Miss Cavendish," he said in a low, taunting whisper. She could hear Neptune's trident being thumped above them, and raucous laughter. Random straightened and took a step toward her. Moira stepped back, heart galloping in her breast. Her mouth felt dry.

"I'll . . . I'll go right this minute if you'll let me pass."

"I think not." He took another step toward her, and she retreated to the dining table.

"Mr. Hawthorne, I don't know what you have on your mind, but you're making me very nervous."

"You do look a little worried," he agreed, continuing to stalk her, his dark eyes moving from her chest to the pink tip of her tongue wetting her lips.

"I won't demand as much as King Neptune," he told her, smiling sensually and sending color into her face and heat throughout her body. "After all, it's my sworn duty to protect the passengers aboard the *Stephen Rule,* even if it costs me a bottle of bourbon."

"I'll buy another for you at the first port of call," she offered quickly.

"I don't think so. That brand you can only get in the States."

"Now, be reasonable, Mr. Hawthorne," she said with as much bravado as she could muster. He had backed her into his cabin and stood squarely in the doorway. She found herself against his bunk with nowhere else to go. He grinned, and she stared at him, waiting for him to do something. Suddenly, he stepped back and pulled the door shut. She heard the lock catch and stared at the portal that trapped her in the first mate's quarters.

"A pleasant evening to you, Miss Cavendish," Hawthorne drawled from the other side. Understanding dawned on her. She should have been relieved that she was safely locked away from the wild goings-on on the main deck, but she was furious! She lunged forward and pounded her fist on the portal.

"Let me out of here!"

"Temper . . . temper . . ."

"Let . . . me . . . out . . . of . . . here!" She pounded harder. She heard him laugh; then the door to the main deck opened and closed firmly. "Hawthorne!" she hollered. The burst of laughter above her drowned her yelling out. She kicked the door, then sat down to nurse her bruised toes.

Hawthorne unlocked the cabin door at dawn. He looked as though he had joined in the celebration on the main deck and remained well into the evening. His dark hair was rumpled, and there were lines about his eyes. His white shirt was open, exposing the hard muscles and dark curly hair on his chest. He leaned against the doorjamb, a thumb hooked in his wide leather belt, and watched Moira push herself up from his bunk, staring at him with sleep-dazed brown eyes. Her hair had come down and was hanging around her shoulders in a curling, unruly mass. Her cheeks were flushed, and there was a vulnerable fullness to her parted lips.

Moira sat up and put her bare feet on the floor, searching for her thin-soled shoes. The bodice of her dress stretched tautly, accentuating the fine curves of her young body.. She glanced up and saw Hawthorne staring.

"You're letting me out?" she asked, finding her shoes and slipping them on. Her voice was huskier than usual.

His eyes narrowed, and then he smiled slightly. "I think you can safely return to your cabin now without fear of losing your virtue, Miss Cavendish." She smiled back at him, her eyes sparkling in challenge.

"I suppose I should thank you."

"You should." He glanced down at the tray he had put inside the cabin while she was sleeping. She hadn't touched it. "Didn't the labscouse suit you?"

She had already had enough of the hash made of salted meat, potatoes, and hard bread to last a lifetime.

"I wasn't hungry."

"The cook passed out on the bow, or you might have fared better. Unfortunately, that was all I could scratch up." He looked her over again. "You should eat more. you haven't gained back all the weight you lost from your bout of seasickness."

Meaning she was skin and bones, she assumed indignantly. "I'll try to remember," she said stiffly. He laughed softly, comprehending.

"What's the matter, Miss Cavendish? Did I say something wrong?"

She let that question slide and looked up at him curiously. "What happened last night?"

"I can't rightly remember," he said, rubbing his neck and sending her a laughing look. "Why do you want to know?"

"Just call me curious."

"Well, I think everyone had a good time, and they're suffering for it this morning. Those who have come to, that is."

"You look a little under the weather yourself, Mr. Hawthorne."

"You sound pleased."

She shrugged, an unpleasant thought whirling in her head. Where had he spent the night? And with whom had he been sleeping? She had seen him talking several times with Monique Beaupré, and that woman certainly would have welcomed him to her cabin. Her cabin mate could have moved in for the night with Jewel. She didn't want to think about it. And after all, why should she be concerned?

Moira looked up and found Random Hawthorne staring at her again. They looked at one another for a long moment. Her heart began pounding like a locomotive, and she saw a muscle move in his jaw. His expression seemed to tighten and become almost grim. Then it changed again, his mouth curving into a mocking, indulgent smile.

"If you don't plan on leaving my bunk, would you mind moving over? I need some sleep."

Moira stood up with a jerk, then gracefully curtsied and indicated he should take his bunk. They moved around each other like two dancers changing position, not touching.

Out on the main deck, men were sprawled everywhere like carelessly scattered cards. There was a rhythm of snores. Moira tripped over a man, and he didn't even flinch. She thought he was dead until she looked closer and saw the slow rise and fall of his stomach as he breathed. Someone was groaning on the poop deck. Someone else was retching over the side.

Moira looked for Daniel among the fallen. He and his cronies were still by the windlass, all unconscious, by the looks of it. She stood above them, hands on hips, and shook her head. And this was what men called fun! She looked at Daniel as he lay sleeping, one arm flung above his head. Kris was snoring loudly. Hadley was beginning to stir.

After all the hours she had listened to them all drawing up their righteous bylaws with such delicate care! They had promised not to drink, carouse, swear, or gamble. And they had promised to respect the Sabbath. Yesterday had been Sunday! It hadn't taken the lot of them more than a few weeks to forget all their grand ideals and proper upbringing. They were young, away from home, and they were going absolutely wild.

A thought came to Moira as she stood looking down at the members of Charleston Mining and Trade Company passed out on the main deck of the *Stephen Rule*. She started to laugh as she walked toward the booby hatch. She'd give the darlings a few hours to revive and then she'd start having her fun. After all, hadn't they all been making merry while she'd been locked in that stuffy cabin?

Jewel was dead to the world when Moira entered the cabin. She was lying on Moira's bunk, half dressed, with her forearms over her eyes, a five-dollar note hanging out of the front of her dress. Moira took some paper from her letter case and climbed up, setting to work. When Jewel began stirring an hour later, she was finished.

"What are you doing up there?" Jewel asked, voice croaking like a bullfrog.

"Oh, just a little something," Moira said, smiling to herself. "How are you feeling this morning?"

"Don't ask. Lousy. Rotten. Sick," she said and lay back down on the bunk. Moira hopped down, her skirts floating around her. She brushed them down. Jewel groaned.

"Not so much noise, if you don't mind."

"Would you like me to get you anything?" Moira asked, pausing at the door.

"A new head," Jewel said, covering hers with a blanket.

Up on the main deck, men were sitting up. Several had their heads in their hands. Others were sitting as though one movement would destroy them. Amazingly, some of the sailors were working. The ship was becalmed, but no one cared—the less movement the better.

Moira found a few nails from a loose crate. Using the heel of her shoe, she tacked up her notice. Then she walked down the deck, smiling and greeting friends, and climbed the ladder to the bow to enjoy the sun and the sea air.

On the main mast was nailed the following:

AMENDMENTS to the BYLAWS
of CALIFORNIA-BOUND
MINING COMPANIES

Section 1. No member shall consume any alcoholic beverage *unless he is sick, well, wet, dry, hot, cold, or just in want.*

Section 2. No member shall use the Lord our God's name in vain *except when he is unable to express his feeble thoughts in any other way.*

Section 3. No member shall carry on immoral activities *unless he is able to do so with or without the express knowledge and approval of the other members of the company.*

Section 4. No member shall gamble with any-one's money but his own *unless he finds himself with a willing fool to finance him.*

Section 5. All members of the company shall honor the Sabbath *unless they find something more entertaining to do.*

Section 6. All members, when not engaged in the work of mining gold, shall be occupied in worthy activities for the betterment of the com-pany, *such as drinking, carousing, gambling, swearing, and fighting.*

Section 7. No member shall act in violence against another of this company *unless another member asks for it. Then it shall be a free-for-all.*

Any breaking of the above rules shall bring about the expulsion of the offending member of the company.

The bylaws remained posted until the next storm washed them down, but by then more than a dozen copies had been made.

Chapter Six

The wind dropped when they were several hundred miles south of the equator. With nothing better to do, three young men raided the mess, and in retaliation the angry cook liberally laced their wine with tartar emetic. The young men suffered for forty-eight hours before their systems returned to relative normalcy. The galley was safe again.

Men played cards, chess, and checkers and made bets on anything, including how many minutes it would be before the wind came up again. Others cleaned firearms, read, and developed latent talents. One man practiced the fiddle until told that to do so might shorten his life. Moira began teaching Jewel French, because the prostitute said it would be good for her business.

Tempers soared with the continued calm. Everyone was impatient to reach California. The heat was almost unbearable, and arguments began breaking out with more frequency, even between men who had been friends at the onset of the voyage. Kris and Hadley had come to blows over a chess game; Daniel had had a shouting match with John.

Moira began to plot mischief.

A farmer from Maine had taken to sitting on the bow of the ship with his fishing pole, ever optimistic that he would catch

something. So far he'd not had even a bite. Bets were on as
to when he would get one, and so far pockets were empty.

Moira sent Kris over the side with a chamber pot to attach
to the fisherman's line. For a while there was great excitement—until the man managed to bring his catch up into view.
When the pot was brought up, the ship's company went wild
with laughter.

Moira's prank didn't improve Daniel's foul temper. Her
presence on the ship was a constant worry to him, and the fact
that she was becoming a leader of sorts irritated him even more.
His sister was supposed to be a lady, and ladies didn't plan
practical jokes or nail up amendments to seriously drawn-up
bylaws—amendments, moreover, that indicated a worldly
knowledge she shouldn't have. Nor should a lady encourage
the men on the ship to swoon at her feet. He began pressuring
Moira to stay in her cabin.

"Propriety be damned," Moira told him fiercely, as much
affected by the heat as anyone else. It was bad enough above
decks with corset and petticoats on, but the cabin was little
better than an oven, and she had no intention of baking for the
sake of his peace of mind. So what if men had their shirts off
and their pants rolled up to their knees? Of course she had
noticed their legs. She wasn't blind, was she?

At that Daniel lectured her even more doggedly.

"Stop yapping at me, Daniel," Moira told him impatiently.
"You'll give yourself a headache." It was so hot she seemed
to be melting, and all he could do was sweat over conventions.
Conventions be damned, and Daniel too if he didn't shut up
pretty soon.

"Yapping!" he exploded.

She swung on him and put her face close to his, almost
touching his nose with hers, and said loudly, "Yes, yapping!"

Several passengers and crew members who had been watching them laughed. She looked around and realized they had
become the center of attention, probably the objects of more
ridiculous bets, and her face flamed. Random Hawthorne had
seen it all and was enjoying it as well. She glared up at Daniel,
then stormed below to sit sweltering and fuming in her cabin.
But she planned her revenge for later. For the moment, let
Daniel think he had the last word.

That night Moira went to the mainmast's rope ladder. She had tied her skirts about her legs to make pantaloons, and her hair was braided down her back. Reaching up, she managed to pull herself onto the lines. The sailors made it look so easy, she thought looking up at the crow's nest, her destination. Someone was up there, looking down at her. She started to slowly climb upward. The ladder shook, and she clung to it tightly, afraid to look down. It was a long way up, she realized belatedly, and after one look down to the deck below, decided it was best to keep her eyes heavenward. If she fell, that might be the way she'd be heading anyway.

When she got to the top, she recognized Ole Peterson at the same time he recognized her. His shocked expression stopped her ascent.

"You're mad!" he gasped, grabbing her arm. He looked more nervous than she was, and she started to laugh. If his reaction was this great, how much greater would be Daniel's when he found out! She stood in the crow's nest with Ole, clutching the ropes and frame for all her life. She was shaking but feeling triumphant. The reason for her climb was pinned to her side, as Ole Peterson was quick to notice. He stared at her corset with frank curiosity.

"I've never been up here, and I wanted to have a look around," she said, grinning at him. She turned and looked out at the ocean. it was beautiful and peaceful, mirror-smooth in the starlight.

"What are you doing with your..." He cleared his throat. Obviously, seeing a woman's undergarment embarrassed him.

"I'm going to hang it up here with the ship's colors."

"You're going to do what?"

"I'm making a statement."

"Is that what you're doing?" He looked at her speculatively. She gave a low laugh. She wasn't going to hurry this. She'd been in cramped quarters for too long, and to be up here in the open air was wonderful. She might stay until Daniel came up to get her down.

Peterson's arm curved around her waist, and she glanced at him with a wry smile. "Ole..."

"I wouldn't want you to fall." He smiled at her.

"You're shaking worse than I am, Mr. Peterson."

He laughed, his breath brushing lightly against her neck. "Pretty girls do that to me."

His technique wasn't much better than Charles Beauchamp's, Moira thought ruefully, but she liked him much better. She subdued the urge to elbow him. It was unnecessary to do anything, for someone was coming up the rope, and Ole removed his arm voluntarily. Moira peered down, then wished she hadn't. The sight of the deck far below made her head spin dizzily and her heart leap into her throat. She *was* crazy! Coming up had taken all her courage. How was she ever going to get down?

Random Hawthorne suddenly appeared. "What in hades is going on up here?" He was standing on the yardarm, having come up with lithe precision and in a minimum of time. He looked furious, eyes glittering, mouth compressed, a muscle knotting in his jaw. Moira swallowed hard.

"She came up for . . . for some air, sir," Peterson answered. There wasn't much room in the crow's nest, and they were both looking very guilty. The first mate looked from one to the other and then came across. He was as surefooted as a cat, she thought enviously.

"You're going down, Miss Cavendish," he told her.

She smiled weakly. "I hate to tell you this, Mr. Hawthorne, but I don't think I can."

"You got up here, you can sure as hell get down. And now!" His eyes swung toward Peterson. "This man is supposed to be on duty."

That got her dander up. "I only came up to . . ." She stopped herself. He might not think it funny to have a woman's corset flying below the ship's flag. ". . . to get some air," she finished lamely.

"Well, you've had it. Now climb down!"

This man isn't reasonable, Moira thought furiously, glaring at him.

"I don't want you splattered all over the deck," he added angrily.

"Wonderful," she said harshly. "Just the words of confidence I needed." But irritation gave her some courage. She looked down and then up at him again. He seemed to be taking a certain unwarranted degree of malicious delight in her predicament. She started down the rope ladder, praying silently. She clutched the ropes so tightly that her knuckles turned white. Perspiration broke out on her face, and her heart felt as though it were beating its way up into her mouth.

Suddenly, she wasn't alone on the ladder. Hawthorne had positioned himself right behind her, his body so close to hers they touched. If he had intended to make her feel more secure, he'd failed.

"Do you feel any safer?" he asked against her ear. She was trembling worse than before, aware of the heat of his body and the musky male smell of him that went straight to her head, the pit of her stomach, and other places a lady shouldn't be thinking about.

"I'm not sure," she hedged.

He put his hand over hers and worked her fingers loose. "Take a step down. Come on, I'm not going to let you fall. If I did, I'd hit the deck first."

"With me on top," she croaked, trying to bring a lightness to the moment.

They started down, and she found it was easier with him behind her. When they were almost to the rail, he swung down and reached up to grasp her firmly at the waist. He set her before him, and she looked up at him, wide-eyed and waiting for the coming storm of reprimand. He didn't say anything, just took her arm and turned her toward the booby hatch.

"Good night," he told her firmly. She sighed in defeat and headed toward her cabin. Turning, she saw him striding in the opposite direction. She stopped, unpinned the corset, and tossed it overboard. She brushed off her hands in satisfaction and went below.

On deck the following morning, Random approached her. She was standing with Daniel and his friends near the bow and nervously watched the first mate's approach, sure that he was going to say something scathing about her escapade the evening before. Daniel was angry with her this morning for coming up on deck again. She gave the mate an appealing look, and he smiled sardonically back, eyes glittering.

"I'd like a word with you, Miss Cavendish," he said sternly, drawing Daniel's immediate questioning glance.

"Is something wrong, Mr. Hawthorne?" he asked and then

looked at Moira suspiciously. "Has my sister been up to something again?"

"Nothing to worry about," the mate said coolly, eyes never leaving Moira. "We'll talk in the officers' quarters," he told her. She flushed at his expression, then followed him. He opened the door and stepped to one side, allowing her to enter first. Moira glanced back and saw her brother staring after them.

"Perhaps if you'd just..."

"Inside, Miss Cavendish. We'll have our conversation in private." She looked up at him and, seeing the uncompromising set of his jaw, the fire in his eyes, did as he instructed. He was feeling fierce about something, and her heart beat more rapidly when he closed the portal behind them, entrapping them in the officers' quarters.

She was more nervous this time than the last, but she looked around, delaying the inevitable. Two doors at the far end opened on stairs that led up to the poop deck and the helm. There were other doors, officers' cabins, the pantry, a small galley. To the left was the captain's cabin, and she could hear him snoring loudly. In the center of the room was a long table and two benches bolted down, where the men took their meals. Slats were nailed on top to keep the crockery in place. There was even a wood stove to keep the quarters warm on a cold night. Not that it was needed now in this hellish heat.

Hawthorne leaned against the mizzen mast, which thrust up through the deck, watching Moira make her minute inspection. She swallowed hard and looked up at him, clasping her hands respectfully in front of her like a schoolgirl called before the headmaster.

"You wanted to speak with me, Mr. Hawthorne? If it's about last night, I promise not to go up the mast again."

He smiled slowly and straightened. Her heart beat faster, her stomach tightened, her breathing stopped. He seemed to take note of it all, assessing her from head to foot. There was a hint of threat in his eyes that did not bode well for her.

"Women are trouble on a ship," he began. "But you, my dear Miss Cavendish, are an absolute catastrophe."

"I beg your pardon," she said in confusion.

"Where shall I begin, Miss Cavendish?" he asked dryly.

She wished he would stop calling her that in that precise tone of voice. "With your first transgression, or your last?"

"How about the one that has you so annoyed with me, Mr. Hawthorne?" she suggested pertly.

"That's simple enough," he agreed. He stepped past her and opened the door to his cabin. Reaching in, he grabbed something and then returned. What dangled on the end of his index finger was embarrassingly familiar. The color started at her toes and worked its way to her hairline with amazing speed.

"Oh."

"Yes, 'oh,'" he mocked her. He looked at the wet corset and then smiled at her, obviously relishing her discomfort.

"How . . . how did you ever get hold of it?" she stammered.

"The same way we retrieved your carpetbags when you first boarded this ship. This"—he lifted the corset—"created much more of an impact, I must say."

"You're assuming, of course, that it's mine," she said, trying to worm her way out of it. He laughed slightly, a husky sound deep in his chest. He looked her over very slowly, his eyes traveling with the speed of a snail over her swelling young breasts.

"That's easy enough to deduce."

"Oh?" Moira said again, drawing her breath in sharply.

"The other four women aboard wouldn't be so quick to throw their belongings overboard, nor would any of them be caught dead in something quite so . . ." He looked at the white silk, lace, and whalebone undergarment. ". . . so virginal."

"And just what do you know about who wears what aboard this ship, sir?" she demanded before she thought better of it. He laughed again.

"You want details? Let's say that I'm judging the women aboard from . . . past experience."

She wished she had kept her mouth shut. "I still don't understand how throwing my . . . that"—she pointed—"overboard should earn such condemnation from you."

"'Condemnation' is a harsh word," he said, "but have you ever thought what goes through a man's mind when he finds something like this floating in the water?" He raised a brow slightly, and his mouth curved in a slow, sensual smile. "It leads him to certain avenues of thought, certain . . . speculations.

And when the undergarment so obviously belongs to a young"—he lifted the corset again, looking at it and then at her—"budding lady, then that makes him wonder if she has cast all discretion to the sea along with her underwear."

Moira felt thoroughly embarrassed. "Of course I haven't!" she stated emphatically.

"Well," he drawled. "I wanted to be the first to find out about that." He still wore that lazy smile that set her pulses pounding.

"I didn't expect anyone to fish the thing out," she insisted hotly. "I hoped it would sink quietly to the bottom."

"Just as you hoped it wouldn't be noticed tied to the main-mast, I presume."

That silenced her for a full minute. His brows rose, and he hooked a thumb into his belt. What could she say about her trip up the mast? Not much, since he obviously knew everything already.

"It's much too hot to wear it," she said finally.

"You could have taken it off and simply put it into your carpetbag."

"And the moment my brother noticed I wasn't wearing it, he would have insisted I put the miserable thing back on again."

"I don't think anyone is going to notice it's missing," he said looking her over again and obviously enjoying the excuse she had given him to do so. "You look—"

"Never mind," she said breathlessly, and he grinned broadly at her discomposure.

"Your brother certainly doesn't dictate what underwear you put on each morning, now, does he?" he asked, needling her further.

"Of course he doesn't. But he notices everything I do. How I dress, how I wear my hair, what I say and do. And nothing suits him."

"No doubt. Poor Daniel is sweating blood over you."

"Well, he needn't!"

"I'm not too sure about that," he said somewhat seriously. "You have a way of stirring things up around you, especially a man's blood."

Moira looked up, startled by his remark, and her heart raced at the look in Random Hawthorne's eyes. The silence between them was anything but comfortable, and growing more charged by the second. She drew in her breath, eyes widening as he took a step toward her.

"Another thing, Miss Cavendish," he said, his voice harder. "Don't send any more men over the side to play practical jokes. It might cost them their lives. There are sharks in these waters."

That information startled her from her mesmerized state. "I didn't know," she said shakily. "I wouldn't have done it if I had. Please believe me. I just thought the distraction might ease tempers a little."

"And it did. But something a little less hazardous would be better next time."

"Assuming there will be a next time."

"Oh, I'm sure of it, Miss Cavendish. Absolutely sure . . . unfortunately."

She was feeling ashamed for having risked Kris's life for something so foolish as a practical joke. Troubled, she looked up and searched Hawthorne's hard features. "I am sorry, Mr. Hawthorne. I promise not to do anything like that again."

A strange smile touched his lips. "Don't look so upset. He came back aboard with all his proper parts still in place." He reached out and touched her cheek with the back of his hand, a tender gesture that contracted her heart for an instant, then sent it racing at an alarming speed. He withdrew his hand almost immediately, a faint frown creasing his brow. He held the corset out to her. She drew a shaky breath and gave a husky, self-conscious laugh.

"What shall I do with it now? I can just imagine the gossip if I left these quarters carrying my corset in my hand."

His eyes danced. "You could always go into my cabin and put it back on again."

"It takes another just to see it laced properly," she said and then blushed. He grinned down at her roguishly, leaning back against the mizzenmast.

"At your service, Miss Cavendish."

"I do believe you're a wolf at heart, sir."

"Have you ever really doubted it?"

"Why don't you just heave it back into the sea this evening?" she suggested. "I really don't want it back."

"You left all your inhibitions in Charleston?"

"Not all of them," she said primly.

He gave an exaggerated sigh of disappointment. "A pity. And such a long voyage with so little to do." He looked at the garment in his hand. "Well, I guess I'll have to be content with keeping this as a trophy fairly fished from the sea," he decided, fingering in a curiously intimate way the silk and lace that had covered her breasts. His eyes moved to her in lazy perusal. "Of course, it would be much more of a prize with the maiden in it...."

"You'll have to be happy with the trappings," she told him and decided the quicker she left, the safer she'd be. "Was there anything else?"

He remained as he was for a prolonged second and then straightened. "Not at the moment," he said with a slight smile. She opened the door as he tossed the corset back into his cabin.

When they were back on the main deck, his fingers curved around her arm. She glanced up at him, cheeks flushing. But she was safely in the open now.

"Do me a big favor, Miss Cavendish, and stay out of trouble for the rest of the voyage." He released her.

She grinned up at him, her eyes lighting with mischief. "Why, of course, Mr. Hawthorne. I wouldn't think of doing anything else, now, would I?" With that, she walked away.

Chapter Seven

The whistling, howling wind was high, whipping the sea into a frothing monster intent on devouring the bark. Struggling to make headway in the Strait of Magellan, the *Stephen Rule* surged upward as waves broke across the bow and sprayed over the slick decks, then plunged down as if into a bottomless abyss.

The crew worked the sails and lines while Random stood steadfastly at the helm. He shouted an order, the veins standing out on his neck, only to have the gale-force winds whip it away. Captain Thackary lay in a stupor below, unaware and uncaring of what went on.

This time, by God, they were going to make it around the Horn or die trying. For several weeks they had fought the winds, rain, currents, and deadly rocks in the Strait, three hundred miles of the most treacherous ocean in the world. Only once had they sought safe anchorage—at the windswept Portugese penal colony, Port Famine. And now patience had run out, endurance was at an end.

Below, every square foot was cluttered with passengers and their possessions. With each roll of the ship, trunks, valises, boxes, and loosened articles tumbled back and forth. The stench of vomit was thick and fetid, and with each swell dozens of groans rose in cadence with the creaks of the protesting ships' timbers. Few were spared *mal de mer;* many would gladly have given a rich mine of gold for one day of calm seas. Others, as Moira had done before, prayed loudly for death and peace.

By the mercy of God, she hadn't become seasick again, even in the worst seas. She had been so sick for so long at the beginning that she believed she would never be susceptible again. Daniel, however, lay in his bunk moaning and in very ill humor. She checked on him frequently. Kris and Hadley roomed with her brother now that the upper decks were too wet and cold for hammocks, and they lay with their faces to the wall, groaning in unison.

Jewel, good sailor as ever, sat in the top bunk playing endless games of solitaire and complaining about the cold. Moira hadn't been out of her cabin for weeks except to eat and check on Daniel, and she was growing increasingly restless. She had slept enough for a lifetime, read everything she owned three times over, and played whist with Jewel until she was sick of the sight of a deck of cards.

The leaking ship creaked and groaned in protest at the storm. Bored beyond toleration, Moira decided to get some air. Jewel was sleeping, and Moira stepped out into the passageway. It was dark and cluttered, making it difficult getting to the ladder. She moved slowly, one hand against the bulkhead to maintain her balance on the rocking ship. She heard someone retching and someone else cursing violently.

Reaching the ladder, she went up two steps. Intending only to open the portal for a breath of fresh air, she reached up. Before she managed a hold, the door opened, knocking her backward with the force of the wind rushing in and the sudden surge of the ship. A heavy spray of seawater cascaded in, hitting her full in the face and chest, flinging her down hard. She hit the deck below with a thump and began to skid backward down the dimly lit passageway. The ship surged upward again, and she stopped with a crash into the first pile of boxes, the top one falling and spilling its contents all over her.

Moira flailed her arms, trying to grab anything to stop herself from going further. The ship reached the crest of the great wave and started its sharp descent. She felt herself sliding in the other direction and gave a sharp cry of warning as boxes and loosened articles came tumbling with her.

"Look out!"

Whoever had had the misfortune of entering the passageway had reached the bottom of the ladder. As the man stepped forward to assist her she plowed him down. She heard him swear as they both skidded and ended up in a heap at the foot of the ladder.

Both struggled frantically to disengage entangled arms and legs. Moira wished she had never left the cabin. She was wet to the skin, freezing cold, and having the greatest of difficulty extricating herself from this great oaf of a man. He managed to sit up and she gasped, recognizing Random Hawthorne. Before she could brace herself between the bulkheads, she was sliding again as the ship rolled. Hawthorne stopped her, holding onto her ankle as he gripped the ladder with his other hand.

"What in bloody hell are you doing out of your cabin?" he roared at her. He swore with such vehemence that color flooded Moira's cheeks, and she struggled to sit up. It was impossible with him hanging onto her ankle. Scooting around on her fanny, she wedged herself in the passageway, sitting back against one bulkhead and placing her free foot against the other.

"May I have my foot back now, Mr. Hawthorne?" she shouted. He released her abruptly. She could see in the faint lantern light that he was very angry indeed. He had several days' growth of dark beard and looked like an exhausted, angry bear.

Moira's hair had come down, and she pushed the wet, tangled mess back, shoving the few remaining pins back in. Then, seeing the ridiculousness of their situation, she started to laugh.

"You might at least ask if I'm all right!" she shouted at him. "You're not exactly light, you know!"

The storm's fury seemed tame to the blaze of temper in his dark eyes. He shouted at her, competing with the howling of the storm above. Thankfully, some of his words were lost in the wind. "What in . . . coming on deck? . . . step . . . washed overboard! Stupid . . . damn . . . woman . . . listen . . . in your damn cabin!"

What she couldn't hear she clearly surmised by his exasperated expression and the movements of his mouth. He had a very nice mouth, she thought, the lower lip slightly fuller than the upper. He had straight, white teeth, and the grooves in his cheeks were deeper when he was angry. He was certainly in no mood to have a pleasant conversation about the weather, she thought, smiling in spite of herself. He was probably frozen to the bone after hours at the helm, and it was understandable that he couldn't, at the moment, see the humor of the situation.

"Stop grinning!" he ordered, seeing that she was laughing with her customary lack of concern. "I'm going to lock you in your cabin and make sure you stay the hell where you belong!"

"I wasn't coming out on deck!" she shouted as loudly as she could, leaning slightly toward him so he could hear her better. "Don't be such a sorehead! I was only intending to open the door for a breath of air!"

Random stared at her and then shook his head, frowning. Thinking he meant he had not been able to hear her, she leaned even closer, putting her hand on his arm and shouting again.

"A breath of air, Mr. Hawthorne! Not a stroll on deck!"

He grinned, the creases dispelling the sternness from his mouth, the flash of anger from his dark eyes. "And did you get it, Miss Cavendish?" he demanded, leaning toward her so that they were very close.

She nodded and then spread her hands wide. "And a badly needed bath as well!" She laughed up at him, then stopped.

Random's eyes took full advantage of the opportunity she gave him, moving down over the sodden clothes that molded her body perfectly, his eyes gleaming with amusement and something more intense. They paused deliberately on the rapid rise and fall of her full, young breasts, then traveled up to her mouth, and finally reached her startled eyes.

"You did at that!" A half smile lingered as he held her gaze. The closeness suddenly took her breath away and set her heart thundering. Moira tried frantically to get up and away from him, instinctively sensing her danger, but her feet slipped as a great wave thrust the ship upward. She cried out in alarm and found herself pitched violently toward the ladder.

Random caught her wrist and yanked her down. She gasped,

finding herself straddled across his lap. Her eyes flew up to his and saw that now it was he who was laughing. Her face flamed as she tried to move away. She could feel his long, hard-muscled legs beneath her soft buttocks and tried to stand up. Random stopped laughing and firmly clasped her slim hips, holding her where she was. His eyes darkened. They stared at one another.

Half frightened and half something else she didn't want to evaluate too closely, Moira looked at him. His eyes moved slowly, taking in her quickened breathing and her dazed look. She became aware of one of his hands moving from her hip upward in a slow, tantalizing caress. His eyes never left hers as his hand lingered over her hip and moved to her swelling breasts. She drew in her breath sharply and then couldn't breathe at all.

No thought of protesting or fighting entered her bemused brain. She was completely befuddled by sensations she had never felt before. His hand moved again, up along her slender, pulsating throat, finally entwining itself in her hair and drawing her inexorably toward him. Her eyes closed slowly as his mouth touched hers in the lightest caress, testing, teasing. He was cold and tasted of salt. He withdrew his mouth and looked down at her, taking in every feature before his mouth again descended on her trembling, parted lips. He pulled her against him, his fingers tightening convulsively in her hair as her lips opened beneath the onslaught of his. His mouth moved over hers in growing passion. The violence of the storm rocked her closer against him, and she felt the tension in his body and the hardness of his desire.

After a long moment, Random pulled his mouth away and pressed it hotly against Moira's neck, where her pulse hammered wildly. Then his lips moved upward until they rested lightly against her temple.

"You should have stayed in your cabin, Miss Cavendish," he said huskily. "It's dangerous out here. You're taking a big chance."

"With the storm or you, Mr. Hawthorne?" she murmured raggedly, wishing he would shut up and kiss her again. She had been kissed before, several times on this voyage, but never,

ever like this. She leaned back slightly and looked at him, the invitation unknowingly clear in her flushed cheeks and parted lips. He drew in his breath sharply.

"Both." Suddenly he pushed her gently away and rose, bringing her up with him. Without his closeness she began to feel the damp, freezing chill seep into her. She shivered. Her teeth began to chatter, and she hugged herself, looking up at him questioningly.

"You'd better get out of those wet clothes right away!" he ordered, putting a slight distance between them. She saw a muscle tightening in his cheek, a faint frown creasing his forehead. Yet nowhere in his face could she see evidence of the passion that had just flamed between them. Her senses were still reeling; she wanted to feel his arms around her as they had been a moment before. He was looking at her so coolly, surveying her, seemingly unaffected by what had just happened. What was he thinking? Had it simply been a stolen kiss for him?

"Do you need help back to your cabin?" he shouted when she didn't move. She shook her head, swallowing the growing lump of humiliation in her throat, squinting her eyes against the burning sensation there. Whatever he was thinking, it was not to her advantage. He looked angry again.

"No, thank you, Mr. Hawthorne. I can manage."

She went carefully along the passageway, stepping over cases and spilled objects, until she reached her cabin door. She glanced back over her shoulder. Hawthorne was gone.

Jewel was still sleeping when Moira entered the cabin. She hastily stripped off her wet woolen dress and pulled on another. When that didn't warm her, she put on another over that one. Then she huddled under the blankets of her bunk.

Closing her eyes, Moira tried hard to remember the sweltering heat of the Tropics. But it was the memory of Random's kiss that finally warmed her enough to sleep.

Chapter Eight

The *Stephen Rule* rounded the Horn after four and a half weeks in the storm-tossed waters of what the sailors called "Cape Stiff." Within the week, most of the passengers were eating again. Winds and seas were still mountainously high and heavy, but they were now making fast headway up the west coast of South America. It was almost two weeks before everyone realized that half the passenger cargo had been jettisoned in the Strait to lighten the overburdened ship. Gone were Daniel's boxes of California Gold Grease and his gold detector. Gone also were merchant boxes of panama hats, mosquito nets, ladies' fripperies, bolts of Irish wool, and sweets intended for the markets in California. It was too late to complain about it, though many grumbled endlessly for want of anything better to do.

Mates and sailors were busily employed in overhauling, refitting, rigging, planing, scraping, and caulking decks. The passengers sat about talking, playing cards and musical instruments, and planning what they would do when they reached San Francisco.

The last of the lamp oil was gone, and everyone was on the lookout for a whaler. Coffee and tea had run out, and the cook had begun brewing molasses instead, which was good for the elimination process but hard on the nerves. Duff was appearing with grueling regularity at every meal; tempers were running high and hot again, but Moira's spirits couldn't have been lower.

Numerous times in the past, she had carried on innocent flirtations with young men, usually friends of her brothers. She had never found herself at a loss for words when speaking to any of them, even following a stolen kiss. Yet whenever Random Hawthorne appeared, she felt trembling excitement fill her while at the same time her brain atrophied. It was a distressing combination. She was not sure how to behave toward him since the episode 'tween decks. She felt embarrassed and ill at ease with him. She should never have allowed him to kiss her in that devastating way. She tried over and over to tell herself that it had simply been a stolen kiss in a stormy moment. It wasn't anything to turn her life upside down. She had been kissed before.

Yet never like that, never in such a way to melt her bones and turn her blood to liquid fire.

She decided there was no reason to punish herself for her natural response to an undeniably attractive man, one who obviously had learned a great deal about how to please a woman. That might not have bothered her half so much had she been the one to end the passionate embrace. But she hadn't. She had wanted him to go on and on kissing her like that. Just remembering it made her hot all over and filled her with a curiously aching sensation. And to make matters even worse, Hawthorne seemed indifferent about the whole thing. He greeted her as politely as he always had, yet he scarcely looked at her now, and Moira felt confused, hurt, and not just a little angry.

Daniel was relieved by Moira's suddenly subdued nature, though Jewel questioned her frequently about it. Moira attributed it to the length of the voyage and the unknown future.

The Magellan clouds and the Southern Cross gave way to the Big Dipper, and the climate grew hotter again. The man who had brought the fiddle was becoming quite expert. Jewel could now speak French fairly well. *"Voulez-vous coucher avec moi?"* was by far her best line, and she could say it with a certain degree of authenticity.

Daniel's funds had dwindled to less than one hundred dollars.

Along the coast of Mexico, freshly washed laundry began to appear all over the ship. Men's underwear flapped in the breeze. Passengers began to shave away the beards they had grown on the voyage, and everything began to be packed neatly away again.

Moira thought more of Jack with each passing week. As soon as the ship anchored in San Francisco, she was going to make plans to head straight to Bootjack and find him.

There was jubilation when the ship began up the coast of California. The low hills eventually grew into well-wooded mountains above a rocky coastline. Moira took to standing at the rail and looking at the land in growing excitement. Soon they would be in San Francisco and she could begin her search. Daniel packed and repacked in growing excitement.

One afternoon, Hawthorne came to stand by Moira during her vigil. She was startled by his sudden company after weeks of hardly exchanging a word. He looked down at her with a faintly mocking smile.

"Are you having your breath of fresh air, Miss Cavendish?" he asked, deliberately provoking her memory of the event 'tween decks. Her color mounted and her pulse began pounding. Did he have to remind her now after she had finally pushed it to the back of her mind? And why was he doing it when he had been avoiding her for so long?

"Yes, Mr. Hawthorne," she said, smiling stiffly, trying to appear poised and indifferent to his teasing. She drew her shawl more tightly around her. "I thought California was supposed to have a mild climate," she said, referring to the heavy mists that had begun to appear.

"Once you're inland," he answered, watching her face. He leaned on the rail, his shoulder almost brushing hers. "California was believed orignally to be an inland paradise," he told her. "It was supposed to be inhabited only by women armed wth solid-gold weapons who hated men."

Moira laughed, glancing at him. "Are you making up this fairy tale, Mr. Hawthorne?"

"It's the absolute truth, I swear," he said, putting his hand up and grinning down at her. "Calafía, their queen, even had an army of well-trained griffins to make sure there were no male invaders. I believe the hapless men that did fall into the women's hands were eaten."

"By the griffins?" she asked with a slight smile.

He looked at her, half amused. "And the women," he drawled.

"Well, Calafía has an invasion of men on her hands now," Moira said lightly, glancing away, disturbed by the suggestiveness in Hawthorne's brown eyes. He laughed low.

"She does at that," he agreed. "But then, I believe the lady was eventually converted to Christianity and learned a proper respect for her betters."

Moira bristled but covered her irritation. "And thus the paradise was spoiled," she replied.

Random laughed, then looked out at the misty coastline. "Daniel is never going to have the chance to put a pan in a stream."

"Why not?" she asked, glancing up at him sharply.

He grinned down at her. "All his time is going to be spent keeping you out of trouble or fighting off the sexually deprived men that populate the gold fields."

Moira's face flamed with indignation and embarrassment. "There hasn't been any trouble of that sort on this voyage," she snapped.

Random smiled slowly, his eyes dancing over her flushed features. "You don't call what happened between us during the storm trouble?" he drawled sardonically, heightening her color even more. "If not, why have you been avoiding me ever since?"

"I'd say that was by silent, mutual agreement, Mr. Hawthorne."

"I thought it wise to keep a safe distance between us," he told her, leaning closer, his mouth close to her ear. "You see, I can resist everything except temptation. And you"—his eyes moved over her face and lingered on her mouth—"are definitely a temptation, Miss Cavendish."

Moira's eyes widened, and her senses ran rampant. Random grinned. "Now, as soon as we arrive in San Francisco, it will no longer be my duty to protect you, and I can give full and proper rein to my more...natural inclinations concerning you."

"Shall I take that as due warning?" Her knees felt shaky.

"As you like." His mouth curved sensuously. "In fact, I think you'd be very wise if you did."

She felt like a mouse before a very hungry cat. He seemed to read her thoughts exactly, for he laughed low again. It was a disturbingly husky sound.

"One aperitif makes me hungry for the entire meal." He patted her hand. "Don't look so frightened, Miss Cavendish. I shall only take very small bites at a time."

They looked at one another for a long moment. Moira wondered if she should believe him. It was a cruel way to tease her if he wasn't serious, for he knew she found him far too attractive as it was. And she didn't want him laughing at her anymore than he had probably done already.

Again it was Random who steered them to a safer channel. His eyes narrowed.

"Are you planning to try your luck panning gold with the rest of the mining company—that Kris, especially?"

"No," she said blankly, feeling shaky and flushed, finding it difficult to pull her thoughts away from the vivid images he had just presented to her fevered brain. "I'm...I'm going to look for my brother Jack."

"So there *is* another brother in California," he said cocking his head slightly. "I thought he was an invention."

"No. We lost touch with him almost two years ago. Daniel was going to look for him but..." She shrugged.

"You thought it best to come along and make sure he didn't get sidetracked by other things," he finished for her. "Have you any idea where this brother is?"

"When he first arrived in California, he worked at New Helvetia for Sutter. But the last letter we have from him came from a place called Bootjack. I've no idea where it is."

"You've got your work cut out for you, then," Random said seriously. "If he isn't where he's supposed to be, there are hundreds of small camps springing up all over California with the rush going on. There could be half a dozen Bootjacks."

She sighed heavily. "I know. But someone must know where

this one is. He mentioned the American River, and that it wasn't far from the fort."

"And you and Daniel plan to lug all that mining equipment around the territory while you're looking for him?"

"We'll buy some horses, of course," she said simply.

Random smiled and shook his head slowly. "You've a hundred dollars a head?"

"One hundred dollars?" she repeated with a gasp, staring at him in an openmouthed manner Aunt Miranda would have abhorred.

"If not higher. But I take it from your present expression that you don't have the price."

"You take it correctly, Mr. Hawthorne. One hundred dollars! That's ridiculous," she said, aghast. "Jack wrote that prices were going up, but I never dreamed—"

"I wouldn't let it bother you," Random said casually, mouth curving slightly. "Chances are there wouldn't be many horses around to buy, anyway. You have to remember that about fifty thousand men have been there ahead of you."

She looked at him for a long, hard moment before speaking again. "Have you any more helpful information to give to me, Mr. Hawthorne?"

He chuckled. "Not much, I'm afraid."

"Heaven be praised for small favors."

"At least you brought the right clothing with you," he told her. "There are several aboard this ship who brought tropical wear, including, if you can believe it, panama hats and mosquito netting."

"You must think we're a pack of fools."

"There's a lot of profit in transporting fools to the gold fields. And I'm no better than the rest. My dreams are as grand and as out of reach."

"Really?" She looked at him with growing interest. "What do you dream about?"

"Why, you, of course, Miss Cavendish. Achingly so, I might add."

She did laugh then. "Am I really supposed to believe that?"

"You don't?"

"Absolutely not." He was not going to have the opportunity to laugh at her again. She changed the subject this time. "Will you be returning to Charleston soon?"

"I thought I'd made my plans perfectly clear a little while ago," he said, that slow, sensual smile drifting across his face as he looked at her.

She took his statement lightly. "Well, you can hardly make your fortune chasing me, now can you, Mr. Hawthorne?" Then she grinned. "Though it might prove interesting."

"Undoubtedly," he drawled, eyes glittering. "I doubt very much if the *Stephen Rule* will leave San Francisco again. Even if she could keep a crew aboard, which is doubtful, she'd never make it around the Horn again without a lot of expensive refitting. We were lucky, damn lucky, to make it this time."

"Then you'll be joining another crew?" she asked quietly, feeling disappointed.

He smiled. "Later . . . perhaps. If things don't go according to my plans." He looked away from her to the coastline.

"Well, I wish you luck in your endeavors, Mr. Hawthorne," Moira said, feeling sad that she would not be seeing this man again once they all reached San Francisco. They would all be going their own ways, searching for their own fortunes.

He looked down at her. "Well, that's some encouragement, Miss Cavendish. I thought you would wish me in Davy Jones's locker after the liberties I took."

Her cheeks flushed. "I could hardly condemn you for that, since I was a willing party, now could I?"

Random started to say something more when his name was called. Excusing himself, he left her alone at the rail and strode toward the helm. Moira watched him and then turned away, tears filling her eyes.

Idiot! She told herself. He's ten years older than you, a lifetime wiser and more experienced, and you're just giving him a few minutes of entertainment.

Moira went below to write to Aunt Miranda. She had sent a letter when the ship had stopped for provisioning at Santa Catarina and another from Talcahuano, and she would have one ready when they anchored in San Francisco.

August 24, 1849

Dear Aunt Mandy,
    There is not much time now before we reach

San Francisco Bay, so I shall make this epistle as brief and informative as possible so that I may post it upon arrival.

Body: healthy but thin.

Mind: in a quandary. How shall I keep Daniel's pan packed until we reach Bootjack?

Occupation: making plans to search for Jack.

Ideas: many and varied.

Daniel: healthy, excited, irritated with my company, packed and standing ready at the rail, and absolutely penniless.

Friends: all well and in a fever to reach the end of this voyage. Jewel will be staying in San Francisco before she makes plans to go to the gold camps. I wish her good fortune. She has been a wonderfully educational cabin mate, and I will miss her tremendously.

Victuals: potted meats (spoiled for the most part) and duff, duff, duff.

Drink: water.

Novelties: none I dare mention.

Pastimes: collecting proposals of one sort or another, two honorable, ten the other kind.

Hopes: to find Jack.

Determination: to find Jack!

Wishes: to have my feet firmly planted on terra firma again and to stop hearing the grumbling, bored, swearing complaints of the male population aboard this miserable, leaking scow!

I love you, Aunt Mandy. I hope you've found it in your generous heart to forgive your wayward niece. You're well rid of her.

> As always,
> Moira

Postscript: Give my regards to dear, lovely Charles.

Chapter Nine

The long and eventful voyage of the *Stephen Rule* from Charleston to San Francisco Bay ended on August 27, 1849. A low, chilly fog hung over the ship when it finally dropped anchor in the murky waters. The loud, jubilant cheers of the gold-fevered passengers announced their arrival in California.

Moira stood at the rail, longing for a better look at the now famous California seaport. All she could see were the ghostly ships deserted in the harbor. There were at least seventy, she calculated, and no hands on any deck. It was strangely eerie to see them all lying fallow, silent and lifeless, their sails furled and masts pointing heavenward. Randon had said the *Stephen Rule* would suffer the same fate.

As the fog cleared, Moira could see the long single pier jutting out into the bay. Beyond the hilly shoreline were numerous adobe structures, hastily erected wooden shanties and shacks and the beginning of two- and three-story brick buildings. No cobblestones here, just dirt and mud.

Confusion reigned as everyone lugged their belongings to the main deck, shouting and arguing as to who would be the first group ashore. Captain Thackary looked around in swaying disgust and retired to his cabin with a final bottle of brandy.

Random was in charge once more. Within moments, lots were made up and drawn, the departure schedule established, and groups waited in an orderly and cooperative spirit.

Jewel Delarue was among the first to go. She came to give Moira an affectionate hug and tearful kiss and a last bit of advice before having her things loaded into the boat. Six men were crammed in with her, and Moira saw with amusement that her cabin mate's spirits quickly soared again. Much of the gold in them-thar-hills would most probably end up in the pockets of that-thar-dress.

Daniel was excited and fidgeting in impatience to be away. Moira watched him with growing, rueful amusement. He couldn't wait to get ashore and head for the gold fields with Kris, Paul, Hadley, and the others. He saw each moment's delay as lessening the chances of finding his fortune. It didn't matter how many thousands had preceded him, and he hadn't so much as mentioned their primary purpose in coming to California—to find Jack.

Finally their call came, and their trunks and bags were lowered. Daniel went down the ladder to the platform where the rowboat was waiting. Moira looked down over the side and gulped. It was a long way down, and that ladder didn't look anymore sturdy or dependable than the ropes to the crow's nest had. She was shaking so hard that she stumbled on her skirt as she started on her way down.

A strong arm circled her waist and hauled her back.

"That would be the quickest way down," Random agreed against her ear, "but I think feet first, by ladder, would be much better, don't you?"

"You startled me!"

"I saved you a dip in the bay," he told her smoothly. "I've a habit of doing that, haven't I?" he said, grinning. "I appear at the most unexpected times. You'd do well to remember that, Miss Cavendish."

She looked up at him, but his expression was enigmatic. "Perhaps it would be wise if we put you securely in the cargo net and lowered you," he suggested. "At least then we wouldn't have to fish you out of the harbor."

"You wouldn't," she gasped. "Would you?" He smiled. "Now look here, Mr. Hawthorne. Let me go!" Before she could protest further, she was tossed bodily over his shoulder and carried down the ladder. She kicked her feet.

"What are you doing?" she squealed. When he reached the platform he turned, spinning her dizzily and making her grab hold of him in a most unladylike fashion, her arms clasped firmly about his waist.

"So help me God, if you drop me, I'll . . . I'll . . ."

Random deposited her with a thump into the boat. She clutched frantically at the swaying sides and glared up at him, red-faced and indignant. He gave her a laughing look and touched his forelock in silent, mocking salute. Daniel was laughing uproariously, which didn't help the situation.

"Aren't you going to thank me, Miss Cavendish?" Random asked. "You're safely down and on your way."

She glared at him, fuming in silence.

"Don't wander off too far," he told her. "Remember what we talked about the other day." They were ten feet apart, and she felt she could safely answer.

"Happy hunting, Mr. Hawthorne," she answered between her teeth. He laughed and went back up the ladder. Moira stared at him for a long moment, torn between anger and misery. He was a disturbing man, and one she wanted desperately. Yet she had another purpose for being here, and that purpose didn't include a flirtation with a man well beyond her experience.

"What was that all about?" Daniel asked. She glanced at him and then away.

"Nothing," she said flatly. "He was just teasing me."

A crowd was gathered at the pier when they arrived. The other women had been surrounded by excited, shouting men and were being escorted down the pier toward the town. Cargo was stacked everywhere, unclaimed or waiting collection. Overhead, seagulls perched on the support posts and screeched.

A man on the pier spotted Moira and gave a rousing shout, pointing at her. Moira glanced at Daniel. His hand tightened protectively on her arm. "Stay close, Mory," he instructed quietly, mouth compressing into combat readiness. "They look like a rough lot."

She had no intention of doing anything but staying close. Most of the men waiting on the pier had long hair, beards, and a wild look about them. They all wore the same clothing, almost a uniform—checked woolen shirts, dungarees, boots, jackets, and sloppy hats, which they were now taking from their heads in a show of respect for an arriving female.

There was some grappling as two members of the Charleston Mining and Trade Company disembarked from the bobbing rowboat onto the narrow platform below the pier. The rough-looking San Franciscans were pushing each other in their haste to get down the ladder onto the platforms and closer to Moira.

"I'll help the lady! Get out of my way, you damn sodbuster!" one man, stronger than the others, said, and jumped onto the platform. Another grabbed his shoulder and propelled him back toward the ladder, bumping him into two more men who were descending. One of the men stumbled sideways and fell into the water. He came up sputtering foul epithets.

"May I assist you, ma'am?" a tall, dark-haired man with hazel eyes and a broad, toothy grin asked, shoving two men aside and stepping forward. He extended his hand and bowed gallantly. He had a New York accent.

"Now, just a minute," Daniel said, rising and placing himself protectively in front of Moira. A large, callused hand planted in the center of his chest propelled him backward out of the boat. With a splash, he went under, popping to the surface a few feet out.

"You lout!" Moira cried, swinging one of her carpetbags as she nimbly jumped out of the boat. She caught the man across the side of his head and sent him into the water, along with the man behind him. She glanced back and saw Daniel swimming toward the platform. Someone grabbed hold of her.

"Let go of me!" she snarled, swinging one of her bags again as she yanked herself loose, only to find another man latching onto her in his eagerness to assist her. Daniel was pulling himself onto the platform, dripping and furious. He looked ready to kill.

"Let go!" Moira shouted and kicked another man in the shins. "Give me back my bag, you brute!" She kicked another a little higher, and the men on the dock fell back slightly. She watched them as warily as they watched her.

"This one's a lady, all right," one of the San Franciscans said in disappointment.

"Well, there are four more of the other kind over there," Kris announced, pointing toward Monique, her two girls and Jewel on the pier. Half a dozen men turned and looked and then ran off toward easier prey. Several remained on the dock, though keeping a safe distance. The New Yorker had climbed out of the bay and was standing on the platform, dripping water and grinning from ear to ear.

"Honey, you're just what I've been looking for!" he said excitedly. He took one step, and Daniel hit him squarely on the jaw, sending him back into the drink again. Daniel then turned and came up the ladder, casting a burning look at the group of men. Moira followed him.

"If anyone else lays a hand on my sister I'll let them have it, too," he growled. His hair was plastered to his head, his clothes were sopping wet and smelling of the bay, and his boots squished with each step he took. But his face said plenty, and the men gave him a wide berth.

"We don't mean her any disrespect," one blond man said defensively.

"I want a wife. I got a cozy little cabin on the American. I'd take good care of her."

"I didn't come all the way to California to get married!" Moira snapped.

The New Yorker was again on the platform. He was rubbing his jaw. "That sounds all right by me. If you don't want to get married, you can just share my bed."

Daniel turned around, and Moira grabbed his arm. He had caught the New Yorker unaware the first time, but he wouldn't be so lucky again. "Let's go," she said firmly. He glared at the man on the platform and then took her arm and steered her down the dock, Kris and Paul ahead with the trunks and cases, Hadley behind with another trunk and case. Moira carried her own carpetbags.

The group following them up the muddy street seemed to grow. The New Yorker's suggestion had been mild by comparison. Some of these men were drunk with rye whiskey or wine and had more detailed descriptions of what they wanted from Moira. Her face flamed as she listened to their propositions. Daniel was furious, but he couldn't fight them all.

They passed numerous shacks that announced their businesses and a large number of saloons and casinos. Eventually they came to a large building that proclaimed good lodgings and food called the Sunrise House.

"In there!" Daniel said, pointing, and the Charleston Mining and Trade Company entered, dumping their gear on the floor. Luckily the crowd of San Franciscans stayed outside. The proprietor, a tall, lean, bearded man in his mid-twenties, came to greet them. He looked delightedly at Moira, eyes widening.

"Are all the men in this town insane?" she asked, breathless after the fast walk up the hill. She was shaking from the ordeal and glanced toward the windows, expecting the foul-mouthed ruffians to come barging into the hotel after her. They were all still out there, unwilling to disperse.

"Not insane, exactly, ma'am," the young man said, smiling. "Just . . . starved for women. You'll have to get used to it. Most women get followed around here wherever they go, even if they're married or ugly as sin."

"Wonderful," Daniel muttered disgustedly and gave her a furious look. "Well, to hell with them. All I want at the moment is a decent bed and a good square meal. I've had enough fish and duff to kill the hardiest man." All the men were in agreement with that.

The proprietor opened the register. "Rooms are ten a night. We've the best beef stew in San Francisco, and only four dollars a bowl."

Daniel and the others froze.

"Do you have any rules against sharing rooms?" Moira asked.

The man laughed. "No, ma'am!"

She looked at the company of young men around her. "So much for spacious quarters." They divided up and rented four rooms. Moira and Daniel took one. As they lugged their possessions up the stairs, they all grumbled about the outrageous prices.

The rooms didn't look much bigger than the cabins they'd just vacated. The beds were lumpy and the sheets hadn't been changed since the last occupants, but at least they weren't bunks!

The stew did prove to be delicious and thick, served with fresh-baked bread and good, strong coffee. It was almost too good for the stomach to tolerate after so long a diet of brick-hard biscuits that made the stomach work to attain nourishment. Daniel and the others ate until they could eat no more, then sat glazed-eyed before the big stone fireplace and asked the proprietor questions. They suggested that Moira leave them alone so that they could have a company meeting.

She returned to her room grudgingly. When Random Hawthorne had made his dire predictions about Daniel's difficulty in protecting her, she had thought them gross exaggerations. Now, after barely half a day in San Francisco, she saw how depressingly accurate they were. She looked out the window. There were some women in the city, mostly of Spanish origin, judging from their dark good looks. And every one of them was being followed by a crowd of men, catcalling and wolf whistling.

Moira had no intention of going along with the unwanted attention. She had come to California to find her older brother. A following of randy, rowdy men didn't fit in with her plans. It was worse than having fifty drooling Charles Beauchamps leering at her. Moira was not yet about to be part of any man's menu.

The problem wouldn't even have existed if she'd been fortunate enough to have been born a man. It wasn't fair that they enjoyed so many freedoms and privileges while a woman was expected to live an exemplary, dull existence, seeing to the needs and pleasures of the men that controlled her. And now, damn their hides, those members of the company were down there deciding *her* future, without *her* consent.

Or thought they were!

Daniel came up several hours later, looking as though the world had come to an end.

"Well, you've done it," he told her in disgust. "I am no longer a part of the Charleston Mining and Trade Company, thanks to you."

"Then whatever you find you won't have to share, will you?" She smiled tightly.

"You've ruined all my plans!" he told her, angry as a petulant child, blaming her for everything that had gone wrong. "I came here to pan for gold, not play guardian to my damn sister!"

"And look for Jack!"

"And look for Jack," he snarled.

"Well, you can do both with me."

"You boneheaded idiot!" he yelled at her. "I can't do either with you! Or hasn't it entered your head yet that your presence makes everything I want to do impossible? You remember those men this afternoon? Well, there'll be more tomorrow, from what the proprietor said. And they'll be everywhere we go. How can I put a pan in a stream with a crowd after you?"

"Just because men are fools who think with their male organs and not their tiny brains is no reason to holler at me!"

"Don't talk like that!" he reprimanded sternly. "You're a lady. Or have you forgotten that fact on the voyage here!"

That did it!

"How is it possible for a lady to remain a lady when all she is able to do is absorb her environment? And what an environment, dear brother. If you weren't drinking on that scow called a ship, you were swearing; and if you weren't swearing, you were gambling. And if you weren't gambling, you were whor—"

"That's enough!"

"Enough be damned!" she snorted, standing up. "You may be my big brother, but you're not very wise. In fact, you're downright stupid! How much money have you left after the voyage?"

He looked nonplussed. "Some."

"How much?"

"Not much," he said grimly.

"Well, I've ten dollars less than I started with. So don't you dare stand there and call *me* the boneheaded idiot, you boneheaded idiot!"

"Now look here . . ."

"Shut up!"

His eyes opened very wide indeed.

"You and the rest of your friends are not going to decide for me what I am going to do here in California. I'm going to find Jack! And as for you"—she pointed a finger at him—"I can get you to the gold fields, because I'm the one that has the money. You lost all yours playing cards!"

"Damn it. You still don't seem to understand! We can't go

anywhere, because you'll have a train of men following you and making obscene suggestions when they can't get their hands on you!"

"I understand everything," she said slowly. "The solution to the whole thing is obvious and simple."

"Really?" He expelled his breath sharply. "Enlighten me."

She let out her breath sharply as well, eyes blazing. "If the men in California are so desperate for women that they'll act like asses—"

"Moira!"

"—donkeys," she amended impatiently, "then I'll just make myself inconspicuous."

Daniel laughed and sat down on the bed, shaking his head. "Making you inconspicuous would be like trying to make a crab walk straight!"

"I don't appreciate the comparison."

"Moira, just look at you, for God's sake!" he railed again. "Black hair, soulful brown eyes, a perfect complexion, and a definitely female shape, even if you lost some pounds getting here. How can you possibly make that combination inconspicuous in a country populated by men? And if all that isn't trouble enough, they'll smell you coming."

"Now just what do you mean by that remark?"

"That French perfume you wear. I certainly don't know a man alive that'd be caught dead smelling of it unless it . . . ah, hell . . ."

"You make it sound like I pour it over myself by the gallon!"

"Good Lord, it doesn't take much. When everyone around you smells like dirt, sweat, and the rear end of a horse, you're going to be like a gardenia in the middle of a garlic field!"

Moira was somewhat mollified by that explanation. Then she began to smile.

Daniel always looked worried when Moira smiled like that. "Just what are you thinking now, Moira?"

"Don't worry. I've worked everything out."

"That's what I'm afraid of."

"All I need is for you to buy these things," she told him and handed him a list she had compiled while he was downstairs being washed out of his company. "Here's the money. I expect change and a receipt."

He gave her a disgruntled look and then glanced at the list. His eyes jerked up to her again. "You're not serious!"

"Absolutely. And I'll make a bet with you now, Danny. We'll be in the gold fields before your friends downstairs are."

"But what would Aunt Miranda say about this?"

"She's not here to say anything. Nor are Mama and Papa. But I am, and I have to survive in this godforsaken territory overrun by men looking for—"

"Never mind," he cut her off. He sighed heavily. "I think you learned a little too much on that ship."

"I was about to say gold, Danny," she said, grinning. He blushed. She sat down and clasped her hands. "It'll work. I know it will. Just buy those things, and I'll be ready by morning. We'll leave before first light."

He looked very doubtful, and then he shrugged. "What the hell," he sighed. "I can't see how else I'll ever get to pan for gold."

While Danny was gone on his errand, Moira went through her things. She decided that most of her clothing was now useless to her except for her underthings. She would leave everything behind and take the chance that she would be able to come back and collect it all at a later date. She found the compact sewing kit in the bottom of one of her bags and extracted a pair of scissors. There was a small mirror above the bowl and water pitcher, and, standing in front of it, she began to cut her hair. The first snip was the hardest. The pile of dark hair grew on the commode. When she had finished, she decided it looked horrible. She rumpled it and shook it and then concluded that however it looked, it felt good. Too bad she couldn't sell the clippings to a wig maker—they would have brought a good price. She stuffed the cut hair into the chamber pot.

Next, she cut off her long, manicured fingernails. Her hands felt clumsy and strange without them.

Daniel returned and blanched when he saw her. "What did you do to your hair?" He was looking at her as though she had grown horns.

"I cut it, of course. What does it look like I did to it?"

"Butchered it. What did you use? A hatchet?"

"I used what I had. My little scissors."

"My God, I thought you were just going to push it up under

your hat, not hack it off!"

She wasn't listening to him, but staring into the small mirror thoughtfully. She rubbed her chin. "Too bad I can't grow a beard." Her eyes teased her brother in the reflection.

"Did you have to cut it so short? It's barely past your ears. Shorter than mine."

She turned slowly and grinned at him wickedly. "Are you hinting you want a haircut, too?"

"Not from your barber, I don't."

"Did you get what I wanted?" she asked, reaching for his bag. She rummaged through, finding checked wool shirts, dark dungarees, heavy socks, long johns, high boots, a wide leather belt, a bowie knife and leather case, a red scarf, a hat, a jacket, and, finally, a backpack.

"Good." She saw he had purchased other nececessities—a pan, a pick, a shovel. "How much did it come to?"

"Three hundred and seventy-five."

Her eyes opened wide. She smiled weakly. "In that case, you can keep the change."

"Keep the change! There wasn't any!"

"Shhhhhhh. Do you want the others to get wind of this?"

"They'd never believe it. I don't think I do. God, what am I getting myself into?"

He grumbled about her plans most of the night, but he didn't talk her out of it. He had spent his last dollar on her shovel. Moira rose early to pack her few usable things into the backpack. She couldn't resist taking the small vial of French perfume but had to leave the blue watered-silk dress and matching dancing slippers behind. She doubted she'd be needing them where she was going.

"Get up, Danny, it's almost daybreak," she said, prodding her snoring brother. "We've got to get out of here before the others."

He was groggy and grumpy from lack of sleep, but managed to pull himself together after a cold spash of water. He looked her over as she pirouetted before him, dressed like a very young man, with curling black hair and sparkling dark eyes.

"Well, what do you think? Do I look like a typical California gold miner?"

He grunted. "A little handsome and slightly effeminate,"

he told her finally. "You can't carry all that stuff."

"It's not that heavy. I've got the pan and shovel secured, and I can carry the pick in my hand."

"It may not seem heavy now, but just wait until you've carried it all for a mile. Come on. Let me have it."

"No. Now listen. It'd raise a few questions if one man was carrying everything for another, don't you think?" she reasoned, hands on hips. He frowned slightly.

"They wouldn't have any doubts about you, but they'd certainly think me strange," he said wryly. He shook his head and then looked her over again.

"If Aunt Miranda could see you now," he said grimly.

"Stop worrying. You don't want to go through what we did yesterday, do you?"

"Hardly."

"Then this, my dear brother, is what you've got," she said, holding her hands wide in a theatrical gesture. "And from now on, call me Mory. It could be a man's name."

He nodded solemnly.

"So?"

"So, what now?" He looked at her blankly.

"So, let's go!" She gestured at him impatiently to move. He gave her a faint salute and opened the door.

Chapter Ten

Moira had never ached so much in her entire life. Her feet were the first to react to the long trek, acquiring blisters over blisters and feeling swollen and pinched inside the heavy, high boots, which also chafed her calves. Her legs became stiff from walking up the hills northeast of the bay, and her skin was rubbed raw by the unaccustomed friction of the coarse dungarees and woolen shirt.

Riding on the crowded ferry across the bay had been easy. She had sat down and put her feet up on a barrel of salted pork until someone reminded her that it was time to give another a rest. The conveyance had taken them up to Benicia, a community of a few shacks and shanties, where they had disembarked due to lack of funds. From Benicia they'd had to walk.

After a mile her back began to hurt abominably with the strain of carrying the pack. She struggled for every breath of air. Never had she thought that a few articles of clothing, one pan, a pick and shovel, and a few miscellaneous supplies could become as heavy as a load of bricks.

Yet she didn't complain. She cursed a lot to herself, but whenever Daniel glanced back with that smug smile, she grinned at him as though this were all a pleasure walk. By late afternoon, she could tell that Daniel's muscles were feeling his load as well, and she had long since lost the ability to look nonchalant. How could she, with perspiration beading a reddened face and each step a plodding, agonizing effort?

They set up their first camp near a stream that meandered through low, rolling hills dotted with oaks. It was overhung by grape ivy and brush, and it took quite a fight to get through the thick vegetation for water. Afterward, Daniel went fishing, having laid a fire for Moira to begin making coffee and a meal. Never having cooked anything before, she wasn't sure how to brew coffee. After several moments of contemplation, she went to the creek to fill the pot, then dumped a cup of ground beans in, stirring them around over the fire until the mixture started to boil. She rummaged around in Daniel's pack for a can of beans, but it took her ten minutes to get it open by pounding a knife into it with her boot. She scooped the beans into the pan to warm over the fire.

Daniel came back with three sizable trout, cleaned and ready for the frying pan. He handed them to Moira, who accepted them with a wrinkling of her nose.

"Oh, marvelous. More fish," she sighed. She looked up at him, eyes laughing.

"But this is fresh, not smoked or salted."

"And not spoiled." She looked at them for a moment and then plopped them into the pan. When their meal looked ready, she scooped beans and fish onto tin plates and poured coffee into tin cups. Daniel took his plate, leaned back against a tree trunk, and sighed. He took his first bite.

His expression changed radically. He stopped for several seconds and chewed again. His jaws moved for a long, slow minute, and then he closed his eyes tightly to swallow. To wash the bony muck down, he took a big gulp of hot coffee. He stopped swallowing the second it passed over his lips. Moira could hear him across the crackling fire, where she was having difficulty downing her own meal.

"Mory," Daniel began slowly, with a painful patience, grimacing down at his plate. "You're only supposed to warm the beans. And there's a grinder and strainer for the coffee." He paused. "And fish are supposed to be fried separately and quickly."

"I'm sorry. I'll do better tomorrow."

He made a sound in his throat. Moira buried their meal a few feet from camp. She handed Daniel a hardtack biscuit soaked in strong coffee. "It isn't any worse than what we had on the ship," she said with an apologetic smile.

"No better either," he said with brotherly ruthlessness. He finished eating and lay back on his blanket, falling asleep almost immediately.

Pulling off her boots, she examined her sore feet, which were swollen and badly blistered. She walked gingerly down to the stream and sank them into the cold water. For an instant they stung painfully, but then they quickly began to feel better.

Moira sat there for a long time, listening to the crickets, the gurgling stream, and the faint evening breeze rustling the leaves in the trees. It was getting cooler, but she didn't want to go back to the fire yet. She needed these few minutes to herself after the long months crowded aboard the *Stephen Rule* with no privacy whatsoever. Now there was almost too much space and air, too much peace and quiet. Her mind wandered to Jack and she prayed that he was all right and that they would find him and be reunited soon.

Gradually, her thoughts turned to Hawthorne. There was no sense in thinking of him or of that devastating kiss. That was now in the past. He had had some fun at her expense, teasing her and provoking her emotions. Now she should forget him and put the experience in its proper place.

When she came back to the fire, Daniel had awakened and lay staring up at the star-studded sky, his hands folded comfortably behind his head. He glanced at her and then pushed himself up, bracing his weight with an elbow.

"You looked depressed down there by yourself."

She shrugged. "Just thinking."

"You sorry you came now, Mory?"

She sat down and stared into the flickering fire, listening to its comforting crackle, feeling its warmth. She put her hands out to warm them and cast him a teasing smile.

"Only briefly, when I tasted dinner," she said. He laughed.

"God-awful, that's for sure. You'd better improve or we'll starve!" He smiled. "Otherwise, how do you feel?"

"You want the truth?"

"Yes."

"My feet are blistered to bleeding. My back aches. My stomach is empty and growling. My head is pounding. Every muscle in my body has died and gone to heaven. Other than that, I'd say I'm in good shape."

He grinned. "Well, I'd say we're in about the same condition," he admitted.

She stared down at the fire again. "I'm not sorry, Danny. Even hurting as much as I do, I feel more alive than I have since..." She thought of her parents.

"I know."

She looked up at him again, hugging her knees, tears springing into her eyes. "Then you've forgiven me for spoiling your plans."

"Almost."

"Wretch," she laughed.

"I'd be lying if I said I had."

"You'd have expected me to stay in Charleston and marry Beauchamp, I suppose," she accused good-humoredly.

"He was pretty bloody awful, wasn't he?"

"An absolute lecher."

"Well, I hope he hasn't entirely chilled your feelings about men. I'd hate to think I'll have you hanging around my neck like a millstone for the rest of my life," he teased.

She had the sudden, unwelcome thought of Hawthorne kissing her 'tween decks, holding her hips so that she couldn't escape the feel of him. The memory made her heart race. Charles had done nothing but look and lightly touch. Hawthorne had been far more bold, and yet it was Charles she thought of as the lecher.

"What's the matter?" Daniel asked.

"Nothing. Just thinking."

"You sure had a strange look on your face. He didn't, did he?"

Moira stared at Daniel blankly. "Who didn't what?"

"Charles didn't make you... you know... not want to get married?"

She repressed a smile and looked at him very seriously. "Well, I thought I could just live with you. Cook, clean, take care of your home... that sort of thing."

Daniel didn't say anything, and Moira chuckled. "Don't

worry so much, Daniel. If worse comes to worse, I can always move in with Jewel."

"Shut up, Mory." He lay back. Then he sat up again. "One thing, before I forget. You're going to have to watch the way you walk."

"All I can think about is managing to place one foot in front of the other. What are you talking about, 'watch the way I walk'?"

"You've got to keep the hip movements to a minimum. You should have seen the ferry operator's eyes when you were walking away from him. He didn't know what to make of a man with a sashay."

She giggled. "I'll try to remember." She sighed, wishing the heat on her face, forearms, and shins would penetrate to her cold backside. "It's too bad he didn't know where Bootjack was."

"Said he thought it was someplace up along here. That's why we're walking."

"It is? I thought it was because we didn't have enough money to get horses."

Daniel was asleep. Moira rested her head on her knees, too tired to even move as far as her blanket. She awakened some time later when the breeze changed direction and blew smoke into her face. She coughed, then crawled around the fire to collapse near Daniel, who was snoring loudly.

Dawn came altogether too soon. Daniel was excited and didn't want to waste time fixing breakfast, so they set off again, chewing on hardtack. They made it to the meadowlands northeast of Mount Diablo. That night they feasted on tough jerky, more charred beans, and a better, though far from tasty, pot of coffee.

It was easier going the next few days across the wide stretch of land and through the wild-wheat-covered hills. Moira kept her feet carefully wrapped, her muscles became more used to the load. She lost more weight.

Daniel shot a rabbit on the fourth day, and Moira promptly burned it to a dark brown over the fire. At least it wasn't smoked fish, duff, or charred beans, she reminded him when he complained bitterly about the burnt offering she had made of his hunting triumph. And her coffee, at last, was digestible.

It grew hotter the further east they went, and Moira thought longingly of the cool mists of San Francisco. Sweat beaded on her forehead and trickled down her temples. More dampened her breasts and the underarms of her rough shirt. She was beginning to smell less and less like that gardenia Daniel had spoken of.

They saw men traveling during the day and the lights of distant campfires by night. Yet they exchanged only brief greetings with fellow travelers and stayed to themselves as much as possible. Farms and ranches were scattered few and far between. They stopped at one, hoping to purchase eggs. They were chased away by an irate woman with a rifle who shouted that she had enough of thieving miners who were down on their luck. The next said he would sell anything they wanted, but his prices were so exorbitant Daniel and Moira went on. The third was more amenable.

A thin, middle-aged woman with a worn gingham dress stood hoeing in a vegetable garden outside a modest adobe structure. A barn stood nearby, far better built than the house. As Daniel and Moira approached cautiously, looking around for her firearm, the woman straightened and leaned on her hoe, watching them. She wiped the sweat off her forehead with her apron and waited for them to state their business.

Daniel did the talking. The woman listened, neither friendly nor unfriendly.

"At least you're not asking for a handout," she said finally and walked toward them. She looked at Mory curiously. "Take off that hat, boy. Don't you know it's rude to stand there talking to a lady with your hat on?"

Mory yanked the floppy thing off quickly, holding it clutched respectfully in her hand, feeling embarrassed and stupid that she hadn't thought to do it without such a brisk reminder. Daniel glanced at her.

"Lordy, you must have broken your poor mother's heart," the woman said, shaking her head sadly at Mory. "You can't be more than fourteen by the looks of you. The youngest I've seen yet."

"Eighteen, ma'am. I had a birthday a week ago," she said, and Daniel cast her a despairing look.

"And not even the hint of a whisker to boast of yet," the

woman said. "Well, it's no skin off my nose if you're fools like the rest of them. Come on and I'll give you something to eat." She pointed at them. "But you're going to have to work for it."

She sent them to the barn to clean stalls and fork in fresh hay. Daniel gave Mory a droll look as she mucked out the horses' stalls. She laughed, leaning on her pitchfork.

"What was that you were saying only a few days ago about a man smelling like the wrong end of a horse?" she asked. "I think I pass now, don't you?"

When they came in, Meg Vanderstrum had laid out the table with mulligan stew, freshly baked bread, churned butter, home-made preserves, and tall glasses of milk recently taken from old Bessie. She sent them to the washbasins just outside the kitchen door, where they scrubbed up to their elbows and washed their faces. Sitting at the table with pewter forks in their hands, they felt the nearest to heaven that they had been since leaving home.

All the while Moira and Daniel ate Meg Vanderstrum talked. She had three sons who had gone off like all the other fools to look for gold. Even her husband Henry was chomping at the bit again, although he had tried his luck in '48, not many months after word got out about Marshall's discovery at Sutter's Mill on the American. A lot of farms and ranches were in a bad way, with the men off looking for a pot at the end of the rainbow. It was clear as a bell to her that there was more gold to be had on this farm than in any of those streambeds in the mountains. Gold miners needed food, and this farm could produce plenty with enough manpower. Would they like to stay and work for her?

Moira explained that it was not so much gold they were seeking as word of their older brother, who had come to California ahead of them. After relating the story to Meg, the woman relented.

"I've heard of Bootjack. It's not more than thirty odd miles from here. Up on the river, I think. About a stone's throw from the fort. The fort's taking lodgers now, I hear. You might just learn more there."

They thanked Meg and went on their way with her blessing and a knotted cloth full of squash, beans, and beets. She refused to take any money from either of them in spite of all her talk about the farm bringing in money from miners.

Daniel and Moira set off in the wrong direction, and it was two days before they finally found the river again. They camped nearby and were suddenly joined that evening by three men on their way back to the coast from the gold fields. Moira jumped, and Daniel dove for the gun lying near his bedroll.

"Hold on, there, gents! Don't shoot!" an alarmed voice said. "We're friends." A big bear of a man stepped forward with his hands out to show them empty. He looked dangerous to Moira. He had several days' growth of beard on a hard, square jaw and shoulders that were too broad for comfort. His clothes were ragged and dusty, and he was packing a load of gear that probably weighed as much as Moira herself.

She realized that she and Daniel must look as rough and disheveled as he did.

"We just want to share your fire," the man said. He had dark curly hair and a pleasant smile. He looked about Jack's age. Moira relaxed and smiled in welcome.

There were two other men traveling with the big dark one. Tad Knap was the youngest, with blond-brown hair and big, puppy-dog brown eyes. He wasn't much older than Moira, but there was a wealth of experience written in the lines about his mouth. He'd been in the gold country for six months, and that was enough for any man, especially when he hadn't found enough gold to feed himself properly.

Manny Delgado was the other, a sailor who had jumped ship in Monterey. Everyone had assumed he was Mexican, and he was tired of fighting the prejudice and having his claims jumped. He was sporting a black eye from his last attempt to hold what was rightfully his.

Sam Rolands, the big man, was a blacksmith from Pennsylvania. He had gotten separated from his company not long after arriving in California. He had had very little luck panning for gold and was now on his way back to the coast to look for work.

Tad cooked dinner, to Moira's infinite relief. Sam Rolands produced a bottle of whiskey and passed it around. When it came to Moira, she realized she could hardly let it pass without raising some questions or being teased, so she tasted the foul stuff. Her tongue burned. Rolands laughed. Moira watched as his Adam's apple bobbed when the whiskey went down. Daniel, she noticed, didn't resist the offers.

Within an hour, Moira noticed with growing consternation that none of them, Daniel included, were feeling any pain. They were enjoying themselves immensely, brothers of the same mold looking for their fortunes, getting coarser by the minute. Moira was learning a great deal about the male animal, and what she was learning was nothing to their credit. Each time the bottle came around, she pretended to drink and then passed it on, leaning back to absorb every word.

Women, of course, were a primary topic, Sam Rolands being particularly descriptive in what appealed to him. It seemed there was a whore in Hangtown who was particularly gifted in her field of trade, and Sam didn't spare them any details about her special skills.

Moira's stunned, red-faced, red-eared silence didn't go unnoticed. The trio believed her to be a virgin boy, ready and now well primed for his first experience with the fair sex. Daniel thought that uproariously hilarious, and no matter how many killing looks she sent him, he simply sat by and enjoyed her growing discomfort at the ribbing she was getting.

The following morning, Moira learned even more than she wanted to know. She stood up from her blankets and turned around, stretching. Rolands stood in full view relieving himself. Moira gasped, swung around, and then didn't know whether to throw herself down and put the blanket over her head or pretend nothing was amiss. The others seemed to see nothing wrong in going about one's natural functions in broad daylight. They were all men, after all. When Moira crept toward the thick brush some distance away from the group, glancing back to make sure they didn't follow, Rolands stared after her curiously and then hollered, "Hey, kid, you got something to hide? You ain't that much bigger than the rest of us, are you?"

The others laughed heartily. Rolands looked at Daniel. "Modest, ain't he?"

Moira was relieved when the trio departed soon afterward and she and Daniel were once again left to themselves. They broke camp and headed up the American. Daniel didn't say much for several miles. He seemed to be suffering from an acute headache. Moira had no sympathy.

She was beginning to wonder if her masquerade was an appropriate idea or not. Yet the more she thought about it, the more certain she was that hearing what plans went on in the minds of men was far better than being open prey to them.

Chapter Eleven

Bootjack was southwest of Sutter's Fort, and Moira and Daniel stumbled onto it quite by accident. It was a community of scattered canvas tents, slapped-together shacks with hastily printed signs, and two or three poorly constructed buildings along a quagmire of a main street. There were countless men tramping around, all looking much the same as the others with whom Moira and Daniel had come in contact during their trek. None of them looked affluent, though back East they might have been physicians, lawyers, professors, or even ministers. Some looked downright pathetic, staggering around and swigging down rotgut whiskey, while a few others were sleeping against shacks.

There was a fight under way near one of the buildings, and men were standing around yelling encouragement while the two contestants battered each other bloody. Moira didn't like Bootjack. She could see nothing on the surface to recommend it, and hadn't the desire to know what was going on beneath the foul facade. Were all mining camps like this one? She couldn't imagine Jack being here, though she searched faces, hoping by some miracle she would find him among them.

Daniel was tired and not feeling well. He had been ill for two days, and Moira blamed it on the whiskey Sam Rolands

had shared. With brotherly predictability Daniel blamed his ill
health on her cooking.

They camped not far outside town, and Daniel begged off
dinner again, stretching out beneath the lean-to they had constructed. He pulled his blanket over him and promptly went
to sleep. Moira was too anxious to find Jack to feel tired. They
had come so far, and now they had arrived at their destination.
She couldn't have slept had she walked a hundred miles that
very day.

After eating some beef jerky and drinking some strong
coffee, Moira decided there could be no harm in going back
to town on her own and asking about Jack. Daniel would be
all right in camp. She had all their money neatly sewn into the
clothing she wore, and there was nothing else of any value she
was leaving behind.

It was still drizzling and she took a blanket with her, draping
it over her head and around her shoulders to keep the wet chill
off. She remembered to walk with legs slightly spread and to
move her shoulders instead of her hips. The effort always
exhausted her, but she didn't want to give herself away when
she was alone.

Most of the businesses she passed coming into town were
involved in drinking and gambling. She began to understand
why so many of the men wandering around looked poor. What
gold they did manage to take from the streambeds and hillsides
they quickly dropped on a faro, monte, or poker table, or
shoved across a bar for a bottle of whiskey. Food wasn't cheap
either, and she hadn't seen a fat miner yet.

The trading post didn't know anything about Jack, so Moira
gathered her courage and went into one of the many saloons.
Boisterous swearing and laughter greeted her ears. She was
damp and smelled of wet wool and dirt, but there were others
that smelled far worse than she.

Moira weaved her way between the crowded gambling
tables to approach the plank bar. A burly man with a polished
bald head and sharp blue eyes presided. He had massive hands,
and his sleeves were rolled up over muscular forearms. What
hair didn't grow on his head grew profusely down his arms to
the knuckles of his fingers. He poured out whiskey for the men

along the bar. Much of it sloshed on the plank, but he didn't bother wiping it up. The place smelled strongly of spirits.

She had to shoulder her way in to find a position, an action that took some bravado on her part. Someone bumped against her on one side and demanded more whiskey, though he smelled well sodden already. He put an elbow into her side and she fell back slightly, giving way. Someone behind her pushed her forward again right into the drunk, who turned angrily and glared down at her. He had bloodshot gray eyes and a ruddy complexion. He looked stupid and dangerous. Moira wished she had never set foot in the place.

"You bump me again, runt, and I'll make you wish you'd never been born!" he snarled. He looked hopeful that she would argue. Moira stared up at him, wide-eyed with fright. She retreated and then wove her way toward the other end of the long plank. Finally she was able to get close enough to put her elbow on the bar, as the others were doing.

"What'll you have, boy?" the bartender asked. "We don't serve sarsaparilla."

A couple of men laughed, glancing at Mory with curious amusement.

"If the kid's old enough to be panning gold, he's old enough to drink."

"Hear, hear," another slurred drunkenly. "Give him a whiskey on me." The bartender sloshed some into a glass and shoved it across to her. The miner to her left paid two bits for it. She looked at him, thanking him in as gruff a voice as she could manage.

"You're kind of young to be out here, aren't you, kid?" he asked, looking Mory over. He was tall and thin, with a dark, well-trimmed mustache.

"I'm looking for someone," she said. "Have you heard of or seen a man named Jack Cavendish?"

"Cavendish? Can't say. Not many men stay around anyplace long enough to give names." He shrugged, sipping his whiskey. "Lot of nicknames. Bonny Jack. Jack Blue. Smooth Jack. No Cavendish, though."

"Oh."

"What's he look like and where's he hail from?"

"He's six two, blond-brown hair, blue eyes, wears a gold-and-onyx ring on his right hand, and he's from Charleston."

"Nope. Don't know him." He looked up at the bartender. "Hey, Nash, you heard of a big gent, blond, blue eyes, named Cavendish?"

"Don't think so," he answered indifferently, shoving another shot glass across the plank toward the bleary-eyed customer opposite him. "How long ago was he here?"

"More than a year now."

"Well, that was way before my time," Nash answered with a laugh. "Didn't even know Bootjack was here that long ago. I've been here just six months. Why you looking for this fellow?"

"He's my brother."

"Well, boy, you're going to have one hell of a time finding anyone in this country. Men are moving all the time, searching for that lucky strike. Not many stay put in any one place longer than a few months." Someone hailed him from the other end of the bar, and he walked away. The man next to Mory looked at her sympathetically.

"He's right, you know. You probably won't find him."

Moira frowned, not knowing what to do now. The man seemed in a mood to talk, and since she wasn't sure where to go from there, she listened.

"I came west with a group of friends from my hometown in Ohio," he volunteered. "We thought we'd come right into California, strike it rich, and run right back home with our pockets full of gold dust. We called ourselves the Felton Mining Company. Worked the Yuba for a couple of months, but didn't make much more than what it cost to live. So we decided to split up for a while and see if we couldn't better our luck." He sighed miserably, staring into his half-full glass. "I haven't seen any of them since." He gulped the whiskey down and raised a finger to Nash for another.

"Wish to hell I'd never come," he said, sipping his fresh drink. "Don't know how in hell I'm ever going to get home again. Haven't got enough gold to buy a horse or buy passage on a steamer to the Isthmus," he said dismally, hardly caring that Mory was even there.

He smiled sadly into his whiskey. "Got a real pretty girl

back home that's waiting for me to come back and marry her. Name's Sarah. She's so damned pretty," he slurred. "Probably got someone wanting to marry her now. Maybe she's married already. Hell. Wish I knew." He sighed, drank the whiskey, and raised his finger again. Nash poured more, taking more gold dust. "Shouldn't have come," the miner slurred. "Should have stayed the hell home and married pretty Sarah and been satisfied with that little farm I sold. At least it was mine. Now I got nothing. Nothing. Not even pretty Sarah." His eyes were drooping and his head bobbing. He swallowed more whiskey, wiping his mouth with a dirty sleeve. "Wish to hell I'd never come," he said almost incomprehensibly.

Moira moved away from the bar. Glancing back with pity at the man, she saw that he was drinking the whiskey he had bought for her. She wove her way back through the tables and went outside into the muddy street and dark night. It had stopped drizzling, and the clouds drifted toward the coast. Stars were beginning to appear.

All along the street, lanterns burned inside tents and shanties. Depressed and confused, not knowing what do do, she wandered, still searching the faces that passed by her. A man slept against one of the buildings. Others milled around aimlessly, talking in groups of three to half a dozen. Others went from bar to bar. Someone played a lively fiddle in another tent saloon. It was growing very dark and much cooler.

A sign at the end of the street captured Moira's attention: Hot Baths $1. She hadn't had a full, hot bath since leaving Charleston! She had used a bowl and pitcher for keeping clean while aboard the ship, and during the long trek to Bootjack she had, by necessity, been limited to bathing hands, feet, and face in the streams by which they camped. She was not hardy enough to submerge herself in an icy stream. Just reading that heavenly sign made her feel sticky, dirty, and sweaty. It was risky. Yet anything worth doing was a risk, she decided. She walked quickly to the door and opened it before she could change her mind.

It was warm inside, and the room was lighted by several kerosene lanterns. There was a large wood stove in the center, and on it was a huge pot of steaming water. There were curtained cubicles all around the perimeter of the room, and Moira could hear the sounds of men bathing. One was singing an aria.

"By gad, man, careful where you pour that scalding water!" one man exploded from behind a curtain. "I've only got one of those, and I want to keep it!"

A Chinese man came out of the cubicle quickly, drawing the curtain behind him. He was wearing a long apron over a dark, loose shirt and pants and had a long pigtail down his back. He saw Moira and bowed to her twice in quick succession before hurrying over to refill his kettle from the pot. He headed to another cubicle, where a man was calling for more hot water. Moira sat on the bench to wait her turn, her heart pounding. Maybe this wasn't such a good idea after all. It was going to be chancy. But her longing to be clean far outweighed her fear of possible discovery, and after all, she could run fast, it was dark outside, and this establishment was right on the edge of town.

The curtain on one of the cubicles was shoved back and a man came out, buttoning up his checked shirt. He pushed it into his pants and then reached for his hat. He glanced at Moira and then walked out the door. The elderly Chinese proprietor came out and bowed to her again, then put out his hand. She put a dollar into it and he bowed again, this time smiling. He had very straight, very white teeth.

"Bath be ready quick, mister. You want smell added, two bit extra. Much cheap."

"What smells do you have?"

"Mountain wood or allspice," he said in his thickly accented English.

"Allspice, please," she said, handing over a quarter. He bowed again and took a small bottle from a shelf. She smiled excitedly, almost rubbing her hands together in delight, hardly able to wait to get into that tub of hot water and wash away the accumulated dirt and sweat of the days of hard travel. When the tub was partially full of steaming, scented, fresh water, the man waved her in.

"You want clothes washed and dried while you take bath, mister? We quick, chop-chop. Only dollar extra."

She looked down at her dirt-stained clothes and thought

about the temptation he was presenting her with. She plucked the short out from her dungarees and looked at it distastefully. Yet giving her clothes over was asking for trouble. If she was discovered, she wanted to have them handy for a run. And besides, if she gave him *everything*, he would know in an instant that this was no man with whom he was doing business.

She shook her head decisively and pitched her voice low. "I'm in a hurry tonight."

He closed the curtain, leaving her alone. Her boots hit the floor, socks following, then her dungarees, scarf, shirt, long johns, and finally, after a quick look around, the tight cloth that she wrapped around her breasts to flatten them. She put a bare toe into the water and slid her foot in with an ecstatic sigh. She was going to love this!

With no time to waste, she washed her hair first, rinsing it in the clean water before lathering herself from her ears down to her toes. She scrubbed hard and fast, a smile of pleasure on her face. She slid down into the water up to her shoulders, then lifted a slender, curvaceous leg and lathered it down to her toes again. She was on the second leg when the curtain parted and a younger Chinese man walked in with another kettle of hot water to warm her bath.

Moira's eyes opened saucer-wide, and she drew in a sharp, frightened breath. Yet she couldn't possibly have been more shocked than the young man, whose eyes fastened on the two pink-tipped white mounds of flesh that were visible above the surface of the water. He stared at her, mouth agape, and then in half panic dumped the scalding contents of the kettle into the tub. Moira let out a pained yelp, rising from the tub and giving him a fuller view of her female charms. He retreated, shrieking Chinese.

Moira dove for her clothes, splashing water all over the floor in her haste. She pulled on her panties and tied her chest-wrap, and was in the process of yanking on the longjohns when the aging Chinese proprietor peeked in for confirmation of what his son was shouting. His eyes seemed to pop right out of his head as he took in the evidence with a glance, then he pulled the curtain shut as though a dragon were behind it. The verbal excitement outside the curtain intensified as Moira pulled up her dungarees and tried frantically to get the buttons closed.

"What in hell's going on out there?" some man boomed from a neighboring cubicle. "I need some more hot water!"

"Hey! In here, too! Chop-chop!"

Her socks on, Moira shoved her feet into her boots and pushed her shirt into her pants. She expected a horde of randy, depraved men to come bursting in on her at any minute. She cursed herself for ever having come in here in the first place and, jerking the curtain aside, ran across the room to the front door. Two startled Chinamen stopped talking to gape at her as she headed out the door. She collided with someone coming into the building and knocked him backward into the mud.

"Hey, you dumb bastard! Watch where you're going!"

She darted to the side and ran toward the woods at the edge of town. She ran for a distance and then stopped to look back. No one was following.

Leaning against a tree, she tried to get her breath back. When she did, she started laughing. Peal after peal of it rang into the night, until she stifled it with her hand. No use attracting more attention than she already had, she thought, giggling. Their faces! Oh, well, she'd steer very clear of that place on her next visit to Bootjack!

The trees cast eerie shadows as she walked on toward the campsite where Daniel was sleeping. She wouldn't tell him what she had done. He would simply rant and rave at her and worry about what she would do next. She couldn't blame him, really. It hadn't been the most sensible thing she'd ever done.

Looking around, she tried to pick out the landmarks she had mentally jotted down before heading back for town. She was sure she was going in the right direction. There was the bluff to the northeast, the curve in the river to the south, and the clump of white oaks to the west. She was in the right area, so where was the campsite?

Moira looked around again, straining her eyes in the growing darkness. If she didn't find it soon she wouldn't be able to until first light. She didn't look forward to a long, cold night without a fire.

She saw what she was sure was the camp, only something was very wrong. She ran toward it, looking around frantically for Daniel. He had been sleeping under the lean-to. Now it was knocked over. The packs had been searched in obvious haste, the gear dumped all around the camp. The pan, pick and shovel were where she had placed them. But a blanket had been tossed hastily to one side.

Daniel was gone!

"Danny!" she called, turning around and staring into the shadows. Her heart began to pound hard and in a painful rhythm of fear. "Danny!" she screamed.

Nothing but the night wind answered.

Chapter Twelve

Moira searched the area in panic. When Daniel was nowhere to be found, she sat down and cried. What had happened? It looked as though someone had come into the camp and turned everything upside down, looking for something. But what? And where was Daniel? Had the intruders hurt him? Killed him? She should never have left camp. She shouldn't have lingered in the saloon listening to that sad drunk. She shouldn't have gone into that bathhouse!

She didn't know what to do. She didn't know where to look. And yet sitting here doing nothing was driving her crazy! She put their gear back into the packs, trying to ascertain whether anything was missing. She had taken her money with her, never completely trusting Daniel with money in his pocket. None of their possessions seemed to be missing. She reerected the lean-to and tried to get the fire going again so that Daniel would see it.

"Daniel!" she cried, standing up and cupping her hands to her mouth. "Daniel!" Tears flowed unheeded down her cheeks. She sat down and put her head on her arms.

Her head came up sharply as she heard someone running. Whoever it was was coming toward her. Panic swept over her. If it was Daniel, he would have answered. Perhaps it was the same person or persons who had torn through their things and possibly hurt or killed Daniel. She didn't want to think further. Standing up, she turned in the opposite direction from the sound and started to run.

She had run barely a hundred yards when her pursuer tackled her, bringing her to the ground with a hard thud. She let out an unladylike grunt and saw stars swirling before her eyes.

"Damn you, Mory!" Daniel swore violently, holding her down with an effort when she began to fight.

"Danny!" she cried, flinging her arms around his neck with a sob and hugging him so tightly he had difficulty breathing. He grabbed her wrists and tore her arms away.

"Where in hell have you been? I've been looking all over tarnation for you! And then I hear you screaming like a bloody banshee! I ought to string you up by your ears for what you've put me through!"

"Oh, Danny!" she sobbed, half hysterical with relief and not in the least worried about how angry he was with her. He shook her hard.

"Where have you been?" he repeated angrily.

"In Bootjack!" she gasped. "I wanted to ask around for Jack. No one has heard of him."

"You idiot! You stupid, numb-brained, addle-witted *idiot!*" He released her abruptly and raked shaking fingers through his hair. "Do you have any idea at all what I've been through in the past two hours?" He sounded close to tears himself. "After those men came into camp—"

"What men?"

"The ones that knocked over the lean-to and knocked me a good one over the head, that's who!"

"Are you all right?" she asked, reaching up to feel his head for lumps. He shoved her hand away angrily.

"I'll live, damn it!" He glared at her. "You're absolutely crazy going into Bootjack on a Friday night! Or any night, for that matter, by yourself."

"I wanted to find Jack."

"We'll find him, but you don't have to go off like a fool by yourself, asking strangers about Jack. You're looking for trouble!" His voice dropped slightly. He sat back with a plop. "I've been worried sick about you, Mory," he said. "When I came to and found you missing, I thought they'd packed you off somewhere and raped you...or... *Hell, don't you ever do that to me again!*" he shouted, anger rising again. "Do you know there isn't even a sheriff in this town? Nothing at all!"

"You mean you told someone you'd lost a sister?" she squeaked, thinking of the bathhouse.

"No! Hell, no! I couldn't find anybody to do with the law, and I wasn't about to trust anyone else!" He sighed heavily. Then he stopped and sniffed the air. After a second, he looked straight at her and leaned toward her, sniffing again.

"By God, you've had a bath!"

Moira giggled. "A very hasty one."

"Where?"

"There's a bathhouse in Bootjack. Right at the end of the street."

"Do you know the chance you took? So help me God, you ever do this to me again and I'll beat you to within an inch of your life! I swear I will. Sister or not! You hear me?"

"Don't worry, Danny. I won't be going back there," she said innocently. He looked at her sharply. He shook his head, looking away.

"Never mind," he muttered. "I don't want to know."

They walked back to camp, and Daniel rebuilt the fire. Moira snuggled down under the blankets while he took a tally of their possesions.

"They got my gun," Daniel said grimly. Then he looked across the fire at Mory. "Maybe it's a good thing you weren't here. If they'd discovered a girl..." He left the rest unsaid.

"What're we going to do tomorrow?" she asked quietly. He sat with a heavy frown on his face, staring into the fire. He looked older than his twenty-one years. Was she really aging him?

"Go into Bootjack and ask around for Jack again. Then, if we hear nothing, we're going to move on and find a place to pan for gold."

"Just like that."

"You came to find Jack. I came to find gold. I'm hoping we'll find both," he said simply, looking at her, the light flickering across his face. He looked tense and defensive.

"Aren't you worried about him, Danny? Don't you feel the

least bit anxious to find him?" she asked, pushing herself up onto her elbow, frowning.

"What good does it do to worry, Mory? If we're meant to find him, we will. Everywhere we go, we'll ask and look. But I'm not going to stay in this mudhold waiting for him and hear how every other man except me came to California and went home with his pockets full of gold!"

Moira lay back down, brow creased. "Maybe I could do the asking around while you do the gold prospecting?" she suggested quietly, staring up into the dark, star-studded sky.

"After what happened tonight? Forget it!"

"But you'd know where I was, Danny, and what I was doing," she reasoned, pushing herself up again and drawing her knees close.

"Would I?" he said dryly.

"You would. And I'd be very careful. No one suspected anything tonight. No one. And I went into a trading post and a saloon, talked with a lot of different men, and even ordered a whiskey."

"Oh, Lord," he groaned.

"I didn't drink any of it."

"Mory, just drop the subject, will you please?" he said, rubbing his temples. "Just stick with me and don't let me out of your sight again. All right? Promise me that."

She realized he was still distraught from having chased around looking for her. Worry lines were etched in his young face. She had done a very irresponsible thing, and he was paying for it. She had worried him needlessly tonight, and he had suffered even worse at the hands of those thieves who had broken into camp while she was gone. He might have been killed. For a while she had been afraid to even think of that possibility, a very real one.

She got up and came around the fire to sit next to him. "I'm sorry, Danny," she said, looking up at him, sincerely remorseful for the anxiety she had caused him. He looked at her, and there was the hint of tears in his eyes.

"You know, Mory, I love you. You're not the only one that feels Mama and Papa's loss, or Jack's. And when you were gone, I thought—" His voice broke, and he shook his head, looking away from her. She saw him swallow hard and draw a long, steadying breath. "Just don't ever do that to me again," he said hoarsely.

"I promise," she said, taking his hand, tears in her eyes. "Would you like to put your head on my lap?"

He did, stretching out near the warmth of the fire. She brushed the sandy-brown hair back from his temples. She touched a lump on the back of his head, and he winced slightly in protest. He looked exhausted and pale.

"I'm tired," he sighed. "So damn tired."

"Go to sleep, Danny." She stroked his hair like a child, and he closed his eyes.

"I thought it was all going to be such a lark," he said just before falling asleep.

He wasn't the only one! She had thought it would be so easy. Just board the *Stephen Rule* and stay out of sight until there was no way to send her back. Come to California and find Bootjack. And there would be Jack, waiting for them with open arms.

She sniffed, brushing tears from her eyes. She took a deep breath. Well, they weren't going to give up easily. They would look until they found Jack. And they wouldn't leave California until they had succeeded!

Smiling slightly, she thought of how Jack had lounged before the library fire, talking about his dreams of having a good piece of land to work. It was every merchant son's dream to have a plantation, and since that wasn't possible for Jack, he had chosen to go west and stake out his own place. There was plenty of land for everyone out there, he said. And someday California would be annexed to the United States of America, he was sure of it.

Jack had left Charleston in late 1847, arriving by wagon train in California in 1948. They had heard from him several times during the first year. He liked California and wrote of the miles of wild wheat that grew on the rolling hillsides, the endless amount of timber growing in the Sierras. He was undecided where to settle and what to do, and so stayed on at Sutter's Fort.

Then gold had been discovered. His letters were filled with descriptions of the rush. Land was forgotten in his quest for gold. He began to move around. Each of his letters came from a different place, and they came together in bunches when a ship came in. The last letter hadn't made much sense. Something about the pot at the end of the rainbow and daring a demon for it. It had come from Bootjack.

Danny was right; Jack wouldn't be in Bootjack now. He would have long since moved on. Yet they had to start somewhere in their search for him. They could ask again tomorrow, and if they still failed, then they would have to move on. They would keep moving on until they heard something.

Danny stirred, and Moira gently lifted his head, slid her arm out from beneath him, and placed a rolled shirt under his head as a pillow. She replenished the fire and went to lie down on her own blanket. She stared into the fire until her eyes closed.

Bootjack was crowded the next morning. Men were coming in for supplies and to raise hell on a Saturday night. There was talk of a strike further up the American, and Daniel's interest in looking for Jack quickly evaporated in his impatience to get his own pan into the streams. Moira bought supplies from the trading post while Daniel bought himself a hot bath. She finished before he did and waited for him outside the asseyer's office, hoping she might hear some hint of where gold was being found.

When Daniel joined her, they headed for the gunsmith to buy another pistol and a rifle. Daniel bought a holster for the pistol and let Moira wear it while he packed the rifle. It felt strange having the weight on her hip, and she was half afraid that it would go off by itself and blow her foot away. Daniel assured her it wouldn't and promised to give her some lessons in firing it as soon as they found a place to camp for the night.

They headed toward New Helvetia, believing that was their best bet for hearing word of Jack. Since he had worked for Sutter once before, perhaps he would head back that way again, or at least leave word of where he could be found. It was worth a try.

The solid walls and open gates of the fort were surrounded by a jungle of tents and lean-tos. A crowd of men in dungarees and heavy cotton shirts gathered within the walls. Moira was too tired from hiking with her backpack and gear to ask anyone anything. She needed a few days' rest, some decent food, and shelter from the unseasonal rains that had hit them three times in the past week.

Sutter himself was off someplace panning gold with his Kanakas, native Hawaiians he had hired, and a few Indian squaws. Moira and Daniel decided to stay at the fort for a few days and made arrangements to sleep in the upstairs quarters for a dollar a night.

They split up for a few hours and asked numerous men if they had heard of Jack. No one had. They met in front of the cookhouse as they had agreed, where they purchased a modest dinner for an immodest price.

They had no idea what awaited them in the upstairs barracks. They entered the dimly lit room and looked around. It was late, and at least a hundred men lay on the floor, their few possessions not far from them. The man they had given their two dollars to had said a space of three feet by seven, but Moira had thought he was joking. There scarcely looked to be that much space left in the entire room. She and Daniel stepped over sleeping men and cursing ones as they searched for a place to lie down.

When they finally did find room near one of the side walls, Moira sat and looked around, appalled. The rough log and adobe walls enclosed a large room carpeted with men. The bodies turned and twisted to find some comfort on the hard wood floor. They groaned and moaned, snorted and cursed, grunted and complained, and made other impolite noises. The multitude of unshaven and unclean males filled the room with the musky odor of sweat, dirt, and horse. There were other smells as well, and she noted the chamber pots around the room.

A young man not far away from her was crying, and his friends beside him were talking in a low whisper. Moira put her chin on her knees and listened to the sounds of the men around her, feeling a mingling of emotions from disgust and annoyance to pity and faint amusement.

All these rough, dirty, foul-tempered, exhausted men had traveled across a continent, or around one, in order to find gold! *Gold!* The promise of dreams come true and of good times to come for anyone with the courage to leave home.

Nuggets the size of your fist just lying around on the ground! She remembered Daniel and his friends reading those reports excitedly in the parlor in Charleston while making their hasty plans to come west.

Moira looked down at her brother's tired face, stubbly with several days' growth of beard, and at his clothing, dirty and rumpled from so many days of wear. He had lost weight as well. She remembered how handsome he had always looked at home, the way the young ladies watched him and giggled and whispered among themselves whenever he treated them to one of his devastating smiles. Looking around her, she wondered how many others in this disreputable-looking multitude had been young, clean-shaven, well-dressed, educated, church-going men from respectable families, loved by pretty girls and the pride of their parents.

After all, she thought with a curve of her mouth, beneath the dirt and grime, the sweat and wrinkled clothes, the shaggy beards and overlong hair was the promise of this great, growing nation. Not much to look at here and now, but they all had big dreams and aching muscles in common. Maybe, just maybe, some of them would beat the tremendous odds and make something of this journey.

She was worse off than any of them. Gone were the silk gowns, flowered hats and parasols, soft dancing slippers, scented baths, the long, thick, silken dark hair that had fallen to her waist. No more operas, symphonies, teas, soirees, and church socials. Here was a girl who looked like any one of these miserable wretches—and smelled as bad, too.

Tired and uncomfortable as she was, Moira began to find humor in all of it. She looked around the room again, at the rows of exhausted young men. She looked at the dismal fort walls where various decorations hung: half a dozen chamber pots on hooks and one toothbrush meant for communal use. No one seemed overly eager to clean his teeth, she noticed!

California or Bust! And probably everyone of them flat busted!

She looked them over again, grinning now. She listened to the snoring. There was a man near the south end of the room who made staccato snorts, while another not six bodies away drew in a long, drum-rattle breath and then hissed it out in an equally long whistle. The sound sleepers were few; the grunters and groaners were plentiful.

Moira could never resist irony, and she began in a low, half-laughing husky contralto the anthem of the gold rush. After three words, Daniel pushed himself up and stared at her, brows knitted together in irritation.

"Will you shut up?" he hissed. Someone else wasn't so polite about it. Moira just lay back, arms crossed under her head, and continued softly, laughingly:

> *"I came from Charleston with my washbowl on*
> *   my knee,*
> * I'm going to Californ-i-a, the gold dust for to*
> *   see.*
> * It rained all night the day I left, the weather it*
> *   was dry,*
> * The sun so hot I froze to death. Oh, brothers,*
> *   don't you cry.*
> * Oh, California, that's the land for me.*
> * I'm going to Sacramento with my washbowl on*
> *   my knee.*
>
> * I thought of all the pleasant times we've had*
> *   together here,*
> * I thought I ort to cry a bit, but couldn't find a*
> *   tear.*
> * The pilot bread was in my mouth, the gold dust*
> *   in my eye,*
> * And though I'm going far away, dear brothers,*
> *   don't you cry!*
> * Oh, California, that's the land for me.*
> * I'm going to Sacramento with my washbowl on*
> *   my knee.*
>
> * I soon shall be in Frisco, and then I'll look all*
> *   'round,*
> * And when I see the gold lumps there, I'll pick*
> *   them off the ground.*
> * I'll scrape the mountains clean, my boys, I'll*
> *   drain the rivers dry,*

> *A pocket full of rocks bring home, so brother,*
> *   don't you cry!*
> *Oh, California, that's the land for me,*
> *A land of milk and honey and my washbowl on*
> *   my knee."*

Turning her head, she saw her brother's baleful eyes glaring at her in the faint light. She smiled sweetly.

"Daniel, I do believe you forgot to clean your teeth tonight," she said to him for final measure. Someone nearby laughed. She rolled over and went to sleep.

They decided to leave the next day, not wanting to endure the sleeping accommodations again. Finding privacy for certain bodily functions had proved difficult in the fort, and Moira didn't want any more trouble in her life than she had already. Before leaving, they asked again about Jack.

Moira queried a man working in the blacksmith area. "Cavendish," the big man with dark hair and ruddy complexion repeated flatly. He shoved the iron into the fire. "Nope, never heard of him," he said. "Why you looking?"

Moira sighed heavily, dejection showing. "He's my brother. I've come all the way from Charleston to look for him. We haven't heard from him for more than a year."

"We?"

"My other brother. He's over there." She indicated Daniel, speaking to a group of men watching a card game.

The big man ruminated on a piece of tobacco while considering her carefully, taking in the dusty clothes, the thin frame, the young face framed by short dark hair, and the wide, brown eyes filled with disappointment. He spat a clear shot into the fire and listened to it hiss violently.

"What's this Cavendish fellow look like?"

"Big, tall, and lean. He's in his mid-twenties. He's handsome. He has blue eyes and blond-brown hair, probably much lighter in the summer. And he has a laugh that's contagious," she said, smiling as she thought about him. "He came out here looking for land, but he got a little sidetracked looking for gold."

The man laughed. "Like everyone else around these parts. He got another handle besides Cavendish?"

"Jack. If he earned a nickname it'd probably have something to do with cards. He's one hell of a poker player."

"You know him, all right." The man grinned, showing poor teeth.

She looked at him questioningly. "Of course I know him. Do *you* know him or know where he is?"

"I've just got your word who you are, and there've been a lot of people looking for Jack Cavendish lately."

"There have? But who?" she asked, eyes widening.

"Jass Whitsell for one. They joined up on the Rubicon for a while after Jack left Bootjack. Or that's what he claimed. They split up there, I guess, because this Whitsell fellow came up here looking for him. Said there had been some kind of trouble brewing and he wanted to warn Jack."

"What kind of trouble?" Moira asked, heart pounding.

"Didn't say and I didn't ask," he answered, turning the hot iron.

"I wish you had," she sighed. "Who else had been asking for him?"

"Fellow named Barilovich. Big dude with an accent— Russian, I think. Mean-looking. Came through after Whitsell. And he had a gent with him. Heaton, I think his name was. Didn't say much for himself, but then he didn't look like much, either. Weasel-looking fellow with dark hair. Didn't look me in the eye once. Didn't like him." He spat into the fire again. "Then a couple days ago another gent comes through here asking about him. Big, dark man, mid-twenties. Smart by the looks and sound of him, and not from around these parts. Didn't leave a name or reason either." He took the shoe from the fire and set it on the anvil. The hammer came down hard, shooting sparks.

"And all of them were looking for Jack?"

"Sure was. Popular fellow, your brother." He gave the shoe several more blows, and sparks flew onto his bib. Moira stepped back.

"Do you have any idea where he is now?" she asked above the ringing of metal on metal.

"Just a guess," he told her, shoving the shoe back into the fire again. "Mentioned the Yuba once. I'd say he was up there." A couple of more blows to the shoe and then he thrust it into the water, where it hissed violently. "They're finding a lot of color up there, they say."

"Where's the Yuba?"

"North of here," he said, jerking his head in the general direction. "Lots of camps along that river, though. You're going to have trouble finding him, boy."

"We'll do what we have to," she said grimly, looking north. "How far is it?"

"Forty to fifty miles, I'd say."

"Is that where this Jass Whitsell headed?"

"Seemed to know where he was going, but your guess is as good as mine, boy. Told him the same as I'm telling you, and he was sure interested in finding Jack fast. It's going to be damned crowded wherever he is when everyone catches up with him."

Moira couldn't have agreed with him more. "There's no way to even know if Jack is on the Yuba," she said to herself.

"No, you're right about that," the man said. "There's always the chance that he got tired of wandering around looking for a stake. That's what happened to me. Gold mining is hard work," he said, sweat beading his brow, his biceps bulging with the strain of his present labor. "Lot of men came here thinking they'd pick it up like fallen leaves under a tree. For everyone that finds a bonanza, there're a thousand who find a *borrasca*."

"A what?"

"*Borrasca*. An unproductive mine," he explained. "He could have put down roots somewhere and started a farm or ranch. He was looking for land."

"Did he ever mention anyplace in particular? He didn't seem to have any one place in mind when he last wrote to us."

"Can't say. I didn't know him all that well. When I arrived here he was getting ready to head out for the streams. Played a couple of hands of poker with him. Damn good. He cleaned Sutter's pants a couple of times at whist, too, from what I heard." He laughed.

That was Jack all right. He and Daniel shared a passion for cards. It seemed to run in the family.

"Wish I could help more," he said, finishing the shoe and walking toward the horse.

"Thank you for what you've told me. It's a help. More than we've had to go on up to now," she said, walking off to rejoin Daniel. He looked glum until she told him what she'd learned. But his mood darkened again.

"You know, Mory, I'm getting pretty damned sick and tired of looking for Jack. He should've left word for us somewhere along the line."

"He didn't know we were coming, Danny."

"Well, he could have written. Damn it, I've been in California for more than four weeks now, and I haven't even put a pan in a stream yet."

"You complained about that before. It can't be helped," she said, wishing he would at least be grateful for the small amount of information they now had as to where Jack had gone. "You will," she added, understanding his impatience.

"*When* is what I'd like to know!" he demanded angrily, hefting his gear onto his back again and looking north with something less than enthusiasm.

"When we get to the Yuba, of course," she said, smiling, lifting her pack and positioning it on her aching back. She wasn't exactly a bundle of enthusiasm herself, and was not looking forward to sleeping on rocky, hard ground and putting up with creeping things, cold, and a constant menu of beans, jerky, and sourdough bread with coffee. But if they found Jack, it would well be worth everything—and more.

Chapter Thirteen

Panning in the rocky river was bone-tiring work, with very little to show for it. Sometimes Moira and Daniel heard of strikes along the river, bonanzas that were found by chance. But there were hundreds more stories of panners with no luck at all. There were tragic stories as well, of men who died of fevers or pneumonia, others who gambled away everything and almost starved to death, others who turned to crime. Yet thousands kept hoping, by some miracle, that God would single them out for the rich pot at the end of the rainbow.

At night, Moira thought longingly of Aunt Miranda and Charleston. She missed them both intensely and sometimes half wished she had never left. Yet she did not regret having come to California to look for Jack. She was having experiences here that she would never have had under Miranda's watchful eye. Moira always smiled at that.

Aunt Miranda would surely faint if she could see Moira now. She had lost weight from the hours of work. Her clothes were ill-fitting, kept on only by the leather belt, in which she had punched several new holes. Her boots were rotten from the river water, and so were the legs of her dungarees. She smelled of sweat, dirt, and dampness. Her hair had lengthened, and her face, neck, and forearms were bronzed like an Indian's.

Her nails were cracking painfully. She had learned to walk like a man and could even swear with gusto when the occasion called for it. Yes, Miranda would faint dead away.

Just before leaving San Francisco, Moira had left a letter for her aunt with the hotel proprietor. He warned that it might be some time before a ship left harbor but promised he would make sure it was posted. Moira left another letter for her aunt at Sutter's Fort to be taken downriver. If Miranda ever received them, she would know that Moira and Daniel were at least safely in California and now searching for Jack along the Yuba. She hoped that the information would set Aunt Miranda at ease, though she had grave doubts about that.

Mining camps were set up all along the Yuba River. In some places whole sides of hills had been washed away in the frenzied search for gold. The river had paid a high price for the riches it possessed, and Moira wondered how many years it would be after these men left before the banks returned to their natural beauty. Several strikes had been made, and the excitement was high. More men poured in every day.

Miners told Daniel and Mory that there had been some miner-tax dispute in Rough and Ready, and the town had actually decided to secede from the union. Moira could scarcely believe it. One town against a nation? It seemed incredible but there were stranger things happening in this country. Men seemed to have gone mad.

Rough and Ready was much like Bootjack with its quickly thrown-up structures and muddy streets. Yet there was more order here than in the other camps. And there was a less depressed atmosphere, since men's luck was better. Fights, shouting, singing, and laughing were constant, and plenty of drunks wandered around. But the camp had an exciting air to it that Moira and Daniel immediately responded.

After weeks of working the river they had a fat pouch of gold, and it was burning a hole in their pockets.

"A bathhouse!" Moira cried excitedly.

"A fandango hall!" they both said in unison. They looked at each other and laughed. It was the first time they had laughed in quite a while, and Moira thought the expenditure of gold would be worth it if it could take the nervous, short-tempered look from Daniel's face.

"Baths first and then the fandango hall," Daniel said.

That afternoon, after they had both enjoyed the bathhouse—Daniel standing guard as Moira took her bath—they decided to spend the night in a hotel. The hotel clerk demanded five dollars in gold dust in advance for a room. He weighed it out on a small scale on the front desk, and Moira watched carefully to make sure they weren't cheated.

The room was small but comfortable, with two narrow rope beds and a commode with fresh water in the pitcher and a washbowl. Moira sighed in delight. But Daniel was in a hurry to go off, having other activities in mind. He was already dividing up their gold dust.

"Where are you going?" she asked, lying on the bed and watching him. He looked excited and his blue eyes sparkled.

"I'm going to buck the tiger," he told her with a confident grin.

"What?"

"Faro, dear sister, faro."

"Don't you ever learn, Danny?"

"I feel lucky." He flipped the small pouch in the air and caught it, stuffing it into his pocket. "By the way, stay around here, will you? I don't want to have to worry about you." He was already halfway out the door. "Just rest and stay out of sight."

"May I go downstairs and have a good dinner?" she asked sweetly, fuming that he was leaving her behind and out of all the fun without so much as one regret.

The door clicked and he was gone, his footsteps hurrying down the corridor. Moira closed her eyes, loving the feel of the simple mattress under her and the smell of clean linen, rough though it was. These things, which she had taken for granted all her life, were now pure luxuries.

She slept several hours and awakened when it was almost dark. Lighting the lamp, she brushed her hair and rubbed a precious bit of lotion into her dry skin. She was hungry. Daniel could throw away his money on a faro table if he chose, but she was going to put hers in her mouth and eat it!

The dining room was jampacked, and she had to wait thirty minutes before there was space for her at one of the long tables. She ordered a big, rare steak, potatoes, and green beans, and filled her cup repeatedly with the rich coffee, which left not even a hint of grounds in the bottom of her cup. She relaxed and enjoyed every bite she took, feeling blissfully content. She was almost too full to move when she finished the steak but decided to order a thick slice of apple pie anyway. Several men around her were grinning.

"When a boy is growing, he sure has a wolf in his belly, don't he?" said one. They all laughed, and Moira, her mouth full, blushed. She shrugged and then smiled, lifting her fork in silent salute as she stuffed in another mouthful.

"He must have two hollow legs," another teased.

She grinned across the table. "They're full now. Right up to my ears!"

They all laughed and then began to talk about their luck, good and bad. Most of the men had been working the Yuba. Some had come from dry diggings, where Moira thought the work must be even harder.

"Have any of you heard of or seen a man named Jack Cavendish?" Mory asked during a lull in the conversation. She had little hope of a positive response and was surprised when one dark-haired man glanced up. He had fine features and hazel eyes.

"I have. Tall, blond gent with blue eyes?"

"Yes!" She sat up straighter. "He's my brother. I'm looking for him—have been for a long time."

"Well, he was up on the north fork not far from Goodyears Bar when I met him. Don't know where he is now." Someone called him and he left before she could ask him what and where this Goodyears Bar was.

"Is that a saloon?" she asked the men remaining at the table, and they all laughed heartily.

"A river bar, boy. When did your ship get in?" She laughed good-naturedly and told them.

"How do I get to it?"

"Cross the Yuba and the south fork, then go on over Ridge Road until you hit the north fork, then head east," she was told. "You go up that way," another said, pointing with his fork as he chewed his meat.

Moira was eager to find Daniel to tell him what she had learned. She headed out of the hotel and down the muddy street, trying to guess where he had gone to play faro. He could be in any one of the casinos on either side of the street. She went into several and didn't see him.

Then she heard music. Good, loud, lively dancing music! It was coming from a fandango hall just across the street. All thought of finding Daniel fled as she headed for the hall.

Pushing through the swinging doors, she saw men dancing around the room with one another. They were laughing loudly, stamping their feet, lifting their elbows up and down like pumps, and whirling around the room in each other's arms. She started to laugh. Most of them were well saturated with whiskey and as merry as they could be without losing consciousness.

"Hey there, boy!" a man called and came over. She recognized the dark-haired man who had seen Jack. "You'll make some fine lady!"

Moira's mouth opened in fright and her eyes widened until she comprehended what he meant. He tied a handkerchief around her arm to distinguish her from the "gentlemen," and then dragged her out among the dancing couples.

"Just follow me, kid," he shouted down at her "and we'll show these damned sodbusters how to really kick up their feet!" He proceeded to make good his boast. Moira had to move fast and lively just to keep up with him as he went feet and elbows first through the throng of whiskey-merry men. She was out of breath by the time the music stopped. Her partner, whose name was Filmore Chase, grinned down at her and pounded her on the back with enthusiasm.

"I told you we'd show them! Didn't I, kid? Come on, let's have a whiskey!" He shoved her in the direction of the bar.

She seemed to have little choice in the matter as they bellied up and Chase hollered his order. Two shot glasses were filled and slid across to them. Gold dust was passed over, and then Chase lifted his glass in salute.

"Here's to you finding your brother!"

She could hardly refuse to drink to that now, could she? She sipped. Chase laughed.

"Swallow it! Come on, down the hatch, kid! That ain't tea you're drinking!"

He didn't have to tell her that! It tasted like panther piss, a term she had heard several times on the river, and one which at this particular moment seemed perfectly apropos. She decided that maybe if she swallowed fast she wouldn't taste it at all.

"That's it! It'll go down easier the next time. Hit 'em up again, bartender!"

She stood as if turned to stone, waiting for the whiskey to come back up, but thankfully it didn't. By the grace of God, the music started again and she didn't have to accept another.

Someone grabbed her arm. "Come on, little fella, I'll give you a whirl!"

The man was of medium size, with bull shoulders and a thick neck. He wasn't as light on his feet as Chase, but he did manage to plow a furrow through the crowd. Things were livening up, and that glass of whiskey had helped relax Moira's caution. She began to really enjoy herself, laughing and kicking up her heels with the rest of them. She hardly noticed the strange look her partner was giving her. She was panting and laughing at the end of the dance.

"What'd you say your name was?"

"Mory Cavendish," she said, having to yell it to be heard above the clamor in the hall. Glasses clinked and whiskey was being poured down parched gullets, including hers.

"Well, Cavendish, you're downright pretty!"

She did her best to look indignant. "Just because I'm not old enough to boast a beard doesn't give you the right to insult me!" The music started again, and the man swung her around. Suddenly, the man's hand left her back and was thrust straight down between her legs. She gasped and jumped back.

"How dare you?" she cried, furious, and slapped him hard across the face. Men stopped and stared. Her partner grinned from ear to ear.

"I knew you weren't no boy! Besides, a man would have socked me!" He made a grab for her. She sidestepped with a squeal of alarm.

"Well, then, here!" she yelled. Her fist caught him across the side of his head. She then got behind him, put her boot to his rear end, and shoved as hard as she could. He went forward, sprawling onto the floor among the dancers. Moira made a dash for the swinging doors.

"Stop that kid!" her partner shouted, jumping up and pushing men out of his way in his frenzy to give chase. *"He's a girl!"*

Sudden pandemonium broke out in the hall. Everyone was shouting and bumping into one another. "A girl?" "Where?" "Who?" "Get out of my way!" *"Catch her!"*

Moira was through the doors and had taken three sprinting steps toward the open street when she collided with someone entering the hall. The confrontation knocked the wind out of both of them and sent them flying down the steps and into the muddy street. Above her she heard rapid footsteps on the boardwalk. Men were shouting. Whoever she had hit grabbed her roughly by the hair, pulling her head back sharply. She found herself staring straight into the dark, glittering eyes of Random Hawthorne.

Moira gasped.

"Fancy bumping into you, Miss Cavendish," he said dryly before shoving her to one side. Getting swiftly to his feet, he laid a blow on the first miner who came close, sending him reeling backward into the others, who fell then like dominoes. The fight was on! Men swarmed into the street, shouting and falling over one another, sending blows in any and all directions.

"There she is!" someone shouted, and Moira scrambled for her life, going between legs and over fallen bodies. Someone grabbed her, and she found herself being rolled over and over in the mud, wrestling with her captor until she was able to wriggle free. Men fought all around and over her. Someone was sent sprawling and flattened her face first into the mud. Sputtering, she pushed herself up and wiped the mud from her eyes, trying to see her way clear of the mob.

A strong hand grabbed her and yanked her forward. She didn't have time to fight as she was dragged into an alley between two shacks. They ran in the darkness behind a building and passed another dim structure. She heard a door jerked open and found herself being pitched hastily inside a building that, with one good, deep breath, proved to be a stable.

"Now, just a—" She got no further. She was forced down, a big hand clamped hard over her mouth. Hay bales hid her and her captor from anyone who might look in. She struggled in panic and tried to shout through the hand.

"Shut up, Moira, or you'll have every member of that rabble in here taking turns on you," Random hissed against her ear. She froze, heart lashing her ribs, both from the run and from his closeness. He kept still, listening, holding his breath. They remained like that for several long moments. Then slowly he released her.

Moira sat up and started to sniffle.

"And just after I had a bath!" she moaned.

Random sat back against the bale of hay and started to laugh.

Chapter Fourteen

Moira lifted her arm and sniffed at the muddy sleeve with growing dismay. It wasn't just mud that was drying on her face, her clothes, and in her hair. A lot of horses and mules traveled up and down the main street of Rough and Ready, and most of them left their calling cards. She grimaced miserably and then glared at the grinning Random. She could see his teeth in the dark!

"I don't see what's so funny, Mr. Hawthorne!" she fumed.

"No, I don't imagine you do at the moment," he agreed with a chuckle. "But give yourself time, and you'll see the humor in it!"

"I doubt that," she said, sighing in disgust. She was irritated that they had met under these circumstances. She scratched at her hair and clothes. She was beginning to itch all over.

"There's a trough right over there in the corner if you'd like to get cleaned up," Random suggested mildly, leaning back against the bale and resting his forearms casually on his raised knees. He was enjoying this immensely, she thought angrily.

"Not with you around."

"I promise to close my eyes, Miss Cavendish," he said.

"I don't think I could trust you to do that," she retorted.

"And besides, I'd still have to put on the same horrid clothes again."

"I could go and get you a change," he suggested dryly. "I need one as well."

"Oh? And where could you do that?"

"You do have another set of clothes in your hotel room, haven't you?"

"Yes, but I've no intention of telling you where I'm staying."

"No need to do that, since I already know," he drawled.

"You do? How?" she challenged.

"Daniel told me."

"You've seen Daniel? Where is he?" she asked, remembering suddenly the good news she had to impart to him.

"At a faro table losing all his gold dust, the last time I saw him," he told her. "Not a very sensible young man, your brother."

"Well, it doesn't surprise me," she said with a sigh.

"He told me you were waiting patiently at your hotel room, behaving in a very circumspect way. I was on my way to pay my respects to you when I heard the commotion at the fandango hall." He grinned again. "I had a sneaking suspicion who might be at the bottom of it, and you certainly were, weren't you?"

"It wasn't my fault that man needed his ears boxed!" she said hotly, her face flaming as she remembered how uncouthly that miner had discovered her sex.

"Well, I'm amazed you've gotten away with your ruse for so long," he commented, eyes moving slowly over her, then rising to her startled eyes.

"I'm hardly a picture of feminine pulchritude at the moment," she said with a self-conscious laugh, trying very hard to ignore the rapid pounding of her heart. Random looked astonishingly good to her. His hair was slightly longer than on the voyage, curling well over his collar. The creases on either side of his mouth deepened in amusement.

"No, you're not at that," he agreed. "In fact, you smell like the south end of a northbound horse."

"I don't need the reminder, thank you. I'm closer to me than you are," she said ruefully.

He laughed. "Well, go take a dip in the trough over there while I go and collect some clothes for you." He stood up and then looked down at her. "I wouldn't leave here for a while if I were you. There are probably men still combing the area looking for you."

"Then it would hardly be wise for me to take everything off and climb into that trough, now, would it?"

"Maybe you should wait until I get back to protect you," he suggested, mouth curving upward suggestively. He left before she could find a proper retort to that. She went over to the door after he left and listened for a moment.

The music had started again at the fandango hall, and she could hear various other sounds of merriment and drunken revelry going on. No one seemed to be searching the area for her. She supposed that the other miners probably thought her crude partner had drunk too much whiskey and lost his mind. A girl in a mining camp? Absurd! At least that's what she hoped they thought.

When she put her hand in the trough, she found the water icy. She wouldn't have been eager to put herself into it even if it had been warm and sudsy. A horse nickered near by and poked its head through the rail. She put her hand to its velvety nose and stroked.

Random returned a few minutes later carrying some clothes and a blanket. He handed something to her. "I thought a little soap might be welcome."

"Yes, thank you." She looked at him pointedly. "You did say you would close your eyes," she reminded him.

"I'll wait outside the door," he told her, and she smiled in gratitude. He was a gentleman after all.

Moira stripped off her soiled things quickly and, steeling herself, climbed into the trough to rinse and scrub off the mud and dung. She dried herself off with the blanket, which felt very rough against her skin and put on the fresh clothes. He had even brought her another pair of lace panties, she noticed with great embarrassment. He hadn't brought a camisole, however, so she had to wear her shirt without anything under it.

She rinsed out her dirty clothes and wrung them out, wrapping them in the blanket before leaving the barn. Random was leaning against the wall, waiting for her. She was grateful that he was there.

"I've got to find Daniel now. I was on my way to look for him when I . . . got sidetracked."

Random laughed low, and Moira stiffened defensively.

"I have some news of Jack!" she told him angrily. "A miner in the hotel said he saw him up on the north fork of the Yuba."

"And you thought to celebrate at the fandango hall," he said dryly, grinning.

"I wasn't celebrating!"

"You were tipsy, Miss Cavendish. I could smell whiskey on you when you mowed me down on the front steps."

She sighed exasperatedly. "I only had a few, and not by choice."

"It would be wise if you waited for Daniel at the hotel room."

"But he might not be back for hours!"

"He'll be back sooner than you think. I already told you he was having a run of bad luck. He didn't have much gold dust left when I saw him."

"Then all the more reason why I should find him. We don't have very much as it is, and we worked hard for that!"

"You'll wait at the hotel," he told her firmly. "And I'll go looking for your wayward Danny boy." He was no longer smiling. She had the urge to argue his highhanded decision, but acknowledged there was sense in what he said. There had been altogether enough excitement for one night.

Random took her up the back steps into the hotel and waited until she was inside the room before leaving her. About thirty minutes later, he returned with Daniel in tow. Her brother looked sheepish and very ill at ease. He wouldn't look her in the eye.

"How much did you lose, Danny?" she asked grimly. Random leaned against the door, arms crossed over his chest, watching them.

"All of it."

She sighed. "That wasn't very smart."

"You'd better tell her the rest," Random said in a low growl.

"Tell me the rest of what?" she asked, looking from one to

the other. Daniel's face was very red, and he glanced uneasily
at Random, now unrelentingly silent.

"Tell me the rest of what?" Moira repeated, alarmed. Daniel
sighed heavily, sat down on the narrow bed, and ran agitated
fingers through his long, light brown hair.

"I took your gold dust."

"What? No, you didn't. I watched you divide it," she said
faintly, not wanting to believe him.

"After I lost my share, I came back here and took yours,"
he said, his shoulders slumping.

"Oh, Danny," she moaned. So much for sleeping in a bed
and eating a couple of square meals.

"And when I lost that, I put our claim up."

"Our claim? You can't be serious! Who would be interested?"

"I told them we panned all that gold in one day."

Moira stared at him aghast. "And this man believed you?"

"I guess so. He accepted it. It was only after I lost that he
wanted to know the details and see some paper. And when I
didn't have any and told him where it was, he got... a little
nasty."

Random gave a hard laugh. "You're damned lucky they
didn't string you up. Telling men there are good digs when
there aren't any is one of the biggest sins in this country, and
a good way to get yourself killed."

"Well, Random paid up for me. If he hadn't, you'd probably
be one brother short by now."

Moira just looked at him in exasperation.

"I thought I was going to win," Danny added, seeing her
look and feeling some defense was necessary. "And I think the
table was rigged."

"I could quite easily string you up myself," Mory said furiously. "You idiot! All the weeks we slaved for that damn
gold and you've thrown it all away in one night! How could
you be so stupid, Danny?"

"You don't have to go on about it, Mory!" he retorted hotly,
blue eyes flashing. "I feel bad enough as it is!" Random gave
him a hard look, and Daniel turned bright red. He put his head
down and sighed.

"And how are we supposed to get any supplies?" she demanded. "Tell me that, Danny. Or pay Mr. Hawthorne what we owe him?"

"We'll figure something out. Just have a little trust, will you?"

"Trust?" She gave a sniff. Then, remembering her news, she added, "And just when we had some word of Jack!" She felt perilously close to tears, tears of abject frustration and misery. All she could see ahead were more weeks of wet, cold feet and hands and an aching back.

"Jack? What about Jack?"

She told him. "But a lot of good it does us now to know! By the time we pan enough gold to get the supplies we need to reach Goodyears' Bar, Jack will be somewhere else. Daniel, I could gladly wring your neck!"

"Well, why don't we just leave for there in the morning? I don't see what the big problem is!" he said, his pricked conscience heightening his irritation.

"And what do we eat on the way? Pine nuts and miner's lettuce?" she demanded.

"That'd be an improvement over your burned beans and flapjacks!" he retaliated, bringing a blush to Moira's face and an amused laugh from Random, still standing by the door. He uncrossed his arms and stepped between them.

"I'll stake you," he told them.

Moira glanced up in surprise and then smiled gratefully. "That's kind of you, but a losing proposition on your side."

"I don't think so," he said, and there was a disturbing light in his eyes as he looked at her.

"I'm curious how much it cost you to save my brother's neck for him," she said.

"About a hundred dollars in gold."

She went pale and sank weakly down on her bed. She looked across at Daniel, who was fiery red.

"It was a loan!" Daniel said defensively.

"A loan! Loans are expected to be repaid, and how do you expect us to pay back a *hundred dollars in gold!*"

"Would you rather they had dragged me out and hanged me?" Daniel fumed.

"Let me think about it for a minute."

Daniel sucked in his breath and promptly exploded. "You've been nothing but a damn pain in my neck since I discovered you on the ship. You've ruined my plans, destroyed my intestines with your cooking, and made my life a misery keeping you out of trouble, and I don't want any criticism from you or—"

"Shut up, Daniel." Random spoke with cool, quiet authority. "It wasn't Moira who made a braying ass of herself at a faro table. You got yourself and her into trouble, not Moira."

"She's put me in plenty of trouble before," he said with feeling, and she remembered how frightened for her Danny had been in Bootjack.

"And will probably put us in more before she's done," Random agreed with a wry grin, provoking a sharp, questioning glance from Moira.

"Us? You're going along?"

"Of course. Where else did you think I'd be? I've got to keep track of my loan."

Moira wasn't at all sure whether that disclosure pleased or worried her. "I didn't think about it at all."

He laughed, a low, husky sound that sent her pulses hammering. "Well, you'd better think about it, Miss Cavendish."

"I think it's great!" Daniel said enthusiastically. "You can help me keep an eye on her."

"That's my general plan," Random said, looking her over. Moira blushed fiercely.

"Will you also keep my brother away from the faro tables?" she asked sweetly.

"After tonight, your brother can watch out for himself," he said, glancing pointedly at Daniel.

"I learned my lesson," Daniel said seriously. Glancing across, he looked at Moira sheepishly. "I'm sorry, Mory. It was stupid, I admit, but once I got started, I couldn't seem to stop."

"Like Papa," she said sadly. "I'm glad they didn't hang you."

"So am I," he said, putting his hand to his throat.

"You've both had quite a night in town, I'd say," Random commented, looking at the two of them.

"Yes, well, there's no need to talk about all that this evening, is there, Mr. Hawthorne?" she said quickly, not wanting Daniel to begin a lecture on her indiscretions. Hawthorne grinned at her knowingly.

"There's always a price for silence, Miss Cavendish," he taunted, arousing Daniel's full interest.

"What'd she do this time?"

Random merely smiled and declined to answer, raising his brows slightly in Moira's direction. Daniel looked at her narrowly, then rubbed the back of his neck.

"Never mind. Don't tell me. I don't think I want to know."

Random winked at her, then stood near the window, hands on hips. "I'll take care of getting what gear and supplies we need for the trip to Goodyears Bar. We'll leave before dawn tomorrow. I'll meet the two of you at the north end of town by the pine grove. Leave by the back stairs so no one will see you. After tonight, I don't think either one of you should be seen in this camp again."

They nodded. Moira looked up at him. "But how will you get everything we need tonight? It's late, and everyone is gone from the stores."

"You let me manage that. All you need to do is be where I told you, when I told you. And stay out of trouble in the meantime. Have you got that?"

Moira stiffened at his tone. "I'm hardly going anywhere at this time of night. Nor is Daniel."

"I'm glad to hear it," he drawled with a wry smile. "I suggest you both try to get some sleep. We're going to do a lot of hard traveling tomorrow." He looked at them both to make sure his message had gotten across. Neither said anything, relieved to have someone who knew what he was doing taking charge.

"I'll see you in the morning, then," Random said and strode to the door. As he opened it, Moira spoke.

"Thank you, Mr. Hawthorne," she said faintly.

He turned slightly and looked at her, eyes twinkling, mouth curved slightly upward. "Don't thank me yet, Miss Cavendish. You don't know yet what I want out of this particular partnership."

Moira was about to ask him what he meant when he walked out, closing the door firmly behind him. She looked at Daniel, who shrugged.

"I guess we'll find out soon enough, won't we?" was his only comment, and then he set about doing exactly as Hawthorne had suggested.

Moira, however, couldn't sleep a wink. She couldn't stop thinking about Random Hawthorne. He disturbed her, and that very awareness of him frightened her a good deal. She had never in her life felt ill at ease with a man, having been surrounded by brothers and their friends since early childhood. Yet Random made her feel addled every time he looked at her.

Why had he decided to stake them? It made no sense to her at all. He knew it had taken weeks for them to gather the meager amount of gold dust Daniel had so quickly disposed of at the faro tables. As for Moira herself, he had been acutely aware of her ability for misadventure from their first meeting on the *Stephen Rule*. Why should he wish to become partners with such walking catastrophes? Surely he could travel faster and accomplish more by himself!

She wanted to believe it had something to do with her and the words he had said on the ship. Yet he hadn't looked greatly pleased to run into her again outside the fandango hall. And when he might have taken an opportunity to kiss her outside the stable after she had bathed, he hadn't even touched her. He'd looked upon her with mocking amusement, if not brotherly annoyance.

He might be able to forget easily what had happened between them, but she wasn't so lucky. Every time she looked at him she remembered the way he had kissed her during the storm. She knew that he would have kissed Jewel or Monique Beaupé under the same circumstances, and probably would have enjoyed doing so much more. Since she was a lady, he had left it at a kiss. It was humiliating that it was she who had wanted that kiss to go on and on.

Moira was sure, though, that Random found her attractive under certain circumstances. Still, he obviously thought her a very young, troublesome, distressingly irresponsible girl who was bent on one misadventure after another.

It wasn't going to be at all easy traveling with Hawthorne under any circumstances.

Chapter Fifteen

Moira and Daniel arrived at the prearranged meeting place in the pine grove well before dawn, but Hawthorne wasn't there. They waited for well over an hour and began to wonder if it had all been some terrible misunderstanding when he appeared astride a healthy-looking buckskin mare, leading two saddle horses and two mules behind him. The mules were well loaded with gear and supplies.

"How did you ever do it, Mr. Hawthorne?" Moira gasped in awe.

"Who the hell cares how he did it?" Daniel cried, accepting the proffered reins of a sorrel and swinging up with delight. "If he stole the lot, I couldn't care less. But my feet will be in your debt for life, Random. By God, it feels good to be on a horse again!"

"You didn't, did you?" she asked Random.

"Didn't what, Miss Cavendish?" Random asked with a crooked grin.

"Steal them."

"I bought them. I even have a bill of sale, if you'd like to see it."

She wondered where he had gotten so much money. Had he had such good luck already? She couldn't help but think of the money these animals and supplies must have cost Random. She mounted with more care than Daniel, calculating just how much money she was riding. This horse had cost at least one hundred dollars in gold, and the mules must have cost even more. The gear the mules carried looked as if it had cost a tidy sum as well. All that, plus the hundred dollars in gold they already owed Random Hawthorne, put them firmly and deeply in his debt.

"What's bothering you, Miss Cavendish?" Random drawled, smiling at her as though he knew exactly what she was thinking.

"It occurred to me that we'd better find a gold mine if we're ever going to pay you back for all this," she admitted, her face pale.

"Don't worry about it now," he told her, turning his horse northward. "We'll work it all out so that everyone benefits in some way." The devil was dancing in his dark eyes.

They stopped only a few times during the day, taking brief respites only when absolutely necessary. To save time, they ate hardtack and beef jerky on the way, and made almost thirty miles by nightfall. They set up camp near a creek that wound down through thick pines, madrons, and alders. While Random and Daniel unpacked the mules and unsaddled the horses, Moria set about gathering firewood and toting water for the preparation of their evening meal.

Daniel had grown used to her less-than-perfect culinary abilities. However, Hawthorne glanced at her sharply as soon as the first bite crossed his lips. She felt the color surging up into her face. Daniel was downing his food as fast as possible, undoubtedly of the opinion that if you ate it quickly enough it didn't have the chance to touch the taste buds.

Random swallowed. Then he shook his head disbelievingly and started to laugh. "And I thought your brother was exaggerating!"

As Moira's face grew hotter, Daniel worsened things. "And she's improved, believe me," he said, grinning at Moira's poisonous glance. "You should have tasted her first pot of coffee!"

"Thanks just the same," Random said, looking at her.

Moira looked at the two of them resentfully. She was exhausted. Her rear end felt worn to the bone, and they sat there laughing at her cooking. Did they think she liked it? Did they think she enjoyed the chore?

"I shot a rabbit on the way to Sutter's Fort. A nice plump one! And she burned it until there was hardly any meat left!" Daniel went on, recounting the worst. Random set aside the tin plate with her ill-cooked meal on it and lounged back against the saddle.

"I wondered why the two of you were so thin. Now I know."

Daniel grinned, casting a quick glance in Moira's direction and getting a glare back. "Wait until you see her flapjacks," he warned as she struggled between hurt pride and murderous fury. "They look something like a discus and taste about as good!"

Hawthorne laughed and Moira rose abruptly, putting her hands on her hips and glaring at the two of them. "Since my cooking is so bad it shrivels your poor, sensitive tongues, you can fight it out between you which of you will do it from now on, because I quit!"

"You can't quit. You're the only woman in camp, and cooking is women's work."

"Not anymore it isn't!"

"Oh, Moira, if you'd just be a little more careful . . ."

"I'm not going to cook anymore!"

"We were only teasing," Daniel said, now trying to mollify her.

"We were?" Random asked in pretended surprise.

"You can both starve to death before I'll put another pan on a fire!" she fumed.

"I hope that's a solemn promise, Miss Cavendish."

"Now, wait a minute, Random. I can't cook," Daniel said.

"Then it looks as if I'm elected the new chef, doesn't it?"

Moira relaxed. "All right. I'll unsaddle the horses and see that they're watered, fed, and curried." When Daniel didn't say anything, she glared at him. "And what are you going to do, brother dear, besides sit around on your hindquarters and laugh at other people's efforts?"

"Set up camp, I suppose."

"And do the washing," she told him.

"Oh, no! I won't do the washing! That's for women!"

"What would you have done if I hadn't come along?" she

asked. "Waited until your clothes stood up by themselves and then bought new ones?"

"I suppose I'd have washed my things, but since you did come along, you can do it!"

She looked squarely at him. "Nope."

"Moira . . ."

"I suggest we all do our own washing," Random put in, enjoying their exchange.

"That's fair and simple," she agreed, and then glanced at Hawthorne. "Oh, and Mr. Hawthorne, I shall try very hard to be more charitable about your culinary talents than you've been about mine."

His mouth twitched. "Thank you, ma'am."

Moira gathered the tin plates and cups together with a clatter and headed for the stream to wash them. On her way back, she cooled off. She saw Random hauling their packs into the trees and securing them there with ropes.

"What are you doing?" she asked, stopping to watch him heft the last one up and tie it.

"Making sure the bears don't get to our food," he told her, finishing his chore and turning to look at her.

"Bears? Around here?" She looked around, suddenly wary. "I thought they were up in the mountains."

"We're in the mountains."

"And we can expect bears prowling around?"

"Does it worry you?"

"Well, shouldn't it?" she asked in surprise. "I mean, if you've put everything up there and they come into camp really hungry, won't they decide to feast on us instead?"

He laughed. "Maybe."

"I don't see what's so funny!" Hadn't he laughed at her enough for one evening? She turned away and started to walk off. Random caught hold of her arm.

"If you're that worried about it, you can always sleep by me," he suggested in a low voice. She felt his warm breath against the curve of her cheek and trembled.

"And that'll keep all the bears away, I suppose," she retorted with a faint, nervous laugh. She took a step away and glanced up at him. He released her and grinned.

"It might just take your mind off them."

She blushed. "It probably would at that," she agreed, thankful for the darkness. "But I'm not *that* worried."

"I see," he drawled, smiling. "Better the bears nibbling on your tender parts than me, Miss Cavendish?" Her face burned. He had aroused her senses and imagination, and looking up at him, she tried to think of some appropriate light retort, but failed. Her mouth felt dry suddenly. If she had thought he was even remotely serious about following through on his insinuations, she was soon disabused of that notion.

"I'll see you safely back to camp," he told her easily, and did exactly that and no more. When he stretched out beneath his blanket on the opposite side of the fire and promptly fell asleep, Moira felt a mingling of disappointment and irritation. She watched him for a long time, feeling a tightness in her chest and a growing warmth in her midsection and lower regions.

Devil man! she thought wildly. He was only teasing her, playing with her. Well, two could play that game, as she knew from experience.

Hawthorne proved to be an excellent cook. Moira was surprised and a little piqued at the discovery. She watched how he prepared things, taking mental notes so that if she should ever be required to cook again she would know something about it. It looked simple enough. All you had to do was keep the pan out of the fire and turn the flapjacks before the tiny bubbles solidified. But she would withhold final judgment until she tasted some meat or stew.

Goodyears Bar was only a few miles away from their camp. They arrived there early and found the camp almost deserted. It was Monday, and the men had returned to their claims on the rivers and in the mountains, some probably still suffering from their camp entertainment.

"You stay with the horses and mules," Random told Moira. She was ready to protest, but he looked at her in a way that brooked no argument. Daniel went off in one direction, Random in the other. Moira sat in ill-tempered silence waiting for them to return with some news of Jack.

It was almost an hour before Daniel returned. He had learned nothing. They waited for Random to return.

"He's gone upriver," he told them when he finally appeared,

and his news lightened Moira's spirits considerably.

"Then we're on the right track?"

"Looks like it."

"How long ago did he leave?" Daniel asked, swinging up into the saddle again.

"A couple of weeks ago," Random told them.

"But that's wonderful news! We're catching up, and he's all right!"

Random looked at Moira's happy expression and seemed about to say something, then didn't. He glanced at Daniel as he mounted his buckskin. "We'll head upriver and do some prospecting. We can stake a claim if we find something that isn't already taken."

"What about Jack?" Moira demanded in surprise.

"He'll have to come back this way in order to get supplies," Random told her. It sounded reasonable, but she wanted to keep looking. She didn't feel she could argue, however, since it was Random's money that had gotten them this far. And he seemed to know what he was doing.

They rode most of the day and then camped a little north of Union Flat. It was rough country, and when the sun went down it got very cold. Moira ached all over, but she fed and watered the horses and then curried them. Daniel had set up camp, and Random was preparing the evening meal. Whatever it was, it smelled delicious.

Finishing her duties, she made sure the animals were secured for the night, then walked back toward the fire, where the two men sat drinking coffee. Daniel looked up as she hunkered down, putting her hands out to the warmth.

"You look tired, Mory."

She shrugged. "No more than anyone else, I'm sure."

Random scooped some dinner onto a tin plate and put a slice of sourdough bread on it. He handed it to her without saying anything, and she accepted it with a smile of gratitude. She glanced up at him as she ate. He was very quiet and thoughtful, and she wondered what was bothering him. She was afraid it had something to do with what he had learned about Jack today. She ate her dinner in silence, studying him. He seemed completely unaware of her. She poured some coffee. Daniel got up and left the fire to check the horses and mules and raise the packs into the trees. Moira gathered the tin plates together.

Random still hadn't said anything. She went down to the river and washed the plates and cups and hooked them on a branch to dry. Daniel was asleep when she got back to the fire.

"There was something else today, wasn't there, Mr. Hawthorne?" she said. He glanced up at her sharply. "What else did you learn about Jack?"

"What makes you think I learned anything more than what I told you?" he countered, pouring himself another cup of coffee and meeting her eyes steadily.

"I'm not exactly sure. Just a feeling I have. Don't you think we've a right to know everything? He's our brother, you know."

Random rested his forearms on his knees, looking across the fire at her. "No complaints about the cooking?"

"You obviously know what you're doing, and it was delicious. But can we get back to the subject at hand? What else did you learn about Jack in Goodyears Bar?"

"I'll tell you everything you need to know."

"Then you are keeping something back! What?"

He looked at her without answering, and she let out her breath angrily. "I want to know," she told him, keeping her voice down so she wouldn't waken Daniel.

"Why don't you just go to sleep? You look dead tired. If you're not careful, you're going to get sick."

"You're the one that's been driving us so hard!" she retorted. "And if you think you can get me off the subject so easily, think again!"

"Trying to get you to do anything is like fighting nature," he said.

"Then I'll make a few guesses," she said slowly. "Does it have something to do with the men that were following Jack? Barilovich and Heaton, I think their names were. And one other named Jass Whitsell. We learned about them from the blacksmith at Sutter's Fort."

Random looked at her for a long moment before answering. "Well, they're still following him. Barilovich and Heaton, at least."

"Did you find out what they wanted from him?" she asked worriedly.

He gave a slight shrug, cradling the tin cup in his hands.

"Random, please."

He raised his cup to his lips, looking at her over the rim. "You know that's the first time you've used my Christian name?" He smiled slightly, eyes teasing.

"Tell me!" she said, not to be put off. He sighed.

"You're a persistent puss, aren't you?"

"I'm not as much a fool as you seem to think," she said resentfully.

"Whoever said I thought you were a fool?"

She had no intention of getting off the subject again. "I saw you and Daniel talking earlier this evening. Whatever you found out today, you discussed with him. And I've a right to know as well."

"Then why don't you ask Danny?" he suggested blandly.

"Because he's taking his orders from you."

"Then maybe you should learn to trust me as well," he told her.

"This has nothing to do with trust!" she said in growing frustration. "You're just making me more and more certain that something is seriously wrong!"

"Moira, just calm down," he told her, and she could see he thought her nothing more than a hysterical child. She breathed in slowly and stood up.

"All right. You and Daniel can keep your little secrets. But I'm going back to Goodyears Bar tomorrow and find out for myself whatever it was you learned today."

"Oh, no, you won't," he told her in a low, taut voice. He looked irritated and in no mood for further discussion.

Moira looked squarely at him and saw the warning glitter in his dark eyes. She had never backed down from an argument with either of her brothers, and the fact that this man was not a relation made no difference. In fact, it simply fueled her determination.

"Don't make any bets on it." She turned and walked off into the darkness. She heard a tin cup tossed down angrily and glanced back to see Random standing up and striding toward her. Every inch of his six-foot-two frame looked taut with anger.

"Where in hell do you think you're going?" he demanded,

catching up with her and jerking her to a stop. She pulled away, furious.

"To check the animals," she told him tightly. "They're my responsibility, remember?"

"Danny checked them already. They're fine. Now go back to the fire and get some sleep," he ordered imperiously. She glared up at him and took a deep breath, curbing her rising temper. She would have her opportunity later.

"All right, Mr. Hawthorne," she said coldly and started back toward the campfire. He stepped in front of her. She looked up at him and could see clearly that he knew what she was thinking. Silence and no further argument did not mean acquiescence. It simply meant a change of tactics.

"You aren't going anywhere out of my sight, Moira. Do you understand me?"

"Perfectly. Tell me what you learned today and there won't be any need for me to go back to the Goodyears Bar. But if you won't, you'll have to hog-tie me to keep me from going." She meant it.

"Don't think I won't."

They looked at one another, taking each other's measure. Random let out his breath. "You stubborn little bitch," he said hoarsely and pulled her into his arms. Her head was thrown back by the suddenness of his embrace. She didn't even have a chance to take a breath before his mouth covered hers in a punishing kiss that sent her head spinning. His hands moved, one sliding around her waist to draw her forward and more tightly against him, the other twisting into her hair to tilt her head up. His mouth descended on hers. She trembled against him as his tongue ran along the edge of her teeth, attempting to open her mouth to him. She pushed her arms up between them and shoved as hard as she could. His mouth broke away from hers and she gasped, feeling faint from the consuming kiss.

"It's not going to work, Random," she murmured.

"What?" he demanded hoarsely, leaning down and kissing the gentle curve of her neck. She shook, her heart thundering, and again pushed him away.

"Let go! Damn it! Let go of me!" she cried, knowing exactly what he was doing and wishing she didn't. Tears filled her eyes as she glared up at him resentfully. "Do you think I'm an idiot? You think that just by kissing me you can make me forget all about everything? About Jack? Well, it won't work!" Her voice cracked and she whirled away from him. He yanked her back.

"Is that what I was doing?" he asked dryly and then laughed harshly. "Well, it's as good an excuse as any."

His fingers curved around the back of her neck, jerking her forward, and he kissed her again, ruthlessly parting her lips and possessing her mouth. She moaned, fighting him for a moment, then finally melted against him, her hands sliding around him and feeling the rippling muscles of his back. Her body arched instinctively closer to his, drawing a deep groan from Random. He kissed her until she was pliant and consumed with sensation and desire for him.

He drew back slightly shaking his breathing shallow. "I think I could make you forget everything but me for a while," he said, tilting her face up and lightly brushing her swollen lips with his thumb. She was having difficulty thinking at all and looked up at him in a daze. Why had he stopped?

He shook her slightly. "Listen to me, Moira," he said, sliding his hands down over her shoulders holding her away from him. His eyes moved to her parted lips and down to her heaving breasts and then looked back at her face. A muscle in his jaw tightened. "Your brother is in a lot of trouble."

"I've ... I've suspected as much." Was that hoarse voice really her own? She swallowed and cleared her throat. "But why won't you tell me what's going on?"

"I suppose I'll have to tell you or you'll run off and probably land yourself in a mess of trouble," he said wryly.

"It's about those two men, isn't it?" She looked at him closely. Random released her and rubbed the back of his neck wearily, looking down and meeting her eyes again.

"Barilovich and Heaton are claiming that your brother ambushed and murdered their partner down on the Tahualamne."

Moira stared at him, stunned. "Jack wouldn't kill anyone! I know he wouldn't!"

Random said nothing, and she became more vehement. "He wouldn't!"

"Moira, whatever the truth is, those two men want to catch

up with your brother in a very bad way. And they don't have friendly intentions."

"Then we've got to find him first and warn him!"

"Jack already knows they're after him."

"How can you be sure?"

"Because he's doing a lot of traveling. The man who runs the general store said he was pretty jumpy as well."

"How could he remember something like that?"

"Because Jack drew a gun on a man who had done nothing more than walk up behind him a little too quietly."

"You're telling me my brother shot someone in Goodyears Bar?" she gasped.

"He didn't fire on the man, just pulled his gun. He tried to laugh it off, but the merchant said he could see sweat breaking out all over his face."

She had known something was wrong. She had sensed it. There were plenty of reasonable explanations for why they had received no letters for so long. He might have been in the mountains for months at a time; the letters could have been lost— so many things. But she had sensed something was wrong. She hugged herself against the growing chill of knowing that somewhere out there her brother was being hunted down by two men who wanted to kill him. "So what do we do?" she asked quietly, looking up at Random. She could feel the tears forming under her eyelids.

"There isn't a lot we can do. We're going to head up a little further and then stop."

"We're not going to keep going until we find him?"

"We can't. In a few more weeks it's going to be snowing up here. There have been a couple of mild storms already. We've got to build a cabin and lay in supplies for the winter, unless you and Daniel prefer to go back to the coast until spring."

"No!"

"Then there's not much choice."

"But what about Jack?" she asked, frightened. "We can't just forget about him while we're scrounging and looking for gold!"

"We wouldn't do him much good by freezing to death with the first snows."

"But I can't just sit by knowing two men want to kill him!" she said brokenly.

Random reached out and took her shoulders again. "Listen to me," he told her harshly, the lines deepening around his mouth and eyes. "Your brother is on the run, and he's not going to leave messages all over the countryside for us to track him down. For God's sake, think, Moira. He doesn't even know you and Danny are in California! And if he did, would he come for you, knowing he's got a couple of men hunting him for blood?"

She took a ragged breath and in growing despair stared off into the darkness. "It's just that I've come so far to find him, and we're so close . . . so close."

"Too close could get you killed, and I'm not going to let that happen," he told her, letting her go. She looked up at him and smiled weakly.

"You're right about Jack. He wouldn't come anywhere near us as long as there was a chance he would get us caught in any crossfire. He always fought his own battles, even as a boy." She looked out into the darkness again, feeling a constriction of pain and fear in her throat. "Only this time . . . this time, there might be too much for him to fight alone."

Chapter Sixteen

Nothing in Moira's previous experience had prepared her for the powerful, almost terrifying majesty of the Sierra Nevada. Nothing was by halves in this great country where even the trees grew into giants so tall she had to throw her head back to see their tops, which touched heaven itself. The pine cones from the smaller trees were as long as her forearm, while, illogically, those from the giants were the size of the end of her little finger.

The plunging ravines and gorges dropped away, taking her breath and heart with them. Even the Yuba itself seemed to increase the tempo of her existence as it wound down like a writhing, primeval beast from its snowbound source high in the towering mountains above them. The river, ever fed by smaller streams, rolled and churned downward, roaring in raging passion over jutting granite beds, bone-chillingly cold, merciless, and beautiful in its violent fury.

Men of lesser courage, or perhaps better sense, were already heading down out of the mountains, leaving their claims and seeking a safer haven for the coming winter months. Once the snows came, anyone remaining would be trapped, with no chance of returning to the lowlands and the coast.

The river narrowed as they neared its source. Random

stopped them just above the junction of Frazier Creek and the
Yuba, saying they would build a cabin there and bring supplies
up from Sierra City, through which they had passed a few days
before. If Jack was along the river, or up one of the many
small streams that fed it, he would have to pass this way to
return to one of the camps for supplies. Moira wanted to go
further, search more, but Random vetoed her, saying that there
was no time left. They would have to take the chance of in-
tercepting him. Above them loomed Haskell Peak, eight thousand feet above sea level and already snow-capped, warning
of an early and severe winter. They had to ensure their survival
before they could worry any more about Jack's whereabouts
or the two men hunting him.

Random chose a small clearing among the pines overlooking
the Yuba. From the top of the rise small lakes to the northwest
could be seen. It was a pretty spot, peaceful and well-situated.
They'd be able to see those men who decided to go back
downriver to a safer clime.

They set to work chopping down trees to build the log cabin.
Daniel was a novice with an ax, and his hands were blistered
within an hour. Moira's fared no better as she used a hatchet
to chop away the branches from the fallen trees. She wrapped
Daniel's hands carefully, but as she watched him later, each
swing of the ax brought a grimace of pain to his young face.
But no Cavendish was a quitter.

She was bone-tired by midday and sat down on a fallen tree
to rest. She found herself mesmerized by Random as he
worked his shirt off, the muscles of his bronzed, sweat-covered
back rippling with each swing of the ax. He had removed his
neck scarf and tied it, Indian style, around his forehead to keep
the perspiration out of his eyes. The muscles in his arms bulged,
and Moira found her body responding against her will to the
mere sight of him working out in the open in this wild country.

Feeling her gaze, he stopped, leaning on the ax for a moment
as he met her eyes across the clearing. She stood and returned
to her work, her mind in torment. She felt him watch her for
several moments before he returned to his work.

How much worse was she going to feel when they were
living in the cabin? How much worse when the snows came
and she couldn't escape his company at all?

Of course, Daniel was with her. So why was she worrying so much? Hawthorne was not the sort of man to...to what? Take advantage of what she herself was feeling about him? She was more than half in love with him already. Why hadn't she thought of this before, and not insisted they all remain up here so that they could find Jack?

"Coming down!" Daniel shouted, standing back to watch a big pine make its slow descent. It crashed through other, smaller trees before it hit the ground and set off a red dust cloud. Random downed two more before Daniel was half finished with another, then called it quits for the day. The sun was going down; shadows filled the clearing. He took his shirt down from a branch and shrugged into it, not bothering to button it as he strode toward Moira at the campfire.

Once the men had begun work, Moira had agreed to take over the cooking again. She had watched Random carefully during his preparations and found that she could emulate him well enough to turn out a tasty meal. She had even become adept at making sourdough, being sure to keep enough stored to start another loaf the next day. She was squatting on her heels, stirring beans in a pan, when Random came up.

"Smells good," he said and gave her a teasing smile. She was all too aware of the broad expanse of naked chest covered by dark hair. She swallowed and looked down again, blushing at her wayward thoughts.

"I'm learning." She felt tense when he watched her so closely. His eyes narrowed slightly.

"Something bothering you, Moira?" he asked, hunkering down and picking up a cloth to protect his hand from the scalding coffeepot as he poured himself a cup. Her breasts began to tingle. She felt shaky.

"No. Should there be?" Why couldn't she make herself sound casual?

"You've been quiet all day," he said, lounging back against their packs.

"Where's Daniel?" she asked changing the subject abruptly. She looked desperately for her brother.

Random shrugged. "Down getting cleaned up at the river, I suppose."

She stirred the beans some more, avoiding Random's dark,

thoughtful gaze. "How big will the cabin be when it's finished?"

He didn't answer for a moment, and she looked up at him. He was smiling slightly, eyes twinkling.

"Fourteen by twelve," he told her and drank some of the coffee. He held the cup up slightly. "Darn good."

"That's all?"

"What do you want me to say? It's the best I've ever tasted?" he teased.

"No! I mean the cabin," she said angrily.

"We don't need any more room than that. It should be quite . . . cozy." He was smiling again. It would be smaller than she'd thought.

"Cozy," she repeated under her breath. Without looking at him, she was aware of the long, strongly muscled legs stretched out toward the fire. "What . . . what are we going to do when the snows come?"

"Stay inside where it's nice and warm."

"And . . . what else?" There, she had said it. Her face flamed, and she didn't dare look up at him, knowing he would see her embarrassment in the firelight.

"Whatever you want to do, we'll do, Moira." Something in his tone made her eyes jump up to his, and the smile on his face made them drop back down again quickly. *Damn him*, he was laughing at her again.

"You know what I mean."

"We could play cards, read, whittle wood, pan on good days, hunt, laze around in bed—whatever keeps us sane. Or did you have something special in mind?"

"Like what?" she snapped.

"You tell me," he drawled smoothly.

She didn't dare look up at him this time. What he meant was clearly in his voice, and her body, traitor that it was, was already responding to it. She took a deep breath.

"I've been thinking . . ." she began.

He chuckled. "So I see." He raised one leg and rested his forearm on it, watching her closely. She breathed in slowly.

"I'm not sure staying up here is such a good idea after all."

"Why not?"

"Well . . . because . . . we won't really be able to look for Jack," she said lamely.

"That's not your reason and you know it."

"And you do, do you?" She glared at him. He just smiled, and she looked away. "Maybe . . . maybe we should go back to the lowlands and see about work, and then come back in the spring," she suggested, trying to sound reasonable.

"No." He wasn't smiling now.

She looked at him. "Why not?"

His face was implacable. "Because I said no."

"That's a reason?"

"Enough for you."

"Says who?" she retorted, angry again. He smiled, but his eyes were hard.

"We're staying right here, Moira, just as we planned. It's a little late for you to retreat now."

"It isn't too late until the snows hit us!"

"What are you really afraid of, Moira? That I'm going to build two beds and take you into one while your brother watches us from the other?"

She gasped. "Of course not!"

He laughed low, but without amusement. "Liar." They looked at each other across the fire, and she saw his eyes darken and the muscles of his face tighten. Her breathing quickened.

"I . . . I just don't think staying up here is a . . . good idea," she repeated in a low, husky voice.

"You're afraid of me," he stated flatly. She frowned slightly, lips parted. She wasn't as afraid of him as she was of the emotions he stirred in her. He wasn't looking for a wife, that was certain. And during her months of observation aboard the *Stephen Rule*, she had seen and heard things that made her acknowledge that men had certain basic needs that required satisfaction from time to time. Hawthorne was very definitely male, all male. And since she was the only female within miles, it was logical for her to assume that he was going to inevitably look upon her as a means of relieving his needs. Especially when they were cooped up together in a fourteen-by-twelve cabin for months on end!

Random seemed to take her silence as confirmation. He stood up abruptly and looked down at her with dark impatience and contempt. He tossed his empty cup beside the fire and strode out into the gathering darkness. She watched him go, feeling an aching regret in the pit of her stomach.

She'd speak with Danny. Maybe she could convince him that she'd changed her mind and that waiting in the lowlands would be better than staying up here.

Daniel came running back up to the campfire a few minutes later, just after she had worked out what she would say to him. His hair was wet and he was shivering, but his eyes were filled with glittering excitement.

"Look at this!" He thrust his bandaged hand toward her. She glanced up at him, startled, and then looked at what he held. Four gold nuggets the size of peas lay in his open palm. She caught his excitement.

"Where'd you find them?"

He laughed. "I just picked them up while I was washing. Can you believe it? God, right there under my nose, as easy as you please." He laughed again, triumphantly. "I think we've really found something big up here!"

"I was just going to ask you about going back downriver."

"Going back? Are you out of your mind?"

"Winter is coming. Maybe staying up here isn't such a good idea."

"Hell! Can't you make up your blasted mind?" he said impatiently. "A week ago you were fighting tooth and nail to stay up here looking for Jack when I suggested we go back."

"Well, I've finally seen the sense of all your arguments."

"Forget going back. I've found gold, Mory. *Gold!*"

"And what if you don't live through the winter to enjoy it?"

"We'll live. Random knows what he's doing. He grew up in Maine, and it gets damned cold up there. That cabin is going to be tight as a drum. We can work our claim on good days and by spring have a fortune, while the rest of the argonauts are down in the lowlands losing their gold to faro dealers or hotel keepers."

Random was coming back up the hill. When he came close enough to the fire that she could see him, she realized that he had gone to the river to bathe. The chilly water had apparently not restored his good humor at all. Daniel saw him and went hurriedly to share his find. They returned to the fire together. Random didn't look at her.

"We'll build the cabin first, then we can do our mining," he told Daniel firmly. Moira scooped out helpings of beans in silence, not looking at either man. Daniel was too excited to notice the undercurrents going on, or, if he had noticed, to care. After she had finished her dinner, she took a towel and a bar of soap and headed for the river. It was almost completely dark now, and she had little time. The dust up in these mountains stuck to one and became part of one's clothing and skin, and she felt grimy after working all day.

She felt better after having washed thoroughly and quickly in a small, ice-cold pool behind a big boulder. She came out shuddering and dried hastily, then donned fresh clothes.

Coming back up the hill toward camp, she listened to the wind in the big trees and the roar of the river behind her. The flickering light of the campfire beckoned, and she saw Hawthorne sitting back against the packs, looking down toward the river. Daniel was sleeping already. She stopped and let the darkness protect her as she watched Random.

What did she know about him? He had been a capable, well-respected first mate, a man of quick, good judgment. She knew also that she was not the only woman who found him attractive.

She was cold, but didn't want to go back to the fire yet. She didn't feel able to face Random at that moment with what she was feeling. She turned toward the horses in the rope corral Random had made around some trees. Her mount whinnied as she approached, and she held out her hand, allowing him to nuzzle her with his velvety nose. She climbed over the ropes and took up the currycomb, which hung on the tree. She stroked the smooth, warm neck, the back and haunches, gaining warmth from the closeness of the animal. She continued for quite a while and then rehung the brush.

Climbing back over the ropes, she heard a noise and started. "Everything all right?" Hawthorne asked, leaning his tall frame against a redwood and watching her.

"Fine," she said shakily. "You frightened me."

"It wouldn't be the first time."

"I'm not afraid of you," she denied quietly.

He let it go. "You were gone a long time."

"Just thinking."

"I think you've been thinking too much lately," he said flatly. "You can trust me, Moira."

She gave a faint, self-conscious laugh. "But can I trust myself?"

She heard him draw in his breath sharply, then give a low, throaty laugh. "You shouldn't say something like that to me, of all people."

"You just said I could trust you," she said lightly, the darkness giving her courage.

"I did, didn't I? My first big mistake."

"Are we making the right decision, Random?"

"We'll know in the spring, won't we?" he said, apparently unconcerned. "As soon as the cabin's up, I'll go back downriver and bring up enough supplies to get us through the worst of the winter. Then we can sit tight and watch. Your brother is up here someplace, and sooner or later he'll have to come back down."

"And the others?"

"They may have gone back already."

She sighed. "I wish we knew for sure."

"You'd better get back to the fire. It's getting damned cold out here."

They started walking back together, and she glanced up at him. "What are we going to do about the horses this winter?"

"You worry about everything, don't you?" he drawled. "Just leave it to me."

"I don't seem to have much to say about anything anymore," she said ruefully. He glanced down at her and smiled.

"Not a lot," he agreed without remorse.

They had enough trees felled by the next afternoon, and Random set Moira to organizing their gear and supplies while Daniel gathered stones for the fireplace. Random split sections of log for shingles and notched them so they would fit firmly together for the walls of the cabin. The spaces between would be filled with adobe and sod. By nightfall Moira was too exhausted to think of anything, or to care that Random was looking at her with faint amusement. She served up dinner and promptly fell asleep without eating her own.

By the end of the week, the cabin had been raised, complete

with stone fireplace, plank floor, shutters for glassless windows, and built-in beds. It wasn't much by Charleston standards, but it was everything to them who had built it. It meant life when the dead of winter came.

Moira stood inside, admiring their handiwork. She had packed the walls with adobe and sod while Random had put up the shingles. Daniel had brought their gear and supplies in from the outside shelter. Last, Random had constructed shelves to hold their supplies.

"Well, what do you think of your new home, Moira?" Random asked, glancing at her over his shoulder as he secured the last shelf.

"I'm proud of it," she admitted without embarrassment. The glow in her eyes made him grin. Her hands were blistered beyond recognition. She had used muscles she hadn't known existed. But she was proud.

"Be it ever so humble," he said.

"Better than my sea cabin, and a great improvement over hard ground and a blanket," she told him. "Do you think they have windowpanes in Sierra City?"

"I'll find out when I go down tomorrow."

"You won't change your mind and take me with you?"

He finished the shelf before answering, then turned and put his hands on his hips, looking her over. "No. I've enough to worry about leaving you up here with Daniel without wondering what in hell you'd be up to in Sierra City while I got supplies."

"Trusting soul, aren't you?"

He smiled. "Experience makes a man wise."

"If I promised to behave?"

"Maybe . . . in the spring."

"In the spring?" She stared at him. "Just what do you think you're doing. Keeping me up here indefinitely?"

He grinned wickedly. "That might not be such a bad idea. It'd be one way of keeping you safely out of trouble."

She didn't say anything for a long moment, wondering just how serious he was. "How long will you be gone, Random?"

"About a week."

Her shoulders sagged slightly, and she looked away so that he wouldn't see how depressed the news made her.

"You're going to miss me?" he needled.

"We'll manage."

He laughed and went out.

Daniel came in from the mountains with a deer late that afternoon. Random strung it up in a tree and butchered it. They skewered the torso and turned it over a great fire in front of the cabin. When it was roasted they sat cross-legged in front of the fireplace inside and ate until they were too full to move. No one seemed to have anything to say. After a walk, Moira got into her bunk bed and wished them good night. Tired as she was, it was a long time before sleep came. Random was less than six feet away from her in a bed against the other wall. He lay on his back, one arm flung above his head, sleeping deeply. The hard lines were smoothed out and he looked very young and incredibly handsome. She wondered how old he really was. She sometimes thought he was close to Jack's age; at other times he seemed older. There was a maturity about him that her older brother had never had.

She wondered where Jack was and how he was faring with those men after him, then realized that those thoughts would keep her awake all night if she allowed them. She turned her mind to happier images.

Tomorrow she and Daniel would begin working their gold claim. And by spring, perhaps, they would have found Jack and have enough money to return to Charleston.

Random left at sunup, taking the pack mules with him. Moira watched from the cabin door, feeling an ache in her stomach. He didn't look back as he entered the copse of trees below them.

Daniel barely took time for coffee and leftover sourdough bread before heading for the river to begin working the claim. Moira straightened up the cabin and followed him soon afterward.

They worked continuously until afternoon, Daniel so excited he refused to stop for lunch. Moira went up to the cabin and put together a meal of leftover venison and sourdough bread and beans. When she took it down to Daniel, standing knee-deep in the icy water, panning in a frenzy, he told her he wasn't hungry.

For the next five days, Daniel panned in the river every

daylight hour. At night, when it was too dark to work anymore, he would drag himself up the hill and collapse onto his bunk, too tired to eat. Moira grew alarmed. Couldn't he see what he was doing to himself? He had lost weight and looked pale with exhaustion. His stomach had begun bothering him, and diarrhea had started the day before, keeping him drained of energy. Still, he wouldn't quit working, though he agreed to eat something whenever she brought it down to him.

"We've got to work as much as possible until the snows start!" he told her, angry that she was persisting in nagging him about how he was overworking himself. "In a few weeks we won't be able to work at all because of the weather. I want to get as much of a poke as I can now!"

"It'll be there in the spring, Daniel."

"Spring, hell!" he snapped and yanked up the pouch he kept safely under his bunk. "Just look at what's in here! Do you realize I've panned more in six days than we did the whole first three months we were in California! And you're telling me to stop!"

"What good is it all if you lose your health?"

"I'm not going to lose my health!"

He simply refused to listen, yet another victim of gold fever. Moira worked beside him most of the day, and when it became too much for her, she sat on the bank and watched.

Men still came down from the streams above them, though they were now few and far between. It snowed one day and burned off the next. Two groups stopped to camp in the clearing below them. Daniel watched them with an eagle eye to make sure they didn't go near his diggings. They left early the following morning. When questioned about his luck, Daniel invariably told them that it was middling, enough to keep them going and that was all. He was wary of strangers in the extreme. The miners believed him and traveled on, telling him it would be wise to head downriver as well. Daniel always said that there was nothing downstream for them and they'd just wait out the winter up here, having already laid in supplies and built the cabin.

A week came and went with no sign of Random. Moira began to worry. Had something happened to him? Were they going to end up staying here in the wilds all by themselves without Random's knowledge and experience to keep them alive? Daniel wouldn't even listen to her when she suggested they start downriver to look for Random before it was too late.

"He can take care of himself!"

Daniel's entire personality seemed to have changed with his gold strike. The more gold he found and put into his pouch, the more fevered he became to find more. Moira began to hate the very sight of the yellow metal.

A fortnight after Random left, two men came to the cabin. Moira was coming up from the river when she saw them coming out of the cabin. She glanced back at Daniel, still knee-deep in water, then decided they weren't anything she couldn't handle.

Remembering to stride like a man, she came up the hill, watching them. She saw that the smaller man had seen her first and was warning the other. The big man turned as she approached, and the first thing she noted as she stopped ten feet away were the cold gray eyes that evaluated her. He had shaggy, shoulder-length brown hair and a full beard and carried a heavy pack on his back. From first glance it obviously didn't contain mining equipment. He had a long rifle and wore a pistol holstered on his right hip, a buck-horn hunting knife on his left. Well-armed, she thought.

The smaller man was swarthy, with dark eyes that avoided hers. He was nervous. He kept wetting his lips through his bushy black beard and shifting from foot to foot. For the first time Moira regretted her rash impulse to handle the situation on her own. There was something menacing about these two men.

"What were you looking for in our cabin?" she demanded.

"How long you been up here?" the big man said.

"Now, look," she began, and then decided better of it when the gray eyes turned almost silver. "Almost a month. Why do you want to know?"

"We're looking for someone. You see anyone pass by here in the last few weeks?"

Moira's heart began a painful thudding. She knew who these men were. The accent! The big man was Barilovich, and the other was Heaton. She could feel the color draining from her face and the muscles of her body tensing.

Barilovich was watching her carefully, eyes narrowed. His nostrils flared as though he could smell her growing fear. "I asked you a question, boy," he said and moved slowly toward her.

She tried to calm herself and look normal. "There've been a lot of men passing by here. Fewer the last ten days or so."

Barilovich stopped a couple of feet from her. "Any with light hair and blue eyes?"

She hesitated and made a decision. Perhaps she could help Jack even without finding him. "A couple."

She saw that Barilovich had a tic near his right eye. Heaton was looking at him, eyes bright.

"Why you looking for him?" Moira dared, taking a male stance that Daniel usually held when talking to someone.

"He killed a man. Shot him down in cold blood when his back was turned. Down on the Tahualamne about a year ago."

Moira's heart thudded harder. She felt a flare of violent anger at the man's accusation, knowing full well that Jack was incapable of such a vile crime. Though Barilovich looked more than capable of it himself.

"That so," she said tightly.

Barilovich was looking at her with hard, cold eyes. "He's about six foot. Plays poker. Speaks educated." The last words were said with a slight twist of the man's thick lips.

"Does he wear an onyx-and-gold ring?" Moira asked after a deliberate, thoughtful pause. The silver eyes glittered ferally. He uttered a guttural affirmative.

"My brother was working on the river when he came by," Moira improvised, hoping to throw them off the scent. "He looked pretty tired. Asked for some supplies. I gave him a few cans of beans, and he headed out again."

"Which way?"

"Downriver. Said something about heading for Sacramento during the cold season. I asked him if there was any gold upriver from here. Said he hadn't had any luck."

Something she had said didn't sit well with Barilovich. The eyes narrowed again, boring into her until she felt color start to rise to her face. He noticed.

"Don't you believe me?" she snarled, pretending for all her

life that his hesitation was an insult to her integrity. Men took such easy offense when their honor was at stake. He looked at her furious expression for a moment and relaxed slightly.

"How long ago?" he questioned impatiently.

She raked fingers through her hair as Daniel often did and rubbed the back of her neck as though in concentration.

"Five, maybe six days. Can't be sure about it."

"Be sure." There was an implied threat she couldn't miss, and she swallowed hard.

"Six."

Barilovich's eyes widened, and there was an almost wild look about him. Heaton had turned sharply to stare at him again.

"But how in hell could he—"

"Shut up!"

Heaton obeyed immediately. Barilovich was staring at her. She could feel sweat breaking out on her forehead and beneath her arms. He didn't believe her. Or if he did, there was something she had said that was bothering him.

"You're sure it was six days?"

She couldn't back down now or they would know she was lying. They'd want to know how she came by information about the onyx ring. "I'm sure," she said with a firm nod.

"What would he be heading back to Sacramento for?" Heaton muttered.

"Maybe to throw us off again," Barilovich answered without looking at him. Moira wished he would look somewhere else besides right into her eyes as though trying to penetrate her very brain. She moved restlessly and then gave him a hostile look.

"You never did say what it was you were looking for in our cabin," she said stiffly, attempting with bravado to cover her increasing fear. She'd even gone so far as to put her hand on the handle of her pistol.

Barilovich grinned, showing big square teeth that were not in the best of condition. "This," he said and pulled one of Daniel's gold pouches from his pocket. Holding it out, he wagged it in front of her in challenge. The night before Daniel had brought it up and instructed her to hide it, but she had forgotten all about it and left it sitting on Random's bunk.

There hadn't been any reason to worry about someone stealing it. Luckily Daniel had hidden the rest of the gold beneath the floorboards.

"You lousy thief!" she cried, taking an angry step toward him. Then she reconsidered the incautiousness of her action. She saw Barilovich move, and her heart stopped.

The blow luckily glanced off the side of her head as she jerked instinctively back. Yet it sent her reeling, and she hit the ground with a hard thud, pine needles and dirt scraping her face. She felt herself being dragged back up. Barilovich yanked her forward so that her face was close to his, so close that she could smell his rank breath as he spoke between clenched teeth.

"This is just a taste of what you'll get if you've lied to me, boy." He sent a hard fist into her midsection. He hit her again, then let her drop in half-consciousness to the ground.

"If you've lied to me, I'll be back. And I'll rip your cock off and make you eat it. Remember that." He kicked her hard in the side. "You hear me, boy?"

Moira passed out.

Chapter Seventeen

It snowed lightly that afternoon, the tiny white flakes dropping silently from a gray sky. Moira, lying unconscious on the hillside above the river no more than twenty feet from the cabin, didn't feel them. The snow melted on first contact, and then, as the earth gradually chilled, it stuck, layering a soft white blanket over everything. Moira roused once, but when she tried to move fainted from the pain.

The jangle of horses' bridles and gear entered her unconscious. She heard voices, familiar and yet distant.

"How's it been going?" Hawthorne asked. Daniel laughed and told Random excitedly about the amount of gold he had been able to mine during the past two weeks. In the fading light and with the soft blanket of snow over everything, they walked right past Moira without seeing her.

"Damn, but I'm tired. Where's Moira?"

"Probably in the cabin. Haven't seen her all day."

"She sick?"

Daniel laughed. "Just lazy."

The horses snorted and shook against the bridles. Random and Daniel unloaded everything in front of the cabin.

"Moira!" Daniel shouted, expecting her to come out and help. Silence. "Moira! For Christ's sake..." He threw open the cabin door and peered in. The fire was out, the cabin ice-cold. He looked around curiously and then back out. "She's not in here."

"Well, where in hell is she?" Random demanded harshly. The two men looked at one another, perplexed and then worried. It was Random who acted first, his face tight with anger.

"Moira!" His voice carried through the silence of the forest, echoing back. More silence.

"Sweet Jesus, I haven't seen her all day," Daniel repeated, white-faced, looking frantically around.

"You were supposed to keep an eye on her, for God's sake!" Random said savagely. He moved away from the horses and stood, indecisively raking the area close by with his sharp gaze. Then he saw something out of place on the hillside, something that hadn't been there before he left. It looked small but familiar. A harsh sound came from his chest as he started to run. He went down on his knees when he reached her.

He turned her gently and heard a low moan of pain. "Moira . . ." Her head fell back against his arm as he lifted her, showing him the swollen discoloration of her face and the blood from her scrapes.

"God, what happened to her?" Daniel cried, coming forward and staring down at his little sister cradled gently in Random's arms.

"You tell me," Random said grimly. "Get a fire going, fast!"

"What about the horses?"

"Damn the horses! She's half frozen, you stupid bastard! Now move!" Bootsteps hurried away.

In a haze of pain and semiconsciousness, Moira was dimly aware of being brought into the cabin and lowered to the bunk. A shudder wracked her body. Her vision was blurred. When Random moved her slightly, the pain increased until she could hardly breathe. He pushed the hair back from her face, turning her head very gently to examine the wounds. He muttered something violent under his breath.

"Put some water on to boil," Random ordered, his eyes never leaving Moira. His hands moved and he began unbuttoning the front of her jacket, pulling it back off her shoulders.

She groaned in protest, tears welling into her dark eyes as they opened to look at him. His face tightened. Next came the loose, checked wool skirt. She felt it being opened.

"I don't think you ought to be undressing my sister, Hawthorne," Daniel said sternly, coming over to the bunk. Random turned on him violently, lashing out with a fist that knocked Danny backward. There was a loud crash as he hit the floor with a grunt.

"Your brotherly protection comes a little late!" Random snarled through his teeth, hands bunched at his sides, eyes blazing down at Daniel, who was now pushing himself up and shaking his head in a daze. "Get out of here and see to the horses before I decide to beat the living hell out of you!"

Daniel stumbled out the door.

Random returned his attention to Moira. As gently as he could, he removed the rest of her clothing, his hands moving slowly over the pale, soft skin, finding the tender spots, seeing the ugly bruise across her ribs and side where Barilovich had sent the final kick. He took several blankets and wrapped her warmly in them. With a cloth moistened in warm water, he carefully cleaned the blood from the scrapes on her face. With care, using his knife, he removed the broken pine needle splinters that were ground into her cheekbone. When he dabbed on brandy to disinfect her injuries, Moira gasped. She stared up at him in a daze of pain.

"Rand . . . ?"

"Shhhh . . ." He laid a finger to her lips, staring into her swimming eyes. "I don't want to hurt you, but it's got to be done."

Her face felt as though it would crack if she moved one muscle. She winced and sucked in her breath sharply as he finished. "Barilovich," she said softly.

Random frowned. "Don't talk now, Moira. You've got a couple of cracked ribs."

"Hurts . . ." she whispered faintly.

"Try to sleep."

She closed her eyes against the throbbing in her head and sighed, allowing the blackness to return without a fight. It was a long time later that she awoke. She turned her head, and a flash of fire went through her skull. She groaned and then tried to push herself up. The pain in her side made her gasp and lie back.

"Don't move," Random told her, leaning over her. He looked dog-tired, his face pale and drawn.

"I've got to move sometime," she managed, giving him a weak, apologetic smile.

"Give yourself a few days."

"When did you get back?"

"Yesterday afternoon."

She closed her eyes for a second. "I'm glad."

"You missed me?" His voice had a teasing tone, and her cheeks colored. She opened her eyes and looked up at him.

"I could have used a little help yesterday." She gave him a faint smile. "I don't think I want to pretend to be a man anymore." The laughter was extinguished from his eyes.

"You'd have fared a lot worse if they'd known you were a woman."

"I don't see how."

"Don't you? Well, don't talk anymore, Moira," he told her flatly. She looked up at him again.

"I was worried about you. You said you were only going to be gone a week," she told him. It hurt to talk, but she didn't want him to move away from her. She wanted him to touch her. She wanted him close. She wasn't afraid when he was close.

"I had to go farther downriver than I thought. All the way to Marysville to find what I wanted."

"The windows?"

"I got them." He smiled. "And a few other comforts, enough to keep us going until spring. I haven't even an ounce of gold left."

"Daniel has several pouches hidden under the floorboards," she told him tiredly. "Barilovich and Heaton took one I'd forgotten to hide."

"You didn't confront them, did you?"

"I didn't accomplish much," she murmured, mouth trembling at the memory.

"Christ preserve you!" he muttered savagely, looking completely disgusted with her. "I thought you had some brains!

You should have stayed out of it and away from them. What did you think you were doing?"

"I didn't know it was Barilovich and Heaton, for goodness' sake. It was only after Barilovich started talking that I realized who it was from his accent!"

"Clever girl."

"I wanted to throw them off Jack's trail."

"Wonderful. And did you?" he said derisively, eyes glittering angrily down at her.

"I think so," she said slowly, and then in fierce defensiveness, "And it was worth what he did to me if I did!" She tried desperately to ignore the pain in her ribs and side, the way her face felt.

"Just what did you tell them?"

"When they described him, I said a man fitting that description, wearing an onyx-and-gold ring, had come down from the mountains about six days before. I had given him some supplies because he looked in a bad way, and he had headed downriver for Sacramento. I even added that he had said the luck had been poor upstream."

"And they believed you."

"I . . . I think they did. Heaton seemed bothered by something, but Barilovich seemed to go along with my story. Then when I asked him why he'd been in the cabin, he dangled Daniel's gold in front of me. I called him a thief and tried to take it"— Random muttered something under his breath that Moira pretended she hadn't heard—"and he hit me. When he stopped . . . he said if he found I'd lied to him, he'd come back and . . ." Her face turned red.

"Never mind. I get the general idea." He looked grim. "The next time I leave this camp, for whatever reason, I'm taking you with me."

It hurt to grin. "I told you you should do that once before," she managed, her eyes mischievous.

"You did at that. Go to sleep now, Moira."

She awakened later when Daniel came in from his work on the river. Random wasn't in the cabin. Moira pushed herself up into a sitting position, wincing from the pain in her ribs. Her head wasn't throbbing anymore, but the bruised, scraped skin across her cheekbone felt very tender. She glanced across

at Daniel as he sat tiredly on his bunk, transferring gold dust
from his handkerchief into a pouch before concealing it beneath
the floorboards. She saw the dark bruise and swelling along
his jawline and frowned.

"Barilovich?"

He smiled wryly. "Hawthorne."

"Random? But why?"

He gave a humorless laugh. "Never mind. It's not important!"

"But I want to know! Why did he hit you?"

"Because I objected to him taking all your clothes off."

Moira sat stunned for several seconds. "What?" she said
faintly. She glanced down and found she had on a long checked
wool shirt over long johns and dungarees. Perfectly suitable,
not exposing a thing. She looked up again, perplexed, and saw
her brother's amused expression.

"He put fresh clothes on you *after* he found out how badly
you were hurt," he told her unmercifully. Her eyebrows shot
up like the wings of a bird taking sudden flight.

"He what?"

"Well . . . in his defense, he had to find out how badly you
were hurt, and the only way to do that was to look for himself.
You've got a couple of very bad bruises, from what he said."

"He . . . looked?"

"And felt, too, undoubtedly, since he said you've got several
cracked ribs."

"I . . . hope . . . you're . . . joking."

He rubbed his chin. "Does this look like I'm joking?"

The door opened and Random strode in, arms loaded with
firewood. He dumped it beside the fireplace, then brushed off
his hands. Sensing the tension in the cabin, he looked at Moira
and then at Daniel, then back at Moira, and gave a taunting
smile. She couldn't look at him. Her face flamed with embarrassment. Thankfully, he didn't say anything but went about
putting more wood on the fire and setting up the roasting spit
for a rabbit he'd shot. The silence in the cabin could have been
cut with a knife. Moira stood up shakily, her face still flushed.

Random was still hunkered down before the fire, but he
caught her movement and turned on his heels to look at her.
"Where are you going?"

"Outside."

He stood up, and her face flamed even more. "I don't need an escort," she said stiffly.

"That's a matter of opinion," he returned dryly.

"Then let me put it this way. I don't need company for what needs doing!"

Daniel watched the exchange with obvious relish, leaning back on his bunk, one foot raised.

"All right," Random agreed. "But if you're not back in ten minutes, I'm going to come out for you, *whatever* you're doing."

She turned away abruptly and fled the cabin, standing outside and wondering how she was possibly going to ever regain some measure of dignity again. She couldn't even squat now without his permission! She walked to the woods. A few minutes later, she started back. She saw Random walking toward her and stopped.

"I haven't been gone ten minutes yet," she told him defensively.

"No. But I wanted to talk to you... alone."

Moira stood uncomfortably in front of him, unable to think of anything but the fact that he had seen her naked. He smiled slightly, shaking his head.

"What are you worried about, Moira? That I took advantage of you while you were unconscious?"

"Was it absolutely necessary to..."

"Absolutely. And I'd a good idea already what was underneath what you wear, so don't go supposing that I saw anything of any great surprise."

"Thanks for telling me," she said stiffly, wondering if he'd said that just to make matters worse. He laughed.

"Would you like it better if I told you that the mere sight of you naked took my breath away. It did, you know."

She gasped. "I'd like it even better if you told me you didn't do what you did, Mr. Hawthorne!"

"Mr. Hawthorne," he mocked her laughingly. "So, we're back to that, are we? It's a little late for formality, I'd say. Wouldn't you agree? You called me Rand once when you were asleep..."

She started to step past him, embarrassed beyond description. He moved in front of her, his laugh low and husky.

"Put your mind at rest, Moira," he said softly, leaning toward her, too close for comfort already. "I looked . . . and I touched . . . but I didn't take."

She stared up at him, wide-eyed. The intimate tone of his voice, the way his eyes drew and held hers, took her breath away. He smiled slowly. "When I make love to a woman, I want her eyes wide open, knowing what she's doing, and fully conscious of what I'm doing to her."

Moira drew back sharply, heart pounding wildly, heat surging up inside her like a furnace.

He grinned. "I see you understand me."

She gulped hard, almost audibly. "Well, thank you for being such a gentleman," she managed with some asperity.

"Only when the occasion demands it," he said wryly. He took her arm. "Now, let's go back to the cabin before we add pneumonia to your list of problems."

Chapter Eighteen

"Will you please speak to him, Random? He won't listen to me at all. Every time I even try to talk to him about it, he explodes. And I'm worried. He's lost so much weight and he's got a fever, though he won't admit it even to himself," she said worriedly, sitting with Random on the hillside above the river. They watched Daniel working below with the Long Tom he had constructed, while Random ate the lunch she'd brought down for them both. Daniel had refused to eat, not wanting to take time away from his claim.

"I've already tried," Random admitted grimly, brows drawn together as he kept an eye on Daniel. "He's not listening to anything, and there isn't anything we can do about it."

She sighed heavily. "He's changed. I hardly know him anymore. The only thing that matters to him is . . . gold."

"It does that to people. They can't see anything for the glitter of it. It's called gold fever, and your brother has a bad case of it. Maybe incurable."

"How do we get through to him?" She looked desperately at Random. "The only time he leaves his work is when he has to because . . . because of the diarrhea and when it's too dark to work anymore. He hardly eats anything. He's lost so much weight he looks emaciated."

"Short of tying him down and forcing him to eat, what do you suggest?" he demanded impatiently. "Daniel's a man, Moira. He makes his own way, his own decisions. You can't change that."

She put her head on her knees and sighed shakily. "A man can be an awful fool."

They sat in silence for several moments. Moira looked up at Random again. "What good will all that gold do him if he's lost his health? Tell me that."

"Sometimes it's not the spending that matters. It's the challenge of accumulating it."

She looked at him appealingly. "Please, Random. Please talk to him again." He looked at her worried face for a long moment, then he smiled gently, reaching out to slowly trail his fingertips over her soft cheek. The bruises and scrapes had healed, leaving only faint marks that would eventually go away entirely. She stilled beneath his touch, her lips parting slightly as worry gave way to desire. Random's fingers moved to her lips, his eyes following caressingly. Restlessly, he shifted his weight. Then he drew his hand away, his face tightening almost in anger. He stood, and she heard him draw in his breath.

"I'll try again, Moira," he told her without looking down at her. As he walked down the slope, her eyes followed him in confusion.

Always, when they drew close, when feelings intensified, he pulled back. He teased, taunted, mocked, and provoked her. He protected her. Twice he had kissed her, closing off all consciousness of anything in the world save him. Yet she felt she had not touched him in any lasting way.

Moira had fallen in love with Random Hawthorne. She'd faced that fact some time before, and being in love with him, she was overly aware of his every word, his every expression, his every look. Her body responded to the subtlest of movements from him, and she suffered a thousand agonies, understanding that while he found her somewhat desirable, his feelings apparently went no deeper. When he had kissed her aboard the *Stephen Rule*, it was because of proximity. When he had kissed her after leaving Rough and Ready, it had been to allay her questions, to silence her arguments. That knowledge hurt unbearably, but it was better to arm herself with the truth than blind herself with illusions.

Moira left the men working at the river and went up to plan the evening meal. Entering the cabin, she looked at the big tin bathtub in the corner and smiled slightly. Random had gone all the way to Marysville to buy it at the same time he had bought the windows for the cabin. He felt something for her if he would do that; perhaps not love, but something.

Later, she heard Daniel shouting. She went out and looked down the hill. Random was standing in front of her brother, his hands on his hips, listening as the younger man ranted. Daniel's chin jutted out as he talked, and he gestured toward the river and then the cloudy sky. She could guess what he was saying; he'd said it often enough to her when she tried to reason with him. The snows were on them, the last storm had left deep drifts that weren't melting off, and it wouldn't be long before he couldn't work at all. Then he would rest.

Daniel turned away and Random grabbed his arm, jerking him back like a spoiled child. He said something, his face stern. He talked for several minutes, jerking his head toward the cabin, where Moira stood watching, then released Daniel impatiently. Daniel hadn't replied, but he looked angry. As the two men started up the last stretch of hill before the cabin, Moira went in.

Neither said anything when they entered. She could feel the tension between them. They ate in silence, but at least Daniel ate. He was pale afterward and left the cabin. He came back some time later, even more pale, and stretched out on his bunk. He lay there, staring, for a long time. There was a faint flush across his cheek that indicated his fever had risen again. Moira longed to put a cooling rag on his forehead, but she knew that to do so would make him angry. She looked at Random, who was lying on his bunk, a hard expression tightening his face.

"Random, I'd like to talk to my sister. Alone," Daniel said finally, sitting up. Random turned his head and looked at the younger man for a long minute, impatience in his eyes. He sat up in a smooth movement, eyes never once taking in Moira's tense form near the fireplace.

"All right," he said flatly. "Just try to remember something, will you, Cavendish? Your sister's worried about you out of love, not for any selfish reason."

He left them alone. Daniel looked angry at what Random had said and looked over at Moira.

"We're going to get something settled."

"Danny . . ."

"I don't need or want a nursemaid."

"No, you just want to be left alone to work yourself into an early grave. What you do need is some good common sense! You wouldn't listen to me, so . . ."

"You told Random to talk to me," he finished for her, mouth twisting bitterly. "I'm a man, damn you, not a baby. And I'll do what I damn well please."

"Danny, you've lost far too much weight—"

"Aren't you listening to me?" he shouted at her in a fury. She flinched, and tears sprang into her eyes. His face tightened and paled. "You don't understand. You just don't understand. . . ."

"Then explain it to me," she pleaded.

"It's simple. I want to go back to Charleston with so much gold no one will ever look at me with smug pity again."

She frowned. "But who does that now?"

He gave a hard, humorless laugh. "You know the facts, but it never really touched you. Pa gambled everything away . . . everything." He looked at her, eyes tortured. "Do you have any idea how I felt having everyone know that? It was bad enough with Aunt Miranda paying for my last year at the university. But *everyone* knew. Paul, Kris, Hadley, the lot of them—they all knew about Pa. Their parents knew long before we did. God . . ." He lay back, staring miserably.

"I never knew you were so bitter."

"Bitter?" he said hoarsely, looking at her. He pushed himself up and looked at her squarely, his face pinched in pain, his eyes bright. "Ashamed . . . I'm ashamed. Cavendish used to stand for something in Charleston, something besides what it does now—gambling debts and foolhardiness. Money is still owed all over the city . . . at almost every club Pa ever entered. I don't suppose you can understand what that means to me."

There was a long silence between them as he looked away.

"Can't I?" she said quietly.

Daniel looked back at her and frowned.

"Nothing really changed for you, Moira," he said flatly. "You didn't have a dowry, but you're beautiful. You could have married Charles Beauchamp and still have been the toast of Charleston though your father had been 'Gambler' Cavendish."

"For all his faults, and in spite of the debts he left behind, Danny, he was our father, and I loved him."

"I could have wished for a stronger one."

"So you wouldn't have inherited his gaming spirit?" she asked sharply. "Is it Papa you hate or just that part of him you see in yourself?"

"What do you mean?" he asked.

"The way you gambled everything away in Rough and Ready. The way you're gambling your life away now."

"I'm not gambling now. This is a sure thing. Or haven't you really looked at what I'm taking out of that river?"

"Danny . . . Danny . . ."

"You could get on a ship and go home and within a fortnight of arriving be married to Beauchamp."

"The price would be too dear."

"What price?" he said cuttingly. "That for everything a woman could want or ask for she give herself to a man?"

"For my life. In exchange for money I'd forfeit every dream, every hope, and all my self-respect. As a man, you have a choice about what to do with your life, where you go and how. If I'd stayed in Charleston, or if I went back even now, what choices would I have? Aunt Mandy would parade me like so much horseflesh before any marriageable man until one decided to take me off her hands for good." She gave a painful, tremulous laugh.

"You want to go back before all the rest, richer than all the rest. All right, I can understand that. You want to have so much wealth behind you that it'll outshine what people remember about Pa. All right, I can understand that, too. But Danny, what good is it all if you kill yourself in the process?"

"I'm not killing myself," he said wearily.

"You are . . . now. Only you can't see it. And I'm sorry if I sound like a nursemaid . . . but I love you. I love you, Danny," she repeated. "All I want is to find Jack and have what little family we have left together again." She smiled as her eyes filled with tears. "And if we manage to bring home a million in gold dust, so much the better. I wouldn't mind the luxury of being as free as any man to make the choice of what I do with my life, either."

He smiled. "Since when didn't you take the choice, given it or not?"

Holding back the tears, she looked at him seriously. "I'll work the Long Tom every hour you rest, if you want. I'm not saying give it all up, just give yourself a few days, a little time."

He sighed, defeated. "All right. I'm too damn tired to argue anymore."

"Thank God for that." She smiled at him playfully, pushing the hair back off his forehead.

"God's got nothing to do with it. It's my decision," he insisted, with a lopsided grin.

"You feel warm," she said, her hand on his forehead. He brushed her hand away and pulled her down to hug her.

"I'll be all right," he said hoarsely. "And when we go home, it'll be all right, too. You just wait." His hold loosened. "God, I'm tired. So damn tired," he said thickly. She kissed his cheek.

"Then sleep, Danny," she whispered. He did, losing consciousness almost immediately. She sat on the bunk and looked down at him, so thin and flushed. He was sick, but at least now he had agreed to rest for a day or two. A day or two couldn't make that much difference to his dream.

Moira went outside to find Random. He was standing not far from the cabin, leaning against a redwood, staring down toward the river. He didn't look at her until she was standing right next to him.

"What did he say to you?"

"He said he'll rest for a day or two," she told him in relief. She breathed deeply of the cold mountain air. When she exhaled, she could see her breath clouding in front of her. She shivered slightly.

"You ought to go back in to the fire," Random told her flatly, not looking at her. She looked up at him, sensing something was wrong but not knowing what.

"Random..." She reached out and touched him. She felt

his muscles tighten. "I . . . I want to thank you for talking to him." She drew her hand back and looked up at him.

"He couldn't fight both of us and himself for long," he said. "A couple of days of rest and some fresh meat will do him a world of good." He looked down at her. "I'm going hunting tomorrow."

"I'll keep an eye on things here."

"No. You're going with me. I told you that once before. Where I go, you go."

"But Danny?"

"He should be all right if he uses his common sense. He won't want you fussing around him."

"No," she sighed. "He won't."

"We'll go upriver a ways. Maybe we'll see some sign of your brother. We won't go far, and we'll be back by nightfall." He sounded curt and distant. Moira studied his face. His mouth was tight, and a muscle worked in his jaw.

"Is something wrong, Random?"

He put his head back against the redwood and closed his eyes. His voice was hard and dispassionate when he spoke.

"Just go back inside the cabin, Moira." It was almost an order, and she paled at the rejection. Her chin tilted slightly.

"All right, then. Good night." She turned and walked back to the cabin.

Chapter Nineteen

While Random readied the horses the following morning, Moira stayed in the cabin to speak to Daniel, who was still stretched out on his bunk.

"You promise to rest?"

He yawned widely, then grinned at her, seemingly more himself after a long night's sleep. "I promise," he said easily. "Don't worry about me. I'm going to eat that breakfast you've prepared for me over there and climb right back into this bed and sleep some more. The only reason I'll get up will be to make the usual hundred trips to the bushes."

"We'll bring back some good fresh meat and maybe even some wild vegetables, if we're lucky."

"How would you know a wild vegetable from poison ivy?" Daniel needled.

"I wouldn't, but maybe Random will."

Daniel frowned. "You think Random has the answer to everything, don't you? Moira, don't—"

"Don't what? Fall in love with him?" She smiled slightly. "You needn't worry. He's been most discouraging."

"You'll find someone better suited to you back in Charleston," he said looking at her seriously.

"Better suited? Have you taken a good look at me lately?"

She laughed and then looked at him more seriously. "And what's wrong with Random? Are you such a snob that you look down on seamen?"

"There's nothing wrong with Random. It's you and Random together that bothers me. He's . . . he's . . . hell, I don't know. I can't put my finger on it."

Moira looked bleakly toward the open door of the cabin and sighed. "I think I know what you mean. Just when you think you've scratched the surface, you find another layer, and what's there is just as elusive as ever."

"Just be careful with him."

"Don't you trust him?" She looked at him in surprise.

"Oh, I'd trust him with my life. I just don't trust him with my sister."

She gave a faint laugh. "Well, I don't think you need worry about your sister, either. I'm not what one would call a beauty, looking the way I do. And he . . . well, he doesn't have anything in mind on that score anyway."

"Well, don't sound so disappointed about it."

"Disappointed?" She widened her eyes deliberately. "Why would I be disappointed?"

Random was mounted outside. "Mory!" he shouted, and she stood up. Bending over, she gave Daniel an affectionate kiss on his forehead.

"Rest and eat."

"Aye, aye, Cap'n," he said mockingly, giving her a salute.

Moira mounted up beside Random, casting him a questioning glance. He was studying the cloudy sky, a faint frown on his face. He looked at her, and there wasn't even a hint of softness in his eyes.

"You stay close to me. Do you understand?"

"Yes." She pressed her knees against the animal's side to move closer to him. "How far are we going, Random?"

"As far as we have to to find game. Most of it's been chased out of the area by the miners, so we'll go up and back." He indicated northeast. "With any luck we'll be back long before nightfall." He made a clicking noise with his tongue, and the horse moved.

They rode for a couple of miles, Random finding signs of

game as he went. Several times he stopped and dismounted, squatting down to look more closely at what he found. After inspecting one particularly large set of tracks he stood up and rubbed the back of his neck. He gave Moira a self-mocking smile.

"I haven't done this for years," he admitted ruefully. "Not since I was a boy."

She smiled down at him. "Well, I've never done it. Have you found something?"

"A couple of bear tracks."

"Bear?" She gulped.

He grinned up at her. "They don't look fresh." He mounted his horse in one swift motion, and they went on. They were more than five miles from the cabin when he drew rein. She could see a small creek not far away through the trees, and there was a small stretch of grass. There were snow patches on it already. Random dismounted and tossed her the reins.

"Stay here with the horses. Don't go anywhere. Don't do anything. Just sit quietly and wait. Understand?"

"Yes, sir," she said stiffly in response to his curt orders. He pulled the rifle from its scabbard on the saddle and walked into the woods.

He was gone for so long that Moira finally got tired of sitting in the saddle waiting. She dismounted and tied the reins of the horses to a low branch and went to sit beneath a big pine, keeping her eye on the meadow beyond.

Something moved, she was sure of it! There it was again! A buck! It was standing right on the edge of the meadow, still in the shadows. She looked around, trying to spot Random. Looking back, she saw the buck was still there. He was twelve points at least!

Where was Random? Here was the game they needed, and he was off somewhere doing God knew what! She got up slowly and went back to her horse, reaching up for the rifle tied securely to her saddle. She pulled it out slowly and then tiptoed back to the tree where she had had a clear view of the magnificent animal. He was coming out of the shadows, one tentative step at a time. Daniel had shown her the rudiments of firing the gun, but she was no marksman. Yet she couldn't let the buck pass. And he was so big, how could she miss? It would be like firing at the broad side of a barn.

She reached the tree and raised the gun, sighting along the barrel, holding her breath as she put her finger to the trigger. The buck took another step and she fired, the sound cracking through the forest, echoing on. It was a clear miss. The animal gave one powerful leap and began to bound in panic across the meadow. He had taken two flying leaps when another shot rang out. The animal seemed to stop in midair and then dropped, blood streaking from its chest. It jerked several times and then lay still.

Random appeared across the meadow. How had he arrived clear over there when he had gone in the other direction, she wondered bemusedly. He bent down and checked the animal, then stood and strode purposefully toward her. She swallowed hard, seeing his darkened face. He was furious, ragingly furious!

"What in hell did you think you were doing?" he roared at her, ripping the rifle from her hands and putting it back in its scabbard. He sheathed his own and then glared at her, his hands on his hips, legs splayed.

"I didn't know where you'd gone," she stammered. "And the deer was just walking away."

"You damn near lost it for me!"

Her temper rose in the face of his. "How did I know you'd even seen it?" she yelled back. "You went that way!" She jerked her thumb toward the woods behind her.

"Well, no thanks to you, we've got a deer."

She sucked in some air. "Thanks to me, it ran right into your sights!"

He gave a hard laugh. "You didn't come within a mile. All you did was scare the hell out of him. And don't try telling me that you intended for him to run in the direction he did!"

She glared up at him.

"And when I tell you to sit and wait, that's exactly what I mean! No more and, damn it, no less! Do you understand me?"

She gave a defiant shrug of her shoulders and started to turn away, then found herself yanked back none too gently to face him again. Her eyes widened at the fierce expression in those dark eyes.

"I said, do you understand me?" He spoke more quietly but with far more menace. She swallowed hard, feeling the bite of his fingers into her upper arm.

She nodded. "Yes." Her voice was a nervous rasp. He seemed satisfied, releasing her abruptly and turning away to pull the rope from his saddle. He didn't look at her as he went back across the meadow. With obvious effort, he hefted the heavy, dead animal across his back and carried it to the trees. Then he roped the hind legs and pulled it slowly up over a branch so he could gut it.

Moira watched him work for several moments. Well, she had learned something more about Random Hawthorne. He had a violent temper and he disliked being disobeyed. She sat down near the meadow and leaned back against the redwood to wait for him.

The air had grown colder, and she shivered slightly. Looking up, she saw that clouds had filled the sky. They were moving fast, bunching together, darkening the air. More were coming from the northeast.

Random came back for the horse. He glanced at her briefly and went back to lash the deer over the back of his mount. As he started back, she mounted up.

"We'd better get a move on," he told her flatly. "There's a storm coming up." Moira said nothing, but followed him obediently.

They hadn't gone more than three miles when the wind came howling down from the mountains, bringing a hard-driving rain with it. "Over there," Random shouted at her, indicating a pile of rocks up against the mountainside that formed a shelter. He left her with the horses while he checked to make sure nothing on four paws was living there. He came back and lifted Moira down from her horse, on which she had been huddling, a shivering mass.

"Pick up as much wood as you can while I see to the horses," he told her curtly, and she obeyed. She had gathered enough for a good fire by the time he came up with the provisions they had brought for the day's hunt—food, a couple of canteens of water, the guns, a couple of blanket rolls, and the saddles. He dumped everything near her and set to work building the fire.

"How long do you think it'll last?" she asked, teeth chattering.

"I wouldn't know," he said. "Not long, I hope. I didn't come prepared for a heavy storm."

"Can't we make it back? We can't be far from the cabin. Not more than a couple of miles."

He shot her an angry look. "If we could see anything, I'd say fine."

She stiffened at his tone. "Well, excuse me for asking!" He muttered something under his breath that Moira hoped she hadn't heard correctly. He started the fire, then stood up and started out of the rock shelter. Moira stood up quickly and took a step after him.

"Stay here," he told her, eyes glittering.

"Where . . . where are you going now, Random?"

"To get more wood. We may be here all night." He left her standing there staring after him. She sat down again, close to the fire. She rummaged through their things to see what they had to eat. *Beans!* God above, beans. She had had enough to last her a lifetime. Digging deeper, she found beef jerky and hardtack. She looked at their larder and grimaced. With all that fresh venison just waiting to be roasted . . .

Random came back and dumped more wood on the ground. The rain had turned to a blizzard, and snow flakes frosted his dark hair and clung to his eyelashes. Such long eyelashes for a man, she thought, looking at him. He looked cold, stiff, and uncomfortable.

"Come closer, Random," she said. He did. He sat down beside her and gave her a rueful smile.

"Thanks. I was afraid you'd want me to stay out in the cold for my behavior this afternoon."

She smiled, eyes mischievous. "Isn't that where growly old bears usually stay?" she teased.

His eyes sparkled angrily. "You deserved that and a lot more. When I tell you to do something, you do it!"

Her mouth tightened and then twisted wryly. "Sorry I even brought it up."

"Well, you did. And I'll tell you something else while we're about it. There's a good reason for any order I give you. I don't do it just as a test of your common sense. Someday, Moira, your life could depend on doing exactly what I tell you, when I tell you."

"It was just a deer, for heaven's sake."

He let out his breath in sharp impatience. "This time. But would it have mattered if it had been a cougar or a bear, or Barilovich and Heaton? You'd still have blundered into something you couldn't handle. In this case, it was just a deer, as you put it. But, damn it, I knew what I was doing. I knew where that buck was. I told you to wait and do nothing, and you almost got in the way. Next time it could be something a lot more important!"

She sighed, recognizing the sense of what he was saying, though she badly wanted to deny it. She did have a way of getting into trouble without realizing how or why. Barilovich was the worst incident, but the fandango hall could have been catastrophic for her as well.

"I'm sorry," she said simply. He reached out and ruffled her hair like a kid brother, a gesture she did not appreciate.

"All right. No more about it. Just don't ever do it again." In spite of his teasing manner, she knew he meant it.

They ate little and stayed close to the fire. They could see the horses from where they sat and the deer that Random had tied high in the tree out of the reach of predators. By the time the storm let up, it was too late to start back down for the cabin. Random went out and collected more wood. When he returned he leaned back against the boulder opposite Moira and closed his eyes.

Moira couldn't sleep. She was exhausted and miserable and so cold she sat shaking even with the fire blazing before her. She looked at Random, wondering how he could possibly sleep.

"Random?" It was scarcely a whisper, but he opened his eyes and looked at her. There was nothing in that dark gaze to tell her what he was thinking. "I'm cold," she said and a shiver emphasized her statement. His jaw tightened. He sighed.

"Come here."

She felt stiff with cold as she stood and crossed the few feet between them. He pulled her down to sit in front of him between spread legs, her back against his broad chest, and wrapped his blanket tightly around them both. She snuggled as close as she could to the warmth of his hard body and sighed contentedly. Then she leaned her head back.

"Better?" he whispered huskily against her hair.

"Yes," she murmured, a faint smile curving her lips. She rested her forearm on his muscular thigh and heard his sharp intake of breath. His arms felt so good around her. Little tingles of warmth traveled through her. But she wasn't any more sleepy than she had been before. In fact, she was wide awake, deliciously aware of his closeness.

"You're still shaking." His voice was deeper, the warmth of his breath fanning her temple. Her heart started to pound in slow, hard beats. Her stomach tightened. She didn't breathe as his mouth moved downward to her tender earlobe. His lips opened, and his teeth nibbled the soft, sensitive flesh. She gave a faint gasp and his arms tightened around her as if he expected her to escape from the arousing touch. When she didn't, his tongue trailed down to the pulse throbbing wildly in her throat as he shifted her weight slightly. Her head was thrown back against his arm, and his mouth moved back up her throat and along her jawline.

"Warm me," he whispered before taking her mouth. Her lips parted instinctively and he deepened the kiss, opening her mouth to his thrusting tongue. She moaned deeply and realized she was not the only one shaking badly.

Random's hand moved tantalizingly from her throat downward. Buttons gave beneath expert fingers, first those of her heavy coat, then those of her leather vest, finally those of her woolen shirt. When warm fingers came into contact with heated flesh, she closed her eyes and made a faint sound of surrender. His mouth lowered to taste and arouse, and her fingers pushed deeply into his thick, dark hair. He raised his head after a moment, breathing hard.

"Moira..." He looked at the way her eyes were half closed from the sensations he had fanned into blazing life. He looked at her parted lips, and his mouth returned to hers in passionate possession and promise. His hand moved down over the soft, full, swollen young breasts to the waistband of her dungarees. Another button gave, then another, and another. She felt the strength of his fingers as he spread them across the smooth, quivering flesh of her abdomen. He hesitated.

"Rand..." she appealed, all the pent-up passion of her young body revealed in the whispered name. He groaned.

"Shhh. Let's just warm each other."

"I'm warm enough. I want..."

"Shhh..." He kissed her again, and what started as a means of silencing her turned into a devastating possession. The depth of his need was almost painful. He drew back again, shaking hard.

"God, what have I started?" he muttered hoarsely. "I came up here with you to keep you out of harm's way, and I can't keep my hands off you."

The frightened whinny of the horses broke them apart. The horses whinnied again as both tried to pull away from their ties near the tree. There was another sound that raised the hair on the back of Moira's neck.

"Wolves," Random said, coming to his feet quickly and leaving Moira sitting on the hard ground, buttoning her clothes. He grabbed the rifle. "They're after the meat."

Moira scrambled to her feet, fingers working the buttons in haste. He turned back. "Stay here!" he ordered, eyes fierce with command.

"But..."

"Do as I say, damn it!"

She stood staring after him as he ran toward the panicked horses. She saw dark shapes moving on the hillside below them and held her breath in fear. Random hesitated and raised the rifle. It cracked once. She heard a canine yelp of pain and saw a wolf hobble toward the forest. Another darted forward, growling. The rifle cracked again. That wolf dropped. The others retreated, disappearing like shades of the devil. There was a howl not far away. Another answered. Moira shuddered.

Random went to the horses, reaching up to grab the ropes, murmuring soothingly to the rearing animals. The next howl was farther away.

It was some time before the horses settled down and Random was able to return to the fire. He rested his rifle next to the boulder, within easy reach, hunkered down, and put his hands out to the flames.

"Will they come back?"

"I don't think so. They'll look for easier prey."

He didn't look at her as the flames flickered across the hard planes of his face. He looked grim. She stood and took a tentative step toward him. He glanced at her sharply.

"Stay where you are," he told her flatly, a muscle moving in his cheek. She frowned slightly.

"I just thought—"

"We'd take up where we left off," he finished for her. "I don't think that would be very wise. The wolves might not save you a second time around."

She gave a faint, self-conscious laugh. "I wasn't thinking of—"

He interrupted her again. "It's not going to happen again, Moira."

She didn't move. She felt she had been slapped in the face. "Why not?" she dared.

He let out his breath. "A lot of reasons. Not the least of which is the fact that you're just not ready."

"Meaning what? That you think I'm a child?"

He didn't answer and he didn't look at her. She blinked rapidly, keeping the tears back. She felt angry pride fill her. She drew the blanket more tightly around her and tilted her chin up.

"Well, *Mister* Hawthorne," she said coldly, "now that you've made me suitably ashamed of *my* behavior, I think I'll try to get some sleep."

He looked at her then, his eyes hard and angry. "Don't push me."

She turned her back on him. "I wouldn't think of it," she muttered hoarsely, tears running down her cheeks.

She did manage to sleep a few hours. Random awakened her at first light, and they started down for the cabin. It took them barely an hour.

All was quiet when they rode down through the trees to the clearing. No smoke was coming from the chimney, but it was scarcely past dawn, and Daniel was probably still sleeping.

He was not in his bunk. Moira came out of the cabin and marched past Random, who was seeing to the horses. He looked at her sharply.

"So help me God, if he's working that damn claim again, I'll kill him!" she muttered in angry frustration. She crunched through the snowdrifts toward the river below.

She saw him before she was halfway down the hill. She gave a sharp cry and started to run. "Danny!" she screamed. It was too late.

Daniel had fainted from his fever, collapsing barely a foot from the Long Tom, and had drowned in a puddle scarcely five inches deep.

Chapter Twenty

Random stood in the doorway of the cabin, blocking Moira's exit. "Where do you think you're going with that?" he demanded, indicating the double-edged ax clutched in her two hands and held across her body.

"Get out of my way!" she ordered. He looked at her haggard face, the trembling mouth, the wild, dark eyes, and stepped slowly aside. He watched her as she passed him and walked down the hill.

The ax was almost too heavy for her to wield at all, but grief and fury gave her the strength she needed. She laid on the first blow, tipping the Long Tom. She swung again, splitting it down the middle. She went on swinging the ax until the Long Tom was nothing but a pile of splintered wood. And still she swung the ax. When she finally had no more strength to even lift it, she let it drop to the ground and fell to her knees, pounding her fists on the ground that Daniel had valued above his life. Now he rested, about a hundred feet from the cabin beneath a simple cross with his initials and the dates of his birth and death carved on it. Six feet of dirt makes all men equal, whatever their dreams and hopes, whatever their father's debts. Moira stayed on her knees in the dirt for a long time, sobbing until there were no more tears left.

She raised her head and looked around her, then sat back slowly on her heels.

"Jack!" The name reverberated through the forest. Silence. She drew in as much air as she could. "Jack!" Her voice broke. Her shoulders sagged. She stood up and waited for a long time in the hope of hearing an answer, any answer. Perhaps he was dead already. Dead like Danny.

Nothing. Slowly, she turned and walked back up the hill. Random was sitting beneath a pine tree, his forearms resting on his knees, his head bent. She stopped and looked at him. He raised his head. The lines were deeply etched around his eyes and mouth, and his face was pale beneath the tan. He stood up, shoving his hands deeply into his pockets, and looked at her squarely.

"Do you blame me, Moira?" His eyes were dark and unfathomable.

"Why should I?" she asked, tired beyond bearing.

"For taking you away from Danny. For making you go up the mountain with me when you wanted to stay here and look after your brother."

She closed her eyes, feeling drained of strength and emotion. "Do you think it would have made any difference?"

"No. Maybe. I don't know. It might have." He sighed heavily, rubbing the back of his neck. "It's what you think that matters to me now."

"Then I don't think it would have made any difference. And if I blame anything, it's gold. Dirty, stinking, filthy gold." Her voice broke. She looked away.

He looked down at her and she looked back, their eyes meeting and holding. She saw something in his eyes that brought sudden tears to her own. She shook her head. "No, Random I do *not* blame you."

Random looked away from her and then up at the sky. It was stormy, the air cold. His breath came out in a cloud. Already, snow was beginning to fall again, piling up on the drifts of the previous days.

"Another storm," he said quietly. Moira stood there, not thinking, not feeling, looking at nothing. He stood looking down at her a moment and then folded her in his arms like a child. She snuggled close to him, feeling a hard lump in her throat, a deep lingering pain of loss in her chest. He stood for a while with her tightly against him, close and safe, then walked back into the cabin.

Random cooked a thick venison stew that night, but Moira couldn't eat any of it. She sat in silence on her bunk, legs crossed Indian style, staring off into space, her mind filled with Danny. Random lay on his bunk looking up at her, a deep frown of concern creasing his brow. She finally lay back and closed her eyes, sleep coming with welcome grace. For a few hours it was dreamless, and then the nightmares came.

Danny stood before her in his shroud, marked with the red dust of the Sierras. "Do you know what you've done to me, damn you! You've killed me. I'd have been with Kris and Hadley and Paul and the rest if you hadn't come aboard the *Stephen Rule* to ruin all my plans. This would never have happened to me. I'd have found my gold and come home to Charleston a rich man to make the Cavendish name mean something again!" He stretched his arms wide. His face was ghastly gray, and worms had begun crawling out his eyes and mouth. "Your fault! Your fault!" He kept repeating those words over and over as the worms devoured him and he crumpled into the open pit a few feet from the cabin.

"Danny . . . Danny . . . Danny!" Her cry was a moan at first, that gradually rose to a terrified wail. "Danny!"

"Moira! Wake up!"

She opened her eyes to find Random standing beside her bunk, his hands biting into her shoulders as he shook her to consciousness. Her face was wet with tears, her eyes wide with fear and pain. She realized with a rush of relief that it had been a nightmare, and then she began to cry. Deep, wracking sobs shook her.

"My fault," she groaned. "If I hadn't come along, he'd have been with the others . . . he'd be alive!"

"Stop it."

"My fault. It's true!" she screamed at him and then fell back as Random slapped her hard across the face. Her cheek burned, and she stared up at him in a daze. His face was pale, his eyes watchful. She drew in a ragged breath, and her muscles went limp.

"I'm sorry," she managed shakily, eyes blurring. She put

her forearm up to cover her face, ashamed that he had seen her so out of control. He pushed her arm back, his fingers firmly around her wrist, and forced her chin around so that she had to look at him.

"Moira, he fainted. You had nothing to do with that. He promised to rest and take care of himself, and we got caught in a snowstorm. He pushed himself too hard. And it was by some quirk of fate that he fell in that puddle the way he did. He didn't die because of anything you did or didn't do," he told her with stern authority.

She closed her eyes, seeing her brother's dead, bloated face before her, and moaned. "He just wanted to make up for what my father had done, for what Cavendish had come to mean."

"You can't blame yourself," he said harshly. "He was a full-grown man. You couldn't make decisions for him. You tried to make him see reason, but he was too caught up in that claim down on the river."

She stared up at him in an agony of grief, anger, and pain. "It's not fair!" she cried. "It's just not fair. He was only twenty-one! Twenty-one, for God's sake."

Random's face was pale and tense. "I've known younger men to die with even less reason." His eyes grew distant with some long-ago pain now brought to renewed life. "My younger brother was hardly twelve when he died of appendicitis. Not an easy or pretty way to go. And two sisters not even in school died of influenza. . . ."

"Oh, Rand . . ." she murmured in abject apology for having been the cause of his remembering such things. She sat up and put her arms around him in a spontaneous gesture of compassion. His body went rigid. She drew back.

"I'm sorry . . ." she choked out.

His hand came up quickly, curving around the nape of her slender neck, then plunging deeply into her hair, pulling her toward him again. He held her tightly when she tried to pull back, his other hand sliding around her waist. The embrace was hard, and she didn't know whose heart was pounding so hard and fast that she was trembling from its force.

"Moira," he murmured. "If I could take away the pain, I would. So help me God, I would." His voice was rough and husky. She knew he understood what she was feeling, and she needed his closeness tonight. And if it meant swallowing every ounce of pride and begging him, she would, and worry later about regaining her self-respect. Her arms slid around him again, hugging him close.

"Hold me, Rand," she said softly, tremulously. "Stay here with me . . . and just hold me . . . please . . ."

She felt him take a deep, shaky breath before he answered in a gentle whisper, "All right. If it's really what you want . . ."

His hand stroked her back until she relaxed, and then stretched out on the bunk, pulling her against him beneath the thick blankets. Her body molded easily, naturally to his, the soft feminine curves pressed to his harder contours. He breathed in slowly and then let it out. After several moments, Moira's eyes closed, and she slept.

The nightmare recurred, but a gentle stroking hand and softly murmured words made it move off into oblivion, not to return again. She awakened in the faint light of earliest morning to find Random's legs across hers and his arm tightly looped around her waist. His head was turned toward her face, his deep breathing fanning her sensitized skin.

She looked at him for a long time, a tenderness so strong welling inside her that it squeezed her chest with painful longing. She *loved* this man. She knew next to nothing about him, but she was in love with him. She loved everything about him—the way he looked, the way he moved, the way he spoke, even the way he smelled. She loved the feel of him next to her, the warmth of him against her, the hard strength of his body, the rough stubble of beard he hadn't shaved for several days now. And she wanted him to love her in the same consuming way. She wanted that so badly she ached.

Turning her head away, Moira closed her eyes, not wanting to acknowledge all the other feelings that were stirring her to full wakefulness. She might be just eighteen, but she had a woman's body, a woman's longings, a woman's love, if he could just see it. She was ready for him.

She looked at him again, wondering what he would do if she turned fully against him and kissed him awake. What would he do if she touched him? Her heart thumped crazily. Slowly, she leaned forward, lips parting. His mouth was barely an inch away. She closed her eyes. She touched him very lightly. He didn't move. She drew back, looking at him, tears of overwhelming emotion filling her eyes. She drew a shaky breath and felt his hand tighten, drawing her closer in his sleep. She leaned close again and kissed him. He made a sound in his throat and his hand moved up slowly to possess her full, young breast, bringing a faint gasp of surprise from her. He moved slightly, and she became aware that he was very much aroused, though still asleep. Her heart started pounding hard and fast. He was murmuring something, his hand gliding down from her breast over her abdomen and lower. Her nerve departed.

"Random . . ." she murmured, and his eyes opened slowly. They were dark and dazed as he looked at her for one still moment, a faint smile on his face, and then full comprehension hit him. He pulled himself away and stood up, muscles tight, face turned away.

"Sorry about that," he said flatly and reached for his coat. He left the cabin, a blast of cold air coming in as he left.

Moira wished she hadn't awakened him. She could still feel the tingling places where he had touched her. She got up slowly, hands pushing her disheveled hair back from her face. She looked down at her wrinkled clothes and grimaced.

She heard the crack of an ax against wood outside. She looked longingly at the tin bathtub in the corner, and then decided a simple washing would have to do. Soon, she hoped to be able to sit in that tub filled with warm, sudsy water. But not now. There were too many things to be done.

She washed and changed clothes and then set to work making breakfast. The aroma of strong coffee filled the cabin. Random was still chopping wood. She opened the cabin door and carried a mug of coffee out to him. He glanced at her and set the ax aside, the same ax she had used yesterday by the river to destroy Daniel's Long Tom. She looked past him to the grave, now covered by snow, the cross not even visible after last night's storm. Random took the coffee, and she looked up at him again.

"Thanks," he murmured, sipping the scalding brew. He looked at her and then away.

"Don't we have enough wood already?" she asked tentatively.

"I thought I could use the exercise," he said, his tone reminding her of the reason he had left the cabin so abruptly. Color flooded her cheeks, and she smiled slightly.

Moira looked up toward the mountains. "I don't believe Jack is up there."

Random sipped his coffee, looking at her over the rim. "Why have you changed your mind?"

She looked at him, eyes wide with pain. "Because, if he's up there still, he'll die. And I don't want to even think about losing another brother."

Random tossed the rest of the coffee away. "You said Jack came west by wagon train. He learned a lot about the country on that journey, Moira. He worked for Sutter at New Helvetia and acquainted himself with the land there. He's lived on his own for several years. He knows California. If he's up there, he'll survive. He knew what he was doing when he headed that way. It's just a feeling I have, Moira, but he had a reason for going up the Yuba with those two men on his trail. Maybe to throw them off or lead them into a trap. I don't know. But I'm sure he knew exactly what he was doing."

She wanted so desperately to believe that. It sounded like Jack. He had always thought things out. He hadn't been the impetuous boy that Daniel had been. Even his reasons for coming west had been logical and reasonable. As far as she knew them. "But how do we find him?"

"I don't know," he told her bluntly. "If he doesn't come back this way, if he goes across the mountains or doubles back another way . . . I just don't know, Moira. Maybe we won't find him. But even if we knew exactly where he was right now, we still couldn't get to him. We're just going to have to sit tight until spring."

Moira moved closer, reaching out to touch him. She placed the palm of her hand against his chest, feeling the hard strength and comforting warmth. "I'm . . . I'm very glad you're here with me," she said, her eyes softening as they met his, telling him far more than she wanted him to know. His darkened to blackness, and a muscle tightened in his jaw.

"It'd be pretty damned lonely up here if I weren't," he said grimly. Then he raised his hand, his fingers lightly tracing her cheekbone, trailing down and finally caressing the full vulnerable curves of her lips. "I'm going to keep you safe, Moira," he said huskily. "I promise you that. Only"—he smiled lop-sidedly, eyes faintly teasing—"I don't think I can stand sleeping on that bunk with you again."

Moira flushed and then gave him a mischievous smile. "I thought you were utterly immune to my charms, Mr. Hawthorne."

"Not quite," he said. His hand had come to rest on her shoulder and he dropped it, aware of what his touch was doing to them both. He picked up the ax and went back to work. Moira watched him for a long moment and then slowly walked back to the cabin.

Chapter Twenty-one

Sitting on a rock amid the trees above the river, Moira looked at the whitened landscape. It was quiet, unnervingly quiet. She wished Random had stayed around this morning. Her mind was full of Barilovich and Heaton and she felt dangerously alone, though reason told her they wouldn't come back up now that the snows had come.

Random frequently went off on long walks in the forest, telling her that if she needed him she was to fire the pistol once. He wouldn't be so far away that he couldn't hear that. She badly wanted to fire that gun now and bring him back to her. But what possible reason could she use when he did return? That she was lonely? That she just wanted him to sit on this rock with her? That she needed his presence even though he seemed loath to stay for any length of time with her?

They spoke little when they were together. His silences seemed to stretch longer and longer, and he hardly looked at her. She had tried to draw him into conversation, and he had answered her and been polite as always, but he wasn't interested in light talk to while away the time. He always seemed to be working, chopping wood, hunting, whittling utensils and plates and bowls for the cabin. He seemed always too busy to notice her.

It hurt, for she was all too damnably aware of him, and she relished his company, even when he said nothing and didn't seem to know she existed. She loved to look at him, though she did so furtively. She was glad of his presence, even though his thoughts were obviously elsewhere most of the time.

Moira had begun to be piqued by his coolness. They were alone up here in the Sierra Nevada wilds, and he seemed to care less that she was the only female within miles. He might as well have been bunking with another man for all the attention he had shown her lately. He carried on mild, general conversations with her during the evenings, then, he would lie on his bunk, say a curt good-night, and turn his back to her.

She had difficulty sleeping. She would find herself looking at that broad expanse of back, the long, well-muscled legs, the firm buttocks, and think the most improper thoughts.

Moira always needed something to keep her active—some plan, some mischief to keep her mind occupied. And now was no different. In fact, now it was even more important. She couldn't allow herself to dwell on Daniel's death, for she would become too depressed. She couldn't think of him without tears and that hard, painful, choking sensation in her chest. She tried to think only of the good times, the happy escapades they had shared, the tender, brotherly moments, and to forget the turmoil and bitter arguments of the past months. Yet it was an uphill battle, and Random's long absences didn't help.

She decided to wage a campaign against Random Hawthorne, to make him fully, uncomfortably aware that she was a woman and not to be ignored. She began by taking Daniel's shirts and dungarees apart and working on a dress like the ones she had worn in Charleston. It was slow, tedious work, because she lacked experience. She kept it hidden when Random was around, but had a goodly part of each day to work on it when he was gone. She experimented with her hair, trying different styles, brushing it to a high sheen. And all the while she plotted against him.

Moira finished the dress early one morning while he was out and decided this was the day to set her plan into action. He had taken the rifle with him, intending to hunt. She thought he would probably be gone for two hours, and that gave her enough time to set the scene for teaching him a lesson about ignoring women.

She toted buckets of snow inside and melted them in the great pot over the fire. Then, bucket by bucket, she filled the tub to the right depth. She put up a curtain of blankets around it. Finally, she stripped off her men's clothes and sank with a sigh of pure pleasure into the warm water and leaned back for a long soak, sure that Random would be returning shortly.

A sharp, single rap at the door announced Random's return from hunting. He had done that since the beginning, a gesture of politeness that Moira had always appreciated. She smiled and said absolutely nothing as he walked in. His time had come, and she was going to make him squirm!

She heard him stop just inside the door and could almost feel his eyes on the curtains that hid her. Trusting him implicitly, she was not the least bit worried by the situation and was, in fact, enjoying his discomfort immensely, for she could sense it without even seeing him.

"Why didn't you tell me you were taking a bath?"

"You don't have to leave," she said sweetly from behind the curtain, hearing him move back toward the door. Her grin widened. With an effort, she kept her voice neutral. "I'll be finished in a few minutes. I know it's very cold out there and was snowing just a little while ago. You can't see anything, so just stay inside where it's . . . warm."

"Hell," he muttered in a low voice she wasn't supposed to hear. He set the rifle in the mount over the fireplace, and she heard his restless poking at the burning log.

"Disappointed you can't see anything?" she teased lightly. She could almost feel his discomfort, gentleman that he was. But he deserved to feel uncomfortable after so many days of practically ignoring her very existence. Eager to get on with her plan, she scrubbed herself vigorously. She heard him swear again and begin pacing like a nervous cat.

"Would you like to join me?" she called innocently.

"Don't tempt me," he snapped. He shoved something into the fire, and Moira heard a burst of sparks. The cabin was getting warmer. Hot, in fact.

Finishing, Moira picked up the bucket of warm water beside

the tub and poured it over herself before stepping out onto the cold planks to dry off. "It felt so good to rub away all that dirt," she said in a husky, seductive voice, toweling herself off with one of her men's shirts. "I'll warm some fresh water for you, Rand," she offered. "You haven't enjoyed this tub yet either, and I can tell you, it's pure, unadulterated heaven," she purred.

"I could use a bath," he agreed flatly. "I smell like . . ."

"Like what?" she asked sweetly.

"You ought to know, living in close quarters with me."

She grinned and pitched her voice low as she spoke. "The way you smell has never bothered me," she said, which was very true. "In fact, I rather like the way you smell."

She almost laughed out loud at the silence that followed that statement. She put on her lawn pantaloons and soft silk camisole. Then she pulled on her Sierra creation, the dress made of checked wool and blue and brown dungaree material. A wide, neat leather belt cinched her waist. It looked very nice, even if it wasn't made of the best materials. She brushed her hair and shook her head to fluff it about her shoulders. She added the final touch, perfume from the precious vial she had saved and kept deep in her pack. She assumed an expression of innocence, then parted the curtains and stepped out.

There was a definite span of time before he spoke. "What in hell do you think you're playing at?"

"What's the matter?" she asked, pouting. "I thought you'd be pleased to see me . . . out of pants."

A faint flush rose to his face, and his eyes blazed. "Like it? I don't need any damned reminders that you're a woman."

"No?" she said, her brows rising fractionally. "Well, that's nice to know." She smiled up him. "I didn't think you'd noticed enough recently." Continuing in a soft tone, she said, "Now, if you'll just get rid of that dirty water, I'll begin on yours." She walked over to him, moving sinuously. His eyes widened in surprise.

"My God! You're even wearing perfume!"

She leaned toward him, lowering her eyelids. "L'amour Toujours," she whispered in a deliberately husky, suggestive manner that made him narrow his dark eyes again. She restrained another grin. "Isn't that wicked, Rand?" she asked innocently. "Aunt Mandy would have had the vapors to know I'd even known of such a brew, let alone possessed a whole vial of it. The woman I purchased it from claimed it makes men wildly passionate." She parted her lips slightly and looked up at him, tongue lightly touching the edge of her teeth. "Do *you* like it, Rand?"

He didn't answer, but he was looking at her with a perplexed and less-than-pleased expression on his face.

"I've had it all along," she went on, turning away and then glancing back at him over her shoulder in a provocative manner that tightened his mouth to a firm, hard line. "Hidden in my pack, just waiting to be put to good use. But I only put a little bit here"—she turned back to him, touching her neck—"and here." She smiled, trailing her fingers down over her breasts.

"Well, you can just put it away again," he said tightly. "It's wasted up here."

She put her hands lightly on her hips, moving them the way she remembered Monique Beaupré doing on the ship before jolly, drunk old King Neptune. "Oh, I wouldn't say that."

His face darkened in anger. "Damn it, Moira. This is hardly the time or place for a—"

"You look positively worried, Random." She moved toward him slowly, the sway of her hips pronounced, and reached up to finger the buttons of his shirt front. "What do you think I want to do to you?"

He shoved her hand away abruptly. She laughed then in spite of her resolve. "Are you actually blushing, Random Hawthorne?"

"Now look!" he exploded.

"Surely a big man like you isn't afraid of little old me, are you? I'm perfectly innocent. Never been touched by man nor beast." She gave him a bawdy wink.

But she had pushed Random too far. He picked her up, shoved her through the curtain of blankets, and dumped her unceremoniously into the cold bathwater.

"Cool off!" he told her grimly. She sputtered and then screamed, laughter having turned to rage. Random stood for a moment looking at her, hands on his hips, legs spread, and

then he seemed to see the humor in the situtation at last. He
laughed and laughed. She grabbed the sides of the tub and
pushed herself up into a standing position, tears of fury brightening her dark eyes.

She punched him hard in the chest, and he laughed harder.
He blocked the punch she aimed at his nose and with a firm
hand on her head forced her back into the tub again.

"What's the matter? I thought you said the bath was *heavenly*."

"If you've ruined my dress, I'm going to take some of *your*
shirts apart and make another."

He pulled her up out of the tub and set her on her feet,
grinning at her furious face. "I suggest you dry off and get
your *pants* back on again."

Her chin tipped up. She looked at him defiantly. "I'll dry
off, and then I'll hang my dress in front of the fire and sit there
naked waiting for it to dry!"

The wet material clung to her body, the chill hardening her
nipples. Random had noticed, and some of the laughter had
gone out of his face. He picked up the shirt she had worn
before and shoved it rudely at her.

"Oh no, you won't," he said flatly. "You'll do just as I
said."

"If you don't like it, Mr. Random Hawthorne, you can just
go outside and freeze your . . . your . . ." She cleared her throat.
". . . Yourself to death," she finished lamely, not having the
courage to say what she really wanted frozen.

His mouth twitched. Some devilment had lightened the darkness of his eyes. He reached out to finger the buttons on her
soaking dress as she had fingered the buttons on his shirt a few
minutes before. "Maybe I can help you get this thing off." He
unlooped the top two before she slapped his hands away, face
flaming with indignation.

"Keep your hands to yourself."

"Now, just a few minutes ago I was getting a definite message from you that you'd welcome my hands on you . . . and
anywhere I happened to want to put them." He leaned toward
her, smiling slowly. "You even asked me what I wanted you
to do to me," he said huskily. "Well, I could tell you,
Moira . . . in detail. And I could show you, too."

Her face was burning. He was turning her joke around, damn his hide.

"I was only teasing."

He smiled slowly, tauntingly. "What I want you can't give me with all these clothes on you," he whispered, moving closer. He wasn't actually touching her, but she felt as though he was, and her heart thumped against her chest.

"I was only teasing!" she said loudly and gave him a shove backward. She felt only the solidity of his chest. He straightened and looked down on her, no longer laughing or smiling.

"I'd like to know why you felt you had to go to such lengths!"

"You've been ignoring me for days," she said sharply. "I wanted to get even for the way you've hardly said a word, the way you've gone off by yourself for hours on end, and practically engraved on my forehead what a dull, poor companion you're stuck with for the winter!"

He gave a harsh, humorless laugh. "If you had any sense at all, you'd know why I've been going off for those long walks in the cold!"

"Oh, I know, all right!" she fumed up at him, dabbing herself dry with the shirt. "To get away from me, that's why! You've made that perfectly obvious!"

He muttered something violent under his breath as he rubbed his neck in angry frustration. "To be truthful, yes! I was getting the hell away from you!" he growled at her. "But not for the reason you think. It was either go out and walk, or chop wood, or freeze myself to numbness, or . . . or, . . . Damn it, Moira, I'm a man. And you're too damned desirable for your own good." The last words were said as a harsh, flat statement.

Her eyes widened in disbelief. "You're trying to convince me you've been ignoring me because you find me *attractive?* And they say women are illogical!"

He let out an exasperated breath. "Well, what in hell do you think I feel, shut up in this damn cabin with you barely six feet away?"

"Well, I find it hard to think that, that's for sure," she retorted. "And since it's just the fact that you're 'shut up with me,' I'm not to mistake this grand passion of yours for anything other than unfortunate proximity. *Any* woman would bother you! After all, men do get these nasty little urges, don't they?"

"You're treading on mighty thin ice," he said between his teeth.

"I'm supposed to be flattered, I suppose, that you think I'm desirable, simply because I happen to be the only female within a hundred miles of here. Well, thanks very much, Mr. Hawthorne. You've made me feel wonderful!"

"Apparently you've never gotten any kind of message from me at all! You seem to have forgotten my kisses entirely!"

"Weren't they intended to shut me up?" she replied, eyes sparkling as she gave him a bald grin. "Try it again."

"Don't go flinging me any provocative challenges, Moira. I'm churned up enough now to curdle from your little performance a while ago. And one kiss could lead to . . . to a multitude of other things. And you, Moira Cavendish, might just find yourself spending the winter in that bunk over there with your legs spread."

She gasped, afronted. "Don't be crude!"

"Crude?" He gave a sharp, angry laugh. "I'd say I was being plain frank!"

"Well, you needn't be quite that frank!" She was blushing again.

"I wanted to get my point across to you, and you didn't seem to be hearing anything I was saying!"

"So go back to being your unsociable self. I don't care!" she cried. Then she sat down on the bunk with a thump. He sat down slowly on his and stared at her. Moira looked over at him.

"Couldn't we compromise?" she suggested.

"Compromise? How do you compromise in a situation like this?"

"If you won't ignore me, and if you'll take me with you on your walks, I promise not to . . . flirt with you." Color came up into her cheeks again. "We could try to entertain one another a little for the next few months."

"It's thoughts of entertaining one another that are causing me to sweat buckets now," he muttered grimly, and she started to laugh. "It's not funny, Moira."

She sighed and gave a faint shrug. "Well, I'm hardly immune to your attractions, Mr. Hawthorne," she told him impishly, "though I'm sure that is highly improper to admit. We'll just have to contain our lust for one another and behave in a civilized manner, now, won't we?"

He gave her a wry look. "You know . . . you've given me one hell of a pain in a certain part of my anatomy."

"Your neck?"

"Lower."

"Well, Jewel would have told you to go out and dip it in the snow."

He chuckled. "I knew it was a mistake putting you in with her. You learned too damn much coming to California."

"Daniel said the same thing."

She now felt remorse for having been so forward. Things were difficult enough up in these cold mountains without her throwing herself at Random. But it was hard to ignore her constant, throbbing awareness of him. She looked up at Random through her lashes. How could she possibly make him understand without also making him think her an utter fool?

"I get so lonely," she told him huskily. "When you're gone, I imagine all sorts of things happening to you. I don't know what I'd do up here without you."

He smiled slightly. "Well, I'm glad to know I've finally made myself indispensable to you."

She laughed faintly and looked squarely at him. "Utterly."

His eyes darkened. Her heart began to pound.

"If I promise solemnly not to pester you, will you stay here in the cabin more?"

"Being in here with you more often could prove dangerous."

Sensations were spiraling through her. Her lips curved faintly. "I'll take the risk."

She saw the blaze in his eyes before he banked it again. He squeezed her shoulder. "Get out of your wet clothes and sit by the fire. We've some serious talking to do."

Back in her dungarees and wool shirt, Moira sat cross-legged on the floor. Random prodded the logs and then sat on the floor as well, his back against the fireplace, legs stretched out in front of him. He looked at her, and she felt suddenly uneasy.

He put his head back, his face taut.

"What is it, Random?" she asked, worried.

He sighed. "I should have told you this long ago," he said

heavily, looking at her steadily. She waited, knowing that whatever he was about to say would affect her greatly.

"Moira, I'm married."

Her face went deathly white. Her eyes widened in shock. She felt a pain so intense she could hardly breathe. He looked at her, and she saw the pain reflected clearly in his own face.

"I should have told you sooner. . . ."

"Married . . ." she murmured hoarsely and gave him a weak, self-mocking smile. "I should have known a man like you would be."

He leaned forward slowly, face drawn, eyes intent. "Moira . . ."

"The blond lady in Charleston?" she managed, past the thick lump in her throat.

"Blond?"

"I saw you with her at the opera. She's very beautiful." His wife would have to be.

"You mean Clarissa," he said thoughtfully. "No. She's not my wife."

"No?" Her eyes went wide.

His face tightened. "She's just someone I . . . saw when I was in port," he told her flatly.

Everything inside her went still. "You mean you slept with her?" she muttered faintly.

"Yes."

"Oh." She closed her eyes for a moment and then opened them to look at him again, frowning. "You aren't the proverbial sailor with a woman in every port, are you, Random?"

His mouth had a faintly cynical twist. "There have been a lot of women in my life, yes."

"And does your wife know?"

"Probably. She wouldn't care if she did. She's gotten everything she wanted anyway." His voice was hard, bitter.

"I . . . I don't understand."

He let out a long, weary breath and leaned back. He drew his legs up and rested his forearms on them. He was pale, and there was a hard, cold look on his face that was different from any expression she had seen before.

"Laura is a few years older than me," he told her. "I met her when I was a very gullible nineteen. She was . . . hell, to be blunt, she was very good in bed, and at that time, I couldn't think past that fact."

Moira put a shaking hand over her face. "I don't think I want to hear anymore."

"No. I don't expect you do. And believe me, Moira, I wish to hell I didn't have to admit to you what a blind, stupid fool I was!" He sighed harshly and rubbed the back of his neck.

"I married Laura because she said she was pregnant with my child."

"Random, you don't owe me any explanations."

"Just listen to me, Moira," he told her hoarsely, eyes bleak. She looked at him, biting down hard on her lip. She nodded slowly. He frowned. "I never meant to hurt you. Believe that."

Her eyes filled, and she fought the tears down. "I know."

He didn't say anything for a moment, and then he continued in a low, taut voice. "I'd been to sea for three months. When I came back, I went to Laura. She told me straightaway she was pregnant. I didn't question her, but I was pretty stunned. I hadn't thought of the possibility."

"No?" She was surprised at that.

"Christ..." he muttered, raking fingers back through his hair. "I get mad every time I think about this."

"What?"

He looked at her, the lines about his mouth deep. "Laura was...sophisticated. I was under the impression...even as green as I was...that she was taking care of things so the eventuality wouldn't arise."

Moira stared at him. "Is that possible?" she couldn't resist asking.

"There are ways," he said flatly.

"What ways?" She leaned forward, curious.

"Abstinance during certain times of a woman's monthly cycle. Withdrawal. A silver half-dollar inserted in—hell." He stopped. She saw a faint flush of red spread across his face. "I didn't start this conversation to teach you how not to get pregnant, Moira."

She smiled faintly. "No. But you never know when such information might come in handy."

Random's face darkened ominously. "I don't find that one bit funny."

She thought of how many times he might have told her about his wife and hadn't. She lifted her chin, meeting his gaze squarely. "What makes you think I meant it to be?" Something flickered across his face that made her wish she could take the words back. She regretted her impulse to strike out at him. Her face softened apologetically. "You were telling me about your wife and baby."

"Maybe we ought to leave it for another time."

"Rand . . . please . . . I'm sorry . . ."

She saw his chest rise as he took a long, deep breath before going on. "The baby was born six weeks before it should have been if it had been mine. When I questioned her about it, she broke down and admitted that it had been someone else . . . some adventurer she'd been in love with and who'd run out on her again."

"Oh, Rand . . ."

"I took her back to the family farm, and we tried to make a go of the marriage for about two years. Then I went back to sea. My parents had died by that time, and I made all the necessary arrangements for someone to work the farm for her. A couple from New York. I came back a year later and found Laura sleeping with him. . . . His wife had gone back to her people. I left, and I haven't been back since."

Moira felt sick. She looked at him and felt overwhelmed with her desire to reach out to him. She leaned forward and saw him stiffen.

"I don't want your pity, Moira," he told her angrily.

She wove her fingers together, staring down at them. Finally, she managed to ask him what was troubling her. "Why didn't you divorce her?"

Random didn't answer for so long, Moira glanced up at him. His expression had hardened, and his eyes were distant.

"Random?"

He gave a harsh laugh. "I decided all women were alike, and there was no reason to go to the trouble and expense of ridding myself of a wife that gave me a certain degree of protection against other women like her. A man can only have one wife. Since I'd no intention of ever getting involved with a woman again, save on a physical level . . ." He shrugged. He looked at her intently. "In my own defense, I limited my affairs to women who understood that everything ended when I walked out their door." His mouth tightened. "It's never been my practice to seduce virgins."

She already knew that much about him. Her cheeks grew hot, and she gave him a self-mocking smile. "Even when they're more than willing," she agreed.

"Even when they're more than willing."

"Have there been a lot of us?" She smiled more lightly.

"A few, but you're the only one that's ever given me so many bad moments."

"Bad moments?"

"Hellish ones. You've a way of looking at a man..." He shook his head, his smile wry. "I knew you were serious trouble that first day I took you to your cabin."

"You've always been cool and in complete command of yourself."

He laughed. "I haven't been in command of myself since I first laid eyes on you." His eyes darkened. "You make the devil's brew with a man's insides, Moira. You knew exactly what you were doing to me a while ago, and I've seen others suffer agonies over you as well. That young pup, Kris what's-his-name, for example. And I had to threaten Ole Peterson with keelhauling if he put his hands on you again."

"Kris and Ole were always perfect gentlemen," she said in their defense. "And I don't think I like that 'devil's brew' reference."

His eyes softened in amusement. "I'll bet you had all the young men madly in love with you back in Charleston."

"Dozens of them," she quipped.

"Most girls are married by your *advanced* age."

"I'm not 'most girls'."

He grinned. "On that I can agree."

She stiffened. "I've never encouraged any serious involvements."

He laughed outright. "What's that supposed to mean? That you encourage the pleasures without the commitment?"

"I do not!"

His smile was sardonic. "The truth is, you're a tease, Moira Cavendish."

She raised a brow at him, eyes twinkling. "Would you have

it another way, Mr. Hawthorne?"

"If things were different, I've have you every way there is," he told her, and her face flamed.

"Rogue."

"Take the warning."

She sighed. "I suppose I *should* be thankful that you're not a man to take advantage of a situation or a girl's . . . inexperience," she said.

Their eyes met and held. The silence lengthened. There was no laughter in either of them. Moira's lips parted in a silent intake of breath as heat filled her body. Her eyes widened and deepened almost to black, and a faint flush stained her cheeks. She saw the muscle tightening in his jaw, and his face grow pale and tense. The most private places of her body began to tingle with instinctive awareness, and she trembled slightly.

"Sometimes it's very hard to remember all those clear-cut morals my aunt drummed into my head back in Charleston," she said huskily. His eyes burned over her.

"You're worth more than an affair," he told her harshly. She saw his hand curl, the knuckles showing white. She ached inside, and the cabin seemed far too close and warm.

"You shouldn't have told me so much about your wife."

"Why not?" He frowned, not understanding.

"If I thought you were in love with her, she'd have made a much better shield."

He froze, his eyes hot. She saw the rapid pulse in his temple and knew what she was doing to him.

"I'm not going to make love to you," he told her.

Tears stung her eyelids. "Because I'm a virgin? It's a curable disease, I've been told. And once done, would my not being a virgin make me different . . . less valuable as a person?"

"I couldn't make love to you just once," he told her, and she heard the tremor in his deepened voice. "I wouldn't be able to let you off that damn bunk for days . . . and there wouldn't be any question as to whose baby you'd be carrying."

Her body felt like molten fire. She could feel the blood surging through her veins, swelling her breasts, swirling down into the depths of her womanness, turning her liquid with readiness.

"And I couldn't marry you." His words dropped like stones in the cabin."

"Random, I—"

He stood up abruptly. "That's enough, Moira." He turned toward the door. It was dark outside.

"Where are you going?" she asked in alarm.

"To get some venison for a stew," he told her and went out. The meat was stored deep in a snowbank close to the cabin, but it was a long time before he came back in. She was still sitting forlornly by the fire. She looked up at him apologetically. He gave her a gentle smile, but said nothing.

Hunkering down, he pulled the pot across the rod, positioning it over the hot glowing coals, and tossed in chunks of meat. She took the knife from his hand and turned the meat, browning it before dipping the ladle into the water bucket and pouring it into the pot.

Random hadn't moved away. He was still very close to her. She turned her head slightly and looked at him shyly, a faint flush in her cheeks.

"God...Moira..." he whispered, and her lips parted as his head slowly descended toward hers.

There was a high-pitched scream from outside. Random straightened with a sharp, swift jerk.

"What was that?" Moira gasped, eyes wide and frightened.

The scream came again, louder, closer. Moira heard the horses' high, terrified whinnying. Random grabbed the rifle from its mount above the fireplace. In two long steps he was at the door. He swung it open, letting in a blast of icy air. Moira stood up and moved toward him. He turned back abruptly.

"Stay inside."

"But..."

"Stay inside!"

Another scream pierced the cold night air, and Random was running, cocking the rifle as he went.

Chapter Twenty-two

"What are they?" Moira asked, bending down to look at what Random was studying. A half mile northeast of the cabin, Random had found something in the snow. He straightened and looked around grimly.

"Puma tracks."

"Puma?"

"A mountain lion."

"Is that what killed the horse last night?" she asked, standing up to look at him in wide-eyed concern. He glanced at her.

"Just calm down."

"Calm down? But those footprints are so big! Are you sure they're not a bear's?"

"Would it make a difference?"

"Well, bears are herbivores, you told me. Now, a lion..."

"Definitely a carnivore, as he's already proven," Random said. "Most bears are deep in hibernation right now."

Moira looked around, half expecting the puma to come leaping out of the thick woods. "Do you think he's going to come back?"

"Pretty good chance he will," he said, shouldering his rifle. "I only winged him."

"Well, what do we do?"

"We?" He grinned at her. "Ready to jump right into deep water again, aren't you? What did you have in mind for *us* to do?"

"I don't know. You tell me."

He started to walk back toward the cabin. "We wait and watch, and if he comes around again, we do our best to kill him." Moira fell into step beside him. He was walking rapidly, and she had to stretch out her legs just to keep pace with him in the deep snow. It didn't take long for her to become exhausted with the effort. She was puffing hard. Finally, necessity overtaking pride, she reached out and grabbed his arm. "Slow down, Random. Your legs are a lot longer than mine."

He stopped and gave her an apologetic smile. "You're out of shape."

She gave him a grimace. "Thanks."

"On second thought, I can't really tell." He grinned, looking her over again. The heavy jacket and hood obscured her figure.

"Go on," she said, gesturing. "I've got my breath back now." He gave a laugh and took a couple of steps away from her. She reached down and scooped up some snow and packed it into a firm ball. When he noticed she wasn't beside him, he turned, and she hit him squarely in the chest. He jerked backward in surprise and then gave her a threatening look as he dusted himself off.

"You asked for it," she said, laughing. "I was aiming for your head!"

He bent down, and she gave a shriek of playful laughter as she headed for the cover of trees, ducking behind one just in time as a snowball burst on the trunk. She stuck her tongue out at him.

"Terrible shot, Random. Really poor. No wonder we haven't had any fresh meat lately!" she taunted while she hastily made an armory of snowballs.

"Come on out, you little coward!"

"I'm not stupid! Now, you, on the other hand . . . just standing there," she said and let fly another snowball as he bent to scoop up some snow. She made a perfect hit. He shook his head to get the snow out of his ear. Then he apparently decided against the flinging match and came after her.

"No fair!" she shouted and started to run. He tackled her

before she had gone ten feet and shoved a handful of snow down the back of her coat. He released her and she sat up, laughing and pulling at her coat to get the snow to drop through, shivering. Random stood above her, grinning.

"You did start it," he told her.

"You don't play by the rules!"

"Rules! Haven't you ever heard 'All's fair in love and war'?" He laughed. "Well, it's war, Moira. You declared it on me. Don't go complaining because you're losing!"

"All right. Truce." She raised a hand. "I know when the enemy has conquered me." He reached down and hauled her up. As he was turning away, she bent quickly and grabbed his boot. He barely managed to catch himself, and by the time he had straightened Moira was already running downhill toward the cabin. He caught her and pushed her down, pinning her to the ground as he dumped handful after handful of snow on her writhing, laughing form. Then he let her go.

"Now behave!"

She wiped the snow off, feeling its chill almost freezing her skin. But she was light-headed from the physical activity so long denied her. "We'll call it a standoff," she grinned.

"A standoff? Why, you . . ." He made another grab for her, and she jumped back and started running again. She could hear him coming and tried darting back and forth. She felt his fingers touching her coat hood and turned sharply to one side. She stumbled, and Random crashed into her, sending her flying forward. She came down hard on something hidden beneath the snow, it striking the side of her head. She lay there stunned, gasping for breath.

"Moira, are you all right? Damn it, enough fooling around!" He turned her over gently, his face pale and tense.

She sat up with his assistance and nodded. "In a minute," she muttered, still seeing spots in front of her eyes. He pushed the hair back from her face and saw a lump already growing.

"Are you sure you're all right?"

"What did I hit anyway? A rock?" She looked over at the shape beneath the snow, and her heart and breathing stopped. "Oh, God . . ."

The snow had made the body look like just another lump on the hillside. But where Moira had landed, she saw a patch of heavy brown wool and buttons. She lunged toward it and began uncovering the dead man's face.

Random stared at her for a split second, aghast at what she was doing, before he reacted and yanked her back. "Don't, for God's sake, Moira."

"Jack!" she cried, jerking away from him and lunging back toward the frozen body in the snow. "It might be Jack! Oh, God, no!" She cleared the snow from the man's face, and a harsh sob rose in her throat. She sank back with a thud, eyes shut tightly. She swallowed hard, feeling her stomach rising.

"Is it?" Random asked, his hand hard on her shoulder. She shook her head. The man had dark hair and a thin, aquiline face. His mouth was slightly ajar, dead eyes open and almost picked clean by some scavenger. Something had begun to eat away his cheeks and lips, and the result was a grotesque grin.

"Moira, go on back to the cabin and let me take care of this," Random ordered as she turned away, pale and shaken.

"I'll . . . I'll help you," she murmured thickly.

"Do as I say just once, damn it!" he growled, pulling her to her feet. Her head spun dizzily. Seeing the pallor of her face, Random let out his breath and pulled her forward against him. "I'm sorry. Damn it, I'm sorry, Moira." She leaned against him, tightly grasping his thick coat.

"I'm . . . I'm afraid I'm going to be sick," she admitted miserably and pushed away from him. She stumbled over to a tree and put her arm around it to steady herself as she vomited. A moment later, she walked a few feet away and sank down into the white snow, picking some of it up and rubbing it over her face.

"I'll wait for you here, Random," she said faintly, keeping her face averted as he went back to the body and uncovered the rest of it. After a few minutes he came back and gestured for her to go on down the hill. She entered the cabin and sank down on the bunk, still feeling faint and ill. She tried to block out the man's face, half devoured, staring and grinning at her, but failed. She should have listened to Random and not looked. All he would have needed to know was that Jack was blond.

"I'll be back as soon as I can," Random said, grabbing the pick and shovel to dig a grave. Moira made no offer to help. She nodded solemnly and watched him close the door. It was almost two hours before he came back. He looked half frozen and exhausted. His face was taut, and he didn't look at her.

Moira had coffee waiting and a tub of warm water. He said nothing as she pressed a mug of the hot brew into his chilled hands. He took a sip and looked up at her with surprise.

"I thought a little brandy might thaw you." She smiled gently. She had known he kept it in his pack for medicinal purposes. She thought that this was one of those times when a little brandy would do a lot of good. Random said nothing, but finished the coffee. She stood in front of him and began unbuttoning his heavy coat.

"What are you doing?"

"I have the tub full of hot water for you," she said. She could tell he didn't want to touch her and she understood why. It had taken quite a washing for her to get the feel of death off her.

"I'll do it," he said grimly. She moved away. He got up wearily and went behind the blanket barrier. She heard him stripping off his clothes and then stepping into the tub. He scrubbed for some time.

"There are some clean clothes hanging on the hook, Random," she told him, bending before the fire to stir the pork and beans. She wondered if he would be hungry. She wasn't.

He came out a few minutes later, dragged the tub outside, and dumped the water, then put his dirty clothes in a heap in the tub for later washing. He sat on the bunk and watched her.

"I'm sorry you had to see that," he said flatly.

She didn't say anything for a moment. "How did he die?" she managed finally, her voice choking.

"Can't tell for sure," he said, then stopped. She closed her eyes, sure of what he meant by that. The animals had already been hard at work on the body, making it next to impossible to surmise the cause of death. What was death to one animal meant life to another. It was how nature worked.

She heard him move restlessly, and she tried not to think about her churning stomach.

"He looked emaciated," he began again. "I'd guess he was starving and collapsed from the cold."

Moira put a shaking hand up to her eyes. "Another two hundred yards and he would have seen our cabin." She turned slowly to look at Random, whose face was lined with tension. "I wonder who he was? We can't even notify his family."

Random looked at her. "Jass Whitsell."

Her eyes opened very wide. "Jass Whitsell!" she exclaimed. "But he was following Jack! How do you know it was him?"

Random reached into his pocket and extracted a frayed envelope with some writing on it. Moira jumped up and snatched it from him, staring at it. It was addressed to Jass Whitsell, New Helvetia, California, and had been sent from New Hampshire in early February of 1849. From the markings on it, it had come around the Horn.

Moira quickly opened the worn sheet and read it.

> February 4, 1849
> Meadow Haven, N.H.

My beloved Jass:

You have been gone from me too long, and I have begun to fear that you have forgotten me entirely. Do you remember what you said to me the day you left? You promised you would love me always and come back soon very rich, so that Father would approve our union without a single reservation. Unless you hurry, my love, no amount of gold will undo the tie that Father will use to bind me to Franklin.

He came to call the same day you left me and spoke for some time with Father in the library. I know not of what they spoke but can well guess. He has come often since, and with Father's blessing. I have managed thus far to keep my promise to you, but Father has become increasingly difficult. The merest mention of your name sends him into a terrible rage. Please, Jass, come home to me before it is too late.

I care nothing about the gold. Is it so important? If you were here, I would defy God Himself to go away with you. Father does not understand that I would rather die than be wife to any other man but you, my beloved.

Your last letter made so little sense to me. Who is Jack Cavendish, of whom you speak so much? Why must you find him again? And I do not understand what you mean by "the source of all California riches." Is this man and this source so important that you must delay coming back to me?

I must end this letter, my darling. Chester leaves today for California by way of the Horn. He is the only friend I can trust and will bring this to you without fail. Everyone else is afraid of Father and tells him of my every word and deed.

Please, my love, I beg of you. Come back to me soon. I am so desperately unhappy without you.

Yours forever,
Mary

Moira refolded the letter slowly and put it back in its envelope. She sat down on her bunk and began to cry softly, the frayed envelope clutched in her hand.

"What do we do now, Random? What do we do?" she asked, her voice quavering.

"We sit and wait," he said flatly. "And if Jack doesn't come out of the mountains, we go back to Sutter's Fort in the spring and see if we can find this Chester."

"But we don't even know his last name," she said dismally. She looked at the letter again. "And what do we do about . . . Mary?"

"Write to her and tell her that Jass Whitsell died in early December of 1849 just south of Haskell Peak," he told her. "She doesn't need to know anything more than that."

Moira drew back her head and looked at him tearfully. "She needs to know that he was still carrying her letter with him and that it was worn out with reading," she said tremulously. "She needs to know that. A woman wants to know if she's loved. She'll want to know he still loved her enough to read that letter over and over until the paper was almost worn out." She closed her eyes, seeing a mental image of the young girl who longed so desperately for her Jass to come home and take her away from a domineering father determined to marry her to a man she didn't love. And she kept seeing the man on the hillside, half eaten by animals and birds, a man who would have been a nameless skeleton by spring had she not fallen over him while playing with Random in the snow.

Now she would have to write to this Mary and tell her that Jass would not be coming home for her, not ever, and that she would have to do as her father wanted.

"I hate it!" Moira cried. "I hate it!" She dropped the letter and hunched her shoulders, crying into the palms of her hands. Random stood up and came over to her, putting a gentle hand on her shoulder. She looked up at him almost angrily.

"How can I write and tell this girl that her Jass isn't coming back? How can I do that, Random? And she wrote that he mentioned Jack. He wrote so highly of him, they must have been friends, mustn't they? He couldn't have been bad like Barilovich and Heaton. He must have wanted to help Jack. Oh, Random, I'm so scared." She trembled, tears running down her cheeks. "Just when I think I'm getting close, when I feel we'll find him safe, then something happens! Danny's gone. And I can't lose Jack, too. I just can't!" She held tightly to Random's forearm. "Why did they ever come out here? Why couldn't they just have been satisfied with what they had?"

Random sat beside her on the edge of the bunk. "Moira, it's not the nature of a man to be satisfied if there's any chance of bettering himself."

She turned toward him, eyes flashing. "Bettering himself? Is Daniel bettering himself six feet underground? Is finding gold *bettering* yourself? How does having it make a man any better? I could name you a dozen men in Charleston, almost as rich as the Astors, living in their fine river plantations with their hundreds of slaves, and they're worthless excuses for men. Charles Beauchamp for one!" She stood up and moved with frustration and anger to the fireplace. She put her fists against the mantel. "Daniel's dead—for what? Jass Whitsell's dead—for what? For gold. It all comes back to gold." She almost spat the words.

Random moved to stand behind her. He put his hands on her shoulders and swung her sharply around to face him. "Daniel's dead because he wanted to repay your father's gambling debts and make the Cavendish name command respect again. And this Jass Whitsell wanted gold to marry his girl, Mary, and buy her father's approval."

She threw back her head, defiant in the face of his explanations. "And they're both dead now, aren't they? The Cavendish name is as black as it ever was when Daniel boarded your ship in Charleston, and Jass's Mary will spend her life with another man, a man she doesn't love but of whom her father approves. So you tell me what they accomplished by their dying, Random. Just tell me!" Her voice broke.

He looked at her with sad understanding. "Neither of them came here to die."

"But they did, didn't they? Needlessly, stupidly. Don't you see? It's all so senseless, meaningless. All these men out here grubbing around in the dirt for quick riches, making themselves sick with hunger and work, living no better than animals."

He shook her slightly. "It's not the gold. It's the dream, Moira. Some things are worth dying for. Your family name, the girl you love . . . Maybe you don't understand that, but there are some dreams worth all the risk."

"You're right," she flared. "I don't understand. I don't understand why Daniel couldn't have had his dream and his life as well. He could have, and so could Jass Whitsell. It was all right there, right in the palm of their hands, if they hadn't become so fevered, so crazy for it all at once," she went on tearfully, the pain of her brother's death reviving with the added sadness of Jass Whitsell's tragedy.

"Moira . . ."

"He's dead," she said, mouth trembling. "And so is Jass Whitsell, damn it. And he might have told us something about Jack!"

Random pulled her roughly into his arms. "I made a big mistake bringing you up here," he said hoarsely, holding her tightly against him. She could hear the hard pounding of his heart and clung to him in her grief and fear. "You were dead right when you said I could have talked you out of it," he continued huskily. "But it was too soon. I wanted more time . . ."

He stopped, and she heard his heart pounding harder and

faster. He took a shuddering breath and pushed her away slightly. She tilted her head back to search his face, her hands flat against his chest.

"Time for what, Random?"

He looked down at her, eyes dark but with an element of regret. "Moira..." He barely whispered her name as his head slowly descended. Cupping her face in his hands, he brushed her mouth gently. His eyes burned into her, making it impossible for her to move away from him.

"I want you, Moira. I have from the very first moment."

She reached up and pulled his head down, kissing him with all the innocent passion and love that had been growing in her since she had first met him aboard the ship.

"I love you...I love you..." she murmured against his mouth, and her lips parted beneath his. She could feel the tension in his body, the tight control he was exerting over himself. His hands moved up and down her back, then pushed up into her hair. His thumbs lightly traced her ears as he plumbed her mouth with his tongue. She moaned. He pulled her even closer, fitting her curves to his body, and she began to tremble with excitement and a vague fear. He made a sound deep in his throat, and his kiss became more demanding and sensual. His hands moved down over the small of her back and lower. Then his fingers curved over her hips and pushed her back.

His breathing was ragged, and his eyes were glazed. He looked at her and grimaced. "Damn, every time I touch you, I want you so badly my guts ache."

She smiled, her mouth feeling full and tender from his possession. "I love you, Random Hawthorne," she repeated more clearly than before, looking him squarely in the eye, and then seeing the sudden flare of triumph and satisfaction that admission brought him. "And...I want you in the worst way," she went on in a tortured voice. He smiled, half mocking, half tender.

"Don't you think I know that," he whispered huskily. "I've known that since we were aboard the ship. You show everything you feel, or almost everything. And whenever I've kissed you, the storm waves have come at me with drowning force."

She stepped closer to him, her face full of hectic color, her lips parted as she looked up at him pleadingly. He put his hands on her shoulders.

"No, Moira."

"Oh, Rand," she murmured, her heart and her need there for him to see. His nostrils flared and his face tensed with restrained desire. His fingers tightened on her shoulders.

"Let's talk," he suggested. She saw the pulse pounding in his temple, the beads of perspiration breaking out. She reaching up daringly and touched his face, lightly stroking her fingers down and across his lips. With an intake of breath, he closed his eyes for an instant and then opened them to stare down at her feverishly.

"I don't want to talk," she said in a low, throbbing voice. She could feel the growing heat of his body.

"Neither do I." He kissed her hard, punishingly hard. His hands tightened painfully, and she knew he was fighting himself more than her. She wrapped her arms around his waist, pressing herself against him, giving everything she had to the kiss.

"You make everything so damn hard, Moira," he rasped, his fingers trembling as they raked into her hair to draw her head back so he could look at her. He searched her face and then groaned. "Impossible, in fact." And then he was pulling her toward the bunk, drawing her down with him and stretching out beside her so that every part of their bodies was touching. And still it wasn't enough. He was vibrating, and she could feel the rapid, thundering beat of his heart against her own.

"God . . . I want to love you . . ." he rasped.

"Do it," she begged him, opening her mouth beneath the onslaught of his. She heard him groan again as he accepted her offering, almost smothering her with the power of his passion. His fingers dealt easily with the buttons of her shirt, pushing it aside to expose the full, swollen young breasts to his questing mouth. She drew her breath in sharply as he kissed, nipped, and sucked at the hardened peaks.

"Just a little . . . I'll love you just a little," he murmured against her flushed skin. "I won't take everything from you," he moaned, and she felt the last covering of civilization come off her, beneath his expert hands. She lay quivering against him, feeling the heat of his body through his clothing as she lay naked for him to see.

"Beautiful," he breathed hoarsely and worshiped her with his hands, mouth, and tongue until she twisted against him, losing her shyness and letting her hands rove possessively over him.

"Rand . . ." She could hardly breathe, her body was so filled with clammering sensations and intense heat. Her fingers sought the buckle of his belt, hanging on to it as though it was a lifeline that would help her through the sea of churning needs swelling in her awakening body. "Rand . . . please . . ."

"Shhhh." He took her wrists and drew her hands away from his pulsating body, raising himself up enough to see her flushed face and dark, smoky eyes begging him to finish what he had started. His face was a hard, chiseled mask of desire.

"I can't stand it anymore . . ." she moaned, shaking her head, the power of the new feelings bringing a sob from her throat. "Just love me . . . please . . . love me."

He released her hands, and with one hand he began to unbutton his shirt. Then he slid his hands down over her body and parted her legs so that he could kneel between them. She hadn't believed that her heart could pound any harder or faster.

She watched him strip the shirt off and toss it aside. Her gaze moved over his broad, firm, bronzed chest, covered with dark hair. He unbuttoned his pants. Her eyes widened slowly.

"Oh, God . . ."

He heard the virginal fear in her voice and leaned over her. He kissed her slowly, his lips teasing hers.

"There's nothing to be afraid of, Moira."

"I . . . I can't help it. Oh, Rand, I want you so much, but you're so—"

"Shhh . . ." He took her mouth again, slowly easing his body onto hers, keeping her legs widely spread. She was shaking. "Easy," he whispered.

He pushed himself up to look down at her. "Do you want me to stop?" She stared up at him and saw what it had cost him to even say it. She knew that whatever agonies he would suffer, if she said no he wouldn't take her.

She slid her arms around him and smoothed her hands down over the rippling, tense muscles of his back, raising her hips in an instinctive gesture of total submission. He drew in a tortured breath and then his mouth devoured hers. With one deep thrust he took her. Her body stiffened in pain, and he held her pinioned. His mouth moved from hers, kissing her eyes and then traveling to the curve of her neck.

"It hurts," she moaned.

"It won't in a minute. Try to relax." He kept kissing her, stroking her until she was the one to move beneath him.

"Oh, Rand..."

Her tone told him all he needed to know. The rhythm built slowly, gently at first, then became more demanding. When she cried out, her body arching up, her head going back, he withdrew. She felt his hands tighten painfully and heard him groan. His body was taut, and then he shook. After a moment, he relaxed against her, his head on her breast.

She stroked his hair. "Why did you leave me so quickly?" she murmured hoarsely, her voice unrecognizable to herself.

"So you wouldn't take my seed," he said with a sigh.

"But it hurt you."

"Not physically."

"Oh, Rand..." She started to cry. The aftermath of their lovemaking left her weak and yet filled with an overpowering tenderness. He raised himself up, looking at her, and his face softened. He shifted his weight so that he was beside her, and drew her tightly into his arms, kissing her gently.

"I love you, Moira Cavendish."

They remained in one another's arms for a long time. Finally, Rand drew back. He sighed heavily.

"There's more going on in this thing with your brother than we can understand," he said. She looked at him, her lethargy slipping away.

"But I thought you said Jass Whitsell died of starvation and cold. Didn't he?"

"I can't be sure."

"Do you think he was murdered?"

"I'd be making a guess. I couldn't tell much, Moira. Anything could have happened to him." His hair was disheveled. "I should have gotten you safely down to Sacramento before the snows, even if I had to drag you by the hair."

She smiled slightly. "I'm glad we stayed." She reached up

and caressed him. She loved the feel of his skin, of the hair on his chest. "Besides, Barilovich and Heaton went down-river," she muttered.

"Your brother may still be up there someplace. Or he might have gone back."

Something in his tone and the look on his face made her eyes widen in shock. "You don't think Jack killed Whitsell, do you?"

"He could have."

"You know he wouldn't!" She pushed herself up, eyes holding his.

"I don't know anything, Moira . . . and especially not concerning your brother."

"Then you can take my word for it! He wouldn't kill anyone. And besides, Jass Whitsell must have been a friend if he wrote so highly of him to this Mary."

"That letter was written almost a year ago, Moira, so Whitsell's letter to her was written at least six months before, possibly earlier than that. Eighteen months at the very least. A lot of things can change in less time than that. A man can change. Especially if he has men hunting him down like an animal."

"Barilovich and Heaton could have come back up here and killed him," she said, disturbed by what he was saying.

"They could have. But if that trail you sent them on has already been found to be a wild-goose chase, they'll want to know how you knew so much about Jack Cavendish before taking you apart limb by limb."

That prediction sent a frightened shiver down her spine. All her warmth dissipated, and she just looked at him. He frowned heavily and let out an impatient breath. Then he reached out, drawing her close.

"I promised to keep you safe, remember? And I meant it. I'd die before I let anyone hurt you, Moira."

She sighed, leaning back slightly to look at him with soft, glistening dark eyes. "All very nice to hear, Random. But there are two of them and only one of you."

He smiled dryly. "There are two of us. I'm going to teach you how to shoot."

Chapter Twenty-three

"It's hopeless. I tell you, it's absolutely hopeless," she groaned.

"It wouldn't be if you'd stop saying that over and over," Random said with scarcely veiled impatience. "Just concentrate."

"Random, we've used almost twenty shells, and I haven't hit a thing I've aimed at yet. I can't see properly with one eye shut. And my shoulder hurts!"

"Then leave both eyes open if it'll help. And keep the butt pressed into your shoulder the way I told you instead of holding it loosely. Here, like this!" He repositioned the gun as she stood in tight-lipped obedience. "Now, see if you can hit that damned tree."

She looked up at him. "If I hit it, will you have enough mercy to let me quit for today?"

"All right," he relented. She concentrated, prayed, and pulled the trigger, feeling the kick of the firearm against her bruised shoulder. Random was right. The more firmly you held the beastly thing, the less it bucked. The crack of the gun reverberated in the forest, and by the grace of God, a piece of bark spun off the tree. She grinned up at him and handed over the rifle.

"That's all for today," she said and turned to march toward the cabin. He shouldered the gun and followed her. As soon as they entered the cabin, he handed her the rifle again.

"You're not quite finished."

"Yes, I know," she smiled mockingly. "But I'd much rather clean the thing than fire it, if you gave me a choice."

"Which I won't." He grinned arrogantly.

"You run a mighty tight ship, Mr. Hawthorne," she drawled before plunking down on the bunk and crossing her legs to begin the tedious process of cleaning the gun.

At first she hadn't even liked holding it, sure that it would discharge in her hand or that she would accidentally blow her foot off. Random had begun her training by teaching her the basic mechanics of the rifle. He took it apart and reassembled it, explaining the principles of how it worked. His patience gave her confidence, and she quickly grasped the information. It was simple to clean and assemble the weapon. It was firing the blessed thing accurately that was proving so difficult. It kicked like an angry mule and didn't hit a thing at which it was aimed. So far she preferred the pistol that Danny had purchased for her in Bootjack. At least that was like pointing her finger and firing, and she had reasonable luck with it. Yet Random said the pistol's range was next to nothing, making it useless unless she were planning to face Barilovich and Heaton at about ten feet, face on.

"I'm going down to the claim. Are you coming?" Random asked from the door.

She glanced up. "Let's not work today," she said with a beguiling smile. His mouth curved.

"You want to just laze around the cabin?" His tone brought color into her cheeks.

"If I had a willing partner, I might not mind it one bit," she replied pertly, and he laughed.

"Don't start on me, Moira."

"Let's ride upriver and see if we can find some sign of Jack."

"We've pretty well covered the area as far as we can go."

"I know...but...well, we have at least twenty-five pouches of gold under the floor planks. How much more do we need?"

"Depends on what you want to do with it."

"And what *do* you want to do with it?" she asked, arching her eyebrows.

"Buy my independence," he said, and there was a flicker of something in his eyes that she didn't understand. She wondered if he was referring to Laura. Then he smiled. "I'm going down to the claim. You can take it easy today if you want. But stick close, understand?" He looked down at her like a stern father, and she grimaced.

"Aye, aye, Cap'n."

"I mean it."

"Don't you always?" she muttered in resentment. He looked at her for a moment longer and then left without saying anything more. She finished cleaning the rifle and hung it above the fireplace.

Standing in the open doorway, she looked down the hill at Random. She liked to look at him. He was so handsome, so definitely male, that just looking at him made her feel warm and tingly all over.

But there were plenty of times when that streak of ruthless masculinity bred defiance in her. Just because he was a man didn't mean he always had to have the last word. And just what sort of relationship had they that he had to be so arrogantly high-handed?

It was too beautiful a day to stand knee-deep in freezing water panning for gold, she thought rebelliously. And she was in no mood to rock the cradle while Random shoveled in the dirt. He didn't like her doing it anyway and half the time just had her sitting on the hillside talking with him as he worked. That is, she did the talking, amusing him, while he listened.

It was also too beautiful a day to stay in the cabin. Since finding Jass Whitsell, she had wanted to ride upriver and look around. There were times when she sensed Jack was close, so close that if she rode a few miles north she would find him. She decided she was going to do it. It was time she got over her dependence on Random. She had come to find her brother, after all. And she wouldn't go far.

The silence of the mountains surrounded her as she mounted Danny's horse and turned him toward the higher peaks. The cougar had killed hers. The cat hadn't had a chance to finish the job before Random had arrived, but the horse had been too far gone to save. They had had to shoot it. She pressed her heels into the horse's warm sides and moved forward.

The snow made riding slow but not impossible. She headed straight for the spot where they had found Jass Whitsell partially buried in the snow. She had wanted to go back there for the past week and then ride further north to see if there was any trace of Jack.

There was nothing there to indicate the exact spot where Jass had fallen. Random had brought him back down and buried him beside Daniel. Moira sat silently on the horse and looked around among the trees, then pressed her heels again and moved further on. She was about a mile from the cabin when she began to have a vaguely uneasy feeling in the pit of her stomach and the back of her neck.

There were high, jagged boulders to her left and a steep, tree-studded slope to her right. Someone was watching her. Or something.

Her horse became uneasy as well. He shifted his head to the side, snorting and pulling jerkily on the reins. She looked down the mountainside and shuddered. There wasn't much choice but to go on and see what was ahead, but her heart was pounding in rapid, sickening beats, and the hair on her nape prickled with instinctive fear. Someone was above her. She was afraid to even look, irrationally thinking that not to see danger meant it might go away. If she looked, whatever it was would attack. She knew her logic was that of a child putting its head under the covers.

The horse stopped and then backed away a few steps. He whinnied.

"Easy, boy," she said nervously, patting its smooth, silky neck soothingly. "Don't throw me off now, *please.*" She tightened her legs, but the horse wouldn't move forward. It whinnied again and pranced up off the snow-covered ground.

She heard a growl almost at the same instant the horse reared in panic. Moira's head was thrown back, and she looked up to see something crouched above and then leaping toward her with a powerful thrust of its massively muscled hind legs. She screamed, losing the reins as she went flying backward off the horse. The crack of a rifle broke the frozen air as Moira hit the ground with stunning force. The horse galloped down the trail through rocks and trees, its bridle still jangling after he was out of sight.

"You scream like a bloody woman, boy," a gruff voice bellowed from the trees. She pushed herself up, brushing snow from her face, shoulders, and legs. Her hind end felt battered, and she winced as she stood up to see who had spoken to her.

A man stood within ten feet of her, leaning against a red-wood, and her eyes widened.

Never had she seen such a grizzled-looking character. He was tall, well over six feet, and looked broad and powerful beneath buckskins that were fringed and beaded. He wore a wide-brimmed Spanish hat. His hair was cut raggedly to his shoulders. His beard was full and his brows so heavy that nothing save his nose was uncovered by thick hair. A long knife was in his belt, and the rifle was still smoking in his hand. Cold, winter-gray eyes stared back at her with contempt.

"What you doing up here by yourself?" he demanded in an accent she could not quite identify. Australian, she guessed. She didn't answer but simply stared at him in amazed curiosity.

"I asked you a question, boy. It's polite to answer." The rifle tipped in her direction to prod her to speak.

"I . . . I was looking for someone," she stammered.

"Who?"

After her previous experience with Barilovich, Moira was not eager to blurt out information to this monster of a man, who looked far more dangerous than the Russian.

"I got separated from my brother," she said, sticking to the truth as much as she could. She looked around. "My horse has run off."

"Do tell," he drawled. "You didn't sit him well," he added. She looked at him nervously.

"Did you shoot at me?"

"If I'd shot at you, you'd be dead."

He straightened and walked toward her slowly. She backed away a step, eyes wide with fear. Glancing back, she saw there was nowhere to turn or run. The rocks were above and around. He stopped and looked at her with a sneer.

"Coward, aren't you?"

"You've got the gun!" she flared. He laughed.

"Well, maybe there's something to that little muskrat body of yours," he said. "I'd have liked to put a good blast of rock salt in your arse, boy, for almost getting in my way. I've been tracking that cat for three days."

"What cat?"

"That cat!" He jerked a thumb, and Moira followed the gesture to see a puma lying dead in the snow on the hillside.

"Was he after me?"

He grunted contemptuously. "You just blundered along like the half-wit you are and gave him an opportunity he couldn't resist. Greenhorn on the hoof. That damn cat killed my mule."

"A puma killed one of our horses a few days back."

"You and your brother?"

She hesitated. "We . . . were doing some hunting up here . . . and got separated."

"That's what you were saying." He looked decidedly suspicious, since she had felt it necessary to repeat it. The gray eyes narrowed.

"How long have you been up here?" she asked.

"Why do you want to know?"

"I wondered if you might have seen anyone."

"Wouldn't be telling if I did."

He wasn't a very friendly fellow. "I'm looking for my brother."

"How many brothers you got?"

"Two," she said and knew by his lowered brows that he was convinced now she was lying.

"Got no damn business being up here this time of year, boy."

"You're up here."

"I was on my way back to the valley when that cat got my mule."

"So you're walking?"

He looked at her balefully. "You're full of questions, aren't you?" His beard moved as his mouth opened up in a humorless smile, more of a cold challenge than anything else. Moira gulped. "You looking for a horse to steal since yours has run off?" he asked her.

"I was merely going to say that we have an extra mule you could buy. My brother died—"

"Thought you just got through saying that you had two brothers and were up here hunting with them," he said, eyeing her now with unveiled hostility.

"I have two brothers. One died and the other one I'm separated from." He had certainly taken a bald dislike to her. "We've built a nice cozy little cabin—"

He made a snort of disgust and then spat in the snow.

"Next to the Yuba, just past Haypress Creek," she finished stiffly.

"So you're planning to winter up here?"

"Well, yes."

"Then you're pure stupid." He spat again, and she had the definite impression that he had almost aimed at her.

"We're waiting for someone to come down out of the mountains!" she told him indignantly, disliking him as much as he apparently disliked her.

"Another brother?" His tone was unpleasant.

"I already told you . . . Oh, forget it!"

"I'll buy your mule."

"I'm not sure I want to sell him to you now!" she burst out in annoyance.

"Oh? Why not?"

"Because you've been so . . . so unfriendly," she said incautiously, all her previous lessons forgotten. "I don't like you."

The man grinned broadly, showing straight white teeth and a surprisingly attractive smile. "Well, you've given me a good boost of confidence. I was worried you might take a liking to me."

"Not likely."

He let out a piercing whistle, which made her jump. She heard the jangle of saddle gear as a big black-and-white Indian pony galloped down the trail toward them. It trotted to a stop beside the man, and he slid the gun into the saddle holster before mounting with a springing leap. She expected the horse's back to break from his great size. The man looked down at her.

"Lead on," he ordered. She decided not to argue with him. She had pressed her luck enough already. He didn't speak to her as she walked.

"Haven't seen anyone like you since leaving the big cities," he commented after a half mile. "It's something I could have done a lifetime without seeing again."

She didn't understand what he was muttering about, so didn't reply.

"Your brother anything like you, boy?"

She cast him a stiff look.

"Aren't talking, huh? Well, that's all right by me. You probably haven't got anything to say that I'd want to hear anyhow."

They went another half mile. Moira was tired, puffing with each step, and the wretched man didn't even offer to let her ride behind him. He was obviously enjoying watching her labor through the deep snow. She stopped and breathed in badly needed air. She was getting a headache.

"Soft little dandy, aren't you?"

"Easy for you to say, sitting on your horse!" She started to walk again. He followed slowly on his mount, laughing. The animal blew almost down Moira's neck. The man stayed close and every few minutes hurled another softly spoken insult at her, taunting her for the next few hundred yards.

Random appeared in the woods below them, and she gave a cry of relief.

"Big brother, I presume," the man behind her said dryly as she pushed on quickly through the trees. Random spotted her and strode toward her. She was exhausted, flushed with exertion, and feeling sick. But when he reached her, he didn't notice any of this. His face was a tight, furious mask, his eyes blazing. He swore for almost thirty seconds before he had sufficent control to say what he intended.

"Where in bloody hell have you been?" he roared down at her, fingers digging painfully into her upper arm.

"Did my horse come back?"

"Yes! I've been combing these damn woods looking for you! I told you to stick close to the cabin!" He shook her so hard her head jerked back and forth. "And as usual, you didn't listen!" He gave her another ruthless shake before letting her go.

The sound of the mountain man's horse drew his sharp

attention. He stared narrowly at the man and then took a step toward him. "Who the hell are you?"

"I might ask you the same question," came the cool, amused response. The man leaned forward, resting his forearms on the saddlehorn and looking between Random and Moira. "You couldn't be the brother of this here gelding who's got a mule to sell, could you?"

Random gave her an exasperated look. "Oh, she said we were selling mules, did she?"

"*She?*" The mountain man's eyes swung to Moira and looked her over with renewed interest. "By damn," he breathed, straightening in his saddle. "And I thought . . ." He whipped the hat from his head. "You should've told me, ma'am. I'd have put you up behind me."

"Pure stupid of me not to think of it, wasn't it?" she snapped, glaring at him. She could almost see the flush creep up under his beard.

"Name's Mathias," he said, dismounting. He was easily six feet six, several inches taller than Random.

"Hawthorne," Random said simply. "And this is Moira Cavendish."

"By damn," Mathias repeated, looking her over curiously. "Ain't seen a white woman in almost a year, and that one was old enough to have built the pyramids." He looked at Random. "What you doing letting her wander around up in the mountains? Damn near shot her. She got between me and a cat."

"It's typical of Moira to get in the way," he said grimly, looking at her impatiently. Her mouth tightened mutinously.

"I wanted to see if I could find any trace of Jack," she defended herself.

"She said you had a mule to sell," Mathias repeated. "The cat killed mine."

Random nodded. "We could spare one." He turned to her. "Get something cooking while I talk to Mathias."

She glared at him furiously.

"Go on!" She went, hearing Mathias speaking behind her. "Your little woman give you a lot of trouble, Hawthorne?"

"Enough."

She was bone-tired by the time she reached the cabin. The

horse had come back and was standing near the shelter, his reins dangling in the snow. She put him in the corral with the other horse and the two mules, then went inside to change into her woolen dress. She threw bits of dried salted beef and some canned beans into a pot and stirred angrily.

So Mathias had thought her an effeminate boy, had he? Well, he was going to squirm a bit for that. She dabbed some perfume on her wrists and behind her ears and brushed her hair to a glistening, dark sheen. Glancing out the window, she saw the two men talking about whatever men talk about on such brief acquaintance. They looked as if they had become fast friends.

It was half an hour before Random pushed the door open and walked in. He gave Moira a hard look when he saw she was wearing the dress again. His expression darkened even more when he got a whiff of the perfume.

"What do you think you're doing?" he growled under his breath as Mathias followed him in.

"By damn," the big man said, seeing Moira, and she smiled brightly at him, ignoring Random.

"Are you ready for dinner, gentlemen?" she asked, looking at the two of them. Random looked furious. Mathias had lost his tongue altogether. "Sit down, please," she said, dipping in a polite, graceful curtsy, enjoying Random's growing irritation. He shed his hat and coat. Mathias did the same. Moira ladled out bowls of beans and beef and then sat on the floor with them. Mathias accepted his, his eyes on her, but once he started eating all attention went to his plate. Moira watched in stunned silence as the food disappeared into the man's bearded face. He wiped his bowl clean with his bread before that too made a fast departure down his throat. All in a matter of less than two minutes! Then he belched loud and clear in appreciation.

Moira couldn't suppress a laugh. "I take it you liked it?"

Mathias's ears grew red. "Excuse me, ma'am. I forgot I was in a lady's company."

She grinned. "Would you like some coffee to wash it all down?"

He nodded solemnly. "I'd be much obliged." He wiped the residue of sauce from his beard with the back of his hand and smiled his amazing smile.

She filled a cup and handed it to him. He drank it straight-away without so much as a fliniching of facial muscles. Moira stared. How could he possibly drink scalding coffee like that? His mouth must be lined with granite!

"Thank you, ma'am."

"You want to see the mule now?" Random demanded.

Mathias stood, ready to go, even eager. Moira obviously made him nervous. "Thank you for the fine meal, ma'am."

She rose, too, putting her hands on her hips. "I liked you a whole lot better when you weren't so polite, Mathias."

"I'm not much with the amenities. Been too long since I've been in polite company."

Moira reached out and placed her hand lightly on his arm. The buckskin felt smooth and soft, the arm beneath rock hard, and she smiled up at him beguilingly. "Don't rush off, Mathias. I want to ask a favor of you."

"I already told him about Jack," Random said.

Moira glanced at him and then smiled back at the mountain man. "And?" She looked straight into the clear gray eyes.

"I'll do what I can." Random watched the man's face in silence and then gave Moira a mocking look. He opened the door and let a blast of icy air inside. Moira withdrew her hand as Mathias turned away and followed Random outside.

Standing by the window, Moira watched the two men talking. Mathias listened and then nodded. He said something and pointed toward the mountains. More words were exchanged, and then they went to the animal pen and Mathias selected a mule. There was a moment when the animal refused to budge from the others, but Mathias grabbed an ear and yanked while giving the beast a swift kick in the hind end. The mule came out, and a rope was quickly lashed to the saddle of the pinto. The animal took a nip at the horse, which retaliated by a hard kick into the mule's chest. After that the mule stood docilely by.

Mathias mounted and gave a nod to Random before turning the mount toward the northeast. Random strode back toward the cabin. When he came in he didn't look at Moira. She could see the tension in his body. He was still mad as hell at her, she guessed, and she had been feeding his irritation by attempting to flirt with Mathias. She did owe him an apology for worrying him.

"Random?"

He turned and glared at her, his mouth a hard, uncompromising line, his eyes dark and narrowed. "You ever take off like that again, when I catch up with you, I'll . . ."

The power of his anger shocked her, but also served to raise her hackles in self-defense. Who was he to tell her what she could or couldn't do? He hadn't shown any great eagerness to ride up the mountain and find Jack. And she had come to California for that purpose and that purpose alone. Let him look for gold! It was her brother that she cared about!

"Oh no, you wouldn't," she said giving him the impish, taunting smile that had always frustrated Aunt Miranda and her brothers alike. "You wouldn't lay a hand on me because you're a *gentleman*. And I was going to apologize for worrying you before you blasted me with both barrels!"

If anything, Random grew madder than before. Her pert defense aroused him to pale rigidity. He reached out and pulled her roughly forward, crushing her against him as his mouth covered hers in a punishing kiss. She gasped and tried to pull back but couldn't move within the iron circle of his arms. His fingers in her hair tightened and pulled, forcing her head back. It was all meant as a lesson for her irresponsible behavior and then her taunting defiance of his orders. But Random had forgotten Moira's spirit and passionate nature.

Sensations flooded her young body, and her arms slid around Random's waist. She pressed herself against his lean, hard frame and made a purring sound of surrender. She felt his heartbeat against her breasts as his anger dissolved into something even more powerful. The assault continued, but with a far different objective in mind. Random's mouth became coaxing, teasing, possessive, and Moira's response was to part her lips and imitate the pleasures he had previously shown her by using the tip of her tongue.

"You witch," he groaned, quickly dispensing with the buttons of her dress and opening it, filling his hands with the firm warm flesh of her breasts. Then, impatient, he swung her up into his arms and deposited her on his bunk, joining her there. There was no light play this time, but an urgency on his part to possess her. Moira gave herself with an abandon that took his breath away and almost succeeded in obliterating his control at the last crucial second when his body was ready to give its fertile burden.

"Was that really meant to be a deterrent?" Moira murmured huskily against his temple, lips curving in a mischievous smile.

"Next time I might just beat you instead." He laughed in self-mockery.

She ran her hand slowly down the hard, smooth muscles of his back. "I should get you angry more often if this is the way it will end."

He pushed himself up on one elbow and glowered down at her. "And you can quit using your charms on poor Mathias," he told her, his eyes flashing again. "He's old enough to be your father!"

She raised her brows. "Barely. But is that what I was doing? Charming Mathias?" she asked impishly.

"You know damn well you were. He couldn't get out of here fast enough."

"Because you practically dragged him out the door."

"He was more interested in the mule, Moira," he taunted back. It was true, but Moira was not about to admit it. She smiled instead, watching Random straighten up and reach for his discarded clothes.

"This time."

Chapter Twenty-four

Mathias returned a week later. It was snowing when Moira spotted him coming out of the trees, the mule laden with packs and pelts. Before Random realized what was happening, she threw the door open and started running toward the approaching mountain man.

"Mathias!"

Small icicles hung from his heavy beard and from the fur of his winter coat. His nose was red, and his eyes were narrowed against the chill. Moira struggled through the snow and didn't stop for a greeting. She was panting hard when she reached him, her breath a cloud of vapor before her. "Did you find anything?"

"You shouldn't be out here," he told her gruffly. "And no coat on you."

"Did you find anything?" she repeated excitedly.

"Some tracks," he said briefly and then before she knew what he was about, reached down and picked her up, settling her in front of him on the horse. "You shouldn't be out here in the snow, girl," he repeated firmly, arms around her. She felt the warmth of his breath against her cheek. She looked up at him wide-eyed and turned in time to see Random standing in front of the cabin, looking at them. His face was remote.

261

She felt the muscles of Mathias's legs tighten as he urged the horse forward.

Mathias put Moira down when he was beside the cabin. "Get inside, girl." Then he turned the horse and mule toward the corral. Random went with him without a look at Moira. She sighed heavily.

Random came in a few minutes later and scowled heavily when he saw her in her dress.

"I'd like it better if you wore pants," he said.

"But I am." She grinned and lifted the skirt to show dungarees rolled up to her knees.

"Put your skirt down, for God's sake. Mathias is going to be—"

She dropped her skirt back in place as the door opened and Mathias came in. He bowed respectfully to her. She poured coffee for them, adding a liberal dose of brandy. Mathias drank it appreciatively.

"You said you found some tracks," she pressed, and he nodded.

"Coming southeast toward here," he told her. "Followed them for some miles before the storm hit and wiped them out. When it let up the next day, I tried to find more, but all sign was gone. Guess he made it."

"How can you be sure?" Random asked.

"Well, he was a big man, judging by his tracks. And he was walking sure, like he knew exactly where he was going. He wasn't walking in circles. He's mountain-wise, whoever he is."

"But he's disappeared," Moira said, eyes bleak.

"Until the snow stops. No telling how far he got. Might've gotten further than I looked if he kept going during the storm. Can't say. Couldn't find anything. The snows are covering everything now. In another couple weeks anyone up there won't be coming down until spring."

"Right by us and we didn't even know it," Moira murmured miserably.

"We don't know for sure it was Jack," Random reminded her.

"Who else could it be? Who else?"

"Could be anyone, girl," Mathias said. "There are a few

other foolhardy men still up there who're staying the winter to protect their claims. Or others like me, who just don't like being in big crowds in those camps below and wait until the last before leaving the peace of the mountains."

"He's still alive. I know it." It must have been him, she thought fiercely to herself.

"Then we'll look for him in the spring," Random told her, reaching out to slide his hand over hers. She sighed.

"Spring is so far away."

Random's hand tightened. "There isn't any choice, Moira."

Mathias started to say something and then stopped when he looked at Random. He raised his mug and drank more brandy-laced coffee.

They ate venison, beans, and sourdough bread for dinner, then sat before the fire for a while. Moira cleaned the dishes and straightened the cabin while the men played cards. When they didn't invite her to join them, she sat down on the floor with them.

"I'd like to be dealt in."

The two men exchanged amused glances that clearly said that the logic of poker was far beyond any female mind.

"This is no woman's game," Mathias told her.

She'd never told Random that she had learned poker and half a dozen other gambling games when she was scarcely out of the cradle. Her luck had always held faster than Daniel's or even Jack's, because she didn't allow herself to get into a fever. She was adept at counting cards and had a quick comprehension of odds. But since poker was not considered a lady's game, she had never played it with anyone other than her brothers.

"Why don't you just explain the principles of the game and let me try?" she suggested. "I'm as bored as everyone else cooped up in here."

Random grinned. "Do you mind, Mathias?" Mathias shrugged, obviously not excited about the idea.

Random dealt out half a dozen hands and showed her the game. He went through the deck, making a variety of hands, flushes, full houses, pairs, and tried to explain the general concept of poker. She listened, watched, nodded, followed his lead, and never once gave any indication that she knew as much as he, though he appeared to be an expert player himself. It was all in knowing the cards, understanding the odds, watching the way the others played.

"Think you have the general idea?" He shuffled again. He had nice hands, square and strong, with long, flexible fingers and trim, clean nails. She watched with admiration how deft they were. You could tell a lot about a man by his hands.

"Oh, I think so," she murmured, curling her legs under her and carefully arranging her skirt while watching him flip the cards out to the three of them. She pretended slight confusion when she picked them up. "If I make a mistake, you just tell me."

Random fanned his cards. Mathias did as well. Moira deliberately fumbled hers and then restrained a grin as they both quickly showed her how best to hold them. Random was smiling slightly, amused by her ineptitude. Mathias looked disapproving.

The men discarded, explaining why they had tossed away the cards they had. She sat for a moment, finally deciding to throw in four. Random looked at her hand and explained that she should have kept two. She nodded, listening intently, eyes wide and innocent. The next few hands went slowly, Moira playing her own cards without Random's assistance. Mathias looked grim. They were betting wood chips, and Moira made sure she lost a pile. Random played very well, she decided. Mathias was average, with a tendency to show too much in his face.

When it came time for Moira to deal, she spilled the cards all over the floor. Random laughed, scooping them up and handing them back. He showed her again how to do it as she apologized repeatedly for her clumsiness.

Several times she had excellent hands with great possibilities and had to ruin them deliberately. It was too soon to close the trap. First she had to up the stakes.

"I think I'm beginning to get the idea," she said when she had lost a dozen hands and been allowed to win with a pair of sevens. She had been sure that Mathias had a trio of tens that time, but he had tossed the cards into the pot without turning them up. He was not going to find her so charitable.

"Couldn't we make it more fun if we bet something?" she

suggested with pretended hesitance. "I mean, wood chips aren't very exciting."

Random grinned at her. "You'd better keep in mind that you haven't won a single hand yet, Moira."

"No," she sighed. "Not yet. But I catch on eventually, dense as I am. How about gold?"

"No," he said decisively. "It wouldn't be fair. We'd clean you out of your share in a couple of hours."

"Women don't gamble for money," Mathias grumbled.

Mathias was going to be difficult. "All right. When we finish playing this evening, how about making the overall loser take care of the fire, breakfast, and cleanup tomorrow morning?" she suggested. The two men looked at one another and grinned.

Mathias grunted. "Since you'd be doing it anyway, seems fair enough."

Random nodded, eyes laughing. "Why don't we throw in hot bathwater for the next week as well?"

She hesitated deliberately and then sighed heavily. "Well, it was my idea to bet something worthwhile. I agree. Fire, breakfast, cleanup, and bathwater for a week." He was certainly sure of himself.

"You deal, Moira." Moira shuffled poorly and then tediously counted out a hand for each. Random won the first. Mathias the second. Random two more. They were very smug, she noticed.

"Want to change your mind?" Random asked teasingly.

"It's a matter of honor, isn't it, to keep your bet?" She watched him flip out the cards again and decided it was time to wipe that look off both their faces. She had had a chance to study both of them and knew that when Random had a good hand, he showed it by the tension in his jaw. Mathias's eyes gave his hand away. She smiled slowly, picking up her cards.

She won the next four hands and pretended exuberant surprise. "Are you two letting me win?" she asked gaily, batting her lashes.

They exchanged a look. Mathias dealt.

"I think I'm getting the idea at last," she proclaimed when she won three more hands.

"It looks like it," Mathias grunted, brows knit. Random's

eyes were glinting suspiciously.

Random won the next three hands, and Moira forced herself to concentrate. She won the next two. Random took to watching her carefully, and she concealed a smile. She deliberately widened her eyes when she had a good hand. He picked up on the giveaway mannerism and used it to determine his own method of playing. She used it ruthlessly and won the next four hands. He began to look decidedly irritated, so she let him win the next three hands before suggesting they quit for the evening after the next half dozen. The two men seemed very agreeable, especially Mathias, who was taking the worst beating.

Moira won all six games. She laughed brightly. "Beginner's luck! You're *wonderful* teachers!"

"Small comfort," Mathias growled.

"Oh, don't worry, Mathias. You're our guest, so Random will build the fire and make breakfast in the morning. And he'll warm my bathwater for the next week!" Random looked at her balefully.

She picked up the deck. "I'll have to practice shuffling." The deck made a smooth riffling sound that made both men narrow their eyes. She spread the cards in a smooth line on the floor and with a mere flip of her finger rolled them back in the other direction, sliding them together and picking them up, then shooting them like rifle fire into one hand and returning them perfectly to the other. She made a waterfall and then held the deck up before them, fanning them wide and closing them with one hand, as if by magic. Calmly, but grinning blatantly now, she set them on the floor. "Yes, I think I need a little more practice. It's been too long since I last played. I'm a bit rusty."

"You devious little bitch," Random said in a low voice, grinning. "We've been had, Mathias."

"And not even a royal flush to do it," Moira agreed with a bow of her head. "Gullible, gentlemen. In poker, it is wise never to underestimate an opponent . . . or a woman's intelligence."

"Never trust one," Random said.

Moira leaned back and tapped her finger thoughtfully to her lips. "Venison steaks, I think. And biscuits."

Random raised a hand, pretending to take a swing at her.

They talked late into the night. With enough brandy under his belt, Mathias became loquacious. He had come from Australia in 1848 before word of the gold rush had reached his homeland. He had come to trap and sell furs and to satisfy the wanderlust that had been in him since he was a boy. His parents had been sent to Australia from England for some crime invented by their rich employer. They were dead now, but four brothers and five sisters still lived in the Outback.

Random talked of the sea, the storms of the Atlantic, the ports of call around the world. Moira listened raptly, absorbing everything he said with the hunger of a woman in love. It was what he didn't say that captured her imagination, for there were hints of wild adventures at which she could only guess. And women—she was sure there must have always been women.

Later, she lay back on her bunk, and let the men's low-pitched talk flow over her. They liked and respected each other. Their men's talk now excluded her. Closing her eyes, she slept, dreaming of Charleston and Jack.

They were riding along the river, and Jack was laughing at something she had said. He turned in his saddle, and she couldn't hear what he was saying. He looked excited as he spoke, pointing at something she couldn't see. He spurred his horse forward, disappearing into a haze of clouds, his image still faintly visible yet out of reach.

"Jack," she moaned and turned over. "Jack."

Her eyes came open. The cabin was silent. She looked around in faint confusion, still drugged by sleep and the vividness of the dream. *He'd been so close*. He *was* close. She sensed it. There had always been a special bond between them. She felt certain he was close now.

Random lay asleep on his bunk, one arm flung above his head. Mathias lay stretched out on the floor, a pelt blanket over him. He pushed himself up on one elbow.

"You all right?"

She nodded.

"Your brother?"

She nodded again.

"This is no place for a woman. Get your man there to take you back down out of the mountains."

She sighed. "I don't know, Mathias."

"You're being pure dumb, girl."

"Jack may come down from the mountains yet. I can't leave."

"From what you've said about him, your brother got the sense to be down out of the mountains by now. That was probably him I was following. Just get on your horses tomorrow and go back with me. Nothing more simple." He jerked his head toward Random. "Hawthorne's staying here for you."

"Did he tell you that?"

"Didn't have to."

"He's never suggested we go back."

Mathias didn't say anything for a moment, then he let out a hard breath. His eyes narrowed. "This is a good place to keep a woman. No fighting over you. Safe. But he should have married you first."

She frowned. "I'm not up here to be safe. I'm up here to find my brother."

"You sure about that? That may be your reason, girl, but is it Hawthorne's?" He looked at her long and hard. Then he lay back down and closed his eyes. Moira lay still on her bunk, thinking.

She was quiet the next morning. She kept thinking about what Mathias had said. When he went out to ready his horse and mule, she looked over at Random who was poking the fire.

"Mathias suggested we go back with him."

He looked up. "No reason to do that. We've got all the supplies we need to sit out the winter comfortably right here. Men go back to eat and keep warm. We don't have those problems."

"Mathias thinks the man he followed may have been Jack."

Random straightened, eyes darkening. "How could he know that? And when did you two talk all this over?"

She looked at him steadily. "I'd like to know for sure, Random."

Mathias came in and looked at the two of them, feeling the tension. He told them he was ready to head on down the mountain trail. Moira looked beseechingly at Random, but he ignored her. His face was hard and aloof as he bade good luck to Mathias. Moira made a move toward the door. Random closed it. He leaned back against it, arms crossed. His eyes were cold.

She bristled at his high-handed behavior. "I want to ask Mathias something," she told him stiffly.

"Mathias is leaving."

"I know that. Couldn't he wait for a while until we discuss this?"

"There's no need for a discussion," Random told her, unwilling to make any compromise. "The decision was made a long time ago."

"That's not fair!"

"What do you mean, fair?" he retorted angrily, pushing away from the door to stand over her. "There's nothing fair about life in general, Moira. You do what makes the best sense."

"Sense! You're just issuing me an order without even considering—"

He cut her off. "It makes no sense for us to go back down into the valley." She drew in her breath.

"It makes sense to me! That was probably Jack who went right past us two days ago. We could catch up with him, find out what's going on!"

His mouth twisted sardonically. "Plant an idea in a woman's head and she think it's a blessed certainty! Mathias can't tell you for sure that was Jack walking out of the mountains! How could he?"

"I'd like to find out if it was!" she fumed.

"And if we caught up to this . . . mystery man and found out it wasn't Jack, what then?"

"We'd come back here and wait."

He gave a harsh laugh. "Typical woman's thinking! By the time we got down to the valley and found out it wasn't Jack, it'd be too late to come back up here!"

Moira's temperature rose by several degrees. "You'd rather we sit here and wait for the spring thaw, however many months off that may be! And if it was Jack, God knows where he'd be by then!"

"*I frankly don't give a damn about Jack!* I want to keep you safely out of harm's way, and staying up here is the best way to see to it. Down there, you'd bloody well search out some kind of trouble!"

Moira's eyes sparked. "In case you've forgotten, Mr. Hawthorne, I came to California to find my brother. And with or without your help, I intend doing just that!" She took a step closer to him. "I didn't come to hide safely away in a mountain cabin."

By now his own temper was fully aroused. "Have you forgotten about Barilovich and Heaton? You sent them down, remember? And now you want to blunder right into them again. Make some sense!"

"Oh, God," she gasped in sudden apprehension. "What if Jack runs into them!"

"You don't know for sure it was Jack!"

"I *feel* it was!"

"Woman's intuition, I suppose," he sneered.

"Mock all you like, damn you, but if it is Jack, I've put him in tremendous danger!"

"He knows those men are after him."

"I've got to go." She swung away, reaching for her pack. Random jerked her back.

"You're staying right here. You're not going off on some wild-goose chase because of some ridiculous suggestion that those tracks may have been Jack's."

"I'm going to find out one way or the other!" she told him, determined.

"The hell you are!" He shoved her roughly onto her bunk. "You're staying right here with me!"

"I'm beginning to wonder just why you want me up here!" she cried in frustration.

"That should be obvious!"

"Oh, it certainly is, Mr. Hawthorne! You think you own me! Well, you don't! And if you think you can keep me here so . . . so you'll have a woman to warm your winter bed—"

"If you'll remember, I didn't push you into my bed, you *threw* yourself there!"

Her face went red and then white. "Well, I'm climbing out as of here and now!"

"When you gave yourself to me, you became mine," he said through his teeth.

That did it. Moira's temper erupted like Vesuvius. *"I don't belong to anyone!"* she yelled at him. "I wasn't Aunt Miranda's to dispose of as she saw fit, and I'm not yours either! Besides, Mr. Hawthorne, you're already spoken for, whether you like acknowledging that or not! And God knows how many other women there are scattered around the world waiting for your ship to sail in! I certainly don't! Maybe you've got a couple dozen children as well, or have you ever bothered to stay around long enough to find out!"

His face was white and hard, his eyes burning like black coals. She thought he might hit her, but it made her no more cautious. She jumped off the bunk, facing him.

"Get out of my way, Hawthorne!"

"You're going to listen to me!" He shoved her back roughly. She clutched the edge of the bunk. Chin jutting out, she looked up at him defiantly.

"That's all a woman is to you, isn't it? A chattel! Well, I'm not your possession. I'm not anyone's. You picked the wrong woman if that's what you wanted. *No one owns me!*"

She darted past him, and he reached for her. She jerked away, banging into a shelf on the wall and sending the canned goods cascading to the floor. He caught at her shirt.

"Sit down, damn it!" he roared.

She was too furious to listen to anything. Her body shook with rage. He was trying to prevent her from reaching Jack. He was trying to hold onto her like a piece of merchandise. Just like other men, he thought a woman belonged to a man like his horse or mule!

Her fingers caught on the coat hanging near the door. She shoved her arm in the sleeve. He pulled it off and flung it into a far corner. She kicked him hard. He swore and released her. She tried for the door. His fingers latched onto her belted pants, hauling her back in as he kicked the door shut. She twisted and squirmed, shrieking her rage at him.

"Damn it, Moira! Shut up and listen to me!"

She tripped over the planks and fell. He fell on top of her, trying to pin her down. She reached for something, anything, and her fingers closed on a can. She swung it hard and cracked him across the head. His eyes widened in shock and then he slumped, unconscious, and rolled off her. She sat up, panting heavily from the fight, and stared at him.

Blood oozed from a cut, staining the hair at his forehead.

She gasped, getting to her knees above him.

"Rand?"

He didn't move. She began to shake violently, staring down at him, and for one agonizing, horrified moment she was sure she'd killed him. She touched him lovingly, and started to sob, then saw the rise and fall of his chest. Anger filled her again. He was all right; now she could go!

She stood up, fists balled at her sides, glaring down at him. *Insufferable male!* But she couldn't leave him bleeding. She snatched up a cloth and ripped off a piece, and tied it around his head. She should tie it around his neck, she thought, fuming. She looked around, trying to decide what to do next. She began to hastily stuff things into her pack. Throwing the plank aside, she plunged her hand in and pulled out her share of the gold and put it into Daniel's pack. She yanked on her coat again, and gave Random one last, burning look. He groaned. His eyelids fluttered. He stirred.

Moira opened the door and went out, slamming it thunderously behind her.

It was snowing again, but that wasn't going to stop her! Nothing short of a blizzard would, and probably not that either. She marched through the thick drifts to the animal shelter and dragged out the reluctant mare, throwing on the saddle. She lashed her packs to the cantle and mounted, aiming for the river trail, where Mathias's tracks could still be made out in the snow.

The horse was not eager to move, and Moira slapped the reins hard over its rump. The snow flew up from the horses' hooves into Moira's face as it lunged down the hill.

She didn't notice the cold for the first few miles, her anger heating her blood. But gradually it began to seep in. It began to snow harder, the flakes clinging to her head and shoulders, catching on her eyelashes so that she had to keep brushing them away. She drew the coat more tightly around her, wishing she had gloves. Her fingers were stiff and chilled. But the discomfort began to force her to acknowledge the foolhardiness of her actions. She knew she should turn back, but pride kept her going. Random Hawthorne was not her keeper! She was here to find Jack! And she couldn't do that sitting by a warm fire all winter, not when he was more likely than not far ahead of her on the trail.

Oh God, let it be Jack.

The horse stumbled, and she almost pitched into the deep snow, catching the mane at the last second and hauling herself up again. She was sobbing and didn't even realize it.

The snow was increasing, falling at a rate that almost blinded her. She could still hear the river and continued to follow the trail broken by Mathias and his mule. The snowstorm was quickly obscuring it, and she felt growing worry the farther she she went.

She had been crazy to run out of the cabin, but she couldn't go back now. The cold had penetrated her coat, and even hugging herself and shoving her hands into the heavy sleeves did little to keep her warm. She was shivering and couldn't stop. She ached with cold, and it seemed to be penetrating her very bones. She felt stiff and slow, sluggish.

She rode for what seemed hours. Mathias's trail had long since been obliterated by the steadily falling snow. She continued following the river, hearing its fierce roar as it churned down out of the mountains. Sooner or later she was bound to find someone, some shelter where she could get out of the cold.

The mare moved steadily, Moira's mind was a blur. She was so tired she wanted to sleep. She could only think of Random and Daniel and Jack. *Jack. Jack!* It seemed they were all lost to her at once, and she couldn't bear it anymore.

Through the trees up ahead of her was the cloudy image of a man on horseback, a mule following. She thought she was dreaming. The man turned his head and looked back. She couldn't make out his face beneath the wide-brimmed hat. Her horse quickened its pace to reach the others, and she slid slowly from the saddle and landed in a snowbank.

Someone was hauling her out. "What are you doing, girl?" Mathias demanded, lifting her. He wrapped her in something heavy, then rubbed her roughly, hurting her. "Don't go to sleep!" He shook her.

"I'm going back with you, Mathias."

"Where's Hawthorne?"

"At the cabin . . ." She started to crumple.

"Stand up!" He yanked her up straight. "Come on! Jump up and down! Move!" He pulled her along, making her move in a circle.

"I'm tired," she protested.

"You've got to get your blood moving. Pure, plumb stupid woman!" He pushed her along. "Thought you were in love with him."

Her face convulsed, and it was a moment before she could speak. She was out of breath from the workout. "It's a woman's prerogative to change her mind." She was going to be no man's possession. Tears blinded her.

Mathias didn't say anything for a long time. "You warming up?"

She gave him a bland look. "Yes."

"Well, don't build up a sweat. It'll freeze on you when we ride."

"I'm all right now."

He threw a pelt at her. "Wrap yourself up in that," She did. He lifted her back into the saddle. "We've got a few more miles to go before we can stop for the night."

"I won't be any trouble, Mathias. I swear."

He gave her a disgruntled look. "Girl, you *are* trouble." He took her reins and tied them to his own saddle horn. She put her head down, hiding it in the furry pelt. Her horse moved on.

Chapter Twenty-five

Mathias took Moira to Sierra City, where he installed her in a hotel room above a gambling casino and bar. The din kept her awake until the wee hours of morning, her head throbbing with tension and worry.

Random would come after her. She could be as sure of that as she was that the sun was going to rise in the morning. She was terrified what his retaliation would be for the crack on the head she had given him. Not that he hadn't deserved it, she thought in angry defense. But he wasn't going to just let that slide.

Unreasonable as she knew it was, she was concerned about him as well. She remembered the cut on his temple and the blood and worried that perhaps the blow had been more serious than she'd thought. What if he was still unconscious? What if he had come to and tried to find her and collapsed in the snow? She remembered Jass Whitsell and shuddered, tears of remorse and worry burning in the back of her throat.

Mathias had no intention of going back when she suggested it. "You crazy, girl?" he growled. She confessed what she had done, and he gave her a disgusted look.

"Pure stupid," he muttered before slugging down a third of a bottle of brandy. "Pure, plumb stupid. But I doubt he's dead.

Too tough, that one. No, Hawthorne will do all right, though I'm not so sure about you when he catches up to us."

She hadn't needed him to say that. She was already sure of it.

"What'd he do to you, girl?" Mathias asked in a gruff, fatherly voice that indicated he had a great deal of concern for her. Moira's face turned bright red, and he mumbled under his breath. "Thought he was a gentleman." He took another long draft from the bottle and wiped his mouth with the back of his hand. He pointed at her with the hand that held the bottle by its neck. "You were right to run away, girl. No good staying with a man who enjoys the pleasures without due process of holy matrimony. By damn, you did right."

She turned away in misery. She couldn't tell Mathias he was wrong, that he had gotten the incorrect impression of what Random had done to make her leave.

Random had been right, but it didn't change anything. The more she thought about Random and her relationship with him, the worse her head ached. Who did he think he was, ordering her around continuously. No, she wasn't his as he'd claimed.

"You still love him?" Mathias asked, watching her. She lifted her chin, and her dark eyes flashed.

"I'd rather not discuss Mr. Hawthorne."

Mathias grunted, and it could have meant anything from understanding to annoyance.

"We'll leave for the American River tomorrow morning at daybreak," he told her, not asking her opinion. She didn't care where they went.

The trek to Sacramento was arduous, the weather miserable, the land unyieldingly rugged. Moira didn't complain. She sat in the saddle for hours, her rear end feeling worn to numbness until she climbed down and it came back to painful life. She cooked their first meal, and Mathias grumbled something under his breath. He seemed to do a lot of grumbling to himself. She knew she was a nuisance to him, but there was nothing she could do about it, and she tried not to feel guilty.

Each night when they camped, Mathias had no difficulty falling asleep in spite of the cold or rain. He looked like a great, hibernating bear under his blanket. Moira envied him his peace of mind. She lay awake for hours in their lean-to, torturing herself with thoughts of Random. She reasoned she was better off away from him. All he expected was to have a woman who accepted him as her master while he was conveniently free of commitment. He'd told her he wasn't going to divorce his wife because it protected him from other women. Well, obviously he looked upon her as just another conniving woman as well—probably looking for bed, board, and a personal bodyguard against randy miners! Well, damn him to hell!

She probed her pain the way a dog licks an open wound. Closing her eyes, she tried to blot out his presence, but the pain locked in her throat, choking her. Rolling over, she pulled the blanket up and pressed it against her face so that Mathias wouldn't hear her crying.

"I'll love you just a little—I won't take it all," Random had said the first time, but he had taken everything. He had been honest, at least, for a little was all he had really wanted. Not her heart. Not her soul. Just her willingness to give her body, to do what he expected until he tired of her and went back to his ship. She had assumed a great deal. She'd been a fool.

"Just a little," he'd said, but you can't fall in love just a little. Love wasn't a made-to-order flirtation that could be easily dissolved when it became too demanding for either party. She *loved* him. If she didn't, the pain wouldn't be so intolerable. He had told her he loved her. Had he meant it? She had thought so with all her heart at the time.

Damn him! She glared into the darkness. He had known she was falling in love with him. He could have stopped it at the very beginning by telling her the cold, hard truth. But he hadn't.

Cursing Random wasn't going to ease the hold he had on her, even now with miles between them, nor the knowledge of his marriage. It was that cutting knowledge that hurt Moira most. Distance wasn't going to make any difference, either, nor was time. She had run away from him for nothing, because everywhere she went, Random's presence loomed hugely, painfully, in her mind. She carried him with her.

The rain started again, the fourth time in five days since they had left the high snows of the Sierra Nevadas and the Yuba River. It started slowly, a light pattering on the canvas, a soothing cadence that eased Moira's tension. Then the deluge began, pounding down on them, streaming over the sides of their shelter and filling the moat Mathias had dug around them for just this eventuality. Soon the moan was filled and the water began creeping in, dampening the blankets and packs. Moira curled up tightly on her side, too exhausted to care about the discomfort. Finally she slept.

Mathias drew in rein at the crest of the hill and waited for Moira. She brought her horse in close to his and looked down at Sacramento below them. She drew in her breath in surprise.

"I can't believe it!" she breathed in amazement.

It was so different from when she and Daniel had passed through in August. In just a few short months the entire scene had changed. This was no longer a camp of sixty to seventy scrap-lumber and canvas dwellings scattered beneath the river oaks and sycamores. It was a sprawling community.

It was dusk of a drizzly, overcast day, and the tents below were illuminated from within by the kerosene lanterns. They glowed all around.

"It's beautiful," Moira said and smiled at Mathias.

Mathias grunted some reply and then made a click with his tongue. The pony moved down over the gently undulating hill toward the town below. Moira followed.

Tall-masted ships were in Sacramento harbor. She could just see Sutter's Fort and the cabins and tents packed around it.

When they reached the huge camp and rode down the muddy street along the river, Moira stared around her in growing wonder. This was a world she had never seen, never dreamed existed. It was disgusting and marvelous at the same time, and she laughed delightedly.

Old ships sails had been confiscated and made into tents that housed gambling casinos, bars, and stores all along the street. Booth shops stood open to the passersby, showing their many wares. Signs hastily painted and often misspelled were hanging everywhere. The place smelled of mud, horse dung, and rotting canvas, with a few welcome whiffs of food.

"Am I really hearing a string orchestra?" Moira gasped, quickening her horse's pace to come up next to Mathias. He pointed to a big tent, the Round House.

"I want to go in!" she said excitedly, and he looked at her, his expression a clear indication that she had lost her mind. "Oh, come on, Mathias! Where's your sense of adventure?"

"Food in the belly first, girl," he said practically. "And that's no place for a lady. Just listen to the rabble."

"I am! Isn't it wonderful!"

He grunted something. They passed other structures made of cast-off materials—the Stinking Tent, the Plains, the Humboldt, the Mansion, Diana's, Lee's Exchange. There was noise and excitement, swearing and preaching, laughter and shouting.

Mathias was heading for Sutter's Fort, but veered off and stopped before a gristmill that had been converted into a place called the City Hotel. They dismounted and stepped into pandemonium.

Mathias flattened Moira roughly against the wall as someone was thrown bodily out the door. Someone else was flung after him with admonishments not to come back if they couldn't behave like proper gents. Moira ducked under Mathias's arm to see what was happening, and he grabbed her by the scruff of the neck and pulled her back, while at the same time his foot came up and propelled a man back who had just been flung toward them in a fight. With another shove, he plowed into the teeming crowd, hauling Moira after him.

"This way!" he shouted above the din, moving her through the throng of men wearing the familiar look of wild desperation and forced gaiety. Moira wove between tables of miners waiting for spring weather. Once in the eating section and seated at a long bench, Mathias glowered at her.

"By damn, girl, you almost got yourself into it back there."

"I only wanted to see what was happening," she defended herself. "You didn't have to wring my neck."

"One more step away from that wall and you'd have been squashed flatter than an empty tick, girl." He glanced up at a harried man delivering meals, whacked his arm against the table, and roared loudly. "Over here, by damn! We're just in and hung—gry!"

Moira laughed. "Mathias. There are others ahead of us. Wait your turn."

He frowned. "I'm hungry and I don't aim to sit here until hell freezes over before I eat." He waved at the man imperiously, glowering at him. His size alone demanded immediate attention. "Over here, by damn!" He pounded on the table again.

Miraculously, food appeared a second after he lifted his fist. He turned his head and grinned at Moira. She grinned back, picking up a fork. Who was she to complain? When in Rome . . .

"Dig in." She did. Never had beef stew and vegetables tasted so much like ambrosia! And all the while she was eating she watched the chaotic scene around her. She wondered how much gold dust was being poured onto those gaming tables and how many of the miners would be dirt poor by spring. Most, she guessed.

The noise in the City Hotel was almost excruciating after the quiet of the mountains. Moira drank in the excitement like a person dying of thirst. She laughed and filled her senses with the sounds, smells, and sights of the place. It was the first time she had felt even half alive since leaving Random lying on the plank floor of the cabin two weeks before. Glasses clinked, men shouted and laughed, and there was a low roar louder than the Yuba itself. The smells of tobacco, whiskey, dirt, and sweat weren't entirely displeasing to her.

"Look at them all," she murmured in amazement. "Gold dust is going across those felt tables like a waterfall. Those men are losing in minutes what it must have taken them months to accumulate."

"They're bored, and bored men are stupid," Mathias said between bites from a second plate of food. "Waiting for spring, they got nothing better to do than gamble and whore, if whores are around, and both pastimes don't come cheap."

Moira watched the excited, hope-filled faces, the rapt looks of the card players, the forced jubilation, and felt pity. By spring these men wouldn't have the poke they had started with, and they would be working the streams and dry diggings again, praying for a bonanza. And how many would succeed? How many would return home with pockets filled? How many, like Daniel, would be buried with shattered dreams below a simple wooden cross? Too many.

Mathias glanced at Moira, seeing her intense concentration. "What are you thinking, Moira?"

"I was just wondering—" she said and stopped, a faint

frown creasing her brows. Daniel's dream could still come true. Her eyes sparkled. Mathias frowned.

"Don't go getting any wild-hare ideas. As soon as we fill our bellies, we're getting out of this hellhole."

"And going where?"

"Haven't decided," he grunted. "But this isn't a place for a lady."

Moira groaned. "You're worse than my aunt. The rules for a lady's conduct just don't apply out here, Mathias. I appreciate your concern, but to anybody here, I'm just another miner. Let's keep it that way."

"What are you planning, girl!?" he demanded, eyeing her warily.

She smiled at him, sipping the hot coffee remaining in her mug. "There's no reason on earth why some of that gold dust shouldn't trickle into my pouch, now, is there?"

He frowned even deeper.

"I play a good hand of poker."

"Oh no, you don't," he said sternly, following her line of thought.

"Why should you object?"

"Because I brought you down here. I got responsibility for you."

"I'll release you from that responsibility right now," she said impatiently.

"Nope."

"You're being stubborn. You've been grumbling into your beard for the past two hundred miles because you got stuck with me. So now you're getting unstuck!"

"The answer is still no." He leaned toward her, glittering with warning, but Moira had long since learned that Mathias's bark was worse than his bite. She smiled up at him, eyes twinkling.

"You can stay with me as my bodyguard if you like. I'll cut you in for thirty percent of my winnings."

His expression grew thoughtful. "Fifty percent."

"Forty."

"Deal." They shook hands, grinning at each other.

Moira grew serious. "You know, Mathias. I've lost a lot

out here in California. One brother is dead, another is lost and probably dead as well. And . . . Random . . ." Her mouth tightened. "Well, I'll tell you this. I'm going to get something out of this experience. When I go back to Charleston, if I do, I'm going to go back filthy rich."

Chapter Twenty-six

Mathias was very good at taking care of sore losers who lost their pokes to Moira. She looked like a boy, and many men didn't appreciate being made a fool of by a child. When anyone started to argue, Mathias appeared at her elbow, and words died in men's throats with one look at that six-foot-six, 270-pound muscled frame.

In three days, Moira had won more than five hundred dollars in gold. She was tired of the City Hotel and moved on to other pastures.

"Easiest two hundred and fifty I've ever picked up," Mathias said, and Moira grinned at him.

"Two hundred," she corrected him. He shrugged.

"Never was much good at arithmetic," he muttered, but his eyes were laughing. "I've got to quit calling you 'girl.' I got a couple of very strange looks back there."

"Mory will do just fine. Even for a gelding."

Their partnership proved to be extremely profitable. Within the space of a week, Moira had made almost as much gold as it had taken her, Daniel, and Random to collect during their entire time on the Yuba. She felt sadness, though, in that knowledge, for Daniel had worked himself to death for something they could have had with ease. She should have thought of all this before.

There were moments when she felt guilty for what she was doing, making gain off someone else's loss. Mathias would have none of that sentiment. He couldn't see why she was having an attack of conscience simply because her wits were sharper than those of most of the men she played against. And winner or not, most of them were playing to while away the time until spring came. Entertainment was expensive, especially if you chose to sit in on a card game.

Seeing how much money she stood to gain, Moira tried to think of ways to use it. Daniel had wanted to repay their father's debts. It was the honorable thing to do, and she would do it in his name. As for herself, her desires had always been the same. Freedom. When she went back to Charleston, she wanted to be able to make her own decisions and not be at the mercy of Aunt Miranda's machinations. If and when she got married, it was going to be to someone she loved or she wouldn't marry at all.

Random.

The thought of him made her ache. She doubted she would ever feel that way about anyone again. And if she did, she would be twice as cautious as she had ever been before. Loving someone hurt. But she wasn't going to think about him. She was going to make lots and lots of money, enough to allow her to do so many things she wouldn't have time to think about him.

Easier said than done.

Every time she saw a tall, dark-haired man, her heart jumped into her throat. It was part of the reason she was afraid to stay in one casino several days in a row. She still had no doubt that Random was looking for her. She could feel it, as though his anger sent out strong waves toward her. If she ever did set eyes on him, she had prearranged with Mathias to hold him at bay until she could make a run for it. No use dying young if you didn't have to.

"You're going to have to face him sooner or later," Mathias said.

"I don't see why," she said stubbornly, the mere mention of Random making her squirm.

"Because a man like him doesn't give up."

"Enough failures and he'll have to."

Moira liked the Round House best of the Sacramento casinos. She didn't particularly care for the explicitly erotic pictures that were painted on the canvas walls, though they sometimes distracted her opponents and obviously were of great interest to the men drinking at the bars. But she did like the elegant touch of cut-crystal bowls filled with cigars, lemons, and peppermints. The string orchestra was not the world's best by a long shot, but it brought back many good memories of Charleston and the soirees she had attended. She could close her eyes and pretend she was there in one of her friend's ballrooms, dancing with a handsome young man. The young man, unfortunately, always developed Random's features.

She played at the Stinking Tent as well, though she preferred the others. It was made from a ripe old sail, for which it had been named. The Plains, on the other hand, seemed to appeal to those men who had come to California by way of one of the many wagon trains. On its tent walls was an interesting collection of trail scenes.

She often returned to the City Hotel, the rough palace owned by the famed Samuel Brannan, who stayed mostly in San Francisco, where he was developing vast holdings. She had only glimpsed the man a few times and thought he lived up to the stories she had heard about him. Many men were in awe of him, but few knew of his more larcenous side.

Mathias shared a story he had heard from a man at the bar. Brannan had come to California with a large group of Mormons and was in fact their religious leader. He was to answer to the Church, collect tithes, and organize his people. But the distance between Brannan and Brigham Young proved too great a temptation for the young entrepreneur. He collected the tithes but did not answer to the Church. When one of the elders demanded the funds, Brannan told him, "When the Lord can sign a receipt, I'll turn over the money." He was still collecting gold intended for the Church and using it to finance such personal ventures as the City Hotel. Moira had heard he was building another pleasure palace in San Francisco. The man had gall.

Mathias admired him. "If men are fools enough to give him a tenth of their workings, then they deserve what they get.

Hell, the Bible says the meek shall inherit the earth. I've always believed it. The meek get trampled, trodden on, shoved onto their faces, and that's just what they get—dirt up their noses. The Good Book also says God helps those who help themselves, and by God, Brannan is helping himself to the Church's gold."

Moira didn't see what was so funny about it, but in her own manner she enjoyed taking winnings from the City Hotel. Whatever she took away from there, she saw as taking from Brannan's own pocket.

The rains kept coming, making the land a murky swamp, swelling the river. The men in the tents were jubilant with the approach of Christmas. With each day that brought the holiday closer, the men seemed to drink and laugh more, only a closer look revealing the loneliness and longing for home in their reddened eyes. They all wanted to forget they were thousands of miles from friends and family.

Moira was no different. She kept thinking of Jack, crying over Daniel, and wondering where Random was. And Aunt Miranda was more often in her mind. She even wrote her a letter and sent it downriver on one of the sailing ships that brought supplies up to Sacramento from the coast. The letter was filled with false happiness, brave promises, and defiant plans for her return to Charleston. She couldn't bring herself to write of Daniel's death of her failure in finding Jack. Nor did she mention Random Hawthorne.

Mathias built a sturdy shelter near the river within easy walking distance of the many casinos. It didn't look like much, but it kept the rain out. He carried the gold dust Moira won in a special belt around his waist until they could turn it over to an assayer with a safe.

Gaily decorated Christmas trees were beginning to appear on the bars at all the casinos. The orchestra at the Round House played carols, which the patrons sang with more gusto than pitch. Moira tried to enter into the spirit of the season, but failed. She was tired and depressed. When she managed to keep from thinking of Random during her waking hours, he intruded upon her sleep.

Sitting at a poker table in the Round House, Moira concentrated on her cards. She had won several hands and lost the last two, making her about even. She kept her expression bland

and her hat pulled down to shadow her face. Mathias was at the bar watching over her, talking to a thin man with hawkish features and brown hair. Men were singing "Joy to the World" near the orchestra, and others were laughing raucously at one of the tables near an erotic picture on the east tent wall.

Moira felt someone watching her. Her muscles tensed, and she felt hot and then cold. Trying not to show any emotion, she glanced up. A man was standing about ten feet away, staring at her in amazement.

She stared back, eyes widening with recognition.

"The dealer wants your bet, kid." The player next to Moira prodded her with a sharp elbow. She glanced at him and then stood up, tossing her cards into the pot before turning abruptly away. Mathias, at the bar, straightened when he saw her abrupt action. The man who had been staring at Moira walked toward her. There was a deep frown on his face. His sandy-colored beard was neatly trimmed, his blue eyes clouded.

"Moira?"

She grinned and tipped her hat up and stood in front of him, hands on her hips.

"Hello, Kris."

Chapter Twenty-seven

Kris stared at her in a state of shock. "We've been looking all over for you for months and never once thought of this." He gestured toward her men's clothes. "We couldn't figure out how you got out of the hotel without raising some kind of excitement. Not a word, not a letter. Just disappeared."

"Daniel said you washed him out of the company."

Kris looked uncomfortable and embarrassed. "Well, we were concerned . . ." He cleared his throat.

"Didn't want the added burden of Daniel's little sister, did you? Yes, I know, and believe me, I understand. But in case you didn't notice"—she leaned toward him conspiratorialy— "no one knows I'm female." Her eyes laughed up at him.

He grinned back. "You do look just like a thousand other miners." He glanced around brightly. "Where's Danny?"

At Moira's silence, he looked back down at her. "What's the matter? Has he lost his poke again?"

"No, Kris," she said, her eyes misting. "His life. Danny died up on the Yuba River two months ago."

Kris stared at her in disbelief and then looked away. She saw him swallow, and tears moistened his eyes. "Damn," he muttered. "He was a good friend. And that makes two now."

"Two? Who else?"

"Paul died on the Mokelumne."

"How?"

"Miner's complaint. He just wasted away." They stood silently together amid the chaotic noise of the casino.

"There's someone I want you to meet," Moira said. "He's a friend." She laughed slightly. "My bodyguard, actually."

Having seen that she was in no immediate danger, Mathias had relaxed against the bar again. His glass was refilled with strong, raw whiskey, and he studied Kris from a distance, thick brows lowered. The young man was very handsome, tall, and well-built, and there was an air about him that bespoke blue-blooded stock.

Moira led Kris to the bar. Mathias straightened. His cold gray eyes speared Kris, who stared up at him in silent awe.

"This is Mathias," Moira said as though she were pointing out a national monument. She grinned up at the glowering mountain man, who had taken an almost belligerent stance before her and Kris. "And this is a very old and dear friend from Charleston, Mathias . . . Kris Westwood."

Kris was still staring up at the towering man. He swallowed hard. He realized the mountain man boasted a pair of shoulders that would have challenged Atlas, and he didn't look the least bit friendly. Those eyes staring out from the bearded face made him feel like a pinned bug.

"He really doesn't bite," Moira said. As though in contradiction, Mathias bared his teeth in a sneer. Moira prodded him. "Don't you dare make a liar out of me."

Kris looked between the two, thinking what an unlikely pair they made, Moira small and slender with big, dark laughing eyes and curling hair, and this great bear of a man, rough and rugged on the outside and probably worse within. Yet there seemed to be a camaraderie between them, a real affection.

Moira bellied up to the bar and called for wine. Kris could scarcely believe the change in her. She even stood like a man and kept her voice low and husky. When he met her eyes he saw she was laughing openly at him.

His mouth curved wryly. "It's a little hard to take in."

"So I noticed. But nothing has changed *under* these clothes," she said, teasing him to a hot blush.

Mathias pinched hard and she let out a yelp, looking at him in stunned surprise.

"That'll be enough of that," he told her. Kris started to laugh, and Mathias glowered at him over Moira's head. Kris abruptly stopped laughing.

"Will you stop staring at Kris like that, Mathias. You're acting like an old bear with his paw in a trap. Kris is a friend."

"Do say."

"Yes, I do say."

Mathias grunted and returned his attention to the whiskey, which disappeared down the hatch with one tip of a big, hairy wrist. The shot glass looked like a thimble in his hand.

"Where are the rest of the boys?" Moira asked with interest.

"Scattered around Sacramento, losing their pokes, more than likely," Kris told her, nursing a whiskey. He smiled at her lopsidedly. "We don't have all that much to lose anyway. Didn't have much luck."

Moira smiled smugly. "We did."

"You did?"

"Daniel made a strike not long before he died."

"And you *left* it? Why?"

Moira flushed, thinking of Random. "It's winter, remember? It's only raining down here. But up in the mountains it's snowing, and I don't mean a few inches."

"But you're going back up in the spring."

"I haven't decided."

Kris looked at her and then across at Mathias. "You made a real strike and you're *not sure* you're going back to work it?"

Moira grinned. "I'm getting rich right here, and not even getting my hands dirty," she told him.

"Playing cards?"

"You sound surprised."

"Well..." He looked uncomfortable, and Moira's mouth tightened as she remembered some of Daniel's bitterness.

"Just because my father was unlucky and Daniel was as well doesn't mean that I am, too."

"I wasn't thinking of your father or Danny, Moira."

"Then what?"

"It's not really my place to say this, but I don't think it's proper for a lady to be playing poker, let alone be in a place like this."

"Save your breath," Mathias muttered. "You're talking to one mule-headed woman."

"And what would you have me do?" she asked, looking at the two men, her mouth a hard line, her eyes sparkling with angry challenge.

"There are any number of things a woman can do, even out here," Kris said vaguely.

"Go back to Charleston and marry some rich man," Mathias told her without hesitation, resurrecting Charles Beauchamp's moldly image. She sniffed in derision.

"Well, if you'll excuse me, gentlemen," she said and left them staring after her.

"Hell," Mathias muttered, watching her march furiously away.

"I think she's mad at us," Kris said, draining his whiskey.

"Do tell," Mathias grumbled.

It was raining outside, but it did nothing to cool Moira's hot temper. She stalked down the muddy street and entered another casino. Mathias caught up with her just inside the tent and put a heavy hand on her shoulder.

"Don't go getting all huffy."

She gave him a glittering glare. Kris was standing there watching her, and she cast him a withering look.

"Two things I want out of this particular venture, Mathias, with or without your disapproving partnership. Number one"
—she raised a long, slender finger—"I want enough money to look for Jack until I find him. And number two"—she raised another finger—"I want enough money to guarantee me freedom from narrow-minded males like you two." She turned and stalked off to the nearest poker table.

"Whew," Kris breathed. "I should've kept my big mouth shut." With a grunt Mathias headed for the bar.

An hour later, Moira was slightly richer and definitely in better spirits. She walked over to Mathias and Kris, busy holding up their end of the bar. Kris glanced at her with a tentative smile, testing the waters, and she beamed up at him warmly, glowing from her triumph at the poker table.

"We've enough to have a real Christmas celebration tomorrow," she announced.

"With your percentage?" Mathias growled.

"I docked you for your suggestion a while ago," she said without the least twinge of conscience. "Yours will go for the liquor. I'll buy the food." He grunted and cast Kris a narrow-eyed look.

"Can you get the rest of the Company together? We'll meet at the River Savoy tomorrow evening for Christmas festivities," she told Kris.

"The River Savoy?" Kris said blankly.

"Our place," Mathias grunted, glowering balefully at Moira, who ignored his ill temper.

"We've a proper place on the American," Moira said, seeing Kris's speculative glance at Mathias. Did he really think she was sleeping with this giant? "Mathias designed and constructed it himself. It consists of canvas and discarded lumber. There are *two* rooms and a cooking area. And the whole place is dry."

With the endless rains that had come, that in itself was a minor miracle. Kris looked suitably impressed. "Wish I could say the same for where I'm living. The tent leaks like a sieve and smells like it's rotting off the poles." He took Moira's arm, looking at her intently. "By the way, your cabin mate is here in Sacramento."

"Jewel?"

"Yes. She's living someplace on the outskirts of the camp. But she said she's going to be dancing with the miners at the City Hotel Christmas celebrations tomorrow night. Brannan has found eighteen women."

"Dancing! Why didn't you tell me?" She looked at the two men and laughed. "This might not be such a bad Christmas after all!" The raucous singing of "Adeste Fidelis" seemed to confirm that.

Sutter's old gristmill had been turned into a paradise of soft lantern light, with decorations that glittered and holiday music. A score of loud, excited California gold miners were being plied with champagne. Gold dust poured across the poker and faro tables and bars, and the noise intensified when each woman entered.

Moira arrived, making nineteen. She stood between Mathias and Kris, wearing a hastily made gingham dress. It was far from the height of fashion, but there wasn't a man there that cared. Any woman in these male-populated camps was a sensation. Moira had made the neckline low, though still within the borders of propriety. She had curled her hair with rags the night before. Kris hadn't been able to prevent himself from staring at her, and he was a gentleman! Mathias had glowered disapprovingly, fatherly as ever.

Moira knew that Jewel would be at the hotel decked in her finest satins and lace. Within two minutes of entering, Moira pinpointed her ex-cabinmate, locating her by the crowd of men around her. Someone pushed through to tell Jewel that a friend of hers had arrived, and Jewel parted the sea of men to come to Moira. She was dressed in red and black, with outrageously fluffy long feathers dancing on her head. The dress was brilliant, provocative, and yet not a bit indecent. She had a magnificent figure, as every man in the hotel could see.

"Moira Cavendish, as I live and breathe!" Jewel cried, a group of randy miners in her wake. She threw her arms around Moira and hugged her, oblivious to the men's surprise that a known prostitute could be on such friendly terms with a young lady. Jewel drew back and clasped Moira's hand, looking her over.

"You look like you're on your way to the Charleston Opera."

Moira laughed. "You do lie so well, Jewel."

Jewel winked. "Where in hell have you been since we docked in Frisco?"

"All over." Moira grinned. "But mainly on the Yuba."

"Well, I made it to Sonora, but it was getting too wild even for me," Jewel informed her. "Two murders, a stabbing, half a dozen brawls, and one man lost in a mudhole!" She laughed.

"A mudhole?"

"Right on the main street of town. Dropped in and never climbed out."

"Well, you certainly look well for having been there."

"Rich as Croesus!" Jewel laughed again and glanced around

pointedly at the grinning, avid faces of her admirers. "Business is booming!"

Moira giggled. "So I can see."

Jewel grew serious, leaning forward and squeezing her young friend's hands. "I was sorry to hear about Daniel."

Moira's happiness dimmed, and she nodded in acknowledgment. "We're not going to talk about anything unhappy tonight, Jewel. It's Christmas Eve, and we're only going to think about good times and happy memories."

"Agreed." Jewel smiled in understanding and then whispered breathlessly in Moira's ear, "Who is this gorgeous giant beside you?" When she drew back, her eyes were on Mathias, and they were sparkling with unconcealed interest.

Moira had never thought of Mathias as "gorgeous," but then, beauty was in the eye of the beholder. She glanced up at the mountain man to gauge his reaction to Jewel and was amusingly surprised. He seemed dumbstruck, but there was definite fire in that usually cool pair of gray eyes.

"Mathias, I'd like you to meet another good friend, Miss Jewel Delarue."

Mathias just stared. Jewel smiled slowly and stepped forward, moving her shoulders in a seductive way. "Mathias," she said, testing the name and appearing to like it. She looked him over slowly from the top of his head to his toes, stopping once midway, her brows rising faintly. He didn't move, but he was making his own careful inspection and obviously liking what he saw. Jewel stepped closer and hooked a long, slender finger into one of his buttonholes. She tugged lightly, and Mathias leaned toward her, dipping his head as though her finger controlled him.

"You're the biggest man I've ever seen, Mathias," she said in a low, husky whisper. "Are you big . . . everywhere?"

Mathias colored beneath his beard, and men close enough to hear what she had said grinned at one another. Others were craning forward to hear and see what was going on.

Mathias, recovering his composure, retorted honestly, "Getting bigger every minute, Miss Delarue."

She laughed appreciatively and looped her arm through his. Gazing up at him, she promised, "In that case, I'm not letting you out of my sights!"

Kris drew Moira away, concerned over what her innocent ears might be hearing, but she laughed in delight.

"I think they've taken a definite liking to one another," she teased as Kris pulled her firmly into his arms and started dancing away from the rowdies around the pair.

"I'd say that was a fair guess," he agreed, grinning down at her. The music grew louder as more and more dancers joined them. With only nineteen women, there were a hundred men dancing with one another. Everyone was laughing and having a good time, trying with brave desperation to forget they were so far from home and loved ones. It was Christmas, and they were going to be happy if it took a case of champagne per man to do it.

Moira danced until her feet and back ached. Kris watched when he wasn't able to claim her. He had tried once and been quickly informed that he had had his one dance and it was now someone else's turn. Moira didn't dance with anyone twice. When she would have rested, the look on the men's faces prevented her. She knew that for many of the miners she was standing in for a wife or girlfriend left behind, and for others she was one of the few women they had seen in months. She allowed them to gaze at her in simple male adoration. It was heady, and she meant to enjoy every blessed moment of it.

Champagne flowed freely, and the noise grew with each empty case. It was almost deafening in the old gristmill. Spinning around the room, Moira flashed by someone and felt a shock of fright as she recognized the face in the crowd. She turned her head quickly, hoping she had been mistaken. She went around the floor again on the arm of an Ohio farmer. Her eyes scanned the crowd and she saw him again. Her heart started racing.

Her instinct was to flee, run to the closest door, and seek obscurity in the darkness. Her partner looked down at her curiously as he felt her stumble.

"Are you all right, ma'am? May I get you something to drink?"

"I'm fine." She recovered quickly, beaming up at him and trying to ignore the thundering of her heart as they went around the dance floor again and she was brought close to the man who was leaning against a pillar and watching her. She saw him smile slightly when he noticed she was staring at him as well.

Barilovich!

Surely he wouldn't recognize her? He had seen her as a man, dressed in faded, worn dungarees and an old woolen shirt and jacket, and now her hair was curled. She shuddered at the memory of their encounter, feeling his boot cracking into her ribs again.

"Ma'am?"

"I'm sorry," she apologized to her dance partner. "I was just thinking of...of...home."

"I know." He smiled sadly. He looked like a nice young man, with brown hair and hazel eyes. He wore a mustache, which made him look older than he probably was. "I've got a girl waiting for me in Ohio. At least, I hope she's waiting," he added with a self-mocking laugh that didn't go to his eyes. "Haven't heard from her in a long time."

"Letters take a long time getting here," Moira offered encouragingly. "And besides, you're a very handsome man. Why wouldn't she wait?"

"Because she's the prettiest thing east of the Rockies," he told her and then flushed. "No insult to you meant, ma'am."

"None taken."

The music stopped, and a wiry young man from Alabama took his place, followed by a Frenchman who was amazed that she could converse with him in his own tongue. He would have claimed her for another dance had a ham-sized hand not shoved him roughly back amid other men asking a turn.

Barilovich moved in front of her, silver-gray eyes staring at her. "My dance," he said in his thickly accented English, ignoring the grumbling protests all around him from the others who had been waiting. The Frenchman put his hand on Barilovich's arm and found himself propelled back, though the big man's eyes never left Moira's. Hers widened and her face paled. He held out his hand and she accepted it, aware that hers shook in his. He smiled and pushed another man back as he drew her onto the dance floor. Amazingly, the big, bullying oaf could dance!

"What's your name, pretty lady?" he asked, bending his head to speak closely. She felt cold all over.

What was she to answer to that question? *Cavendish!* He'd drag her out of there for an interrogation so fast she wouldn't have a chance to scream. Why hadn't she remembered telling him and Heaton that Jack had headed for Sacramento? Idiot! It was pure luck that she hadn't run into him before this!

"Moira," she said, controlling her expression, smiling up at him through her lashes. Sidetrack him anyway you can, she kept thinking. Don't give him any reason to remember you! She leaned back slightly. "What's yours, Mister?"

"Ivan," he answered looking down from the slim white neck to the soft contours of her breasts beneath the gingham. When he met her eyes again, the smile he gave her was frighteningly purposeful. But at least he hadn't recognized her! "I haven't been this close to a woman for a long time," he told her, and she felt his large hand tighten at her waist, drawing her closer until she felt the brush of his thighs against hers. The chill settled in her and then spread.

"Most men here haven't," she said conversationally. Her hand stiffened against his shoulder, trying to put a little more distance between them. His smile lingered.

"I've got plenty of gold." What was she supposed to say to that?

"Good for you." More than likely he had stolen it.

"How much you want?"

"I beg your pardon?"

"I like my women small. Small, dark-eyed women with nice white breasts . . ."

She was afraid she was going to be sick.

"I saw you looking at me. I'm—"

"I think you're making a mistake."

"No mistake," he said. "I'll pay you well."

She stiffened and could feel anger replacing fear. Repulsive creature, she thought, longing to raise her knee sharply and give him a fraction of the pain he had caused her those weeks up on the Yuba.

His expression had changed. Her silence had irritated him. This man obviously hated to be refused anything, and he probably retaliated for the sheer pleasure of inflicting pain.

"Everybody's got a price," he said ominously.

She was shaking badly, searching desperately for a way out

of this situation. When the music stopped, he didn't release her as the others had done, and she didn't dare protest for the ruckus it would cause. He looked around as though challenging anyone who thought they could take her from him. The music started again. He danced her away.

"How much you want?"

An idea came, and disgusting as it was, she grabbed it. "Ivan, you're an attractive man," she said, voice trembling with what she hoped he would think was passion. "I'll take you to bed for . . . say, twenty dollars in gold?"

"We go now," he said thickly.

"Finish the dance, please," she whispered. He pulled her closer, drawing his hips against hers, and she swallowed at what she felt there. She sighed for effect.

"I hope you don't have anything like the last . . ."

He looked at her blankly. "What?"

"He had . . . well . . . never mind." She shrugged.

"What?" His voice was grim.

"Oh, I wouldn't worry about it. I suppose a good wash would make sure you didn't catch anything after we . . ."

He understood. He released her abruptly, saying something in his own language that she was sure was not a compliment. He left her standing in the middle of the floor. Kris appeared suddenly as she darted for a doorway.

"What's going on?"

Moira grabbed his arm, eyes wide with fright. "Get me out of here, Kris!" He stared at her and then glanced at Barilovich, who was shoving his way off the dance floor and very close to a fight as he reached the bar. Then he looked down at her again, and saw how pale she was and the glisten of panicked tears in her eyes.

Taking her arm, Kris began to push their way through the throng of men trying to detain her. Moira held on, keeping her head low, pretending she was faint and needed air.

"Let the lady through," Kris kept saying, shoving men back. A narrow path opened before them to the door.

"Damn, it's raining again," Kris said, stopping before they went out. A torrent was coming down from the black sky. Moira dove out the door anyway.

"Moira!"

She ran, her slippers sucked off her feet, the gingham dress ruined by the mud and muck that splashed up as she flew down the street. Kris caught up with her, grabbing her arm and bringing her to a jolting halt.

The rain poured down over them, running in rivulets over her face and body. "Moira, what happened with that big bastard back there?" Kris demanded, looking ready to go back and challenge Barilovich.

"He's *Barilovich*," she hissed, her lungs burning painfully from her run.

"Barilovich? Who's Barilovich?"

She shook her head. "Not now, Kris. I've got to get away from here!" She looked around, not sure where she was. It was almost two miles to her tent from here. The rain was drenching them both.

"Come on," Kris said, taking her hand and running down a row of tightly clustered tents lighted from within. Several times they had to stop for Moira to catch her breath, taking shelter where they could. Finally they reached Kris's tent, within sight of the high walls of Sutter's Fort. Tents were jammed together all around them, crowded close to the walls.

Kris ducked inside, pulling Moira with him. He pushed her to a cot, where she sank down gratefully. It was dark inside, and she could barely make out even the shapes of packs and mining gear stacked in one corner. Kris lit the lantern, which cast a soft glow around them. He made a fire in a small wood stove that could be carried easily on mule back. She looked at it and laughed shakily.

"You have some comforts even out here."

"As many as I can, which isn't much." He stripped off his coat, flinging it onto another cot. He looked her over and then picked up a blanket. "You'd better get out of that dress. I'll wait outside." He left, and she let out her breath. Well, she guessed there wasn't any choice. Standing up, she stripped off the ruined dress and pulled the ribbons out of her hair. She picked up the blanket and wrapped it around her. She pulled the flap back and called out to Kris.

"Your turn," she said, grinning at him, and turned her back.

"All right," he said when he was finished, and she turned around. He was looking at her, and she saw the flush in his face and the darkness in his eyes. He looked away, breathing in slowly. "Now, just who is this Barilovich?"

Moira stood closer to the little wood stove, raising the hem of the blanket to expose her calves to the warmth. Kris looked at her, eyes moving slowly from her damp hair down to her white shoulders to the soft curves exposed by the wrapped blanket. He gulped.

"Sweet Jesus," he murmured thickly.

"Barilovich is hunting for Jack," Moira said, unaware of Kris's agitation. She felt bedraggled and not the least bit attractive. And this was Kris, someone she had known since childhood, someone almost as close as a brother.

"I'm not sure why," she went on. "Random was told in Goodyears Bar that Jack had killed a man."

"Wait a minute. Random? You mean Hawthorne, from the ship?" Kris asked, confused. "And who's—"

"Let me explain. I don't know very much, Kris. Apparently, Barilovich and Heaton were up on the Tahualamne sometime in '48 or early '49. There was some sort of fight involving them, my brother, and a man named Jass Whitsell. Jass Whitsell was Jack's partner for a while, but they were separated. When we left the ship, Daniel and I, we went to Sutter's Fort, where we found out that Jack was being followed by all three of those men. Jass Whitsell was trying to warn him about something. Anyway, we met up with Random Hawthorne in Rough and Ready by accident, and the three of us headed up to Goodyears Bar, where we were told that this Barilovich had said that Jack killed his partner on the Tahualamne. Jack was still heading for the mountains, so we followed and built a cabin up near Haskell Peak. That's where Daniel made his strike and died," she said, remembered pain cracking her voice. She breathed in slowly. "We all thought that Jack would have to come back by that route and that we could intercept him. Well, he didn't. But Barilovich and Heaton did, and I told them that we'd seen a man fitting Jack's description heading back for Sacramento. They had no idea who I was, of course. And then Barilovich . . . he . . . well . . . he believed me. That's why he's here. He didn't recognize me as the man on the Yuba. And if he finds out my name is Cavendish . . . or really gets a good look at my face and starts to remember . . ."

"Where does Hawthorne come into all this?"

"I've already told you. We ran into him by accident in—"

"You were living with him up there in the mountains . . . after Daniel died?"

She looked at him impatiently. "Well, I wasn't living on a snowdrift! Oh, for heaven's sake, it was perfectly decent. Besides, he's a gentleman." She turned away, almost having blurted out that he was married. But there were a lot of married men in California, and they were enjoying the few women available.

Kris made a sound of disbelief. Moira turned and looked at him. "We found Jass Whitsell's body about half a mile from the cabin," she continued. "Random wasn't sure if he'd been murdered or not. I went back up a few days later, and that's when I met Mathias. I decided it was time to come back out of the mountains when he told me he had found a man's tracks that had disappeared in the snow during a storm. Jack's probably dead. . . ."

"And where's Hawthorne now?"

"I don't know," she said chokingly.

Silence met her answer, and she turned and glared at Kris defiantly. "What do you want to know, Kris?"

Kris had the good grace to color. "So what are you going to do now?" he said after a long moment. "Go back to Charleston?"

"No," she sighed, sitting on the cot again. The blanket opened over her knees and she rewrapped it absently. "I'm going back to the Yuba in the spring and look for Jack again."

"You just said he was dead."

"I said Mathias told me he could be dead. I won't give up until I know for sure. One way or the other."

"And what about this Barilovich and Heaton?"

"I'll have to stay out of their way."

"They'll head up the Yuba as well, especially if they don't find out anything about Jack down here."

"I suppose so. I'll have to worry about that later. I'll just have to go back before they do and reach Jack before they can."

"If he's still up there."

"Yes." She sighed wearily.

Kris stood and came to sit on the cot beside her. "I'll go back with you," he volunteered, looking at her. She turned slightly and put her hands on his arms.

"Would you, Kris?"

"Yes," he said huskily. He put his hands on her shoulders, sliding them up to her neck. "Yes. Moira, I'll go anywhere you want me to go." He drew her forward and kissed her before she realized what he intended. She gasped, and he took advantage of her surprise to kiss her more deeply and passionately, uncaring that she sat frozen in shock in his arms.

"Kris . . ."

"Moira, I love you. I've loved you for as long as I can remember," he said hoarsely. "I'd do anything for you."

Moira stared up at him, tears welling up in her eyes. His face blurred, and she thought of Random with such piercing longing and pain that she moaned aloud.

"Moira?"

She shook her head. "All I want is to find Jack. That's all. Anything else will have to wait until later."

Chapter Twenty-eight

Following the Christmas celebration, Moira cut her hair again, redonned her miner's clothes, and went back to work at the poker tables. Her luck wasn't good. She was having difficulty maintaining her concentration, constantly on the lookout for Barilovich and Heaton. She had described them carefully to Mathias, but Mathias's concentration wasn't much good either. He had Jewel Delarue on his mind. And whenever she was around, he watched her and forgot that Moira was even in the same casino. Kris had become more her bodyguard than Mathias.

Eighteen forty-nine had come and gone, and the sojourning miners of Sacramento were suffering from their lengthy holiday celebration. The pounding rains didn't help, keeping the streets virtually impassable and dampening spirits as it soaked the canvas tents and seeped into bedding and gear.

Because it was dry, Moira had begun to play more frequently at the City Hotel. Kris knew who Barilovich was and kept an eye out for him. He had spotted him twice and Moira had made a retreat without being seen, realizing that, dressed as she was now, the man might make the connection between her and the youngster up on the Yuba whom he had beaten up and threatened.

Jewel was spending less time in her tent entertaining men and more time with Mathias, gazing bemusedly into his eyes. His hard worldly features were softening, and he smiled often.

Kris was pressuring Moira to marry him, and when he kissed her she sensed a feverish desire for her that repulsed her. Only one man had ever kissed her and made her respond. That man was Random Hawthorne.

Rain was pounding on the Stinking Tent as Moira picked up her cards and fanned them in her palm, studying them and calculating the odds of a winning hand. She looked up and met the eyes of the man sitting opposite her. He was thin, with brown, lank hair and swamp-water-green eyes. He had a beak nose and thin lips, thinner since the last two hands, which she had won.

She discarded three. The bets went around the table. "Too steep for me," one said and tossed his cards onto the table. Moira called and raised another fifty, looking at the man on the other side of the table. His mouth tightened even more.

"I'll see you," he said in a low voice and dumped in the necessary chips. He laid out his hand. A straight flush. Moira's heart sank. She tossed her cards in and stood up. She should never have played this evening. Her mind wasn't on the game. The man grinned smugly, gathering up the pot.

Kris smiled at her as she came up to the bar. Mathias and Jewel moved to make room for her. "Win again?"

"Not much tonight. Cash these, would you please?" she said, handing Kris the pouch of chips. He glanced at her.

"You all right? You look pale."

"Just tired." She moved restlessly, wishing he wasn't so possessive. She asked for a shot of whiskey, and Mathias's head snapped around.

"You'll have none of that, Mory," he growled. Jewel was looking at her with worry.

"What's wrong, honey?"

Moira wiped perspiration from her forehead and stared at the bar blankly. "Just tired." But she felt nervous, tense, sure that something was about to happen.

Everything appeared as usual. Men crowded together at the bar or around the gambling tables, the talk was boisterous, the rain pounded with dull monotony on the tent. She turned away again, leaning heavily on the bar, feeling with a sudden certainty that everything was catching up to her.

"Moira, you don't look well," Jewel said.

Moira drank some of the apple cider Mathias had placed in front of her instead of the whiskey she had ordered. It tasted faintly of wood.

Kris's hand fell hard on her shoulder, making her jump. She glanced up in irritation and was surprised at the grim look on his face, the angry glitter in his eyes. He smiled, but it was a mere twist of his lips. "Your Yuba cabin mate just walked in here," he announced flatly, his young features taut with jealousy.

Moira's heart made a leap right up into her throat. Her eyes opened wide as she turned her head sharply toward the entrance.

Random!

He stood just inside the tent, tall and dark, shaking the rain off. He took off his rain-drenched hat and shook his head. She stared at him, feeling close to tears of relief that he was all right after all. He looked so tall and in control standing there, and longing swept over her.

Moira watched him scan the throngs of men around the poker table, unable to move or think, only to drink in the sight of him. Mathias looked at her and then in the direction of her fixed gaze. Kris was saying something to her in a low, growling voice, but she didn't hear.

She still loved him. And for a few seconds, nothing else but that seemed to matter.

As though feeling someone watching him, Random's dark gaze turned toward the bar. He saw Mathias first, standing tall and conspicuous among the smaller men around him. Then his eyes moved, searching and finding Moira. They caught her, and she shivered at the dark fierceness of that look, her relief smothered by the fear of reprisal for what she had done to him.

"Mathias . . ." she muttered in fright.

"You'd better get the hell out of here, fast," he growled, seeing Random coming toward them with purposeful strides.

"Moira?" Kris grabbed her arm. Mathias moved forward to intercept Random.

"Let go!" Moira yanked away from Kris and saw his startled, confused look.

There was an angry buzz behind her as Random pushed his way past the men standing in his way. Mathias blocked his path, and Moira scurried toward the exit.

"Hey, watch where you're going!" someone snarled at her as she tried to get past a cluster of men in her way. She felt herself being shoved rudely back. There was a crash behind her, and she turned to see Random and Mathias fighting among the tables. The noise rose, men shouting and swearing. Mathias had a hold on Random, wrestling with the younger man, trying to hold him back while Moira made her getaway. Random sent an elbow into Mathias's midsection and then spun around to send a fist cracking into his jaw. The big man stumbled backward, and Random took the opportunity to lunge toward Moira. His eyes . . . Oh, God, his eyes. He was going to strangle her!

Mathias dove after him, bringing him down hard beneath one of the gambling tables. Men moved back as they rolled back and forth, finally knocking the table over. Moira frantically tried to get out of the Stinking Tent before Random reached her. Men were surging toward the fighting pair, shouting raucous encouragement, making boisterous bets on who would win. The younger, leaner man was a skilled and savage fighter.

As a last resort, Moira went down on her knees and crawled through a crowd of men and under a table until she reached a space where she could move. She got to her feet, pushing and shoving past shouting men.

She burst out of the tent and stopped, looking around her in confusion and panic. Her instinct was to run as far and as fast as she could, uncaring of the foul weather. She heard another table crash behind her, followed by a burst of shouting and cheering.

She turned and looked back into the glowing canvas casino and caught sight of Random as he straightened up, a piece of broken chair that he had undoubtedly just used over Mathias's head still in his hand. He glared toward the exit, catching sight of her, and flung it violently aside.

"Oh, God," she moaned in fright, seeing the blaze of rage in his dark eyes as he began shoving his way toward her.

Moira turned and fled down the dark, muddy street, rain

pouring down like a sheet of water from a heavenly bucket. She was almost blinded.

"Moira!!" Random bellowed, emerging from the Stinking Tent and coming after her.

Sprinting, Moira glanced back over her shoulder and saw how his long legs were eating up the distance between them. She turned and plunged headlong into a group of tents, weaving in and out. She tripped and fell into one and heard men cursing inside as the shelter collapsed around them. She scrambled to her feet and went on.

Angry voices and shouts rose behind her, but she kept going, weaving among the shelters and then coming out into another main street of town. She stretched her legs to their limit, lungs expanding painfully.

A hand caught her flying coattails, and she lunged forward as hard as she could, feeling the grip slipping. She was tackled, brought down hard and face first into the muddy Sacramento street.

She choked on the mud and rolled, hitting and kicking. The dark shape came down over her, smashing the air from her lungs with his weight. She grunted, reaching up to scratch up at him. A hand twisted in her hair, jerking her head back. A fist crashed into her jaw.

Moira fell back limply, half-conscious, shocked. Even in her fear of Random's retaliation she had never expected him to hit her like that. Strangle her, perhaps, but not really hit her. She tasted blood in her mouth. She was yanked up by one arm and flung across his shoulder as he strode through the rain. The torrent flowed down over her, washing the mud from her head.

A tent flap was thrown aside, and suddenly she was inside a dark shelter. She was flung down, hitting the ground with a thud that knocked the wind from her again. A lantern was lit.

A dark shape sat down beside her. She was roughly pushed back when she tried to sit up, and then she saw the fierce face staring down at her in the lantern light.

"Now, boy, just what do you know about Jack Cavendish?" Barilovich growled.

Chapter Twenty-nine

Moira shrank back, her eyes widening, her face paling to ashen gray. Heaton ducked inside the tent and stood staring down at her. Barilovich blocked any possible escape.

"So you got him!" Heaton said triumphantly.

Barilovich didn't answer. He was staring at Moira, the tic beside his eye twitching spasmodically. Her muscles tensed in anticipation of another blow, and her heart beat against her ribs. His eyes narrowed suddenly, and she saw his nostrils flare, making him look like a hungry beast of prey. His hand snaked out and grabbed her hair, twisting her head sharply back and toward the light. She let out a moan of pain and heard him say something, a harsh guttural word in his own language. She felt his huge hand at her shirt front, ripping it open, shoving it aside. He ripped off the wrap she used to hide her femininity.

There was a moment of stunned silence within the tent. Then Heaton spoke, moving closer to get a better look. "Holy Christ! A woman..."

Barilovich swung a fist, catching Heaton squarely in the groin. Heaton fell to the ground in a heap, cradling his genitals.

"You stupid bastard! Keep your voice down!" Barilovich growled at him. "Get out of here!"

Heaton crawled to the tent flap, disappearing outside. Barilovich turned back, twisting Moira's hair harder and making her cry out in pain.

"So the boy on the Yuba and the girl with the sailor's disease is one and the same," he said savagely. His face came closer, silver eyes glittering ferally in the lantern light, his lips stretching across his teeth in a snarl. Moira shrank back as far as his hand permitted her, staring up at him with glazed eyes.

"What do you know about Cavendish?"

"Nothing." She gasped in pain as those hard fingers twisted her hair again, threatening to pull it from her stinging scalp.

"What do you know?" He spoke slowly between his bared teeth.

"He . . . he came down the Yuba. I gave him some supplies. He said he was going on to Sacramento," she said, repeating what she had told him before. She cried out again as his other hand sought her breast.

"You're lying, you bitch!"

"No!"

His fingers tightened painfully. "Cavendish never left the mountains! So how do you know about the gold-and-onyx ring he wears? What do you know about the lake?"

"Lake?" she repeated, and he squeezed harder, drawing another cry from her. Tears of pain blinded her. "I . . . I don't know anything. You're hurting me," she cried, and he laughed low.

"I haven't even started on you yet," he told her as his hand left her breast to slide down to the waistband of her dungarees. She screamed. His hand cut it off, and her air supply as well. She bucked, trying to escape the smothering hand. He was fumbling with his clothes, opening them.

She heard something behind them. She looked up in terror as a dark shape entered the tent. Barilovich was dragged back, and Moira saw Random yank the big man around and hit him twice. One brutal fist smashed into Barilovich's stomach and another sent him backward over a cot and into some packs. When Barilovich started to get up, Random hit him again. Barilovich fell back, unconscious, the front of his pants unbuttoned.

Random stood above Moira, glaring down at her fiercely, seeing her shirt pulled open, the dungarees yanked down around her hips. He made a harsh animal sound in his chest, and she shrank back from the savagery in his dark eyes as they swung again to Barilovich's unconscious form. She struggled to sit up, clumsy in her confusion and terror, uttered a frightened cry as Random hunkered down and reached for her. She jerked back, eyes wide.

"Damn it, Moira!" He swore and grabbed her, pulling her up, jerking her pants back in place and shoving her shirttail in where it belonged. He cast another black look at Barilovich and then propelled her before him out of the tent.

Heaton was lying unconscious where he had attempted to stop Random from entering the tent. The rain was pouring down and puddling around him. Moira stared at him until Random grabbed her arm and pushed her forward. She stumbled and started to fall. Random muttered something and paused long enough to swing her up into his arms.

"I don't know how in hell you manage to get yourself into these messes," he snarled down at her. The rain was worse than before, a blanket of wet darkness falling from an angry sky. Random stared into her face and then began to stride from the cluster of tents toward one of the main streets.

There was an old oak and he stopped there, letting her feet drop to the ground and then pressing her back against the great trunk, where they had some slight, small shelter from the wet fury coming down on them.

"I ought to beat the hell out of you for what you've put me through," he growled, face close to hers. It was dark, but she could still see the glitter of unleashed anger in his eyes.

"What did you expect me to do?" she shouted at him, defensive in her hurt and fear.

"Certainly not what you did, you little fool!"

She tried to turn away and was shoved back against the tree again. "You might have died out there!" he shouted.

"I didn't. I caught up with Mathias! So, as you can see, I can manage quite well without you, Mr. Hawthorne."

"Mathias!" He spat the name out angrily. "I hope I cracked his head open for him!"

"Let go of me!"

"Oh, no," he said in a low, menacing voice. "I'm going to hog-tie you this time."

"Is that the usual way you keep your women?"

"Shut up!"

"Let me go!" She struggled, shoving at him with her fists, setting all her strength against him, and finally fell back weakly against the tree, panting in exhaustion.

Random jerked her chin up, and his mouth came down ruthlessly on hers. She groaned in protest, trying to move back from him and finding she was back as far as she could go. He followed her small movement, leaning his hips against hers, rubbing sensuously against her. She moaned, the weeks of dreaming and longing firing her blood to fever pitch and making her melt into him. Her hands spread eagerly over his chest, feeling the rapid pounding of his heart, the burning heat. He drew his head away and glared down at her. Even in the darkness, she could feel the rage emanating from him.

"When I get you back to the mountains..." he warned threateningly.

"I'm not going back with you. I'm not going anywhere."

"Oh, yes, you're going, all right," he told her darkly. "You're going to go all the way back, and I'm going to keep you there until I've finished with you."

"Like your other women, I suppose! Well, forget it, Hawthorne! I came to find Jack, not to keep your bed warm until you decide to go back aboard your ship!" Tears of anger and pain poured down her cheeks. He stopped her again with his mouth. She pushed at him as hard as she could, trying to turn her head away. But it was futile.

"I won't forget a thing!" he said hoarsely when she finally stopped fighting him. "Especially the fact that you tried to kill me up there in the mountains."

"Let go!" she whimpered, feeling the tension of his muscles, the barely controlled rage and passion.

"Let you go? Not hardly. Now now. Not ever!"

She winced, pulling back, but his fingers tightened, yanking her back against him again.

"It doesn't pay to become involved with a woman," he said between his teeth. "It's a damn pain in the gut. And I'll tell you this, Moira. If I can't bind you to me with love, as I intended, then I'll bind you to me in another way just as strongly." And his hand moved down over her buttocks, pulling her even more firmly against him and telling her well enough just what he meant.

There was shouting and sudden confusion around them. Random looked away from her pale face, staring at the men shouting incoherently in panic.

"What in hades . . ." he muttered, his hold loosening.

Lanterns were flickering as men ran in all directions, yelling. Tents were emptying, supplies and gear were being dragged out.

"Flood!"

In the faint light, water could be seen pouring into the streets of Sacramento.

"The river is over the banks! *Run!*"

The rains had swelled the streams feeding the wide artery that moved through the heartland of California, and the river had overflowed.

Random swore under his breath. "What else can possibly go wrong!" he muttered before he started running for high ground, dragging Moira behind him.

Chapter Thirty

Random took Moira to Sutter's Fort, where they found a sliver of space among the hundreds of other homeless men seeking shelter from the overflowing, raging river. It was dark. It was cold. Men were crowded together, miserable, hungry, and in despair, waiting to see what was left of their California dream. There was no way to know how extensive the damage was until morning light, and that was hours away.

They sat in silence among the throng, Random deep in thought, Moira tense and worried about Mathias, Jewel, and Kris. She stood up once, and Random caught her wrist. "Sit down!" he ordered, and when she tried to pull away, he yanked her down with a thump.

"I want to look for Jewel and Mathias," she said with angry frustration.

"Mathias is a survivor, and Jewel is more than likely with him."

"And Kris?"

He frowned deeply, and his mouth tightened. "I don't give a damn about your Kris. He can make his own way."

"Well, I care!" She tried to pull away again, and he jerked her back, eyes darkening ominously.

"What do you plan to do, Moira? Or is this another of your thoughtless impulses that will get you literally into deep water?"

"I can't just sit here, Random. They're my friends, and they might be out there someplace needing help."

He looked at her for a long moment and then relented. "All right. If they're not here by morning, we'll find some way to look for them."

He never said what she expected. She sank back, looking at him in confusion.

"I don't understand you."

He didn't say anything, just leaned back against the wall and rested his forearms on his raised knees. He looked dog-tired, with lines of exhaustion around his eyes and mouth. There were lines she didn't remember. She felt a twinge of concern and then suppressed it.

"I'm not going back with you."

He turned his head and looked at her coldly. "I'm not," she repeated, but his expression made her look away and swallow nervously.

A few minutes later, Mathias appeared in the doorway, scanning the faces in the room. Though it was dark, his size was unmistakable. Moira let out a cry of relief and stood up, only to find her wrist captured by Random again.

"You're staying with me, Mory," he said in a low, uncompromising voice.

Mathias spotted them and gestured to someone behind him. A moment later Jewel and Kris appeared, and they made their way across the room through the sleeping flood victims.

"Thank God, you're all right! We didn't know what had happened to you," Jewel cried, reaching Moira first and hugging her in relief. She saw the darkening bruise on Moira's face and looked accusingly at Random.

"You brute! Did you hit her?"

"The thought crossed my mind."

Kris stepped forward angrily, looking like a wet, bedraggled pup. Moira intervened, knowing he would soon find himself sprawled over half a dozen men behind him if he did something stupid.

"It wasn't Random. It was Barilovich."

"Barilovich!" Kris said. "Where was he?"

"I don't know. He was just . . . there."

Mathias had been standing stonily behind Jewel, looking

at Random. He reached for Moira and Random stepped forward, dark eyes glittering. "You interfered once, Mathias. Don't make the mistake of doing it again."

Mathias pressed Jewel out of the way. "It's up to the girl where she goes and with whom," he said gruffly.

"Not until the girl has paid her debts to me, she doesn't," Random told him coldly. Mathias's eyes flickered to Moira questioningly. She stared at Random in confusion.

"What debts?" she demanded, her face pale. Random didn't look at her but spoke to Mathias instead.

"I don't suppose she bothered to tell you that she stole that horse she was riding."

"I didn't!" she protested.

"Or that she neglected to pay for the supplies I bought for her and her brother."

Moira's face paled as comprehension hit her. She stared at him miserably. Was that why he had come after her? She could hardly deny any of what he was saying, though it had never once occurred to her in her haste to get away from him. She tried to think, but the pain of why he had come after her hit her in the face like a physical blow.

"I left you your share of the gold."

"You left *half* the gold—not quite half, as a matter of fact. Or are you now conveniently going to forget I staked you and Daniel to the Yuba venture?"

"No." She fought back tears of humiliation. If he had wanted revenge for what she had done to him, he had it. This was worse than when her father's debts had been aired for public gossip in Charleston. She just looked at him, eyes bright, clenching her teeth so that her mouth wouldn't tremble for them all to see.

"How much?" she asked.

He looked at her for a long moment, dark eyes giving nothing away. "Let's say an even thousand."

Jewel gasped. Kris started to protest. Mathias stood silently by, watching them both Random still held her wrist and felt the jerk when ne stated the price. Her face was rigid.

Moira ripped her arm away from him, drawing a ragged breath. "You'll have your money, Mr. Hawthorne, just as soon as the sun rises and I can get to it." She turned away from all of them and sat down abruptly before they could see the tears filling her eyes. They moved away uncomfortably and Random sat down, leaning back against the wall again. She could feel him looking at her and kept her eyes averted from him.

Sometime during the night she must have slept, for when she awakened her head was in Random's lap. She straightened and looked at him as he slowly opened his eyes. He looked down at her, and for an instant something blazed to life in his eyes and took her breath away. Then it was gone, replaced by the cool, enigmatic look.

"Has it stopped raining?" she asked, in order to break the growing tension.

"Shall we go and see?" He stood, drawing her up with him, and they made their way over and around people to the door. First light had come, and Moira uttered a sigh of misery as she looked outside.

Sacramento lay underwater like a sodden corpse, only a few bare knees of land still visible. Wagons were covered by water, only their pathetic arched rods protruding above the murky flood. Tents had been swept away as well as supplies and equipment. A great sea of dirty, fouled water spread out endlessly, fed by the still swelling rivers to the north.

Ships in Sacramento harbor were crammed to the masts with the displaced and the dispossessed; the Methodist church was filled to the rafters, as was Sutter's Fort, and still men came begging for a space, for some unspoiled food, for a dry place to lay their heads. Many were sick with fevers. And still the winter rain fell.

Dinghies moved slowly through the watery channels that had been streets, stopping here and there at buildings where the water had reached the first story and survivors were perched on shaky, rotting roofs. Carcasses of dead animals and sometimes men floated past, their bloated bodies grotesque and already beginning to decompose. There was no way to know how many men had perished, how many more would die of ensuing sickness.

Moira was bankrupt.

The flood had carried the assayer's tent and safe away, and the man himself was among the missing. The only gold Moira possessed was that which Mathias split with her from what he wore around his waist in a special belt. Her last pile of winnings had been given over to Kris to cash in, and that too had been swept away in the torrential floodwaters.

Random seemed unperturbed and coolly indifferent to this catastrophe. He obtained a dinghy and took her, Mathias, and Jewel to one of the ships that sailed downriver to San Francisco. Kris had decided to join them later after he found out what had happened to the remaining members of the Charleston Mining and Trade Company.

"So, what now?" Moira asked defensively as they sat on the overcrowded deck of the *Sea Queen*. He looked at her, taking in her pallor and bright eyes.

"We'll go to San Francisco and sit out this flooding. Then we'll head back for the Yuba to finish what we started."

"Are you going to take the gold out of my hide?" she demanded sarcastically. The dark eyes narrowed as he smiled unpleasantly. The look he gave her made her skin tingle.

"Maybe," he drawled. "I've had a taste or two of your hide...and it wouldn't be an altogether unpleasant way to extract payment."

Moira's face flamed, and she looked away. "I've no need to worry, Mr. Hawthorne." She turned to look at him again. "If there's one thing I've learned about you," she said coldly, attempting desperately to equal his aloofness, "it's that you have principles. You'd never take what wasn't offered. And believe me, I'm not offering you a thing!"

She saw the muscle tighten in his jaw and his knuckles whiten on the ship's rail. "Those principles aren't going to stop me from getting what I want...and keeping it."

"Apparently not," she flung back angrily. "Just like having a wife never stopped you from enjoying scores of other women. But then, you always made it perfectly clear to them that you didn't want involvement, didn't you?" Even saying it hurt her unbearably, though she had done it solely to lash out at him.

Random's response was to smile sardonically. "Yes."

Moira felt a knot of pain in her chest. She turned away, her hands clenched.

"You're going to get exactly nothing from me," she managed.

"Who are you trying to convince, Moira?"

The ship made its way downriver and into the bay. Moira slept an exhausted sleep, only to be awakened rudely by the rain on her face. Random reached for her, and she tried to struggle away from his grasp, only to find herself dragged none too gently beneath a blanket and wrapped closely in the warmth of his arms. Her heart pounded painfully, and her breath was constricted. She closed her eyes tightly. It didn't help alleviate what she was feeling, and she choked back a sob.

Random turned her face up to his. She couldn't see his face for it was dark, the end of another devastating day.

"Moira," he breathed, and his fingers touched her face, finding the tears. His fingers slid into her hair, drawing her resistingly forward, his tongue lightly tasting the saltiness. "I swear I'm not going to hurt you," he said huskily. "I swear it, Moira. Just trust me. Give me a little time, and everything will work out for both of us."

"And where am I going to get a thousand dollars?" she asked, deliberately killing the hope that had risen like a phoenix from the ashes inside her. How could anything work out between them when he was married?

"You'll think of something," he said, sounding amused.

"Jewel seems to be making a lot of money in her trade," she said, baiting him, testing his reaction. He chuckled, and she felt his hand on her hip, caressing.

"Yes," he agreed, and she could feel the growing heat of his body close to hers. His hand moved upward, and when she tried to pull back from him, he drew her closer, his arm firmly locked around her. "You were just making me a proposition," he said against her neck, and she shoved her hands up between them.

"I wasn't!" she hissed, keeping her voice down so that the others around them on the crowded deck wouldn't hear. "I was only ... thinking. . . ."

"Well, in that case . . ." He sighed and gave her a little more room beneath the blanket. She could feel him laughing silently, enjoying her discomfiture. Angry tears burned her eyes. She gave a hard jerk and found herself still held unyieldingly around the waist, Random's face close to hers. She could just see the twinkle in his eyes, the firm, handsome features.

"You enjoy teasing," he said quietly, his hand on the curve

of her hip. "Most women do. It seems to give them a sense of power. And I've seen you in action—and experienced it myself. But somehow I just don't see you carrying it through to its intended conclusion with every Tom, Dick, and Harry that has the price."

"Let go . . ." she gasped.

"One man, I'd say," he told her. "That'd be your limit. You'd make a terrible whore, Moira, but one hell of a mistress."

"Is that what you intend?"

"For the moment, it'll have to do," he said casually.

She drew in a ragged breath. "You're an unspeakable bastard, Mr. Hawthorne."

"Why, Miss Cavendish?"

"You imply my consent. And you don't have it!"

"I will."

"You're married," she said, unable to think of anything else. His hand moved over her stomach.

"Many married men keep mistresses."

"Well, I don't want to be one!"

"Don't you? Well, it's a bit late, I'd say. You've been my mistress once already. You'll learn to like it again." His hand moved upward over her rib cage, stealing her breath away. "Tell me, Moira. Why is your heart pounding so hard and fast?" he asked hoarsely, reaching his destination and caressing her breast, teasing the impudent peak. "I can feel it beating through your clothes. Why, Moira?"

"You're cruel," she murmured shakily, unable to muster the willpower to stop him.

"Why? Because I tell you you'd make a terrible whore? Because I know you're a one-man woman?"

"You know why." She couldn't keep the pain out of her voice. He sighed heavily. His fingers left her breast and pushed gently into her hair, his thumb lightly stroking her temple where an erratic pulse throbbed.

"Listen to me, Moira . . ."

She closed her eyes stubbornly. "I don't want to listen to you."

"Why not? Are you afraid something I'll say might change your mind?"

"Because a man like you always knows what to say to make

a woman's resolve weaken," she said defensively. "And you've had a lot of practice at it," she cried, her voice breaking.

People around them had heard her. Movement ceased, and she felt everyone listening. Random's body was rigid in anger, and she felt hot tears rolling silently down her cheeks again.

"When you're ready to listen, we'll talk," he told her in a low, cold whisper only she could hear. "Until then, sulk and be as stubborn and mule-headed as you wish. But I'll do with you as I damn well please." He released her abruptly, throwing off the blanket and standing. She stared up at him, wide-eyed, and watched him make his way to the bow, where he stood with the wind whipping his hair.

San Francisco had changed immeasurably since she and Daniel had arrived on the *Stephen Rule* six months before. It was no longer the sprawling tent camp on the lee side of the hills, but a booming metropolis with endless construction under way. Everywhere, in even the worst weather, could be heard the constant din of hammer and saw. The rain bore down on this city as well and the streets were impassable—not even jackassable, as a sign erected on Clay and Kearny streets warned.

The hills were alive with people representing every continent and race in the world. Moira stared mesmerized at the strange faces and dress of the men that walked through the muddy streets in search of a way to pass the time until mining weather returned. Dark-skinned islanders, Mexicans in their colorful serapes and broad-brimmed hats, pale-skinned, sharp-eyed Easterners looking for a way to make a buck, tanned, salty-tongued sailors, and aristocratic Europeans melted together in the tumultuous city, impatiently waiting for the spring when they could go back to mountain streams and dry diggings.

Jewel wanted to go to the Parker House in search of her friends in the trade. Mathias accompanied her. Random had a different destination in mind. He headed for the docks, taking Moira to an old ship that had been beached and converted into a casino-hotel. A long quay had been built, and it was stacked to the sky with merchandise shipped from the East by speculators. Crates of calico and silk, tobacco, razors, mosquito netting, and panama hats lay rotting in the fog and rain. Later they would be carted up the hills and dumped onto the muddy streets to make them passable.

Two Chinamen, more commonly referred to as Celestials, moved back and forth between bar and tables, carrying trays of shot glasses filled with whiskey and plates of hot, delicious seafood. Moira sat down wearily as Random went to the bar to talk with the old sea captain who owned the establishment. They talked for a long time. Random downed several whiskeys and had food sent to Moira. She ate in lonely silence, watching him and thinking of Danny and their auspicious arrival six months before. She had almost forgotten about her things left at the hotel up the street from the docks.

Random came back with a plate of food and sat down opposite her. He looked grim, his dark eyes distant with unpleasant thoughts. He finished his meal in silence, drinking two more whiskeys before rising and looking at her.

"I'd like to go to Sunrise House," she said. "I left some of my things there before we left San Francisco."

He gave her a brief nod, and they left. She glanced back once as they went up the hill, seeing the forest of masts in the foggy bay, more than before, more coming still.

The proprietor of Sunrise House still had her carpet bags, and Moira sat on a bed upstairs taking everything out slowly and looking at it like a child opening Christmas packages. Random was lying back on the other bed, his head resting on his folded hands, watching her.

"At least I have a change of clothes," she said, a flicker of her old smile crossing her face. He grinned at her, making her heart thump crazily.

"I've ordered bathwater."

"Have you?" she asked.

"Don't you think we could use it?"

"We?" Her eyes widened, as her imagination soared.

"I'm not leaving this room. I know you well enough to realize you'd probably make a rope out of the sheets and go out the window."

Her mouth tightened, and her eyes glinted. "Then you'll just have to put up with the way I look *and* smell."

He chuckled, looking up at the ceiling. "I don't know what you're embarrassed about. I've seen everything you have several times over already."

She blushed hotly. "Time changes things."

He ignored her and went on. "And with your complete and hearty consent—and I don't think it would be unfair to say *encouragement,*" he added unkindly, grinning at her as though that was a very precious memory he intended to relive many times over. "Let's not forget those good times, Moira," he said in a low, soft voice.

"I'd rather they'd never happened!"

"Too bad," he sighed and looked at her laughingly. "You've become very modest all of a sudden, haven't you, Moira? I don't remember this side of you in the mountains."

The tub and water were delivered by four bustling Celestials, and Moira had no time to make an appropriate response. When the servants left, she turned to Random.

"All right, Mr. Hawthorne. There's *your* bath water," she challenged.

He smiled slowly, making her freeze. "Would you help me off with my boots?" he asked.

She looked at him warily and then shrugged. "Why not?" She walked over, turned around, and bent over to help him pull his boot off. Random put one foot on her hind end and pushed. When the boot came off she stumbled forward, saved from sprawling by his hand catching the seat of her pants. She laughed and yanked the other one off. Dusting off her hands, she stood looking at him, eyebrows raised. He wouldn't dare take his clothes off and climb into that tub with her watching him.

She was wrong.

Random stood up from the bed slowly and began to unbutton his shirt, his eyes holding hers. "I wonder if you've any idea what you did to me with all those bathes you took in the cabin," he said in a low, suggestive voice. Moira's eyes widened as he pulled the shirt free of his pants and finished unbuttoning it. His chest was bronzed and covered with dark, curling hair. His muscles were hard and rippled as he stripped off the shirt and tossed it casually onto the bed. She swallowed hard.

"You always sat in that tub, talking so casually, expecting

coherent responses from me while I was going slowly out of my mind lying on that bunk, wanting you so badly I hurt." He took a slow step toward her, dark eyes glowing.

Moira's heart was pounding rapidly. She stared at him and then at the firm, perfect muscles of his chest and arms and at his flat belly. She longed to touch him, to taste the tangy saltiness of his skin.

Random reached out slowly. His fingertips touched her silky cheek and trailed lightly down along the pulsing vein in her throat and lower to the taut, hardened peaks of her breasts beneath the cotton of her shirt.

Her breathing had quickened and shallowed, and she didn't seem to move or look away. She knew she should protest. She knew she should move away.

"Ah, Moira," he whispered with a faint smile. "I'd like you to take off all your clothes for me again. I'd explore every square inch of you . . . every soft, hidden place with my hands and mouth," he said with a seductive softness that completely robbed her of breath. "There are so many pleasures we haven't tried yet. So much to teach you . . ." His hands moved slowly to his belt and he unbuckled it, his eyes still holding hers.

When she realized she was standing and staring at him like a befuddled idiot, she turned abruptly away, putting her hands to her flaming cheeks. He laughed behind her, stripping off the rest of his clothes and tossing them aside. She heard him step into the warm water.

"Would you like to scrub my back for me?" he asked teasingly. She turned and made a run for the door. Random didn't move but sat comfortably watching her from the tub. Her hand pulled at the doorknob. She twisted and yanked harder. She tried several times, and still the door remained shut, securely locked.

"I think you need this," Random said casually, holding up a key between thumb and index finger. She made a lunge for it, and he dropped it into the water between his legs. He leaned back slightly, grinning at her red face and flashing brown eyes. "You can have it anytime you want it, Moira. Just reach in . . ."

She turned away in embarrassment and frustration and sat on the bed. He laughed low. He took his time bathing, aware the entire time of her agitation. She sat in stony silence, trying to ignore the churning desires inside her, forcing herself to keep her eyes from straying to him. Each time they did, he grinned at her, and whistled some tauntingly bawdy song. When he finished, he stood, unembarrassed, and dried himself. Moira kept her hands over her face and heard him laughing.

"Now I wonder if you feel even remotely as I felt when you were bathing," he said, and she turned to look at him angrily. He was dressed again in clean clothes, looking devastatingly handsome after his bath and shave.

"You did that just to humiliate me," she said, eyes bright.

"No." He shook his head, eyes very serious. "It's not my intention to ever humiliate you."

"Then why did you tell Mathias I'd stolen your horse?"

"Because you had, and he was going to butt in again," he told her coldly.

"I'd forgotten," she admitted miserably. "I didn't mean to steal anything."

His face softened at the look of despair and hurt on her face. "I know that, Moira. All you thought about was getting away from me," he said and turned away. "I'll order fresh water for you."

"I'm not going to be some cheap peep show!" she cried, and he looked back at her impatiently.

"Who in hell said you were?" He slammed out of the room, and she heard the door locked from the outside. She didn't even try to open it but sat dejectedly on the bed. Random came back a while later with the Celestials. The dirty water was toted away and fresh water poured in. She and Random were left alone again. She looked at him, frowning.

"The room's all yours," he said, surprising her again. "I'll be back in one hour. But if you're not out of the tub and dressed by that time, that's your own ill fortune, because I'll be coming in anyway," he warned her. He saw the confusion in her eyes, and his mouth tightened angrily. "Did you really think I planned to stand here and watch you take off your clothes so I could ravage you?"

"I wasn't sure," she admitted with a tremulous smile.

"You're not going to have it that easy, Moira," he said coolly, and she frowned.

"I don't know what you mean," she said stiffly. His mouth

curved, but his eyes belied the smile. He was angry, and she knew it, very angry.

"Well, think about it for a while until you work it out for yourself," he said, going to the door. She sat in silence after he had left, staring at the door he had locked behind him. She was his prisoner and would be so until he had satisfied his desires, whatever they were. The thousand dollars, she knew, was incidental. And he had had no intention just now of bedding her. So what did he want from her?

She sat in the tub, thinking about Jack and her purpose in coming to California. She had lost sight of that when she left the mountains. And she had accomplished exactly nothing. She was right back where she'd started, in the Sunrise House in San Francisco, where she had been the first day she arrived in California.

An hour later Moira was dressed in the blue watered-silk gown when Random unlocked the door and walked in without knocking. She sat on the bed, brushing her hair. Glancing up, she watched him pocket the key.

He leaned back against the door, arms crossed over his chest, and looked her over admiringly. "Are you hungry?" he asked finally.

"Famished," she admitted and gave up on her hair. "I'm going to have to cut it again. It's too long to look like a man's and too short to work with properly," she said, letting it drop to a damp curling mass about her face.

"Just shove it up under your hat," he told her, his eyes critically taking in its disarray.

"I think it would be wiser to cut it before we head back for the mountains," she said softly, her eyes seeking his.

His eyes flickered. "So, you're going to go back with me without a fight?"

"Is there a choice?"

They looked at one another for a moment, neither saying anything. "No," he said. "You'd be going one way or another. But I'm just curious why you're suddenly so acquiescent."

"It's simple, really. I want to find my brother. It was my reason for coming and it's my reason for staying. And since there was no trace of him down from the Yuba, I'll go back." She lifted her chin slightly, her eyes meeting his in challenge.

"I don't care what your reasons are for the moment. We'll get around to sorting out our relationship later."

"There's nothing to sort out, Random."

"There's plenty!" he said in a hard, angry voice. "It'd take me all of five minutes to show you what I mean, but in your present mood, you'd still deny it."

"Don't think anything's going to change when you get me back to the Yuba!"

"Oh, it's going to change, all right," he said grimly. And Moira knew by the look in his dark eyes that he meant every word he said.

Chapter Thirty-one

The men crowding the dining room of the Sunrise House lapsed into stunned, gawking silence when Moira entered upon Random's arm. They watched as she moved slowly across the room, her eyes straight ahead, the gentle sway of her hips riveting their passionate attention. Random pulled her chair out for her and seated her so that she could look either out the window at San Francisco Bay or around the room at the men admiring her.

Moira kept her eyes on the bay. She was never going to get used to the way men looked at her in this wild country. Longing shone out of their eyes with unveiled openness. It was unnerving.

"When will we be returning to the mountains?" she asked.

"In April or May."

"That long?" she said in surprise. "Why can't we go back now?"

"You're so eager to be alone with me again?"

"We're alone here."

Random looked around and then smiled at her. "Hardly."

"You know what I mean."

"The snows are too deep now. It'd be impossible to get back up to the cabin."

"So what are we going to do between now and then?" she demanded.

His eyes sparkled with laughter. "Anything you want . . . within reason."

"You must have a lot of gold with you, if you can afford to put us up here for three to four months."

"I don't plan to," he drawled, looking at the menu. "What would you like?"

"I don't care. I've just lost my appetite."

When the waiter came, Random ordered two big steaks with potatoes and vegetables and a bottle of their best French wine. Moira gave a faint laugh when the man walked off toward the kitchen.

"And how are you going to pay for all this?" she whispered, leaning toward him across the table. "You lost everything in Sacramento just like I did!"

He smiled secretively. "Not quite."

"What do you mean, not quite?"

"A little business venture of mine has paid off rather handsomely," he said without boasting. Her brows rose.

"What business venture?" she asked curiously.

"That hotel-casino we visited on the docks. I own half of it with Svenson. Bought it with him before I left San Francisco. And I also own part of a general store in the center of town— Market Street, I think they call it now."

She gave a stunned laugh. "You were foolish to ever leave San Francisco," she told him. "Why didn't you stay and manage things yourself?"

"Svenson has done well enough without me, and there were other things I wanted to do."

"Pan for gold?" she asked mockingly.

"That didn't work out so badly either, if we get back to that claim before someone jumps it."

"Well, if you're so rich, why don't you book *two* rooms for us . . . and move us into the City Hotel instead of staying here?"

"We're moving onto the *Stephen Rule* tomorrow morning," he told her.

"We're *what?*"

"I've got things to attend to over the next few months, and I don't want to have to drag you everywhere I go. So . . ."

"You plan to leave me on that old relic rotting in the bay?" she cried.

"Something like that," he agreed unabashedly, grinning.

"No."

"As you said upstairs," he drawled, "you've no choice."

The waiter brought their meals, poured their wine, and left.

"Do you own the *Stephen Rule* as well?" she demanded derisively, furious.

"No, but Captain Thackary has left for parts unknown, and the ship, as you say, is rotting in the harbor. There are plans to sink it along with several others and use them as landfill."

"And no doubt, you'd love it if they did it while I was aboard!"

Random grinned, but didn't answer.

"I'm not going to run out on my debts, Random, I swear," she said pleadingly. "Please . . ."

"Hmmmm, I like that." He smiled wickedly. Then he reached across the table and patted her hand. "But think of it this way, Moira. You have your pick of accommodations this time, and you won't have to share a cabin with anyone."

"Not even you?" she snapped angrily, pulling her hand away.

He grinned. "Only if you want to. I'll make sure you always know where I'm sleeping."

She sat silently for a moment, thinking. Then she looked at him face rigid and pale with anger. "All I have to do is scream and tell some of these men looking at me that I need their assistance."

Random's eyes narrowed to slits. "If you think you have things rough now, Moira, you do something like that and see where you'll be."

She met his eyes for a few seconds longer and then had to look away. She didn't know what he would do, but she didn't want to find out. The small scar from where she had hit him stood out lividly, a banner to grievances yet unresolved, and she wasn't going to press her luck further.

Lifting her wineglass, she sipped, glancing at him warily. He was watching her, and she could feel the coiled tension in his body, the ruthless determination to have his own way.

"For the moment, I'll agree to do as you wish, Mr. Haw-

thorne. But you won't always have things your way," she
warned him coolly, her own determination stiffening. Did he
really think she would simply sit on that damned rotting hulk
without attempting to escape? What did he suppose she would
do all day while he was away?

He smiled slowly, eyes amused and meeting her challenge.
He replenished her glass. "I haven't had things my way since
I met you...Miss Cavendish," he said mockingly.

Sipping, she met his dark gaze. "Then if that's the case, I
can't see why you bother."

He didn't answer, but the look he gave her made the color
rush to her cheeks.

The meal was appetizing, and Moira did it full justice. There
wasn't a crumb left on her plate when she was finished, and
she even managed to finish the peach cobbler Random ordered
for her. She sighed with satisfaction and, smiled warmly across
the table at him.

"I'm a glutton," she admitted unrepentantly.

"I like to see a woman who doesn't think it's necessary to
eat like a bird."

Moira grinned. "But I do. A bird eats almost its weight in
food each day, Mr. Hawthorne. Didn't you know that?" He
laughed.

"In that case," he drawled, "I'll flatter you and say you only
eat as much as a horse."

She grinned. "Close enough." She finished the wine in her
glass with a flourish, and Random poured more. She hadn't
stopped to think how much she was drinking, but her mood
was much lighter, even gay, and the rustic, drab room had
taken on a rosy glow. Even the murky bay had a magic quality
about it when she looked out the window. The ships weren't
deserted relics soon to be dispatched to the deep for landfill,
but mystic sea caravans from exciting old-world ports.

"It's beautiful," she breathed, resting her chin on her palm
and looking out at the booming gold-rush town, churning with
not-always congenial citizenry.

"What?" he asked, eyes laughing at her in the lantern light.
He refilled her glass again.

"Oh, everything," she said expansively and gave him a
teasing smile. "Why, Mr. Hawthorne, even you look good to

me in the candlelight. All those hard, cruel, unyielding lines are quite ironed out."

"Are they?" he said, mouth twitching.

"You don't look like the sort of man who would lock a poor defenseless lady away on an old ship at the mercy of God knows what," she told him purringly, her Southern accent very pronounced.

"I'm not."

She sighed in relief. "Thank goodness," she whispered, eyes glowing at him.

He grinned. "You're neither defenseless nor a lady."

Her mouth tightened. "I won't stay there."

"You won't have any choice."

Moira looked past Random at a young man who had been staring at her since she entered the dining room. He was tall and well-built, with dark hair that was curled over his collar and a beard that had been recently trimmed. He smiled at her when he saw she had noticed him. She smiled back slowly and dropped her eyes demurely to the table. Then she glanced up challengingly at Random.

"I might just arrange to have a champion for my cause," she told him smugly.

"If you mean that young pup sitting over there making eyes at you, I wouldn't advise it."

"Why not? He looks about the right size."

"Because I'll knock his teeth down his throat if he so much as comes over here to talk to you," he said in a low voice, smiling at her all the while. His eyes were hard and glittering.

"You're ruthless, aren't you?"

"If necessary."

She sighed despairingly. "And all because I took your horse."

He smiled sincerely. "And damn near split my head open."

"Don't expect me to say I'm sorry!" she flared, eyes snapping.

"Wouldn't think of it," he drawled easily. "But didn't it ever bother your conscience in the slightest that you left me unconscious up there, and that I might have been seriously hurt?"

"No," she lied with aplomb, even managing to meet his

dark, assessing gaze. "Your skull is far too hard to even dent."

He laughed. "You gave it a damned good try," he said harshly.

"Not good enough, apparently," she said, feeling in need of more wine to keep her courage from flagging. The waiter, upon Random's signal, brought another bottle. Moira noticed that her speech was not as clear as usual and that she was having to concentrate hard to make sure her words came out in the proper order.

"So you wished me dead," Random said, smiling sardonically as he filled her glass.

She gasped. "No. That's not true!"

"I should have just grabbed you and kissed you, and you'd have been combing your fingers through my hair instead of braining me with a can of pork and beans. Next time I'll know better," he said.

"I should have used the shovel!"

He grinned, but there was a steely determination in his eyes. "You're never going to get an opportunity like that again," he told her.

"If you'd just let me go," she said tremulously, tears filling her eyes. What was the matter with her? She felt filled to overflowing with emotion all of a sudden and couldn't seem to control it. Her head was spinning. "You think you were hurt anymore than I was," she admitted unthinkingly, unable to even make out the blur of his face. "You . . . oh, Rand . . ."

Random got up, pulled out her chair, and took her arm. "No crying jag here, Moira." She swayed slightly, and his arm circled her waist. As soon as they were out of the dining room, he lifted her. She wrapped her arms around his neck and leaned her swimming head against his shoulder.

"You must have laughed at how naive I was," she sniffled.

Once inside their room, he set her on her feet and locked the door behind him. He stood in front of her, hands on her shoulders. "I never laughed at you, Moira . . . ever."

She looked up at him miserably, swaying and trying to keep her eyes focused on him. "Oh, Rand . . ." She put her hand up against his chest, and her head drooped. "I think I need some coffee."

Her cheeks were ashen, her forehead perspiring. She

couldn't think straight anymore. She swayed, and Random gently lifted her and carried her to the bed. She tried to understand his expression as he put her down. It couldn't be tenderness. She felt miserable and humiliated, and couldn't keep the tears back. And the longing, oh, God, the longing was worst of all. Random frowned heavily as he looked at her.

"All I wanted was to get away from you," she cried. "I didn't want to kill you. I didn't even want to hurt you."

"No?" His mouth curved.

"Well, maybe for a minute or two," she admitted. "But I didn't intend to steal your damn scrawny old horse. All I wanted was to catch up with Jack."

His eyes became steely. "And did you?"

She sighed and shook her head. Then she looked back up at him, angrily. "You don't own me! I'm . . . oh, my head . . ." She put her hands up to her temples.

Random pushed her hands back and stroked the dark, soft hair away from her face. His rhythmic caressing eased her tension. She sighed, opening her eyes and looking up at him. "I don't belong to you, Rand," she said simply. "I belong to myself."

He smiled slightly, and she felt driven to go on.

"Oh, why are you men so stupid?" She pushed his hand away. "You ask for so little from a woman. A warm, willing body. That's all you want." She gave a sob. "So little."

Her lids felt weighted, her body floated, her head spun crazily.

She closed her eyes slowly and sighed deeply. After that, she didn't feel a thing.

Chapter Thirty-two

Moira awoke to light streaming in. When she opened her eyes, slivers of pain shot into her brain. She closed them quickly and tightly. When she swallowed, her mouth felt dry, her tongue swollen, and the taste was what she imagined might be found on the bottom of a birdcage.

Eyes still closed, Moira could hear Random's steady, heavy breathing. She turned her head and opened her eyes carefully. She spied him on a chair, tipped precariously back against the door. On the floor was a half-empty bottle of whiskey.

She sat up slowly and groaned, holding onto her head, sure that it was about to topple from her shoulders and crash painfully to the floor. She squinted her eyes against the head-throbbing misery. "Random?"

The chair thumped to the floor, and Moira saw his whole body stiffen and his face grimace in agony. He swore vilely under his breath, clenching his teeth together. When he opened his eyes, they were bloodshot and glowered accusingly at her.

"What?"

"I think I'm going to . . . die."

He grinned maliciously, coming more fully awake. "You'll feel better after breakfast and coffee."

The mention of food turned her faintly green, and she

gulped. He stood up carefully and walked to the window, throwing it open and letting in a cruel blast of cold, salty air. Moira groaned.

"Splash some cold water on your face," he told her, breathing deeply of the fresh air, half hanging out the window. She was tempted to shove him the rest of the way.

"I said I was going to die, not that I wanted to hurry the process," she snapped and then wished she had whispered. "Ohhhhhh, my head," she moaned, clutching it.

Random straightened and looked at her unsympathetically. He turned and sat back on the still, studying her with amusement. His eyes moved down her body and lingered. She became suddenly aware that she was sitting in her shift and that it was partially untied and exposing more than a little of her full breasts to his avid gaze. She yanked the blanket up, eyes widening angrily.

"You took off my dress!" As soon as the words were uttered, she gritted her teeth against the throbbing in her temples.

"Yes." He grinned.

"Just what went on here last night? I can't remember a thing after we walked in that door."

"After I carried you in. You were incapable of walking on your own steam."

"You got me drunk!"

"Poured it right down your throat, didn't I?"

"No. But you kept refilling my glass!"

He laughed. "Come on. Get out of that bed, or do you want to spend the whole day there?"

"Random!"

His brows rose faintly at her tone, and he relented. "I would hardly make love to a girl with her shift and pantaloons on, nor would I spend the rest of the night sleeping in a chair by the door," he told her laughingly. Then, in a more serious tone, he said, "When we make love again, you're going to remember every minute of it. You're going to be wide-awake—completely stone-cold sober, and you're going to be giving yourself to me every step of the way."

Her face was flaming. "You're sure about that?" she asked derisively, trying to ignore the way her senses had leaped into life at his look and tone.

"I wouldn't be here with you if I weren't," he said simply and walked slowly toward her, eyes glowing. She watched him warily, senses stirring to tingling life, eyes opening wide. He slid his fingers caressingly along her cheek, his thumb brushing the full, soft lips, which parted as she struggled to breathe. His hand moved down slowly. Suddenly the blanket was gone, yanked from her and tossed onto the floor. She stared at him, heart pounding rapidly, half expectant.

"Get up," he ordered and then grinned at her, well aware of her charged emotional state and her failure to stop him from touching her. She flushed and then jumped off the bed, throwing on her clothes and feeling precariously close to a tempest of tears.

Following coffee and a small breakfast, which Moira only managed to consume under threat of force, Random took her to the docks, where a loaded dinghy was waiting for them. Moira didn't speak as Random sculled her effortlessly out to the *Stephen Rule*. Once he saw her safely aboard with the supplies stacked on the main deck, he left her with instructions to "make yourself comfortable." Moira stood at the railing watching him move off into the low fog that surrounded the deserted ships. She shivered and turned away.

The ship was almost unrecognizable. The scavengers had been hard at work stripping the sails and ropes from the masts and even detaching the yardarms. The hatch was missing, and upon uneasy investigation Moira found that so were all the doors in the officers' quarters. When she went 'tween decks, she discovered that many of the walls separating the tiny cabins had been ripped out and carted away to make shelters on the windswept hills of San Francisco peninsula.

Moira stood in the quiet darkness and felt the first crawling of unreasoning fear.

It was like living on a great carcass floating in the bay. Only the lap of seawater on the rotting hull broke the unnerving silence. The darkness inside the ship surrounded her like a shroud, and she found herself hurrying to the end of the passageway and climbing hurriedly to the main deck. She ran to the railing, clutching it, trying to see some sign of life in the fog around her. The ships stood around her like ancient relics in an eerie graveyard. It was silent, and only the faint sounds of wood protesting in the tide came to her ears.

"Random," she said between her teeth, trying to control the rise of fear. He was gone, and shouting his name was not going to accomplish anything. He was probably up the muddy hill by now, mingling with the population of San Francisco. Damn him! Damn him to hell and back for leaving her here! When was he going to come back?

After a few minutes of struggling with herself, she managed to regain some control and suppress her feelings of panic. She was alone. No one was going to bother her. Random probably expected her to be on her knees by the time he came back. And that made her good and mad.

She decided that the best way to maintain her calm was to work. She dragged the supplies Random had unloaded into the officers' quarters and sorted through them. Then she stowed them away in the galley. Random's things she tossed rudely into his old cabin. She took up residence in the captain's quarters. Let him make of that what he would!

Late in the afternoon, she went belowdecks to explore. Perhaps there was something salvageable that the scavengers had missed. Random had brought a lantern and she lit it, carrying it with her, determined not to let her unease stop her.

Shadows flickered around her as she wandered through the deserted ship, peering into the few cabins that remained intact. There was nothing of any value, and the ship smelled of wet wood and other, less pleasant odors. The stuffy air made Moira's head ache, and she began retracing her steps.

Suddenly, sounds above drew her attention. She hurried along the passageway, hearing the hard thud of something on deck. What was Random doing?

She climbed the steps and came out on deck. "Random!" She stopped and stared. There were three men on deck, prying up planks. They froze and stared at her. One grinned lasciviously and dropped the plank he had in his hands.

Another let go of the crowbar he was using to pry up a board and took a step toward her. "Well, if it ain't a little madam," he said under his breath. Moira let out a cry of alarm. She let go of the lantern, and there was a shattering of glass and a burst of flame as the kerosene was ignited.

"Hey! Get her!" one of the men shouted as Moira disappeared belowdecks. She raced along the passageway, bumping into things. She could hear the thud of footsteps above stomping out the fire while someone else came down the ladder after her.

"Come on out, honey," he said coaxingly, walking along the passageway, peering into ruined cabins. Moira scurried further into the ship's innards. She tripped and fell, sprawling into a pile of stacked boards. She heard running steps behind her and scrambled up, her hand closing on a loose piece of wood. She darted into a dark cabin and shrank back against the wall, holding her breath.

"I know you're in there . . ." the man said, amusement and triumph in his voice as he moved slowly in her direction. He stopped in the doorway and looked in. He took another step and she swung the board like a bat, catching him squarely in the face. He fell backward with a thud and lay still.

She stepped over him and then stood still, undecided which way to go. The other two men had put out the fire on deck and were coming down the ladder. She fled toward the entrance to the hold, fear choking her.

There was a loud grunt. "What in hell!" She heard mumbling. "It's Manny. I think his nose is broken." The fallen man was grumbling and groaning as he came to.

Moira hid behind a bulkhead, crouching low, her breathing rapid and shallow. She listened. They were coming again, the one called Manny swearing now and saying in the vilest of terms what he intended to do to Moira once he found her. She clutched the board more tightly. They passed by, and she heard them going down the ladder to the hold one at a time. She didn't wait any longer but darted out and raced back up the passageway toward the booby hatch, tears of panic streaking her cheeks. They had heard her. She could hear them clambering back up the ladder, and one was already in the passageway pursuing her. She scrambled up the hatch.

She came out on deck and looked around, wondering what to do. Had there been a door, she would have been able to lock the three men below. There wasn't. Suddenly she had an idea. Clutching her board, she stood at the top of the booby hatch.

It was the unfortunate Manny who came up first. He received a stunning blow to the head as he emerged and fell backward on top of the other two, sending them down with a great crash and outburst of epithets.

"Has she got the damn crowbar?" one said in alarm. "I think she kilt the poor bastard!"

Moira raised her board again, waiting. It was too quiet down there all of a sudden. She heard footsteps, but they were moving away. She didn't dare lean over and peer down, for she was afraid one of them would grab her and drag her down.

A thud behind her made her jump around in fright, remembering too late the fore hatch available to them.

Random!

Relief washed over her. He was waiting there. When the bigger man came out, he sent a brutal punch into the man's midsection and then flattened him with a fist to the jaw. The man went down like a rock and lay sprawled unconscious on the deck.

The second man wasn't so easy. He came leaping out, expecting to face Moira, and found himself staring into Random's blazing dark eyes. He glanced to the side and spotted his friend. He looked back at Random and raised his fists. They circled each other for a moment, waiting for an opening, then came together with a growl, swinging, clutching, wrestling, punching. There were grunts from both as blows connected. The man opened up a cut on Random's cheek. Random sent a fist into the other man's jaw.

Moira jumped up and down. "Hit him, Rand!"

He did. The man flew backward but didn't go down. Random dove at him, and they grappled with each other, growling like animals as they shoved each other back and forth on the deck, connecting blows when and where they could. Moira sat down and watched, sure that Random had things well in hand now.

Manny tried once more to come out the hatch. Moira clobbered him with the board and sent him head over tail into the ship again. She dropped the board and brushed off her hands.

Random took a left to the chin and a right to the stomach, making Moira wince. But he recovered quickly, hitting the man twice in the midsection and finally smashing a hard right to the jaw. The man went reeling backward, arms whirling.

He hit the rail, which gave way, loosened because of the boards that had been removed. He let out a yelp as he flipped back and plunged into the cold bay.

Moira sighed with satisfaction. The man on the deck was groaning, trying to push himself up. Random hauled him over his shoulder, walked to the rail, and pitched him over. The two men flailed about in the murky water, heading for their rowboat lashed below.

Moira pointed below. "There's another one down there." Random looked at her standing there nonchalantly and strode across the deck. He disappeared below and came out a second later with the bloody and battered Manny slung over his shoulder. The last of the trio went sailing overboard to meet his drenched cohorts rowing toward shore.

Moira put her hands on her hips. "Well, it was about time you showed up to save the day."

Random grinned. "You looked like you were doing all right on your own."

"I wouldn't have been in about five more minutes," she told him frankly. "Come on. I'd better clean that cut before it gets infected."

Random touched his face and grimaced. He followed her into the officers' quarters and sat down, watching her as she poured water into a bowl and dampened a small towel. She came over and stood in front of him, not meeting his eyes as she assessed the damage. She bit down hard on her lower lip as she gently dabbed the cut, wincing as though she were doctoring herself instead of him. He gave a low laugh and took the cloth.

"I'd better do it myself." He wiped the blood away swiftly. He washed his face over the bowl and then dried with a larger towel.

"You look a mess," she told him, sitting on a trunk he had brought aboard the day before. He glanced at her and smiled. He unbuttoned the bloody shirt and stripped it off.

"Have you had a good day, Moira?"

"Oh, a little boring, but otherwise perfectly all right," she countered, eyes glittering. He laughed. He put on a fresh shirt and looked at her.

"Nothing is ever dull with you around," he commented, and then before she could retort, he added, "I brought you a couple of presents."

Her eyes widened. "You did?"

"I'll get them." He went off. She was damned if she was going to follow him like a pup, so she remained sitting on the trunk. He returned a few minutes later with two packages and tossed them on the floor at her feet. She looked at him tight-lipped, not appreciating his jest. He stood in the doorway, hands on his hips, smiling slightly, eyes glinting.

Curiosity won out. She stooped and picked up one of the packages and unwrapped it. Three books!

"They aren't the most exciting reading, I'm afraid," Random apologized, leaning against the jamb. "But they were all I could get. And at least they'll give you something to do while you're waiting for me to come back each day."

She glanced at the titles and grimaced. *"The Battle for Gaul?"* He laughed at her expression.

"Open the other package."

She did, setting the books aside. Her eyes brightened at the second present—writing paper and quills and a bottle of ink.

"Well, that's better." She grinned up at him. "And thank you very much."

Random gave her a slight nod and then left again. He had brought other things to make their quarters more comfortable— a couple of blankets, two chairs, a small table, a mirror, and finally another tin tub for bathing.

Moira prepared dinner, and they sat across from one another at the table, a candle burning between them. She was aware of Random watching her, his dark eyes intent and thoughtful.

"I'm going to leave the gun with you," he said after a moment.

"I thought perhaps you'd change your mind and take me back to shore," she suggested half-hopefully.

"You'd be in and out of more trouble there," he said with conviction. "Out here, you'll be safe."

"Safe! You call what happened today safe?"

He grinned. "I doubt very much if they'll come back after the reception they received. And if they do, you can blast them off the bow if necessary."

"What makes you so sure I won't blast you off the bow?" she demanded angrily. He laughed low.

"Oh, I'm sure you'll consider it now and then," he drawled, not sounding terribly worried. "But then I know what a lousy shot you are." He gave her a teasing glance. "Where'd you put my gear—in the hold?"

"No, in your old cabin."

"And yours?"

She pointed to the captain's quarters with a smug look. He grinned. "I thought as much." He stood up and moved around the table to stand behind her. He put his hands on her shoulders and leaned down to brush his lips against the curve of her neck, making her stiffen. "It's the biggest bunk on the ship."

Moira closed her eyes, trying to fight the tingling sensations throughout her body, and failed dismally. His lips moved to the pulsing vein at her throat, then slid upward, his tongue outlining her ear. She quivered, her head bending back to give him better access.

Random straightened behind her, and she opened her eyes dazedly to look up at him. The smile he wore brought stinging heat to her cheeks.

"You've had enough excitement for one day, I should think," he said and patted her cheek paternally. "Better get yourself off to bed . . . after you've cleaned up the galley."

Chapter Thirty-three

Moira lay on the bunk in the captain's cabin, staring dismally at the ceiling. With the tide coming in, there was a gentle movement to the ship. She listened to the creaks and groans and then sat up restlessly, swinging her legs to the floor. Just being this close to Random was torturing her. She put her head in her hands, battling herself.

Still hurt and angry with him, she also wanted to be with him, to remain on this old wreck waiting for him to come back to her each night. Yet another part of her wanted to flee from him. With a small loan from Jewel, she knew she could gamble and win back the money she owed Random and that he would then have no hold over her. As long as she remained on this ship, close to him, she was at his mercy.

She knew that Random would never force her into his bed. He'd wait for her to come to him willingly, to surrender everything for nothing. And she knew that the longer she stayed here with him, the more certain it was that she would do it. She wouldn't be able to help herself. Just the thought of his lovemaking made her ache. She wanted his love.

She sighed. She knew she had to leave the ship or she would be completely lost. If she waited, there wouldn't be another opportunity. She would give in to him and give herself up like a burnt offering. She stood and moved quietly about the cabin, packing her few things into her carpetbag, feeling close to tears. She pulled on her dungarees and wool shirt and then crept across the officers' saloon to look in at Random in his cabin. He lay on his back, one arm flung above his head, sleeping. His face was turned away from her. She stood for a moment looking at him and then turned away.

Standing at the ship's rail, she looked down at the dinghy below.

"Where do you think you're going, Moira?" Random asked behind her, startling her. She dropped the carpetbag, and it landed with a thud in the boat below. She swung around, glaring at him in the moonlight. He was leaning against the mast, watching her.

"I thought you were asleep," she said accusingly.

"I heard you packing."

She could feel the heat in her face, the anger and frustration welling up. He pushed away from the mast and walked slowly, purposefully toward her. She could see in his dark eyes a glint of barely contained anger.

"Were you planning to leave me marooned out here?" He laughed mockingly at her failure, and her temper flamed to life.

"Why shouldn't I? It's what you intend doing to me!"

"Only until spring."

"How am I supposed to keep myself sane until spring?"

His mouth curved. "What's really bothering you, Moira?"

"I can't stay here!" Her voice quavered and echoed over the water. She shivered against the chill. "Damn you, Rand, I can't!"

"You're going to."

She lifted her chin. "If I have to swim to shore, I will." She turned around and started to swing herself up to the top of the ladder. He reached her just as she was about to pitch herself out. He hauled her down and shook her, eyes blazing.

"Damn it, are you crazy?"

"Yes. I'm going crazy!"

"You're giving me no choice!"

"What are you going to do?" she cried as he dragged her back across the deck toward the officers' quarters. She dug in her heels stubbornly but found herself pulled inside, shoved toward the captain's cabin, and then propelled roughly onto the bunk, where she landed in a heap with an unladylike grunt. Random stood in the doorway blocking her escape. She sat up, gasping for breath, and glared at him.

"There's no door, so you can't lock me in this time!"

"I don't plan to. I'm going to sleep with you." He stepped into the cabin.

That announcement galvanized her to action. "Oh no you're not!" She jumped off the bunk and tried to push past him. He shoved her back and followed her down, pinning her to the bunk without much difficulty. She tried to kick and found her legs imprisoned by his. His smile was taunting.

"I don't plan to make love to you, just sleep. So you can relax and enjoy the extra warmth."

Tears flooded her eyes. "I'm beginning to hate you, Random Hawthorne."

"Why? Tell me, Moira." His fingers interlocked with hers. He shifted his weight, bracing himself so that he was not crushing her. She felt the heat and tension increasing in his body and was aware that he was very much aroused.

"Stop it," she groaned, her body trembling, her breath quickening.

"Stop what?" he demanded. "Stop wanting you? Stop *you* wanting *me?* How?"

"You don't want *me*. You just want a woman, *any* woman. Well, go find one! You've never had any trouble before! But I don't like being *used!*"

His face went rigid. "You insult me," he snarled, his fingers tightening painfully. "If I wanted 'any' woman, if I just wanted to 'use' you, do you think I would have spent weeks searching for you after you left the *Stephen Rule?* Do you think I'd go with you on some wild-goose chase after your brother? Do you think I'd waste time trying to *know* you? Hell, if all I'd wanted from you was your willing body, I could have had that the night of the storm when we were rounding the Horn. *You were ready then!*" He let her go abruptly, drawing away as if to prevent himself from doing violence to her.

"You insult me and you insult yourself! I *love* you, and you're dead right I want your body. Just looking at you makes me . . . Christ!" He raked his fingers through his hair. He was shaking, his eyes blazing in frustration. "But I want more than that from you," he went on in a low, taut voice. "I want everything. *Everything!* When I make love to you, I want to know I've got your heart, mind, and soul. I want your love, damn you. And not the piddling little amount that most women are capable of giving, but everything I know you have to give. And if you're only willing to dole out a portion at a time, then to hell with you. It won't satisfy me. It's as simple as that."

She stared at him, stunned. He looked back at her and suddenly seemed drained. His eyes were bleak.

"If it's *freedom* you want, all right," he said finally, getting to his feet. "If you really believe that giving yourself to a man completely makes you his chattel, takes away who you are— then I'll take you back at first light. I'll take you to Mathias or Jewel . . . or *Kris,* if that's what you want," he said raggedly. "I'm not going to try to keep you." He stopped and shook his head, eyes dark with pain. "What the hell is the use? I'm taking the next ship out of California." He left the cabin.

A lump of misery rose in her throat, and she felt unable to breathe. All those weeks in Sacramento when she had felt only half alive, when she'd been cursing him, when she'd wished she'd never met him . . . and he'd felt the same. He loved her. He really loved her.

"Rand . . ." She pushed herself up and went after him. On the main deck, she couldn't see him, and panic set in. Her face was streaked with tears as she looked all around for him, crying out his name. And then she saw him sitting on the bow, knees raised, forearms resting on them, head bent low.

He didn't look up at her when she reached him. He sat silently, looking tired and resolved. She went down on her knees in front of him, reaching out to touch him. She saw him tense, though he still didn't look at her.

"Rand . . ." She swallowed back the tears and tried to keep her voice steady and clear, failing miserably. "Don't leave. I'll stay here on the ship without any more fuss, I promise, only . . . oh, please, Rand, don't leave California."

He looked at her then, and she could see the bleakness in his face. "It's best," he said flatly. "I should have left a long time ago. I should have realized from the beginning that the only way to end my marriage was to go back and take care of it."

"Oh, Rand," she said painfully, tears streaming down her pale cheeks. "Rand . . . I . . ." She couldn't say anything through the pain in her throat. He stared at her and reached out to thrust his fingers into her hair, pulling her head back slightly so that he could see every emotion on her moonlit face.

"Moira, I thought I could take care of it all by letter. I thought everything would be long settled by the time we got back to San Francisco. But Svenson hasn't gotten anything. There's been no answer to my letters to Laura concerning a divorce. I don't know what in hell is going on back there. And—"

"I don't care," she interrupted, looking squarely at him. "I love you. I love you so much. I don't care about anything else. . . . I . . ."

He pulled her into his arms, seeking her mouth, kissing her with a passion that took her breath away and set her heart thundering. When he drew his mouth away; he was breathing hard. He tipped her face up, his thumb lightly tracing his smooth jaw.

"Moira . . . oh, Moira. I've waited forever for you."

Reaching up, she drew his head down again, curving her arm tightly around his neck and kissing him with all the passion and love she had to offer. He groaned, half protesting against the power of his desire, and then he gave in to it completely, turning her and laying her back on the deck, his body covering hers.

In a matter of moments, their clothes tossed aside, Moira's body wrapping itself instinctively around his, he took her, and not gently. Her fingers clutched him as his mouth took hers in burning need, smothering her soft cry of discomfort at his roughness and sending blinding flashes of light through her impassioned brain. She made soft, husky sounds in her throat that told him more than any coherent words she could have uttered, and she used her tongue to explore and taste his heated, damp flesh, adding her teeth when her need mounted uncontrollably. Her hips arched up hard against him in the ultimate surrender. He thrust his hand into her hair, pulling her head back, and looked triumphantly into her enraptured face.

And then, unable to hold back any longer, Random drove himself into her, fulfilling the dreams of a hundred nights when she had been just out of reach. He took her mouth as he plunged into her, feeling how she melted into him and met every movement of his body with an abandoned passion that shattered his control. And for one moment, when his mind blurred into his body, he cried out in the ecstasy of their mating.

After a long moment, he sighed deeply and raised his head to look down at her, his eyes love-dazed and dark. He kissed her tenderly. "I'm sorry . . . I'm sorry . . ." he murmured against her heated skin.

"Why?" she asked hoarsely, feeling more wonderful than she ever had in her life.

"I couldn't draw back this time."

She smiled. "I'm glad. It feels so much better when I feel *everything*. It's never been finished before." Her arms tightened as she felt him move away slightly. "No. It's too late, Rand."

He moaned softly and kissed her again, gently and then harder. "Oh, God, it's just whetted my appetite for you."

"Oh, Random," she sighed with a faint, dreamy smile, her eyes languorous. "Love me like that again."

He laughed huskily, kissing her eyes closed and her mouth open. "Oh, I'll love you in every way there is," he assured her. She reached up and lightly explored the handsome features and finally drew him close to her again, her lips and tongue moving along his jawline and down to the pounding pulse in his throat.

"Wanton hussy," he said hoarsely, grinning.

She grinned back mischievously. "Yes. Wanting you," she teased. He grew serious.

"There's so much to say . . ."

She kissed him. "Don't talk," she murmured against his mouth. "We've wasted so much time talking."

He needed no more prompting, but this time he made sure the moment lasted. And for a long time afterward they lay entwined, still touching, kissing. Moira sighed. She opened her eyes slowly and saw the star-filled, moolit sky above her. There was so much emotion inside her that tears filled her eyes, running down her temples into her hair.

"God, that was good," Random murmured, his hand navigating every inch of her body with a leisurely wonderment. He started to leave her, and her arms tightened.

"Not yet," she said and he looked down at her face, seeing the tears. "Don't ever leave, Rand. I don't care about—"

He put his fingertips to her lips. His eyes were solemn. "I want to marry you. I thought I'd have everything settled long before we got to this point. I—"

"Rand . . ."

He kissed her hard, silencing her. She knew that nothing she could say would change his mind.

"It's not the right time for us yet," he said, looking into her softened features, her love-filled eyes. She saw the moisture in his, and her heart contracted. Though there were tears in her own eyes, she smiled impishly up at him.

"It's not the right place, either. I think I have a hundred splinters in my backside."

Random stared at her in astonishment and then started to laugh.

Chapter Thirty-four

The torrential rains that had started in January finally let up by February. Refugees from the valley camps began to make their way back to see what damage had been wrought by nature's fury. And they began to rebuild.

Many remained in the coastal communities, intent on waiting out the harsh winter that many years later would be remembered as one of California's worst. As if in retaliation for man's rape of the fertile countryside in his greedy lust for gold, nature had poured down its wrath, engorging rivers, flooding valleys, covering the majestic mountain range with silent, frozen death.

Yet there was bounty in destruction. When the waters receded, men discovered gold washed from the high mountains and left to glitter in a hundred streambeds. Men poured from the coast towns as the rain had poured from the blackened skies. Mining recommenced with a vengeance, even as more rain came and more snow blanketed the mountains.

March saw San Francisco emptying of sourdoughs and refilling with greenhorns disgorged from incoming ships from every part of the globe. French, German, Australian, Chinese, South Americans, all came. Americans in the East were busy forging laws to control the foreigners and fighting for California to become a state.

Prices rose, and new buildings and businesses supplied goods and services catered to an exploding populace. With his profits, Random bought another general store and erected a hotel. The dock casino was expanded. He moved Moira off the rotting *Stephen Rule* and into a small, secure house on Nob Hill overlooking the bay. He hired Mathias to look after her when he was away on business. When Random returned, Mathias departed to continue his hot, relentless pursuit of Jewel Delarue, ever trying to convince her to give up her whoring and to marry him. Pockets full to bursting but relishing Mathias's lusty attentions, she was gradually weakening.

Life was fast and furious in San Francisco in 1850. A day in the coast community was equal to a month anyplace else on earth. It was exciting, exhilarating, unconventional, turbulent, passionate, dangerous—a young man's dream come true.

New factions poured in, bringing their ancient prejudices and sense of justice with them. The goodwill of forty-eight and nine was gone, and a new, churning population erupted with crime and violence. Law was still in the womb, and men enacted their own passionate retributions on one another.

Random tried to keep Moira safe from it all, but she was too inquisitive and adventurous to remain ensconced and guarded on a hilltop while missing what was happening around her. She still searched hopefully for Jack, seeking his beloved face among the throngs, asking for him where she could. Her purpose in coming to California remained unchanged. Until she knew one way or another whether her brother was alive or dead, she wouldn't give up.

It was very late. The bedroom was dark and silent. Moira listened to Random's steady breathing beside her in the double bed. Turning her head, she looked at his profile in the faint moonlight streaming through the window. She would never tire of looking at him. Not wanting to disturb him, she left the bed, moving carefully. She stood by the window and pulled the curtain back to look out.

Since that volcanic night on the *Stephen Rule* when Random had poured out his feelings to her, he had gone back to exerting careful control during their lovemaking. She wasn't pregnant, and he intended to make sure she didn't become so. It was impossible for them to not make love, and the strain of this method of birth control was taking its toll on both of them. For a while, he could lose himself in her, but he always had to drag himself back to reality at the last second in order to protect her from conceiving his child. It affected him physically, but no matter how much she told him it was all right, that love was enough for a child, he was adamant.

What was going on in Maine? What did Laura want? Why hadn't she written to Random? Was she hoping he'd come back to her? Did she really love him, in spite of what Random thought?

Moira put a trembling hand to her forehead, leaning against the wall. She heard the bed creak and glanced back. Random was getting up, and she tried to cover the misery she was feeling.

She didn't need to tell him anything. He drew her to him and stroked her back. "I love you."

"I know."

"It's not enough."

"It is," she said huskily. He tipped her face up and kissed her gently.

"You're more my wife than Laura ever was. Are you doubting me?"

She sighed. "Not you, Rand." She drew her arms around him, pressing her hands against his hard back. "Only . . . she's always between us, isn't she?"

"Listen to me," he murmured. "From the first moment I saw you, I knew everything in my life was going to change. You aroused me like no other woman, you made me laugh and you made me more angry than anyone ever had. You made me feel alive, Moira. And I knew you were attracted to me."

She smiled faintly. "I didn't try to hide it, did I?"

He kissed her. "I think at first it was just virgin's curiosity on your part—infatuation with an older man—but I knew it could become more. So I fed it, nurtured it, fanned it into life.

I wanted you to need me like the air you breathed. But nothing's ever as simple as that. I never meant to hurt you . . . to cause you any pain."

"You haven't."

"Don't lie," he said gently. "I watch you sometimes when you don't know it. I see what this is doing to you. You'd like to put all the conventions aside and let love be enough, but you can't. *I* can't. All that morality has been beaten into our brains."

"What choice is there?"

"I'll go back to Maine and get the divorce. God knows, I've the grounds for one. And if I give her the farm and enough money, Laura won't try to stop me."

"Take me with you," she begged.

He shook his head. "No. It would be a mess. You know it. Divorce is a mess, and there'll be a scandal. You'd be publicly—"

"I don't care! I want to be with you!"

"You can't be with me in this. I'm not going to put you through that. When it's finished, I'll come back and marry you, and we'll start from there and go forward. We won't look back again."

He pulled her close. "God, do you think I want to go? All I want is you—to lose sight and sound of everything in the world except you. The taste and smell and sound of you when I'm loving you . . . the way you look at me sometimes . . . Oh, God, Moira . . ."

He lifted her, and held her fiercely close. Then he carried her back to bed.

For a while they were able to forget everything but their love for one another. For a while they managed to obliterate everything but the feel of soft, warm, giving flesh surrendering to hard, demanding sinew, venturing into the mindless sensation of physical fulfillment.

They lay spent in each other's arms. Random stroked her back as her head rested on his chest. They were silent, both deep in their thoughts, close but distant.

Moira gave a shuddering sigh. His arms tightened. "I have to go back," she said softly. Random tensed.

"Where?"

"To the Yuba." She felt him relax. She looked up at him. "I want to find Jack."

"It's still winter," he said flatly.

"Mathias said we could make it back now," she told him, having discussed the possibilities and risks with the mountain man already.

"Moira..."

She raised herself up. "I have to go back, Rand. I don't know why, but I feel I have to go—now. Not in the spring. Spring may be too late. He'll be lost to me forever."

"Barilovich and Heaton are probably dead. They must have been caught in the Sacramento flood."

"Maybe. I don't know. I can't explain it rationally. Even if they aren't after Jack anymore, there's *something*.... I wish I understood it myself."

Random looked at her. He reached up and combed his fingers gently through her soft, dark hair and searched her face intently. "If I left, you'd go anyway, wouldn't you? Whatever the arguments against it, whatever the odds of finding him alive."

"Wouldn't you if it were your brother?"

He didn't say anything for a long moment. "All right. We'll make plans tomorrow."

"Mathias can take care of everything."

"*I'm* taking you back. Not Mathias."

"But there's so much here to take care of before you go back to Maine."

"Svenson can manage without me."

"The casino and hotel, yes, but what about—"

"To hell with everything else. I'll take you back to the Yuba first. If Jack's there and alive, we'll find him. Then I'll see to getting my divorce."

He pulled her down into his arms again. She closed her eyes, trying not to think how long it would take to "see to his divorce."

Perhaps *years* ...

Chapter Thirty-five

When Moira informed Mathias that she and Random had decided to go back to the Yuba, he insisted doggedly that he come along with them.

"I know damn well every deer trail up there, and you two between you don't know your tails from a hot rock. It's still winter in the Sierras. You'll blunder around, get yourselves lost, and freeze to death, sure as shootin'. You *need* me."

"But Jewel needs you, too," Moira argued, seeing no reason to drag Mathias all that way when she trusted Random's judgment implicitly.

"Jewel!" Mathias grumbled into his beard, showing his real reason for wanting to leave San Francisco. "By damn, girl, I've stayed too long in this critter-infested hellhole, trying to keep track of the number of bare-tailed asses crawling in and swaggering out of her bedroom. If Miss Delarue wants to change her mind and let me make an honest woman of her, fine and dandy, but she can damn well come looking for me this time. I'm pure sick and tired of talking until I'm blue in the face, and being led around by my . . ." He mumbled something while rubbing his nose and scratching his beard, but Moira had a good idea what he meant. She had never heard

Mathias say so much so vehemently before. She suppressed a smile.

"But I thought your courtship was progressing very well," she said encouragingly.

"Depends on what you mean by progressing," he growled. "I know every forest, hill, plain, and crevice on that blasted woman, but not a damn thing about how her addled brain works. Is that what you'd call progress?" he demanded in obvious frustration.

"She cares for you very much, Mathias."

"She *loves* me," he clarified unboastingly. "Told me so herself often enough, by damn. But she says she enjoys what she's doing for a living, and this way she's not being unfaithful to me. Now can you make any sense of that?"

It sounded like Jewel.

"I'm not sticking around while she samples every sourdough and greenhorn she hasn't *ministered* to yet!" he grumbled.

"All you can give is the best—"

"I've been giving her the best I've got since the night I met her, and I'm pure worn-out!" he said before Moira could finish. "By the time I get a ring on that woman's finger, she'll be permanently shaped like a chicken's wishbone!"

Moira laughed, and he gave her a disgruntled look, seeing no humor in the situation.

"Maybe leaving is the best thing you can do," she told him. "She won't think she has you all tied up then."

"It won't make a bit of difference how far I go or where. I'll still feel the same about her," he said glumly.

"You know that and I know that. But Jewel won't know it. I'll lay you odds that she'll decide quickly enough that you're worth a hundred men when she learns you're leaving without a backward glance."

"Who's not giving a backward glance?"

"You're not, if I have to blindfold you. Now listen, Mathias. You just leave everything to me. Don't go and see her. Just let me plant a few ideas in her head to think about." The devil was dancing in Moira's eyes.

Moira went to see Jewel early the following afternoon. Jewel was normally up until almost dawn and seldom rose before three. Moira arrived at two-thirty, when her friend was still bleary-eyed and disheveled.

Moira allowed her enough time to finish a cup of strong coffee before she launched into her news about returning to the Yuba. Jewel sat in an expensive red silk robe one of her many admirers had given her and brushed her long, unruly dark hair with slow, methodical strokes. She sighed heavily.

"So you're leaving San Francisco. I'm going to miss you. When do you think you'll be back?"

"I don't know. It all depends on finding Jack. I have a strong feeling that we'll find him this time. A very strong feeling."

"Well, I hope you do, Moira. I know it was the whole reason you came to California in the first place. It's too bad about Daniel." She reached out and took Moira's hand. "But, honey, you've got Random Hawthorne, no matter what, and he's one gorgeous hunk of male flesh if I ever saw any. And I have!"

Moira smiled, unable to tell Jewel that Random was married and there seemed no hope of a divorce. Some things were better not discussed, even with the best of friends. And she was here for another purpose.

"Well...I've got to get back. I just wanted to come and say good-bye. Mathias is getting everything ready—"

"Mathias?" Jewel perked up, her eyes sharp.

"Oh, yes, didn't he tell you? He's going back with us."

"He's going back with you?" Jewel repeated blankly.

"Yes. I thought for sure he'd told you. He said it wouldn't make any difference to you, that you were very well taken care of." She gave a slight laugh. "He said you enjoy what you're doing and he wasn't going to make a silly nuisance of himself anymore."

"He said that? That lughead. That bearded mountain goat...He just asked me to marry him two days ago."

"You mean Mathias is running out on you?"

"No, I said—oh, damn, never mind what-all I said." She waved her hand and turned away, letting out her breath in exasperation. "When's that stupid Aussie coming back?" she asked nonchalantly, powdering her nose. Moira hesitated and saw Jewel's eyes dart toward her in the mirror.

"He's not," she lied blithely.

Jewel froze. She turned slowly and looked at Moira again, face white, eyes wide and questioning. "Ever?"

"Well . . . he said he had a 'hankering to see the Rockies.' " She looked around the room, pretending not to notice Jewel's sudden distress.

"The Rockies?" Jewel cried. "He's going all the way to the Rockies?"

"Or wherever," Moira said, pretending unconcern. "I suppose a man like Mathias just keeps wandering until he finds something or someone to make him want to settle down. A lot of mountain men take Indian wives. Well, I've got to run." She stood, bent, and kissed Jewel's pale cheek. "Take care of yourself, Jewel." She walked to the door, opened it, and paused, looking back at Jewel sitting hunch-shouldered in front of her mirror. The corners of Jewel's mouth were drawn down.

"I'll tell Mathias you said good-bye."

Jewel still didn't say anything, didn't even look up. Moira closed the door behind her, waited for a long moment with her ear against the panel, and then smiled when she heard a sudden flurry of activity going on inside the room.

An hour later, Jewel arrived at the little hilltop house and presented herself before Moira, asking to see Mathias. Moira pretended surprise at seeing her, but led her to Mathias out in the backyard, where he was organizing supplies for the Yuba venture.

Jewel was decked in her finest, though still looking drawn and pale. Moira had never seen her look anything less than completely confident, but now Jewel looked nervous and agitated. As she went back into the house, Moira saw that Mathias was in the same foul mood he had been in since early morning. He didn't even look up at Jewel, but kept on with what he was doing.

Moira watched the two of them from the window. Jewel said something, and he barely glanced up at her. Jewel said something more. Mathias looked up then and said something back, gave an indifferent shrug, and went back to his work.

"Let's not overdo it, Mathias," Moira muttered to herself.

Every woman has her pride, and Jewel's was taking a bad blow. But then, on second thought, Mathias's had taken a beating since he had met the object of his ardor.

Jewel's shoulders had stiffened. She took another step toward the mountain man, said something more, and Mathias straightened, eyes narrowing on the beautiful young woman with less than encouraging light. He stood there in stony silence. Jewel was doing all the talking while Mathias stared at her.

Jewel talked for several minutes and then stopped. Mathias still said nothing. Jewel stood for a long moment, looking at him, and then she raised a shaking hand to her tear-streaked face and started to turn away.

Mathias spoke then, hands on his hips, without taking a step to stop her from leaving. He didn't say much, but whatever it was it stopped Jewel dead in her tracks. She turned and stared at him. They looked at one another for a long second, and then Mathias's bearded face split with that charming grin. And suddenly, as though on springs, Jewel bounded into his arms. She was engulfed in a great bear hug before her face disappeared in the rough foliage that grew on his face.

Moira turned away, grinning.

Chapter Thirty-six

Going upriver by ship was easy, even though there were still only a few risking the voyage to the flooded-out camps. Winter was in its dying throes, with spring a welcome challenger. In a few weeks, every ship that could be made seaworthy would be carrying frenzied miners back to the digs.

On concluding the first stage of their trip, Random arranged passage on a smaller vessel heading north on the Sacramento. They disembarked in Riego and followed the Feather up to the boom town Marysville, founded by French immigrant entrepreneur Covillaud and named in honor of his new bride, Mary Murphy, one of the survivors of the ill-fated Donner party. With Moira back in her miner's garb, they were given no favors. Random kept her close at his side, his hand firmly on her arm. He found them a small room in one of the clapboard hotels, which he rented at an outrageous price. Then he filled her with good hot food. He didn't touch her. He hadn't since the night they had made the decision that he would be going back to Maine. They left Marysville at dawn.

The journey up the Yuba to Sierra City proved more difficult. Now, on foot and horseback, they found that the snows were deeper, the weather colder and less hospitable than the damp chill of the coast regions. Winter was supposedly on the decline, but Moira had never in her life experienced an environment so harsh.

The high mountain camp was chock-full of bored, raucous miners desperate for diversion, impatient for warmer weather and the chance to return to their digs. They had grown irritated with one another's company, and fights erupted frequently. They were a grubby, dirty, foul-talking bunch of men who whiled away their winter sojourn any way they could. Every place in the camp was crammed to the rafters with men. Despite Moira's practical suggestion that she and Random take what accommodations were available, Random refused flatly to board himself and her in a communal dorm above a casino filled with shouting, fighting, swearing miners saturated with cheap, watered-down whiskey. They camped outside Sierra City in an outcropping of rocks above the river, which roared like an angry beast of prey.

Moira watched Random put more wood on the fire. She wanted him so badly at that moment that she ached with it, her body tingling with longing and need. But he had put more than a physical distance between them, and she didn't know how to breach his defenses. She understood, but she didn't agree.

Tilting her head back against the rock, she looked up at the clear, star-studded night through the veil of pine branches. Everything seemed closer in the mountains. She felt she could almost reach up and touch the North Star, or the Big Dipper.

Random stretched out on the other side of the fire and watched her. The firelight flickered, casting a glow over her features, brightening her dark eyes. He closed his own, his face pale and taut. He rolled onto his back and looked up at the sky.

"I've spent a lot of nights looking up at the stars," he told her.

"Charting your course somewhere?"

He smiled.

"Do you miss the sea, Rand?"

"Sometimes. I love the sound and smell of it, but the life is hard." He looked at her. "Lonely . . ."

She looked back at him. "Make love to me, Rand." She watched his eyes darken.

"I don't want to take any more risks." He frowned. "We've been lucky, Moira. Just lucky."

"We'll be careful," she whispered huskily, standing up and walking slowly around the fire toward him. He sat up.

"You could be gone as long as two or three years," she said, going down on her knees in front of him, opening her shirt, seeing how his face tightened, his eyes darkened. She drew it off her shoulders. "You're not going to separate yourself from me now, Rand. I won't let you. It's not fair."

"Moira . . ." he protested, but she saw how erratic his breathing had become.

She shook her head. "No. I understand what you're doing and why. And I love you for it." She moved closer, reaching out and slowly unbuttoning his shirt. "But I need you. I need you so much." She pushed his shirt back and began to kiss his heated flesh. Her fingers moved down to the buckle of his belt.

"Moira," he groaned, and drew in his breath. He caught her hand, stopping her. She looked at him, lips parting slowly in a soft, inviting smile.

"Love me, Rand."

Over the months, she had learned exactly where to touch, where and when to tease, and how best to ignite his passion. She did so now. He was going to go back to Maine with her memory burned into his brain just as he would be in hers. And she knew it was what he wanted.

Random let her take the initiative, watching her face as she explored him with her hands and mouth, and then, when his passion began to mount too fast, he took command again.

"No," she moaned in protest when his mouth left hers. He smiled and pressed her back, eyes dark as they moved leisurely over her firelit skin and up to her flushed face.

"You're in too much of a hurry." His hands slowly traveled over her body, and her eyes closed as she moved sensuously beneath his touch. "We're going to take our time. I said I'd love you in every way there is, and I'm going to. I'm going to spend all night loving you, Moira." His mouth moved over the silken curves, tasting, drawing low moans of pleasure. His dark head moved down from her breasts.

Two shadowy figures stood unnoticed not far away. Barilovich and Heaton were watching the firelit lovers.

"Hawthorne's well and truly enjoying her," Barilovich growled. "I'd like to do to him what he did to me." He rubbed his jaw, remembering the brutal blow he'd received in the Sacramento tent.

"Man, would I love a taste of that," Heaton rasped, breathing heavily as he stared at the couple on the blankets near the fire, their bodies glistening like molten gold.

Barilovich's face twisted. "All in good time," he said in a low voice. "I'm going to slit that bastard's throat . . . but not yet. Not until they lead us to Jack Cavendish."

Heaton said nothing. The Russian had a lightning temper, which had already cost them greatly. They had tracked Whitsell up here and cornered him. They had had the greenhorn mountaineer easily at their mercy with all the time they needed to get the information out of him that Tupolev had passed on just before he died. But Barilovich had lost his temper, hitting Whitsell once and killing him, ruining their chances of easy and instant wealth. Now they had to track Cavendish, a man of great cunning, and with a thorough knowledge of the mountains.

All those weeks of Tupolev's seduction of the Yalesumni squaw had paid off, until the fool had gotten careless and been caught by the girl's intended in sexual intercourse within shouting distance of the village. All hell had broken loose. Unfortunately, it had been Cavendish and Whitsell who had stumbled on the scene when Tupolev was almost dead after the Indian's torture. He had passed the information on to them instead of his partners in the plot, and again Barilovich had blown his stack and begun the shooting before Heaton had been able to reason with him. They might have struck a bargain with Cavendish and Whitsell in the beginning. Now they would have to wait and watch and then kill Cavendish, the girl, and Hawthorne before they would be able to reap the full benefits of Tupolev's seduction of the chief's daughter.

Darkness surrounded them, making Heaton nervous. "You think they know anything?"

"Nyet," Barilovich said, looking at Heaton contemptuously. "If they did, they would not be wasting time . . ." He uttered

an obscene word in Russian. He looked back at the lovers. Then he jerked his head, and he and Heaton moved off silently into the night to wait.

"I want your baby," Moira rasped against Random's ear. "Give me your baby this time, Rand. Please."

He groaned, his body shaking, his hips pressed in hard possession against hers.

"If I can't have you, I want your baby. Please."

"Moira, for God's sake . . ." He raised his head to look at her and saw the tears running from her eyes.

"Please," she begged, wrapping herself around him, pulling his head down to her and moving wantonly against him, making all his good intentions and plans war with his desire to give her exactly what she wanted. Because it was exactly what he wanted as well.

Instead, Random gave her ecstasy, and then closed his eyes in pain as he drew back.

Moira started to sob. He smoothed her hair back. She couldn't look at him.

He kissed her gently. "Someday, I swear, I'll give you a baby. I'll give you a houseful of babies, but only when I can be with you and watch you grow round . . . when I can be at the birth, be with you to raise them. But not now."

She opened her eyes and looked up at him sadly. His fingers brushed away her tears, but more came.

"Trust me. It'll happen. It will," he assured her. "But when it does, your name isn't going to be Cavendish. It's going to be Hawthorne," he said, fingers pulling at her hair with the intensity of his determination and love. "Whatever you say you want now, I'll tell you this, Moira—our child is not going to be born a bastard."

"Just come back to me quickly."

"I'll move heaven and earth to come back to you, Moira—and hell itself, if I have to."

Chapter Thirty-seven

The further up into the mountains Random and Moira went, the harder travel became. The snows were melting, but the drifts were still mountainously high and, in places, frozen hard. They wove in and out of the drifts near the highest trees above the river, ever climbing toward Haskell Peak.

By the time they passed Haypress Creek and headed the last few miles up to the cabin, they were bone-tired. Seeing Moira's slumped shoulders and the shadows beneath her eyes, Random suggested they stop for the night and go on the following morning. But Moira wanted to continue on, since they were so close to their destination.

It was late in the afternoon when they finally reached the last slope and saw the cabin, half buried, above them. All was silent save the roaring river below them.

They hadn't come halfway up the open stretch when a rifle cracked from within the cabin, the bullet whizzing past them in ominous warning. Random's arm shot out and caught Moira around the waist, hauling her down with him to the snow-softened ground behind the cover of the horses. Another shot sent the horses prancing off with frightened whinnies. Random shoved Moira behind a redwood while keeping her shielded.

"Damn!" he swore, looking after the horses, on one of which

was his rifle. "Stay down!" he ordered Moira. Her heart was pounding fast and hard, but she gave him a wry smile.

"Someone seems to have moved into our cabin."

"And has no intention of vacating the premises," he agreed, giving a harsh laugh. He moved to the edge of the tree trunk and peered cautiously around to look up toward the cabin. Another shot was fired, and he jerked back, an instant before a piece of bark flew off where his head had been.

"Rand!" Moira gasped. She grabbed his coat and pulled him back even further, her heart pounding in her throat at the close call he had just had. "Don't go sticking your head out there again!"

"He can sure as hell shoot, whoever he is," Random said under his breath, half in admiration, half in anger.

"Rand," she protested, fingers tightening on his coat when he leaned over to look again, though in a different position this time. The results were the same. Random swore under his breath.

"What are we going to do?"

He looked at her. *"We* aren't going to do anything," he told her firmly. "You're going to stay put right here while I make my way down to the horses and get the rifle. I'm going to try to circle around."

"What do you want me to do?"

"Nothing. Don't move. Don't do anything. Just sit tight and wait." He gave her a hard kiss and then, crouching down, made a fast run for a tree down the slope. Another shot cracked the cold afternoon air, but missed its mark by a few inches as Random dove for cover. He waited only an instant before going on. He made it to a group of trees before another shot was fired.

Moira watched Random as he pulled the rifle from the saddle scabbard and darted off to the western grove of trees just above the river. She could see him from her position, but whoever was in the cabin couldn't.

Heart knocking hard against her ribs, she sat in silence and waited. But waiting patiently had never been one of Moira Cavendish's strong suits.

Being a woman was the best possible distraction Moira had to offer, and if that would protect Random, she'd use it. She yanked off her coat and pulled off her shirt, then looked up and around for a stick. She spied a branch that could be easily broken from the massive trunk. Reaching up, she broke it off and ripped the lace trim off her camisole, tying it to the stick securely.

Gingerly, she put the stick with the dangling bit of lace out from behind the tree and waved it so that whoever was in the cabin with his rifle sights trained on her would see it. No shot was fired. She swallowed hard, wondering if she dared do more. Nothing ventured, nothing gained, she thought, and tucked her camisole into her pants, cinching the belt more tightly to make her sex in no doubt to anyone looking. She took her hair down so that it hung in a curly dark mass about her pale shoulders. Now that she was with Rand, she hadn't felt compelled to keep it short. She was shivering already, her flesh goose-bumped.

Waving the stick again, she stepped slowly out from behind the tree, Still no shot was fired, and she breathed slowly, her heart pounding. She didn't know where Random was and didn't dare look for him in case the rifleman spotted him before she did.

"We're friends!" she shouted at the top of her lungs, wondering if her voice carried with the roar of the river behind her. She moved slowly closer, waving the lacy banner, moving her hips in a totally female walk, trying to see something, anything, through the window of the cabin. She thought she saw a movement. She kept walking slowly up the hill across the frozen snow, heart pounding faster with each step.

"We aren't here to cause you trouble!" she shouted again. She was close enough for whoever was in the cabin to hear her.

The door opened suddenly, and a bearded man appeared, staring down the hill at her. She stared back, stunned, her heart pounding even faster. She gasped finally, her eyes wide.

The man stepped out, his blue eyes disbelieving, the rifle still clutched in his hand, half raised toward her.

"Moira!" Random shouted, seeing her through the trees. "Get down!" She turned sharply and saw him appear. He rushed forward, rifle raised, and aimed squarely at the man now running down the slope toward her. Moira let out a cry and ran toward the bearded man, waving her arms frantically.

"Don't shoot!" she screamed. "No! Don't shoot!"

But it was already too late. Random fired. The loud crack reverberated in the mountain stillness and the bearded man went down, rolling to one side, bringing up his own weapon instinctively and aiming with deadly accuracy at the man coming at him.

"No!" Moira screamed again and dove the last few feet, hitting the gun from the man's hands just as it blasted. She lay stunned for an instant and then whipped around and saw that Random's stride hadn't faltered. Turning back, she felt almost faint with relief.

"Jack! Oh, Jack!" She cried, her arms coming around him and embracing him so fiercely that he fell back and gave a half-startled, half protesting exclamation.

Random stopped, realizing suddenly who the man was, and stood staring at the brother and sister hugging one another, laughing and crying as they asked questions. Random knew it was foolish to feel jealous, but the look of joy on Moira's face, brought there by someone other than himself, brought a painful twist in his guts.

"Jack, are you all right?"

"Yeah," Jack said, grabbing her shoulders and pressing her back to look her over wonderingly. "What in hell are you doing here? How did you get here? Why aren't you back in Charleston with Daniel and Aunt Mandy?"

"We didn't hear from you for so long! Where have you been! Why didn't you write where you were? We were afraid you were dead!"

"You're crazy to be up here."

"God, I'm so glad I found you!"

Neither of them were explaining very much or answering anything, Random noticed with a faint smile. He walked forward and stood above them. "Did I hit you, Cavendish, or are you too numb from the shock of seeing your sister to notice?"

Jack glanced up, blue eyes sparkling. "No, you didn't hit me." He got to his feet, pulling Moira up with him. He put his arm around her shoulders. "But in about another split second, I'd have put a hole through your head."

Random grinned. "No doubt about it. You're a crack shot."

He extended his hand. "Random Hawthorne," he introduced himself.

Jack released Moira and accepted the hand offered, returning a firm handshake. "I guess you already know who I am," he said, giving his little sister an amused grin and then looking back at Random.

"No doubt about that either," Random returned. Moira was grinning from ear to ear at them both. Random pulled off his coat and draped it around her, leaning down to say in a low, taut voice, "Good thing it was your brother getting the eyefull."

She laughed, faintly flustered. "Well, I had to do *something!*"

"My sister's never been considered conventional," Jack said in affectionate teasing, reaching out to ruffle her hair. "But she's sure grown since I last saw her!" He laughed, raising his brows expressively. "God, Moira, but you're a sight for sore eyes. But what in hell have you done to yourself? Your hair . . ."

She put her hands on her hips and swiveled around for him to get a better look at her. "Setting the fashion, what else? It's called the 'California miner.'"

"We thought it was safer traveling incognito," Random said.

"I've never yet seen a miner dangling lace or sporting women's underwear as he walked up a hill. Not a hair on your chest, but plenty of cleavage. It was a minute before I noticed your face," Jack said, grinning.

"Got your attention, though, didn't I?"

"That you did, little sister," he agreed with a lopsided smile, eyes twinkling. "Is this fellow here your husband?"

Moira's smile vanished, and color surged into her cheeks as she glanced speechlessly at Random.

"No," he answered for her, and Jack's brows went up as he looked at the two of them.

"From what I saw a minute ago, I'd make a sure guess you care about each other," he said, faintly questioning.

"Random was first mate on the ship Daniel and I—"

"Daniel! Where is he?" Jack exclaimed. "Never mind. I can guess. Probably gambling in one of the fandango halls, bucking the tiger. He's too damn much like Pa," he said, and Moira swallowed hard, looking up at Random for help.

"Daniel died in late fall, Jack," Random told him quietly. Jack turned and stared at him, stunned and pale.

"Dead? How?"

"Miner's complaint."

"He fainted and drowned in a puddle right down there," Moira said, pointing to the spot by the river where she had found Daniel beside his Long Tom. "He wouldn't listen. . . . He just . . . Random and I . . . We were up on the mountain hunting when he collapsed or . . ." She started to cry. Both men moved, but Jack was closer and embraced her, hugging his sister against him as they shared their grief. Random stood by, feeling like an outsider.

"He's buried up there," she said.

"Here . . ." Jack still couldn't take it all in.

"We built the cabin you're living in," Random said. "We followed your trail up this far and decided to wait here in the hope that you'd come back this way." Random wanted badly to reach out to Moira, but knew that now she belonged with her brother, at least until he came back from Maine.

"There were others following you," Moira said, wiping the tears away and looking up at her brother. "Barilovich and Heaton."

"I know," Jack said grimly. "But you said *were?*"

"We're pretty sure they drowned in the Sacramento flood."

"Sacramento's flooded?" Jack asked, surprised again.

"Completely. They're rebuilding now, but just about everything except Sutter's Fort and a hospital were washed away in early January," Random informed him. "Barilovich and Heaton were camped near the river."

"Good riddance," Jack muttered and gave a deep sigh. "I'm glad to have those two bastards off my back."

"I suggest we save the discussion for later," Random said firmly, shouldering his rifle. "We need to round up the horses and get them stabled properly before nightfall." Jack nodded.

"What I've got to tell you two will take the better part of a night anyway," he said.

To the north of the cabin was another small camp, rude and hastily constructed. Barilovich and Heaton sat near the fire, warming themselves and cooking a can of beans. Barilovich took a long pull from a bottle of raw whiskey and wiped his mouth with the back of his hand.

"So we've caught our golden goose at last," he said in his thick, Slavic-accented English.

"They damn near killed one another," Heaton mumbled, shaking his head in wonder. "All this time we thought she knew where he was, and she was looking just like we were." He used a piece of canvas to lift the coffee pot from the fire and poured himself a cup. "We've got to tread mighty easy until he leads us—"

Barilovich gave him a cold, vicious look. "Don't worry, Heaton. I'm not going to make the same mistake with Cavendish as I did with Whitscll."

"I didn't say you were. But Cavendish is mountain-wise. Whitsell wasn't. We're going to have to stay real close or lose him again."

"It's going to be easy from here," Barilovich said confidently, leaning back to slug more whiskey down. "We just sit and wait and let him lead us right to where we want to go. And then . . ." He grinned.

The gray eyes of the Russian stared into the growing darkness, glittering with grisly plans. Heaton watched the curve of those thick lips and was reminded of a ravenous wolf, ready to sink its fangs into the throat of its prey.

Chapter Thirty-eight

The cabin was warmed to cozy, amiable comfort by the roaring fire in the stone fireplace. Moira had prepared a meal of salted pork, beans, and the customary sourdough. Now replete, the three relaxed, sipping strong, hot coffee from tin cups.

Jack stood by the fireplace, looking tired but happy. There were new lines about his eyes that Moira didn't remember, and there was a light scattering of gray in his hair that was appearing much too early. Random sat on the bunk, leaning back against the log wall, one knee raised, while Moira sat below him, cross-legged on the floor.

"I'm not sure where to even begin the whole story," Jack said, raking his fingers through his overlong hair and rubbing the back of his neck.

"First, I'd like to know why you left Charleston, Jack," Moira asked. "I know you argued with Papa, but I never understood what it was that sent you away so suddenly."

"It wasn't really sudden, Mory. It had been brewing for a long time. I'd been thinking of leaving home and heading out here for a long time before that last argument with Pa," he said, shaking his head. "I've always been headstrong, but it made me angry—and yes, even ashamed—to see Pa taking the snide remarks and insults without doing anything about it. And all the time, dumping money onto the gambling tables all over the city like there was no end of it. He became a laughingstock, and I just didn't want to stay around and watch the inevitable end. I was too damn tired of defending the family name when . . . hell . . ."

Moira didn't say anything, watching her brother's face, feeling a deep, emphathetic sadness. Their father had been a fool, but a loving one. "Did you plan to come back someday?"

"No. Maybe. I don't honestly know, Moira. I didn't leave under the best of circumstances. I'd been in a fight over Pa, over something said about him, and when I came home I had it out with him because of it. I said a lot of things to him that could never be taken back. I meant all of them. I don't think he'd have wanted to see me again after that."

"But he did," Moira told him quietly. "That letter you wrote about staying in California—he had tears in his eyes when he read it. He couldn't finish it. He just left the room."

Jack didn't say anything for a long moment. He didn't need to—the look of pain on his face said it all. He turned his head slightly, and when he spoke, his voice was filled with emotion.

"I loved him, Moira. But he disappointed me as a man. I suppose I wasn't what he wanted, either. It's too late now to wonder or worry about it."

He looked at her, his eyes seeking understanding. "Whatever the relationship between Pa and me was at the last, I'd have left home sooner or later anyway. That argument merely precipitated matters. I'd wanted to head west since reading Frémont's reports on his expedition.

"Charleston made me feel restless and dissatisfied. I couldn't see myself doing what everyone else was doing— marrying a girl from a proper family and settling into some dull family business, or running a plantation somewhere. The whole idea was stifling. I wanted to get out, find my own life, and not be bound to Pa's the way he had been by his father. And Charleston—it didn't offer me anything I wanted."

He leaned down and poured himself some coffee. "So I left, and headed for St. Joseph. I joined the first wagon train out, traveling with just my horse and a pack mule. I learned a lot coming out here, but the main thing I learned about myself was that I needed space, more space than I could get back East. And I wanted land, lots of good, new land.

"When I first reached California, I ended up, like everybody else, at Sutter's Fort. I worked as an Indian overseer, but I didn't have the stomach for it. The poor bastards were brought in like so many cattle and made to work in Sutter's fields. They were fed from slop troughs like pigs and then herded into airless, windowless barracks at night. And if they dared run away and try to get back to their homes, they were chased down and brought back like runaway slaves. After a year of that, I decided to find land of my own.

"I headed south to Los Angeles, but it was too damn hot and not enough water down there for good farming. So I rode north again and ended up near Tahualamne, where I met Jass Whitsell."

Moira glanced sharply up at Random, but he gave her a silencing look as her brother went on with his story.

"The gold rush had started, so the two of us decided to team up and head into the mountains to see if we could make ourselves a strike. We had fair luck, but spent most of it in Sonora when we came in for supplies"—he smiled slightly—"and other things. Jass spent most of his time talking about and writing to his girl back home. He hoped to make himself enough to go back for her. I had a penchant for the faro tables. I suppose I inherited more of Pa's tendencies than I'd like to admit, though my luck proved better than his ever did."

He sighed. "Anyway, for a while things went on that way. Work a couple of weeks at the diggings, and then into camp for supplies and a little fun. Nothing to brag about, but enough to live on comfortably for a while. But we both were looking for the big bonanza."

He was growing more excited now, blue eyes sparkling. "There were rumors about a gold lake, a main vein of gold that went through the Sierras. There's even an Indian legend. One of Sutter's men told me about it when I first arrived. An old Yalesumni Indian chief had told him the story of a lake high in the mountains. The bottom is pure gold, but the place is guarded jealously by a demon."

"Makes a good fairy story," Random said. "And also helps bring in new settlers."

Jack laughed. "That's what I thought. For years, no one really took it seriously, not until Marshall found color at the mill. There have always been stories of gold in California— since the first explorer days. No one ever found any. A Mexican did uproot some when he pulled up onions under an old oak down south in Placerita Canyon in '42, and there was a gold rush there for a while, but nothing on the scale of what's happening up here now. But according to Sutter's man, that Indian chief really believed what he was saying. He spoke with authority. The old chief said some of his people had gone to this lake and been murdered by the demon who resides there, and since then, his tribe has avoided the place. A lot of men tried to learn where it was, but he wouldn't say."

His eyes were burning now.

"And that brings me to why Barilovich and Heaton were after me." He set his coffee aside and sat on the bunk, leaning forward intently as he continued.

"Jass and I were heading back from our diggings one day when we heard someone screaming. We didn't know what it was all about, other than that someone was in deep trouble and needed help. We approached cautiously, not sure what we were getting ourselves into.

"There was a big man tied down and surrounded by about a dozen Indians. They were torturing him, killing him slowly. They . . . God . . ." He shook his head, pale from the memory. "They . . . weren't quite finished with him when we got close enough to see what was happening. We opened fire on them, killing two and routing the rest, but not before one of the braves gutted their victim. They must have been sure he'd be dead before we reached him, because they didn't try to come back.

"We came down from where we'd been firing. Amazingly, the man was still alive . . . barely . . . but enough to say what he knew." He drew in his breath, eyes wide with excitement, looking between Moira and Random.

"He told us exactly where to find the mythical gold lake."

"And you've seen it?" Moira breathed.

"Not yet. I've been trying to shake Barilovich and Heaton off my trail. I thought I'd succeeded when I headed up here in the fall. I made it as far as the canyon, but the weather got too bad. I decided to come down out of the mountains when

I realized someone was trailing me. I headed back this way during a snowstorm and lost them."

"That was probably Mathias," Moira said thoughtfully. "He's a mountain man we hired to go up and look for you."

"Well, from a distance he looks a hell of a lot like Barilovich. Wish I'd known you sent him. But even if I had I probably wouldn't have come down. Bringing Barilovich and Heaton down on you wouldn't have done you any good!"

He stood up again, restless to get on with his story. "Just after the man told us where to find the lake, Barilovich and Heaton showed up and started firing on us. They must have thought their man was still alive and we'd waylaid him in order to get the information. We didn't stick around to find out. They wanted us dead, that was certain. The man we found—Tupolev, we learned later—had been traveling with Barilovich and Heaton except during his dealings with the Indians. Well, he was dead, and all Jass and I could think of was staying alive and finding out if the story was true.

"We were pinned down for a while, and then I managed to wing Heaton. We got around them. I got a good look at them both during that shoot-out and learned later from a friend at Sutter's Fort who they were."

"The blacksmith?" Moira asked.

"Yes, Smitty," Jack said and went on. "Once we left the scene where the Indians had tortured Tupolev, we decided it would be wisest to split up and meet again in the mountains near the mouth of the canyon that leads to the lake. And that's what we did. There've been several close calls when Barilovich and Heaton have almost caught up with me. I managed to keep ahead of them and then lost them altogether. I don't know where Jass is. He never made it to the canyon. I'm worried. I've found no trace of him since leaving the valley."

"He's dead," Random told him. "We found his body just up from here. We couldn't be sure what happened to him. He'd been dead for some time before we found him."

"He's buried beside Daniel," Moira told her brother quietly, seeing his excitement die.

"Damn," Jack said, hanging his head. He went over to the bunk and sat there, not speaking for a long time, hands clasped between his knees. "Well, if Barilovich and Heaton had found him, they'd have forced him to tell them where the lake was before dispatching him. So I guess Jass died of exposure. He wasn't very mountain-wise. What I can't figure out is why Barilovich and Heaton were down in Sacramento. They knew I'd come as far up as this."

"They did," Moira said and then explained what she had told them when they came by the cabin trying to retrace the trail Jack had left.

He held up his hand, showing the gold-and-onyx ring. "This ring has identified me more than once. You're lucky that bastard Barilovich didn't kill you," Jack said grimly. "He's no better than an animal."

"I know," Moira said, remembering the incident in Sacramento in the tent before Random had arrived. She shuddered. Random reached down and squeezed her shoulder.

"I was going to hole up here for another week waiting for Jass, in case he came this way," Jack told them. "But there's nothing to keep us here now. We can pack supplies and leave tomorrow for the lake." He grinned at Moira. "That is, if you're game to dare a demon."

Moira looked up at Random, whose hand was still on her shoulder. Her dark eyes were sparkling with excitement.

"We're game," Random said, smiling at her.

Maine and Laura could wait a while longer.

Chapter Thirty-nine

It took two days of hard, rough riding through rugged, unyielding snow-covered terrain to reach the canyon that lead to the gold lake. They were high in the Sierra Nevadas, with the silence of the mountains around them and the chance of tremendous wealth just a short distance away.

It was late in the afternoon, the sun already in its final descent, when they made camp, having decided to enter the canyon the following morning. The last part of the trip would be the most difficult, for it involved going in by foot through a narrow, watery channel and then following a trail up a cliff.

Following a simple meal, Jack, Random, and Moira relaxed and talked of the country through which they had just passed. Moira leaned back against one of the packs and closed her eyes. Jack sat across the fire. Random was close to Moira, his hand on her thigh.

"How long have you been together?" Jack asked in a low voice, thinking she was asleep.

"That depends on what you mean, Jack," Random said.

"She's my sister. I don't want to see her hurt."

"She won't be."

"Why haven't you married her, Hawthorne? It's pretty plain to me that you've been sleeping with her."

Random was aware that she wasn't asleep. She felt his hand

tighten on her leg, warning her to stay out of this. She didn't move.

"I'm married already." She heard Jack swear low. "I'll have to go back East to straighten things out."

"Seems that makes them straight enough," Jack said, and she could hear the anger and suppressed violence in his voice.

"It's a long story, Jack, and not one I'm willing to go into with you at the moment. All you need to know is that I love Moira. As soon as I'm able, I'm going to marry her."

There was a long, still silence. "I think you mean it, Hawthorne."

"I don't say anything I don't mean."

During the night, Moira awakened. She lay motionless, listening intently, filled with unexplainable unease. All she could hear was the faint whispering wind through the trees, and yet she sensed something close by, something that was a deadly threat to them all.

She turned slowly. Random was there, restless but asleep. She sat up slowly, looking across the fire. Jack was gone, his blanket flipped to one side. His rifle was gone as well.

She was about to get up when Jack appeared out of the darkness. He grinned at her.

"Nothing to worry about."

"You're sure?" She didn't feel as certain about it as he looked.

"I just checked around. Something awakened me a while ago. Not sure what it was, so I looked. Nothing out there but some nosy possums." He set the rifle aside, but she noticed it was within easy reach. "Go to sleep," he told her. She lay back, pulling her blankets up. When she looked at him again, he was staring intently into the darkness, a hard, pensive look on his face.

Moira awoke just before dawn and saw that Jack was sitting up, his back against a tree, his rifle across his knees. He was asleep. Random was out looking around. When he came back, Jack had roused. Moira had coffee and breakfast ready.

"We'll take the horses in as far as we can," Jack told them. "Tupolev said the canyon narrows down to become a wall. There's a trail through it just wide enough for a man to squeeze through."

They rode half a mile, the horses having difficulty over the snow-covered, rocky ground. The canyon continued to narrow until it ended at a jagged wall of granite. Shrubs and small digger pine had taken root in parts of it. They stopped, perplexed.

"Leave the horses," Jack said, dismounting. He walked along the end of the path, searching for the passageway. He stopped at a clump of trees and brush that hugged the granite, and when he stepped closer, he saw something through the shadows.

"I think this is it," he called, pushing his way through the brush and disappearing. Moira ran toward the spot.

"It's here!" he shouted in jubilation.

"Where are you?" she called, shoving the brush aside and entering. Random followed closely.

The passageway was indeed narrow, and Jack was turned sideways, pressed in between the cold granite walls.

"It's one tight squeeze," he grunted, pushing himself in another foot.

"Are you sure this is what Tupolev meant?" Moira asked. She didn't like the looks of the place.

"Has to be. I didn't find anything else. Come on." He moved in deeper.

Moira could hear water trickling down from somewhere. Random stayed close enough to touch her reassuringly, far enough to give her room to move. It was easier for her, being so much smaller than the two big men.

There was indeed water. A few feet inside the narrow passageway, the rock became slick with it. Moira could feel the chill of it through her boots.

"How much farther?" Moira asked, feeling claustrophobic in the dark, damp-smelling place. She felt the slippery, icy rocks beneath her feet and under her hands as they moved along.

"There's light above us," Jack grunted, and she looked up to see a small crack high above. Two great stone slabs seemed to have been slammed together, leaving only the space that now gave them entry to the mythical gold lake.

"I just want out of here," Moira murmured, frightened and not quite sure why. What if they became trapped?

"I can see the end of it!" Jack cried. "Another dozen feet or so and we're through!"

And suddenly they were. The passageway ended, leading them into a small, bowl-shaped valley.

"An hourglass," Moira said.

"What?" Jack looked at her.

"We've just gone through the neck of an hourglass into the other side."

Only this side was silent, too silent. They stood looking around, sensing something ominous, yet seeing nothing abnormal. Pine, brush, small snowdrifts, a small pond of water near the south end, a redwood forest.

"No birds," Random said, looking up into the trees.

Jack walked among the trees, kicking up the snow to expose old pine cones. "No squirrels either. These cones haven't been touched." He looked around uneasily. "A dead place."

"And there's no lake, except that little pond over there." Moira said and was startled to hear her statement echo back to her. "Pond . . . there . . . there . . . there . . ." Her eyes grew round with fright. Random tensed and grew watchful. Jack ran his tongue nervously over his lips before speaking in a hushed voice.

"We've got to cross over to the other side. There's supposed to be a narrow granite ledge there for us to follow."

"Then it's not in this valley?" Random asked.

"I'm not sure. Tupolev said to follow the ledge until it comes to an end. The lake would be there. I assume he meant to go over that over there," he said, pointing to a jagged cliff that rose from the valley floor.

"Let's go," Moira said nervously. "I don't want to stay here."

They walked down into the trees. The redwoods rose above them. One was so huge that it might have been a seedling during the time of Christ. Everything was deadly quiet. They moved slowly, cautiously, watching for something, not knowing what to expect.

"Holy Christ," Jack breathed. "Look!" He pointed to something lying in the small space between two redwoods. It was a skeleton, in a position of flight. The skull was crushed, and the jaws were open in a permanent scream. Moira shuddered and looked around the silent, menacing forest.

They had not gone more than a hundred feet when they found another skeleton. The spine was broken, leaving the bones lying in an odd position. The top of the skull was gone. Both skeletons were still dressed in some sort of ceremonial breechcloth.

Jack hunkered down near the skeleton, looking at the skull more closely. He stood up, rubbing his neck, looking around. Moira saw uncertainty in his face. He looked at Moira and then at Random. "Maybe we should send Moira back to the other side to wait..."

"Oh no, you don't!" she told them both fiercely, not intending to let them out of her sight for an instant.

Random smiled wryly. "I wouldn't trust her to stay put. Better she's with us where we can keep an eye on her."

"This place..." Jack said, looking around and shaking his head slowly. "It's too damn quiet."

"Well, let's not stand around here talking about it," Moira said shakily, staring down at the skeleton lying at her brother's feet and wondering what in heaven's name was strong enough to do that to a man.

"There's not far to go," Jack said. "This can't be more than half a mile wide." He drew in a deep lungful of air. "One thing seems to be in our favor. We have guns. Neither of those poor bastards appears to have been carrying a firearm."

When they reached the cliff, they found the trail. At the base were two more skeletons.

"Moira," Random said, a hand on her arm, and she looked up at him sharply.

"I am not staying behind, so don't even suggest it!"

"Listen to me," he told her sternly. "Let me go ahead of you. If anything happens, *anything*, you get down off that ledge trail and hightail it across to the passageway. We'll be right behind you."

"Random, I'm sticking to you like pine pitch," she told him. "Both of you," she said, looking at Jack.

"All right. Let's go." Random shouldered his rifle. Jack went first.

The trail was not difficult to negotiate. It was narrow, about two and a half feet wide, spreading out to no more than four feet in places. Once they came to a section that had broken away, and they had to leap across a three-foot gap. The cliff dropped away below them as they climbed higher and higher.

"It seems to end up here," Jack said, the ledge trail curving around a huge, outjutting portion of the cliff. Jack approached cautiously, back against the cliff, peering slowly around to see what was beyond. He relaxed. His eyes glittered excitedly. "It's all right, I think."

They came around the jutting rocks and stood in the open space before a cave. Cold air came from the place, as if the mountain itself was breathing. Three more skeletons lay sprawled at the entrance. All three had the top of the skull torn away. One had an arm missing as well.

Charred torches lay scattered about the cave entrance. Jack hunkered down and collected a few, breaking one into a small pile of sticks. He reached into his pocket and took out two flints, setting to work. Within a moment, he had a small fire with which to light three torches. He gave one to Random and another to Moira, and then lit one for himself.

The entrance to the cave was wide. Inside it narrowed, the cold granite walls coming close together. The ceiling came down low, almost to six feet in places, and then surged upward again to twenty feet above their heads. Twenty yards inside the cave, they came to a section where mammoth boulders seemed balanced on stone pillars. The ceiling domed above.

"They look like giants," Moira whispered. Her voice carried eerily in the shadowy darkness. Somewhere they could hear water dripping steadily.

Just beyond the place they found another skeleton. The jaws were wide open in a silent scream of terror. The neck was broken, and the back as well. The skeleton appeared to have been flung with tremendous force against the cave wall. Gruesome stains were splattered on the wall above the sprawled bone remains.

Moira was beginning to have grave doubts about going further, but she knew also that the two men wouldn't turn back.

"What could possibly do that to a man?" she whispered, her heart thumping.

"Let's hope we don't find out," Jack said. The cold wind of the cave came toward them again like the exhaling breath of a demon. Moira shivered and gritted her teeth to keep from chattering.

They passed through two cave rooms, the first containing limestone formations that looked like waterfalls, the second containing stalactites and stalagmites that had met into great pillars like Roman columns.

"It's beautiful," Moira said quietly. The torchlight made the pillars undulate as Moira and Random walked slowly through the chamber. Jack had gone on ahead, eager to find whatever lay beyond. A narrow passageway opened at the far end of the chamber. He entered it and disappeared around a corner. They heard his voice come back to them eerily.

"My God! Come and see this!"

Moira hurried ahead, Random close behind her. They followed the passageway, twisting once to the right and then around to the left. Then it opened up into a great chamber easily two hundred yards across and a hundred feet high. Moira drew in her breath and held it, staring around in disbelief.

"This is it!" Jack said ecstatically. "Holy Christ! No wonder it's never been found. *A cave lake!*"

Within the great cavern lay a still lake. Water trickled down from the far wall, probably dripping from some surface opening where the snows were melting. The torches cast a golden glow over the water and everything else. Above them, limestone formations hung suspended from the ceiling, but the walls of the cave glittered.

A wide pathway led all the way around the lake, widening in some places. Shelves of stone jutted out from a wall forming a stairway. Yet at the furthest recesses lay darkness again and possibly other passageways that led off to different cave chambers.

Jack ran along the pathway, climbed up the stone shelves, and jammed his torch into a crevice. He pulled his knife and began chipping away at the cave wall. Chunks of gold broke off into his hand easily. He looked at them and laughed jubilantly.

"Gold! Look at it! I'm probably holding a thousand dollars' worth!"

Moira followed more slowly. She set her torch into some rocks about twenty feet beyond the entrance. The darkness at the back of the cavern disturbed her.

"It's a vein of gold that must go right through the mountains," Jack said, chipping off several more nuggets and putting them in his pocket. "A main vein, probably the one the legends say feed the California streams with gold! This is just the beginning! And look how easily it chips off!"

He already had amassed another handful of gold.

"It's incredible," Random said behind Moira, still standing near the passageway that led into the cavern.

"The walls are ribboned with gold," Moira said, looking around. "I wonder how far back this cavern goes," she went on, staring nervously across the lake into the darkness. Somehow, what couldn't be seen was the most threatening. She sensed something back there, some malevolent force.

There was a hard thud and a grunt of pain. Something fell, and Moira swung around and saw Random sprawled on the stone floor. Barilovich stood above him, having retrieved the fallen torch. He jammed it into a crevice to the left. He put his booted foot out and shoved Random into the lake. Then, grinning grotesquely, the Russian cocked his rifle.

Chapter Forty

"Rand!" Moira ran forward, heedless of the gun in Barilovich's hand. She ran into the shallow water, and grasped Random's shoulders, bringing his head up out of the water. She dragged him with great effort to the edge until his chest rested on the stone surface. She knelt and put his head in her lap, stroking his temples. He was groaning.

"You needn't have bothered," Barilovich told her, still grinning. "I'm going to kill him anyway."

Blood oozed steadily from the wound on the back of Random's head where Barilovich had hit him with his rifle butt.

Barilovich gave a mocking, Continental bow to Jack, who stood frozen, watching him, eyes narrowed. "You are an excellent guide, Cavendish. You left us a wide trail to follow."

Heaton had followed the pathway around to the other side of the lake and was chipping away at a long, wide ribbon of gold in the wall. "Holy Mother of God! It's gold, all right!" He spread his hands, showing the nuggets he had chipped off so easily. "There's millions in here! Millions!" His face was wild, his eyes glittering with obscene greed.

Jack waited until Barilovich's attention swung for a split second to Heaton, and then he acted. He jumped from the stone shelves and ran for the darkness at the back of the cavern.

Startled, Barilovich fired instinctively. The shot roared in the cavern, a loud blast of sound that pierced the brain. A rain of limestone cascaded from the ceiling, splashing into the lake.

With Jack's first movement, Heaton had raced toward the back of the cave in an attempt to block his escape. He raised his gun, and Jack stopped.

"Are you crazy?" Jack snarled. "You want to bury all of us under half the mountain?"

"Kill him!" Barilovich ordered, watching Heaton closing on Jack. Heaton didn't pull the trigger.

"Kill him!" Barilovich roared, his voice rising and vibrating through the cavern. Limestone cracked above and fell. More could be heard cracking.

"Shut up!" Heaton hissed, eyes widening in fear as he looked up. Jack swung one leg in a brutal kick that sent Heaton's gun flying into the darkness behind them.

Barilovich swore and raced toward the back of the cave, forgetting Moira and seeing no threat from Random.

As Random pushed himself up Moira scrambled toward his gun, which he had dropped when Barilovich struck him from behind. It was still lying in plain view. She grabbed the rifle and Random took it from her, shaking his head to clear it.

Jack had just sent Heaton flying backward into the passageway with a hard right to his jaw. Barilovich was coming at him like a battering ram.

"Jack! Behind you!" Moira cried in warning. Jack turned and ducked sharply to the right just in time. Barilovich swung the butt of the rifle, missing him. Jack swung his fist low into Barilovich's stomach and then with both hands locked together sent another blow down onto the man's neck as he doubled over.

A scream from the darkness froze them all. Another scream came, louder and filled with pain and terror. A roar such as none of them had ever heard issued from the passageway. There was another scream, and Heaton was catapulted out into the dimly lit cavern. His body flew like a broken rag doll through the air to land in the middle of the lake. He sank below the surface.

There was another roar, and whatever had killed Heaton was moving from the shadows. Jack ran past Barilovich along the pathway. He hadn't reached the stone shelves when the great, shaggy beast appeared from the darkness, growing taller and taller as it went up on its hind legs and roared again in fury.

Dazed by the blows, Barilovich did not move quickly enough. The enormous grizzly came forward with an amazing speed and was on him. The fur shone like molten gold in the firelight as the animal brought its head down and sank its long fangs into the top of Barilovich's head, its immense paws holding the screaming man in his last spasm of death. The golden bear sank its teeth deeper and then ripped away the top of the skull. A fountain of blood drenched the hairy coat. Barilovich was gripped by the shoulder and flung aside as easily as if the Russian had weighed no more than a babe rather than over two hundred pounds.

The bear straightened itself to its full height. The head went back, and the bloody jaws opened in a tremendous roar.

Jack was racing toward the entrance. "Get out!" he shouted. "Get out of here!"

Random had grabbed the torch and Moira's arm, and was yanking her into the passageway that led back to the limestone-columned chamber. "Jack!" she screamed.

"Run!" Random told her, shoving her ahead.

"Jack!"

"He's coming! Run, Moira!"

Jack was behind them with the torch he had grabbed from the crevice in the stone shelves. Their shadows moved like wild dancers on the walls of the cave as they ran. The bear roared behind them, pursuing them through the winding cavern.

Jack stopped and fired twice into the cavern. Moira heard rock breaking away from the ceiling, granite grinding against granite.

"Run!" Random told her, pushing her ahead of him. She was out of breath. Ahead of her, she saw light. She slipped and fell into a depression. Random hauled her out, dragging her along. And then they were out, the sun blazing above them, blinding them after the darkness.

"Keep moving!" Jack shouted, his hand grabbing Moira's arm, pressing her face first against the granite cliff, pushing her along the ledge. Random followed, sending several shots

into the cave. It was collapsing. The bear was roaring its fury within, still coming. The din magnified. Moira could feel the mountain shaking.

"Run! By God, run, Moira!" Random yelled from above her on the trail. And she did. She made it off the trail and fled into the trees. Her foot caught on a root and she sprawled headlong onto the ground, the remaining wind knocked out of her. Jack was ahead of her. Random caught up, grabbed her, and yanked her up as she gasped for air. She found herself catapulted forward by Random's strength and determination to get her to safety. The three of them reached the other side and clambered up the slope. For one terrifying moment, Moira couldn't see the crevice through which they had come.

"Here!" Jack yelled, waving his arm, and they frantically ran toward the opening in the cliff. Jack was inside. He pulled Moira in after him. Random let go of her as she heard the bear roar again, not far behind.

"Rand! Rand!" Her voice rose, echoing around her inside the rock. "Rand!" She tried to go back, but Jack held her fast, his fingers like a manacle on her wrist. He pulled her along, ignoring her protests.

Suddenly Random was there, beside her, his hand reaching for hers. She looked at him, tears of fright running down her cheeks, her fingers locked with his against the damp stone. Behind them they heard the roar of the golden bear. Its great head pushed into the crevice as it growled ferociously, trying to reach them. When it couldn't, it pulled back and rose on its hind legs, blocking out the sunlight, and roared again.

It took them an eternity to make their way through the crevice to the other side. When they came out, they found their horses and mule and those of Barilovich and Heaton grazing calmly.

They stood staring at the tranquil canyon.

"I'd like to see that damn bear squeeze through there!" Jack said, and throwing his head back, he began to laugh triumphantly.

Then they all laughed together, the laugh of three people who had survived a short walk through hell.

Chapter Forty-one

Now that they knew what they were up against, they could take their time making better plans, being better equipped the next time they returned to the cave of the golden bear. They were in no hurry.

Jack had stuffed his pockets full of the rich gold nuggets from the walls of the cave, and with them they would be able to purchase whatever supplies they needed. In a few weeks they would go back to the cave, and when they came down from the mountain this time, they would have more than a few handsful of gold nuggets—they would have sacks of them!

When they reached the slope to the cabin, they saw smoke coming from the chimney.

"Claim jumpers," Moira groaned. Random shaded his eyes from the sun. The door of the cabin opened, and a man came out. He was easily recognizable even at a distance.

"Mathias," Random said and spurred his horse to a hard gallop down the hill, sending snow swirling up around him. Jack and Moira followed. Mathias was waiting for them, standing just outside the doorway.

"Where in thunder have you been?" Mathias demanded of Random when he reined in before him. He looked sharply at the man riding beside Moira. "So, you've found her brother."

"Do you have something for me, or was this purely a pleasure trip?" Random demanded impatiently.

"Svenson sent me."

Random swung from his horse and walked toward the mountain man, eyes glittering.

"The packet's on the table inside," Mathias said, but put his arm across the doorway blocking Random's entrance. "But you'll just have to wait a moment while my wife makes herself presentable for company."

Jewel suddenly appeared in the doorway, buttoning her shirtwaist. "You can let the man pass, Mathias," she teased. "I'm decent."

Mathias grinned back over his shoulder at her. "Barely." He dropped his arm, and Random went in. Jewel came out. Mathias glanced up at Moira's grinning face and shrugged. "I didn't dare leave her in San Francisco," he said defensively. "Didn't know how many gents I'd have to beat off her when I got back."

Jewel gave him a hard punch in the arm and then laughed. "Those days are over, you dumb lughead."

"By God," Mathias agreed, smiling down at her. "Or else," he growled warningly. Jewel looked up at Moira and winked.

A wild, jubilant shout came from Random within the cabin. He appeared with a sheaf of papers in his hand. He grasped Moira by the waist, lifting her effortlessly from her horse, then kissed her in full view of everyone.

Mathias cleared his throat. Jack stared speechlessly. Jewel laughed. "I just *love* to see an affectionate man," she said.

When Random finally released Moira, her cheeks were flaming with color. He laughed, his dark eyes dancing. She'd never seen him look so happy!

"We're getting married!" he told her.

Her eyes widened. "What?"

"Just as soon as we can find ourselves a preacher. Then we'll start having all those babies you've been wanting," he announced to everyone, kissing her again. She blushed hotly.

"Laura answered your letters?" she asked hopefully.

Random glanced at those listening. Jack took the hint, taking up the reins and leading the horses to the shelter below. Mathias grinned, whacking his wife soundly on the bottom. "Inside, woman, and fix some grub."

When they were alone, Moira looked up expectantly. "What did she say?"

"The letter is from a lawyer named Dobson."

"What does *he* say?"

Random laughed. "Just hold on and I'll tell you," he said, pulling her into his arms and kissing her again. He seemed in no great hurry to stop, and she finally pushed him away.

"Tell me," she said impatiently. "There's time for that later."

"Later?" he teased. "You've always been a right-now girl. Are you going to change your tune when you're my wife?"

"Damn it, Random!" she stamped her foot. He laughed again. He looked very young.

"All right, since patience is not one of your virtues. I've been divorced for more than two years."

She stared at him. "What?"

"Seems good news travels very slowly. Just look at the markings on this packet," he said, holding it out to her. "It's been following me all over the globe. It arrived in Charleston just after I'd left. Before that it was in England."

"You're free?"

"Laura filed for divorce more than four years ago. I've been free to marry you all along! All this waiting and stewing in our juices has been unnecessary. Come here," he said and kissed her again.

"But how could she get a divorce?" Moira asked when he let her go. "You didn't do anything wrong."

"I deserted her."

"*After* you found her in bed with another man."

"I'm glad she neglected to tell that part of the story to the court, or I might still be married to her!"

"I hadn't thought of that."

"Apparently, Laura's adventurer followed her up to Maine, intending to pick up where they'd left off. He was surprised to discover a boy who looked like him. He lived there for a while and decided he wanted to marry Laura after all, so she contacted this Dobson. Since there'd been no word from me or of me in several years, he told her to file on grounds of desertion and planted the suggestion that I was probably dead anyway.

"Creditors were beginning to get nasty with her and her lover. It seems they'd run up bills all over the place charging them against profits on the farm. There weren't any profits, because they weren't working the land. As soon as the divorce came through, she married her adventurer and they went back, cleaned out everything of value from the farm, and left for parts unknown. The farm was put up for public auction to pay for bills and past-due taxes."

"Oh, Rand . . ."

"Don't look so upset. I offered her the farm in lieu of a settlement anyway, so she got everything from me I intended."

"But your family's farm . . ."

"I've never wanted to work it, Moira. My parents knew that and understood. They fully expected me to sell it someday and use the money for whatever would bring me happiness. And that farm has given me the freedom to marry you."

She looked up at him mischievously. "I'll have to think this over."

"Think what over?" he said, tugging her hair.

"Whether *I* want to be married to an adventurer."

He kissed her hard, his hands on her hips, pulling her against him. "We can leave things the way they are, if you like."

"No. I've made up my mind," she said breathlessly and grinned up at him.

"That's what I've always admired about you, Moira. It never takes you long to make up your mind." He laughed.

She threw her arms around his neck and kissed him. "Just give me time for a bath and a change of clothes, and we can go down to Sierra City and look for a preacher."

He grabbed her as she was about to dart into the cabin. "I'll only ask one thing of you," he said, pulling her back. She looked up at him adoringly.

"And what's that?"

His mouth twitched. "For God's sake, will you wear a dress when you marry me?"

She grinned. "Of course, if it really makes that much difference to you."

"You won't be wearing anything for long"—he grinned back roguishly—"but I'd like to think I was the one wearing the pants in this family."

She played with the buttons on his shirt, eyes sparkling with laughter. "There's just a slight problem."

"What?"

"I do have that blue gown which would do very admirably for such an auspicious occasion, but you'll have to ride all the way back to San Francisco to fetch it for me."

Laughing, he released her. "I guess it won't hurt for you to wear trousers one more time!"

Epilogue

Random and Moira were married in Sierra City by an itincrant preacher. Moira wore denims, but Random couldn't have cared less. As he had planned, she wasn't in them long after the ceremony anyhow.

While the newlyweds returned to the Yuba River cabin to honeymoon alone, Jack, Mathias, and Jewel purchased supplies and equipment for the return trek to the gold lake. The five of them went back into the mountains some weeks later.

They found nothing.

After searching for several weeks, they gave up.

Random took Moira back to San Francisco, while Jack remained on the Yuba with Mathias and Jewel, having taken over Daniel's claim. It made them all rich. Each spring they went back into the mountains, retracing the directions passed on by the dying Tupolev, trying to find the cave of the golden bear.

They never did, and finally stopped searching, figuring the cave-in must have forever altered the area's appearance.

Several years later, Jack returned to Charleston and paid off, with interest, all his father's debts. Aunt Miranda introduced him to one of those proper, pretty girls he had spoken of so scornfully, and he ate his words and married her. He brought her back to California, built a huge San Joaquin Valley ranch, and called it the Golden Dream.

When the claim finally played out on the Yuba, Mathias and Jewel settled not far from Sierra City. Jewel opened a very respectable boardinghouse, and Mathias operated a drayage company, which brought supplies for sale up into the mountains. Not surprisingly, many of these came from Hawthorne's mercantile chain. Some things never change, however, and once a year, Mathias would kiss Jewel good-bye, leave his foreman in charge, and head for the peace and tranquility of the high country.

Random and Moira prospered greatly from their various businesses in San Francisco, eventually building a financial empire and becoming intricately involved in San Francisco and California politics. Their greatest joy, however, came from three sturdy, handsome sons and two beautiful daughters. The Hawthorne family would be among California's elite for generations to come.

Rumors regarding the gold lake continued to circulate many years after the gold rush. They also generally included a giant golden grizzly who protected the treasure and brought horrible, violent death to anyone entering his domain.

Perhaps someday the right combination of weather and circumstances will enable someone to rediscover the lode.

May God be with them when they do.

Turn back the pages of history...
and discover

Romance

as it once was!